Praise for Bene...

"Impressive firs...

First, the characters are complex - they are not all good or all bad. Good characters do some bad things. Bad characters have some good to them. They come across very human. Second, the setting of the sixties is well-developed, and events relate strongly to today. Finally, it is a very engaging, multidimensional mystery that moves forward nicely and drives to a very satisfying ending. I highly recommend this to mystery readers." ***Goodreads review***

"An exceptional page-turner! The multiple storylines are interwoven so deftly that you want to know more about every character. The novel is Film Noir on the page with the turbulent history of 1968 surrounding it. The characters and their lives are so well-developed that each character deserves its own novel. Gritty, raw, and at times savage, this murder mystery reads like it could have been ripped from the headlines. History, film noir on the page, and realism combine to give you a novel you will not put down until you find out who did it!" ***Amazon review***

"I liked the detailed characters and their individual story lines that eventually came together. The setting of the book in the 60's was very cool and the historical information included added to the feeling of the intrigue of the murder in the small town in New Jersey. It was an easy, enjoyable read and I was anxious to continue reading to find out which small town character was a murderer." ***Amazon review***

"JE Mullane pulls the reader into the setting so keenly that I felt I had truly traveled to Pendale for a visit. I could feel the heat and the tension from the story and even smell the rotting fish and who knows what in Vern and Nora's house. The plot is fast-moving, and Mullane's characters are developed and complex. If you are looking for a compelling mystery layered with societal conflicts that can still be felt today, you will definitely enjoy this book." ***Amazon review***

Also by J. E. Mullane

Beneath the Surface
Disturbing the Dead

BREAK WITH THE PAST

A SEQUEL TO BENEATH THE SURFACE

J. E. MULLANE

WHITE DOG PUBLISHING

In loving memory of my mother,
Gail Mullane

ONE

D amn, Clarke thought. He crouched to peer at the body slumped forward on the kitchen table. Its vaguely familiar face rested cheek-down in a plate of dumplings. He whistled and shook his head. Almost thirty years on the force and this was a first. Protruding from the right eye socket of the corpse was what looked to be the polished wooden grip of an ice pick. Damn.

Groaning, Clarke straightened up. He looked down at the tousled gray hair of old Doc Eichen and considered what little he knew of the guy other than the fact the man's wild hair had always made him think of Albert Einstein. An angry Einstein. Clarke could not remember a single instance of seeing the man when he didn't have a scowl on his face. Now that he thought about it, Clarke recalled an appointment he'd had with the doctor. It had been about twenty years ago. Clarke's own doctor was retiring and Eichen had been recommended to him. One visit to the man's downtown office had been enough; he had the bedside manner of an angry porcupine. Clarke eventually settled on a younger doctor who, like himself, was new to the area, and he still saw him to this day. Yeah, Doc Eichen was a grumpy old cuss, but hell, what a way to go. Didn't even look like he'd finished his dinner.

1

Clarke pressed his hands against his lower back and stretched. He felt a crackle. Scanning the kitchen, he couldn't help but be impressed. And a bit envious. There was easily double the countertop and cabinet space of his own place. His ex, Judith, would have loved it. Until she found something else to complain about.

Yeah, the kitchen was spacious and airy, painted a cheerful yellow, though rather faded upon closer inspection. On a countertop stood a vase of plastic flowers that were coated with dust. The stove was covered with grease spatters. He bent and peered up under the range hood. More dust, more grease, and spiderwebs. It looked like bachelor living. He wondered about the marital status of the victim. Clarke thought he recalled the guy being married, but that was a hell of a long time ago. Things change, he thought sourly.

Clarke walked back through the house. Several framed photos sat on a cabinet in the den. One was of a severe-looking older woman with features similar to the doctor's. Got to be the mother, he thought. Another was of a castle nestled among the rocky outcrops of some mountaintop, a few were of non-descript groups of people. The final photo, set behind the others, was of a striking blonde woman. She looked very young, not long out of her teens, peering directly into the camera, a tentative, almost frightened look on her face. Clarke pondered her relationship with Eichen. They certainly did not look alike, perhaps his wife? But what a beautiful woman like this would be doing with that crabby old bastard was beyond him. He reminded himself that the doctor hadn't always been old. A crabby bastard? Maybe. He glanced at the cabinet surface. More dust.

He pondered what he knew about Dr. Eichen. Clarke could not remember his first name. He vaguely recalled hearing that Eichen and his family had immigrated to the states arriving in Pendale somewhere around twenty-five years ago, among the wave of Europeans desperately trying to flee Hitler and the Third Reich before it was too late. That would place him here about the mid-40s,

Clarke thought. He would need to verify that when he returned to the station. Though Clarke hadn't cared for him, he knew many older citizens of Pendale were patients of the doctor. Maybe it was a generational thing, he thought. Maybe a stern, bad-tempered doctor was the norm back in the day. His practice had certainly seemed to be a thriving one, the office located downtown on one of Broadway Avenue's more upscale blocks. Glancing at the dust he thought, let's hope he was more fastidious at work than he was at home.

He exited the front door through a lovely, paneled vestibule and onto the wide porch. Reaching his squad car, he called for an ambulance, identifying a probable homicide. But really, an ice pick in the eye? Nothing probable about it.

"Oh, dear, that's awful. I'll say a quick prayer," said the voice of the dispatcher.

"Mrs. Barton, remember our talk about proper radio procedure?"

"Oh, yes. Sorry, Captain Clarke. Over."

He sighed, replaced the speaker, and leaned back against the car, taking in the view of the house from the street. It was almost twice the size of his own, painted white, though in need of a fresh coat. The driveway to the left led to a detached garage in the back. What grabbed the eye though were the dark-green awnings and the deep, wrap-around porch. The awnings hung over every window Clarke could see. Longer, wider ones shaded the porch. It put the porch and every window in shadows. Must get pretty dark in there.

At the corner of the porch, where it wrapped around from front to side, hung a swing. Perfect for snuggling close to a special someone while gazing out over the front lawn on a warm summer evening. A front lawn! There weren't too many of those in town, that's for sure.

3

About thirty minutes earlier a call had come into the station from the deceased's son. Rolf Eichen had arrived at his father's house and there was Dad, at the kitchen table, face down in his dinner. When Clarke pulled to the curb, he saw a man standing on the porch, looking forlorn, hands jammed deep in his pants pockets. His face was familiar, but Pendale being such a small town, everyone's face was familiar.

"Mr. Eichen?"

The young man blinked at the sound of his name and turned toward Clarke. He was handsome in a solid, squat sort of way. He was rather short, with broad features, straw-colored hair, and astonishing blue eyes. There were rings under them. His face looked haggard. Shock, thought Clarke.

"Mr. Eichen? I'm Captain Clarke, Pendale Police. You contacted us? Your father. You found—"

"Yes, of course." The man nodded and held out a shaking hand, then stopped and dropped it to his side before quickly sliding it again into his pants pocket. "Yes, I've seen you around town, Captain, and in the newspapers. I'm Rolf Eichen. I called. My father, the Doctor, he's...in the kitchen." He gestured with a shoulder toward the front door, hands not leaving his pockets. "There, ah, seems, it looks like, ah...." He stopped, blinked several times, and shook his head.

"Mr. Eichen, are you alright? Why don't you sit while I go inside?" He took the man's arm and guided him to the porch swing. "Sit. I'll be back in a few minutes. Is there anyone else in the house?" The man blinked again and shook his head. Clarke left him standing before the swing.

Despite the assurances the house was empty, Clarke proceeded with caution. He pushed open the front door with his foot. Hand on his sidearm, he called into the entry vestibule. "This is the police! Hello?" He took a tentative step inside. Almost instantly, Clarke knew the house was devoid of life. There was no definitive logic behind the feeling, it simply *was*. The house was dead. Or at the very least, death was present. He'd experienced the same feeling earlier that summer, in a similar situation. He had entered a different house, it too had been silent, with an almost palpable feeling of death hanging in the air. Still, he moved carefully through the living room, den, and dining room before reaching the open swinging door to the kitchen. Hand still on his holster, he poked in his head and scanned the room. The kitchen table sat in the room's center, counters and cabinets covered most of the walls. At the head of the table sat the body, slumped forward, its face resting on its left cheek.

One eye seemed to be staring at a stray dumpling that had fallen from the plate now serving as a pillow for the dead man's head. The dumpling lay on the table, inches away. It appeared to be rather dry-looking, as did the rest of the meal that adhered to the man's face. A near-empty glass of something with a pale, yellow hue sat directly in front of the plate.

Clarke passed the body and headed toward a set of stairs off the kitchen. Judging by the dried food, the crime appeared to have occurred a while ago, but procedure was procedure. He needed to search the house in its entirety. What Clarke discovered upstairs were two bedrooms, two full baths, and a locked door. To an extra bedroom maybe? He continued walking until he descended the front stairs and found himself back in the entry hall where he'd first come in. Exiting through the vestibule and front door he approached Mr. Eichen, still standing at the swing, hands still in his pockets.

"Mr Eichen?" The man again blinked several times before seeming to notice Clarke. "Would you step in the house for a

5

minute, please?" Eichen looked panicked for a second, then nodded. In the living room Clarke asked, "Does the house appear exactly as you saw it earlier? You haven't taken or moved anything?"

The man shook his head. "No. Oh, I picked up my mother's picture. In the den. Then I replaced it."

"That's the young blonde woman?" Eichen nodded. There was little resemblance between the two.

"Nothing more?" Another headshake. "Fine. We'll be needing a statement from you, sir. We can contact your mother for you if you're unable to do so yourself." Rolf Eichen looked unable to do about anything; he looked ready to keel over at any second. He shook his head.

"My mother passed away earlier this year."

"I'm sorry sir. Is there other family?" He shook his head again. "Alright. Would you come with me to the station? I'll have an officer drive you home when we're through."

The man hesitated, "I'd rather drive myself if it's not a problem. It's just, I don't know...I'd rather do that."

"Are you sure you're okay to drive? You've been through a difficult experience, sir, finding your father like this. Maybe it would be better—"

"No. I'll drive." Adamant.

Clarke nodded. "That's fine. Do you know where the station is?" The man nodded. "You can park on the street or the lot in back. I need to wait here for the medical people. Why don't you have a seat," he nodded to the still-vacant swing, "or maybe just wait in your car. Then I'll follow you downtown."

"Yes. I'll do that. The car, I mean. Wait."

"That's fine, Mr. Eichen." Jeez, this guy's shook up bad, Clarke thought. He couldn't blame him. It's not every day you walk in on your father, face in his dinner, dead.

Rolf Eichen nodded and walked stiffly past him, taking the porch steps slowly, like a man many years older. Clark watched him cross the street and climb into a pale-blue Chevy. He quietly closed the car door and sat staring ahead.

For about the thousandth time in his career Clarke wondered how he would react if a loved one of his died in a violent manner. But that presupposed the existence of a loved one. Clarke thought of his ex-wife, Judith, comfortably ensconced in the steamy Florida warmth, about as far away from him in New Jersey as she could possibly get. There were no kids, a loss he'd often felt, but Judith hadn't. His mother had passed, and his father was in a nursing home over in Flemington. On Clarke's rare visits his father referred to him as Dwight, the name of a neighbor he'd constantly feuded with. There were no siblings.

Clarke walked through the front vestibule and living room. He glanced again at the photo of the delicate, lovely, young blonde. At the kitchen door he pulled a small pad from his breast pocket and began noting all the visible details, again appreciating the abundant counter and cabinet space. He circled the corpse, leaned, and sniffed at the glass of golden liquid on the table. It most definitely contained alcohol. He didn't put his face too close to that of the dead man. However, he did inch a bit closer to examine the murder weapon. He wondered if it would be difficult to kill someone in such a manner. He wouldn't think so, but what did he know? It was certainly out of his area of expertise.

Not much of the weapon itself was visible. The varnished wooden handle was nestled in the doctor's eye socket. A trickle of dried blood ran vertically from its base to a dumpling below. Clarke shook his head and straightened up. Did people still use icepicks? Did they still buy blocks of ice? He hadn't seen an iceman in fifteen or twenty years. Did the profession even exist anymore? Why would someone choose to kill in such a manner? And finally, who disliked the man enough to want him dead?

TWO

Nikki sat in one of the handful of pews in the chapel at St. Mary's Hospital. The blank-eyed statues' plaster eyes gazed down upon her in seeming condemnation, not for the first time, and almost certainly she thought, not for the last. Sitting there alone she felt vulnerable, very much out of her element. She couldn't remember the last time she'd been alone in a church or chapel. She and God didn't seem to be on a first name basis. And prayer? Oh, man...but she was willing to try. For Mrs. G.

Nikki stood, slid her fingers into the tight hip pocket of her jeans, and pulled out a tangled ball of plastic beads on a small chain. "Shit," she muttered, trying to untangle the mess that was the Rosary Mrs. Gorman had forced on her a couple months ago. After a moment she grunted in satisfaction. Okay, she thought, prayer time. Now what comes first? Mrs. Gorman had run through them all with her. Multiple times. None of it seemed to stick with Nikki, like a first attempt at learning a foreign language. Wait. Oh, yeah, there was a long prayer you're supposed to say over the little cross that dangled from the end. She tried to dredge up the name of it. Well screw that, she would never remem— Wait. Where the hell was the cross?

Nikki ran the beads through her fingers, then looked to the floor between her sandaled feet. Are you fucking kidding me, she thought? My first attempted solo with these damn beads and I lose the most important part?

"Son of a bitch," she murmured. An old, pruney-looking senior citizen who must have sneaked in sometime after she sat down, made a disapproving noise and moved to a pew further away.

Back at ya, you old bat, Nikki thought. Damn, where could it have—ah, wait. She again stood and fished around in the same tight hip pocket, pushing her fingers deeper. Pay dirt! She pulled out the small metal crucifix that had slipped off a tiny link of chain.

Okay, here we go. She stared at the rendering of the crucified Jesus, trying to dredge up the words she needed, but came up dry. She sighed. Fuck it. Nikki jammed the cross into a back pocket, then after a moment kneeled and silently begged a God whose existence she doubted, not to take away the one person left in this world she truly loved. Three floors up her landlady and best friend, Rose Gorman, lay a victim of a heart attack.

Nikki had arrived home and banged on the door adjoining her small apartment to Mrs. G's kitchen, a ritual that had become common the last couple months. But instead of the normal call of welcome from the older woman, Nikki heard what sounded like a quiet gasping.

She pushed the door open to find Mrs. G slumped on the kitchen floor, her back against a cabinet, looking paler than Nikki thought possible. She flew to the woman's side.

"Mrs. G! What the fu—ah, damn! Can you hear me? Do you understand me?" There was fear in the woman's eyes as she nodded slightly. "Okay. Don't move. I'm calling an ambulance."

Next to the wall phone, in Mrs. Gorman's careful cursive writing, hung a list of emergency numbers. "St. Mary's Hospital, Emergency" was the third number down. Just below "Police" and at the top of the list, Nikki's own number. Her number that is, before it had been disconnected for non-payment. Why in the world would she need my phone number on the wall when she could just pop her head into my apartment, Nikki wondered wildly. She blinked back a tear as she dialed. Her finger slipped twice but she finally made contact and was told an ambulance was on its way. She ran into her apartment and dragged the blanket off her bed, remembering from somewhere you're supposed to keep victims of, well, victims, warm. She gently wrapped it around her ashen landlady, realizing belatedly it probably reeked of cigarette smoke, a smell Rose Gorman hated. She sat next to the woman, holding her hand, and trying to be reassuring.

"They're on the way, Mrs. G, just a couple minutes. You hang on with me. I'm not letting you go, you hear? I need you to keep me on the straight and narrow. No way I'm ready to be let loose on my own. Trust me, this crummy town is not ready for me to be on the prowl unsupervised." Nikki was aware tears were running down her face as she spoke. She stammered on, "Mrs. G, I know I'm being a selfish bitch, but I can't lose you. You're my best and only friend and you saved my life." The old woman minutely shook her head. "You did. I was dead, worse than dead, and you took me in your arms and gave me my life back. It may not be the best life in the world but hey, beggars can't be choosers, right?" Nikki's smile trembled. How long she talked she had no idea. Finally, she heard a siren in the distance, growing louder. Thank Christ. Did they stop off for a beer on the way?

"They're almost here. I love you, Mrs. G. And if you love me, you won't leave me. Please don't leave me. Okay?" There were tears now in Mrs. Gorman's eyes and she blinked them in affirmation. "Okay, now that we've got that settled, I better let them in, huh?" She kissed the woman's cheek. "Be right back."

Nikki sprinted through the small house and ushered in the ambulance crew, trying to stay out of the way, but needing to remain as close as possible. She watched them take vital signs, administer oxygen, contact the hospital, and wheel her outside. A small knot of neighbor women stood taking in the spectacle.

As they lifted her into the ambulance Nikki called, "I'll be right behind you, Mrs. G."

As the young medic with an impressive afro slammed shut the rear door of the ambulance he turned to her, "You're welcome to be at the hospital, miss, but you won't be able to speak to her for some time."

"Please," Nikki grabbed the man's arm as he turned away, "is she going to be okay? Please say she'll be okay. She's my land—she's my friend, my best friend."

He hesitated and said, "I've seen patients in much worse condition come through just fine. That's not a promise, just an observation, okay?"

Nikki nodded, "Okay," she whispered. "Thank you."

As the ambulance pulled away, Nikki ran into the house. She stopped in the kitchen, looked around and said aloud, "Right. What does she need for the hospital? How long will she be there? A couple days, a week, a month? Fuck! Why didn't I ask the ambulance guy how long these things usually go?" Not that she had any idea of what "thing" had actually occurred. Nikki could think of nothing. "Come on brain! Have I killed off too many damn cells for you to be useful?" She grabbed a paper bag from beneath the sink. Running into Mrs. G's bedroom she yanked open drawers and into the bag she jammed underwear, slippers, a paperback book from the nightstand, *I, the Jury*. Whoa, wouldn't have dubbed you a Mickey Spillane fan, Mrs. G. From the bathroom she grabbed a toothbrush and toothpaste. To be safe she threw in a jar of Noxzema. "What else, what else?" she mumbled, slowly turning in a circle, scanning the room, hoping something would present itself.

"Oh, fuck it."

She snatched Mrs. Gorman's car keys from the green four-leaf clover key rack by the back door. Running to the car she stopped, ran back into the house, and grabbed the handful of cash Mrs. Gorman had stashed in the cookie jar. When Nikki first learned of it, she was disbelieving. Really? The cookie jar? It's a good thing I hadn't known about it a few months ago, she thought. I would have drunk it away in a flash. She then dashed into her own bedroom at the rear of the house and grabbed the Rosary beads Mrs. G had given her, which she'd draped over the bedpost and promptly forgotten about. Almost.

The short drive to the hospital was a complete blank. After prowling the tiny waiting room on Mrs. G's floor, smoking cigarette after cigarette, she was asked rather pointedly if she might not be more comfortable in the hospital's cafeteria. She was assured she could smoke there, too. Jesus, anything to get rid of me, huh? The cafeteria was almost deserted, save for a table in the corner where a worried-looking young mother sat with a small boy who steadily spooned cube after cube of green Jell-O into his mouth. But the smell of steamed broccoli drove Nikki out and she wandered the first-floor hallways until she found herself before the door to the chapel where she now sat, scared to death she might lose the only person in the world who meant anything to her.

13

Her Rosary swam before her eyes. Apostles' Creed! *That* was the name of the long prayer said over the tiny cross. She again dug out the small crucifix and scoured her mind for the words.

"Ugh!" she almost screamed in frustration. This time the oldster in back stood and left.

Nikki scanned the chapel and noticed a small wooden cabinet in the rear of the room. She jumped up, opened its door, and found a small stack of hymnals and Bibles. She grabbed one of each, took them back to her pew, and began frantically leafing through them in search of the words to the prayer that would enable her to properly begin her Rosary to pray for the recovery of Rose Gorman.

THREE

Two hours later she was granted access to Mrs. Gorman's room. It was the first time Nikki could ever remember being a visitor in a hospital room. Her father had briefly been hospitalized years ago after his stroke, but her aunt hadn't allowed her to visit him before he'd died. Just another reason to hope the hag lived a long and thoroughly crappy life. She remembered a couple months ago when she herself had spent a night in the hospital, as a patient. She glanced around the room. Other than the fact she had been in a single room, it looked almost identical.

The bed nearest the door was empty, its thin mattress was draped with a gray rubber cover, no sheets, blanket, not even a pillow. Looks like whoever was here just packed up and blew town, hopefully not horizontally. The institutional-green linoleum floor looked worn from years of foot traffic and beds being wheeled in and out of the room. The walls were as gray as the rubber mattress cover. Mrs. Gorman's pallor matched that of the room. Nikki quietly approached her landlady's bedside. The woman she'd known to be robust, almost larger than life, possessing more energy than she could ever have a right to, seemed to have shrunk in the bed. Just a slight rising and falling of her chest indicated any sign of life. A chest that had impressed the hell out of her the first time she'd seen it.

After first meeting with Mr. and Mrs. Gorman in what was now Nikki's apartment, she and Donald were driving back to his parents' place. They were both excited at the prospect of Nikki renting the small apartment, as well as impressed with the nice couple who owned it. Nikki fiddled with the radio and stopped at that weird new Beach Boys song, the one with the theremin. Something about vibrating. She leaned back and after a second couldn't help but comment, "That was one major league set of lungs on that woman."

His eyes not leaving the road, Donald nodded and gave a long wolf-whistle before bursting into laughter. "They were mesmerizing."

"Hey," Nikki mock-slapped him on the shoulder. "Don't tell me you're getting eyes for the matronly woman and leaving little ole me discarded on the roadside." She stuck out her lower lip in a pout.

Donald grinned and leered at her, giving her a quick once-over. "Well...I suppose I can find it in my heart to make sure you don't feel neglected."

"Oh, you can, huh?" Nikki slid closer on the bench seat. She leaned, breathed into his ear and whispered, "I'd be ever so grateful. And I promise I'll do something for you I've, never, ever, *ever* done before." She brushed her lips against his earlobe before leaning away with what she hoped was a devilish gleam in her eye.

"Yeah?" The effect on Donald was almost instantaneous. He shifted in the seat to create a more comfortable position given his reaction to her promise. "And what might that be?"

Guys, Nikki thought. Freaking incredible. She peeked over her right shoulder to the sidewalk whizzing by. Looking ahead there didn't seem to be anyone coming too close from the opposite direction.

She again put her lips to his ear, and breathily responded, "This!" She threw off her T-shirt and while seated in the confines of the car's front seat, performed a topless "I Dream of Jeanie" haram dance, complete with attempted hip thrusts.

They both howled in laughter, tears in their eyes. Donald braked abruptly before almost running a red light. Seconds later, a horn blared behind them. They looked back and saw two teen-aged boys in a pickup truck, both applauding enthusiastically.

Nikki quickly spun around facing front again, throwing an arm across her chest. She looked at Donald with wide eyes and mouthed, 'Oops.' This brought on another round of laughter. As the light changed and they accelerated away, Nikki gave the boys a regal wave.

After the laughter finally died, Nikki leaned into the backseat where her shirt had somehow landed. "Hey," Donald said slowly, "how about we make a stop at the woods by the old trestle? It's not dinner time yet and I'm sure Mom and Dad aren't expecting us right away. I mean, you're already halfway, uh, there..." he said, grinning at her.

"Oh," she said as seriously as she could, "you're implying since I'm already half-naked and because you plan on having your way with me on a deserted stretch of road, I might as well not even attempt to cover up, is that right?"

With a thoughtful expression, Donald responded, "Yes, I'd say that about sums it up." He nodded and grinned. "You're staying half-naked," he declared.

"Oh, you're the man and you have spoken?"

"Yes, I have spoken."

"Well, screw you, Mr. Man, this woman has a right to whatever the hell she wants and it's not staying half-naked for you." Nikki quickly unsnapped her tight jeans and pushed them and her underwear to the floor of the car. "It's all or nothing and she's telling you to step on the gas before she jumps you and we go off the road and both die a fiery death."

Nikki reached for the foot of Mrs. Gorman's bed, steadying herself. She hadn't thought of that exchange with Donald in, well, certainly not since he'd died. Died in a car accident at college.

"Aw, crap," she whispered to herself. That's the trouble with having a clear head, you remember what you'd rather not. It almost made stumbling through life, blind drunk and oblivious, worth it. Which was exactly how Nikki lived for almost two years following Donald's death.

A bottle of clear liquid hung upside down from a metal pole attached to the bed; a long rubber tube ran from its inverted mouth to Mrs. G's arm. A breathing tube was held in place under her nose with what looked like a piece of scotch tape. There was a small, kidney-shaped plastic bowl on the nightstand. Alongside the bowl was an empty cup with a flexible straw. Glancing around the room again Nikki thought, it's so damn depressing. No color at all.

Flowers. She would get flowers as soon as she could. Anything to brighten up this morgue. Nikki stepped to the window and peered out. Below was a flat, tarred rooftop with a series of exhaust vents and fans. Directly across from her on the other side of that roof was a solid brick wall.

You deserve better than this, Nikki thought. Better than a crappy gray room, a non-existent view, and no flowers. She looked around and saw a chair next to what was probably the bathroom door. She quietly carried it to the side of Mrs. G's bed, sat, and reached to take her friend's hand. She hesitated, not wanting to do anything that might in any way disturb or compromise Mrs. G's recovery. Nikki laid her wrist on the thin bedspread and extended her index finger to gently rest against the back of the older woman's veined hand. She gazed into the slack face of the woman who had, on more than one occasion, saved her life.

A little over two hours later she still sat, barely touching the hand, when a trio of women entered the room. Each looked about the same age as Mrs. Gorman and each was armed with either flowers or some other nick-nack designed to make a hospital patient's stay a bit more palatable. Nikki recognized at least two of the women, but their names escaped her.

In a whisper she said, "Oh, hi, it's so nice—"

"Shhh. Lower your voice!" the taller of them whispered loudly. "You'll disturb Rose." She pursed her lips angrily and nodded to Mrs. Gorman.

Nikki mouthed, 'Sorry.' She walked to the women. "When I got here," she whispered, "I stopped at the nurses' station, and she told me Mrs. G—"

"We spoke to one of the *doctors*," the tall one said, "and we were informed she needs absolute rest. No disturbances. There's no reason for you to be hanging all over her. You should leave and we'll make certain she's comfortable."

Nikki then recognized her. She was Mrs. Gorman's next-door neighbor. Great, Nikki thought, someone more than just a little acquainted with my previous way of life. No wonder she wants me out of here.

"It's Mrs. Ryan, right?" The woman nodded, lips pursed. "It's very thoughtful of you and you other ladies," she nodded to them, "to visit Mrs. G. I'm sure she'll appreciate it. I really wasn't—"

"Young lady," said the shortest and roundest of the three women, "it would be best for you to leave. We're here now and you'll just be a hinderance." She grabbed hold of Nikki's wrist and walked her to the door.

In the threshold, a stunned Nikki yanked her wrist away and said, still whispering, "Alright! I get it, you don't want me here. Fine, I'll take a walk or find something else to keep me occupied."

The third woman, who must have been about the age of the others but sporting a large mop of jet-black hair, muttered barely audibly, "Something or some*one* else."

Nikki glared at her. "Okay, I'll leave. But Mrs. G is my friend, too. I'll come back when I want."

The woman with the hair sniffed and turned away.

"That sniffle better not be a cold, Blackie. You infect Mrs. G with anything, I'll send you and that dead rodent on your head flying."

She heard a gasp as she left the room and made her way to the nurse's station. "Fucking old bats," she muttered. "Like the witches in 'Macbeth,' just not as pleasant." At the nurses' station she waited for the nurse on duty to finish a phone call. The woman was stubbing out her cigarette and seemed to be wrapping it up. Nikki was craving a smoke, as well. She hadn't left Mrs. G's side for over two hours and needed to fire one up soon. Yet another one of her addictions rearing its head.

"You'll have to leave, miss."

"Um, what? I'm sorry, why?"

The nurse had ended her call and spun her chair to face Nikki. "We do not allow drinking on the premises."

"What are you talking about?"

"I was informed that you were behaving in an intoxicated manner and smelled of alcohol. We do not allow that on the premises."

"What? Who would have—" Nikki stopped. The witches. They must have peeked in the room and seen her before she'd noticed them. Then one or more of them dropped this tidbit about drinking with the nurse. Nikki felt her face getting hot.

"I'm not drunk, and I haven't been drinking. Do I smell like alcohol to you?" She leaned toward the nurse, opened her mouth, and exhaled heavily. "I haven't had a drink in over—" Ah, to hell with it, she thought. This well's been poisoned.

"I'll go, but would you please, *please* tell me the condition of Rose Gorman? I don't know the room number but she's three doors down on the left. She's my landlady and my friend." Nikki stopped to collect herself for a second. "Please."

The nurse stared before rolling her chair to a metal rack that held a series of clipboards. She reached and pulled one out. "Edna Byrne," she muttered looking at it, before returning it to the rack. The second clipboard was the winner. "Rose Gorman." The woman's eyes scanned the page. "She is in room three fifteen, *four* doors down, and has suffered a myocardial infarction. She'll need to remain hospitalized for the better part of a week, but with rest and no distractions she should be fine."

Nikki nodded and realized she was close to tears. No way, Nik, she thought, not in front of this bitch. Keep it together. "Thank you," she whispered to the nurse.

"Rest and no distractions," the nurse reiterated.

Nikki nodded again and walked quickly to the elevators. She then turned and pushed through the door marked "Stairs." She ran down half a flight, leaned her back against the wall, and slowly slid to the floor. Sitting on the cold concrete, she burst into tears.

"Thank you, God," she whispered, "Thank you, thank you, thank you. Thank you for not taking my angel from me. I know I'm selfish, but I'd be lost and probably die without her. And what's one more angel to you, right? But she's all I've got. I'll be a better person, I promise. I'm not sure how, but I will."

Eventually, Nikki stood and gingerly made her way down the remaining stairs, through the lobby, and to the parking lot. She slid into the car and felt a sharp pinch on her backside. Jumping out of the car, Nikki reached to her back pocket and withdrew the small metal crucifix.

"Jesus, you sure poked me good." She was about to toss the cross onto the passenger seat and stopped. The Apostles' Creed. "Is this a sign, God?" She looked up to the clouds hanging motionless in the blue sky. "Okay. A deal's a deal. I'll learn the damn thing." She rubbed her backside. "But lighten up on the signs, huh?"

FOUR

The woman's body was lying face down in the sand. Her long, tangled hair lay strewn across her back, shoulders, and the ground. Her feet were bare, and she wore short cut-off jeans, nothing more. One arm lay extended on the sand, perhaps beckoning him closer, maybe warning him away. Waves smacked the beach in a stiff breeze. Not stiff enough though to rid the area of the stench of bloated fish and dead horseshoe crabs that had washed up on shore. Gulls dove to tear bits from the rotting creatures, their cries almost non-stop, piercing his skull. He winced and pulled his uniform shirttail out from beneath his belt and covered his nose and mouth trying to deaden the stench. Just as a young boy had done two months earlier down here at the water's edge trying to ward off the smell as he searched for snapping turtles to bring home and impress his friends.

Oh, God, not another one, he groaned, as he slowly approached the woman, each step a chore in the shifting sand beneath his feet. This couldn't be happening. The killer had been caught and was locked up tight in some psychiatric hospital, never to be released. There couldn't be another victim, there just *couldn't*. Through the blowing sand he saw the fingers of the hand twitch as the woman slowly pulled her arm in toward her body. He wanted to shout to her not to move, don't turn over and please, please don't get up. But he couldn't. He never could. He felt a rising sense of fear, almost panic. The wind felt colder, the waves crashed louder, the gulls' shrieks grew sharper. Still lying in the sand, the woman slowly turned her head and looked at him. Through the hair partially obscuring her face, he could make out her dark eyes and broad nose. She smiled through her mask of hair and slowly pressed her palms against the sand, moving to rise from her prone position.

Stop! No! Please don't! He screamed at the woman, but the wind whipped his words away. He realized he'd been shouting through the shirttails pressed against his face and dropped his hands hoping his screams might reach the woman. She continued pushing herself up, turning slightly away from him, now on one knee, and slowly rising. No! Stop!

She looked over her bare shoulder at him and flashed a dazzling smile that, even beneath her hair, transformed her rather plain face into one of almost beauty. He raised his hands, waving at her. No, Nora! Don't! Please Nora, don't! But Nora slowly turned until she faced him.

Suddenly, he was almost upon her, still silently screaming at the woman. Sand clung to the front of her shoulders, her belly, and thighs. It clung as well to the two ragged, circular wounds carved into her chest. Shreds of tissue hung, streams of blood slowly ran through the sand caked on her stomach, staining the denim of her shorts. Behind her, Kevin saw dark stains in the sand where her chest had been. A screaming gull landed in one, snatched up a bloody morsel and flew off again.

Nora, I'm so, so sorry. If I had known, if I had any idea what might happen, I would have tried to stop it. But his words were wrenched away by the wind and the shrieks of gulls. There were more of them now. The birds hung over them, their shadows blocking out the sun. He could feel the air displaced as they desperately flapped their wings inches above their heads.

Nora Wilson continued smiling and held out a hand, beckoning him closer. There was no question about her intentions now. "I tried to tell you, Kevin. Way back in high school I tried to tell you, but you didn't want to listen." For some reason, despite the roaring wind, screams of the gulls, and pounding surf, her words were very clear and distinct. "I tried to tell you the hell I was living through, but you ignored me."

"No," he tried to say as he stared at her bloody, sand-encrusted wounds. "This hadn't happened then, not yet. This didn't happen until years later. You were an adult, a grown woman and preg—" He stopped.

Nora's smile slowly slipped away. She brought a hand to her ragged chest and caressed one of the gory wounds. "Yes, I was pregnant. I was going to have a little baby. My own little baby," she said quietly, yet still audibly over the surrounding din. An imploring look crossed her face. "How will I feed my baby, Kevin?" Nora Wilson gazed down at the wounds where her breasts had once been. "It will starve." She looked at Kevin; there were tears in her eyes. "Help me, Kevin, what will I do? Please, don't let my baby starve and die." She reached out one gory hand and stepped toward him. "Please listen to me this time, Kevin. Don't ignore me again. Help me."

He tried to back away, his feet sinking into the sand. He felt almost immobilized, sand swallowing his feet and lower legs, reaching his knees. The screeching gulls dropped closer, almost to his head, reaching a crescendo. His silent scream was lost as Nora Wilson's bloody hand gently caressed his cheek. Finally, his screams erupted, filling the waterfront, drowning out even the hungry gulls.

25

Kevin MacDougall sprang up in bed and choked off remnants of the scream. The twisted sheet had somehow wrapped itself around his legs. His naked chest was covered with sweat. His hand flew there, searching for wounds. Finding none, he dropped it to the damp sheet and tried to get his breathing under control. He turned to the glowing radium alarm clock. Three forty-five. He sighed and slowly swung his legs off the bed. No way he'd get back to sleep now. He rose and slowly began pulling the perspiration-soaked sheets from the bed. Second time this week, he thought. I'm getting to be a regular down at the laundromat. They probably think I'm a bedwetter.

He trudged down the short hall to the linen closet and dragged a fresh set of sheets from the shelf. After making his bed he pulled on a pair of sweatpants and T-shirt and headed to the kitchen. He opened the fridge and stared for about thirty seconds before grabbing the milk bottle, and peeling back its foil cap, giving it a tentative sniff. He hesitated, sniffed again, and shrugged. He sat at the worn, Formica-topped table, staring at the milk bottle. Then he rose, looking for yesterday's Star-Ledger. It was right where he'd left it, splayed out all over the coffee table. Everything was always right where he'd left it. One of the few benefits of living alone, he thought. Nobody to move your stuff.

Sitting again at the kitchen table with a bowl of cereal, he searched the paper for anything he hadn't yet read. Race riots in Cleveland, the republicans thrilled about their nominee for president. No surprise there, he thought, law and order Dick Nixon. The democrats' convention in Chicago coming up soon. He wondered how that city's stiff-necked mayor would deal with the inevitable demonstrations. Kevin continued scanning the pages. Vietnam, Vietnam, and more Vietnam. He tossed the news aside and reached for the sports section. Jeez, August and the Yankees were twenty games out of first place. He sighed and methodically spooned corn flakes into his mouth, tasting nothing, until the bowl was empty.

Kevin reached for the ballpoint pen hanging on a string attached to the small calendar on the wall next to the table. He made a check mark on August fifteenth then hesitated. The dream had occurred after midnight so should he mark the sixteenth instead? He counted the number of marks on the calendar going back to June. Thirteen. Lucky thirteen. He decided to leave the fifteenth checked and worry about accuracy another time.

The dreams were always a bit different but ended the same. Him screaming as Nora Wilson, or Rosaria Donez, or on one especially horrifying occasion, Minna Cooper, reached toward him with bloody hands ready to drag him...where? He never found out because he always woke screaming and covered in sweat just as the woman touched his face.

Thirteen. Jesus. Kevin knew they were affecting him, and it was becoming more and more noticeable at the station. Captain Clarke had spoken to him about it on a couple occasions. The last was a rather pointed suggestion that he needed to speak with someone about his issues. The captain hadn't said 'dreams' because Kevin had not yet mentioned them to his captain. All Clarke knew was that there was something very wrong that needed fixing.

"Kevin, what you went through on the Donez case was brutal. There's no way you could survive that and *not* be affected. But you're not going to get beyond it if you don't talk with someone." Clarke gazed up from his desk to his junior officer in both concern and exasperation. It appeared as if MacDougall hadn't had a decent night's sleep in a week and he looked, if possible, even thinner than before. His very boyish face, usually covered in acne, had appeared to clear up a bit, but now looked at least a decade older than its twenty-five years.

"You know I'm not a big touchy-feely, let's-hold-hands kind of person. But I know that traumatized people need to voice their fears and concerns." He opened his center desk drawer and withdrew a business card. "I suggest you call this guy. He works with cops who need help. And Kevin, make no mistake about it, you need help. Consider this a heartfelt suggestion, but if we find ourselves revisiting this subject, it won't be a suggestion. It will be an order, understand?"

Kevin nodded and blinked. "Yes, sir. I understand."

"Kevin," Clarke said quietly, "it was hell. Absolute gut-wrenching hell. The scope of the madness and the fact that the killer was someone who had been close to you your entire life, must have made it even worse."

Officer Kevin MacDougall cleared his throat. "Not that close, sir. More like acquaintances."

Clarke said quietly, "Okay, Kevin. But please remember what I said. Suggestion now, order later."

In the past an encounter like that would have embarrassed the heck out of him. Not now. It was as though a heavy lethargy had enveloped him. It seemed when he wasn't screaming for his life in dreams, well, let's be honest, in his nightmares, he was unable to get emotionally involved with anything. Not at work, home, anywhere. He'd quit going to his summer baseball league, usually one of his favorite warm-weather pastimes. He'd even stopped his visits to the public library. Kevin loved reading the old pulp-style detective novels from decades ago. Raymond Chandler, Dashiell Hammett, and even the newer guy, John D. MacDonald with his terrific detective, Travis McGee. Talk about a guy he'd love to be, that Travis was living the dream, all right. Not that he'd ever shared this with anyone. That would have seemed too...well, weird. But even Travis McGee failed to pull him from this slump.

Kevin rinsed his bowl and spoon, put away the cereal and milk, and wandered into the small living room. He stopped before the old upright piano and dragged his fingers over the keys. The piano had been in his family for almost as long as he could remember. His mother had picked it up second hand somewhere and insisted he take lessons as a boy. After about six months of discordant noise, she threw in the towel and little Kevin was free to play ball with his friends instead of sitting miserably on the piano stool, feet dangling inches off the floor, and frightening the cat with the din he created. He tried a few half-remembered, left-hand exercises on the keyboard. They sounded as bad as ever.

On top of the piano, next to a vase of very dusty plastic flowers, stood a wedding photograph of his mother and stepfather, Paval. Mom looking very plump and happy. And Paval, Kevin smiled, well, he could not remember an occasion when Paval hadn't had a smile on his face. He'd always wished Paval had been his real father, not the thin, dour-looking man he vaguely recalled from old, black and white photos. But now Paval was gone, joining Mom who had died several years earlier. And Kevin was left to face the aftermath of the murders on his own.

MacDougall looked at a more recent photo of Mom and Paval. Mom looking very much plumper and even happier. And Paval, his smile wider than ever. An immigrant from Poland in the mid-50s, he'd met Mom at a VFW picnic. Well, saw her, anyway.

"Kevin," he had said in his heavily accented English, "there am I at beer truck. I am hooking keg to spout when I look and see God's vision before me. Like a statue in a church, she was. My heart, my heart runs fast and faster. She sipped from a cup, a cup of beer, and there was white on her lips and here." Paval then laid his index finger horizontally beneath his nose.

"She had a moustache?" young Kevin had asked, puzzled.

"Yes!" Paval laughed and nodded. "Yes, my God's vision and a moustache! The beer bubbles, ah, the beer...foam! Yes, foam made her moustache! Why, I ask, why could I not be one who gave her this beer? I could speak to this beauty. Why, oh why was I hooking to spout?

"Kevin," he said, suddenly serious. "I had two feelings. Two feelings at one time. Joy to see this vision, so lovely. And so much disappointment she did not have my beer on her moustache. I felt like broke in two! Never had I such this feeling!"

"What happened next?" Kevin was hooked.

"Next? Oh, next she walks away with other woman, a friend. Oh, so much disappointment I felt! Why could she not have more beer? I would be sure to give that beer! I ask friend with me, who was this woman with moustache by picnic table? He tells me Clara. Clara MacDougall. Clara! Such a beauty of name! I learn husband, your father, Kevin, dead in Korea and she has young boy. A handsome young boy!" Paval laughed and roughly tousled Kevin's hair.

What followed next with Paval and his mother was a unique courtship which culminated in Paval showing up one autumn morning with a horse and buggy and taking Mom for a ride down Stevens Street, through town to Adams Park where he dropped on a knee and proposed to her before amused onlookers. Kevin always assumed Mom was probably too embarrassed to say anything but yes, if just to get him up, into the buggy, and away from the crowd. It was then Paval shared he was a blacksmith back in Poland. Being with horses was not unusual for him, they always made him happy.

All Kevin was certain of was that the years his mother had been married to Paval Solciek were, by far, the happiest of her life. In the photo, Paval in a vested suit, hair slicked down, his arm around Clara, and, of course, smiling. And Mom, Kevin smiled at the image, yeah, looking like a vision. A tremendously happy, content image. God, Kevin missed them both.

While walking home from the grocery store Mom had been killed by a hit and run driver. Kevin swore to himself upon graduating the police academy he would one day track down her killer and bring him to justice. No vigilante stuff, kidnapping the person and torturing him until he screamed in repentance before dying a painful death, nothing like that. But righting what was for Kevin, and Paval, a terrible wrong. No one should be allowed to take a life without repercussions. The loss of her had changed Paval, as well. Yes, he still smiled, he was still the father-figure in Kevin's life, the man he loved dearly, but that glow, the light he had always given off, while not extinguished, was certainly dimmed. And then his death just two years ago.

It was so sudden, the guy seemed to be the healthiest person Kevin had ever seen. He never remembered Paval ever having to see a doctor. Until the very end. His passing was a shock and Kevin was surprised to find the hole in his life left by his deceased stepfather seemed to be more cavernous than the one left by his mother. He had not only lost a parent; he had lost, to his belated surprise, the person who had become his best friend.

Kevin wondered if Paval had known just how sick he really was and chose not to burden his sensitive stepson. Lung cancer. Mesothelioma. Kevin had looked it up after the man's death. Almost since his arrival in America, Paval had worked at the

31

Breyerton Refinery, just north of the town, by the bay. It was one of several refineries in the area. A lot of guys who'd worked there came down with lung problems. Something about being subjected to asbestos while working the machinery. It seemed every year the father or uncle of someone from school was diagnosed with it, became bed-ridden, and eventually died, tumors in their lungs, stomachs, you name it. For years there'd been talk of going after Breyerton, making them pay, but it never came to much. And even if it had, would you want to close one of the major industries in town? For decades generations of men had supported families working at Breyerton. Guys that had never made it out of high school knew there was always a job waiting for them there. A job that would eventually enable him to marry, buy a little house, raise kids, maybe even send a son to college. No, even the families of those that died or were dying did not want the factory closed. It was an essential thread in the fabric of the town.

But these people who had died were decades-long employees of the refinery. Paval had not been there anywhere near that length of time. It hadn't made a lot of sense, still didn't. And he went so quickly! In a matter of days, he was gone. The final diagnosis had been so shocking, but hey, Breyerton, the refineries, what can you expect? And everybody's different he'd been told; there was no single timeline for these things.

Kevin remembered an evening, a day or so after Paval's seeing a doctor. Over a dinner of perogies, he'd told Kevin he would be needing to speak with him very soon about an important matter. Kevin was at the tail end of his days at the police academy.

"Does it have to do with finally sharing the recipe for your perogies? Or am I going to have to go to Poland and knock on every door in Gdansk until someone finally helps me out?"

"Funny man you are, Kevin, funny, funny. The recipe is yours whenever you ask. But I will always make the better taste of pierogies. Experience, you know," he added with a smile. "No," the smile was gone, "this is important matter, I think. Important for your new job."

"For being a police officer?" Paval nodded. "Well, I'm not one yet, keep your fingers crossed for me."

"Fingers and toes. All crossed. But not needed. You will be fine officer, I know."

"Thanks, Paval." His stepfather broke into an abrupt fit of coughing and got up from the table, heading toward the bathroom. As he waited, Kevin marveled how Paval always made him feel so good about himself. All the self-doubt he'd battled for as long as he could remember seemed to dissolve in the man's presence. He tried to recall if his real father had ever made him feel this way. He had very little memory of him at all. Just a face in a photograph, one that with each passing day he seemed to resemble more. But he'd be darned if he would look as miserable as he remembered his father looking. No, he refused to live in misery. Lemonade. Make lemonade when you got lemons in life, or something like that.

"Sorry." Paval had returned to the table. He looked down at his nearly full plate and pushed it away. "This cold," he pointed to his chest, "it takes my hunger, too. Ah, well," he shoved the plate across the table toward Kevin. "Now you will eat more and become big, strong policeman, eh?" He smiled, leaned back, and lit a cigarette.

"Thanks, what did you want to talk to me about?"

Paval waved him off. "Later. This is history, bad history. Now is no time for this. Later, maybe when you become big important policeman, yes?"

"Yes."

Kevin gazed out the living room window until the streetlights eventually went off. He rose to shower away the dried sweat from his dream and get dressed, ready to head to the station. He hoped today would be a better day and prayed he'd experienced his final nightmare.

FIVE

Captain Timothy Clarke sat at his desk staring at his oscillating fan wishing it could oscillate a little bit faster. His minuscule office felt like a sauna. Jeez, this had been a killer summer. Clarke winced at his poor choice of words as he reached to a lower drawer and pulled out Officer Kevin MacDougall's personnel file. He gazed at it knowing nothing had changed since last looking at it a week ago. He'd perused it numerous times over the summer since that awful night when they had finally apprehended that crazed murderer.

Born in January 1943, right here in Pendale at St. Mary's Hospital. Father killed in Korea, mother deceased in 1962, an unsolved hit and run. Clarke knew his young officer aspired to catch the driver who had taken his mother, not that Kevin had ever said this directly. Stepfather...what's it say? Paval Solciek died, wow, just two years ago. Clarke had no idea it was so recent. Must have occurred while MacDougall was at the Academy. The cause of death was blank.

He thought of the young officer under his command. Kevin, until recently, had always been so eager to please, willing to go above and beyond. Someone trying like hell to rise above the prejudices ingrained in him by his narrow-minded upbringing, his being subjected to many of the town's bigoted views, biases, and most, but certainly not all, its secrets. That sure was the truth, Clarke thought grimly, flashing back to early summer and the violent deaths of two young women. Two women who "didn't quite fit" in Pendale. And let's not forget the third, Clarke thought. Angela Castille, murdered over fifteen years ago and buried in the killer's yard.

How many times over the years had the murderer sat, feet up, soaking in the sun, all the while knowing half a dozen feet below, rested the grave of the woman deemed not suitable to continue living, not in Pendale, anyway. And the mutilations of Rosaria Donez and Nora Wilson? It's amazing how insanity can be present for years, right before our eyes, and still go unseen. And Kevin had known and looked up to the killer his entire life. His mother had been a close friend. Clarke knew Kevin now questioned how much his mother may have known about the killer's harsh views and beliefs. And he was addressing all this alone. There was no one in his life to share his doubts, concerns, fears.

Well, that solitude was something the two of them had in common, Clarke thought. He wondered what a personnel file on himself might say. Over fifty, hell, let's be honest, well into his mid-fifties with the next big milestone not too far down the road, He'd probably risen as high in rank as he ever would. Before the Donez case had been resolved, he knew there were those who thought he'd risen well beyond his limits. His ex-wife lived in Florida since the divorce, what, almost six years ago? Six years. My God, Clarke thought, I've been a single man for over half a decade. That's a hell of a long time to be alone and celibate, he thought. Not that he hadn't had several opportunities, of course. Well, two opportunities. But the swinging sixties had not translated into much in the way of female companionship for him. He was...what he was. A middle-aged guy with a paunch, working a job for over twenty years trying his best to make his town a safer, better place, whether those efforts were appreciated or not. He sighed and replaced MacDougall's file in the drawer.

He looked at his phone for a long time before reaching for it. "Mrs. Barton, please put me through to Captain Clements at the Newark P.D. Thank you." He knew what he was about to do was going to make some waves, especially for Kevin, but hell, it was time to shake him out of his prolonged lethargy. *Something* sure had to give.

A moment later his phone rang. "Yes. Really, Mrs. Barton? You're certainly a Speedy Gonzalez. Please put him through...Chuck, it's Tim, how are you? You must have been sitting on the phone, getting back to me so quick. Well, I won't keep you from lunch. You know the officer we talked about last week? I spoke to my superiors and—what? Ha! Yeah, I know. Remember 'superiors' is just a word, Chuck. After our last case they've okayed the expense of another officer in little ole Pendale, and I've made up my mind. We gladly accept the transfer from your office. It's a perfect fit for us. Hmm? I wouldn't kid you, Chuck, I'm serious. This is exactly what we need. Yeah, I know there might be some growing pains—oh, come on, it won't be that bad. Well, we're an accommodating bunch here. You'll see." He pulled the phone from his ear as Chuck barked out a laugh. "So, when can we expect—first of next week? Great. Good talking with you, Chuck. Say hi to Ava for me. Hmm? Yeah, absolutely. Dinner sounds good. Any chance of one of her lasagnas? Ha! Yeah, so I'll have to have my waistband let out. It's worth it. See you, Chuck."

He hung up and thought that was that. He'd taken the plunge. What was that old Bette Davis line? "Fasten your seat belts, it's going to be a bumpy ride?" Something like that. Well, we'll see.

SIX

"Hey, Mrs. G," Nikki called through the open door that separated the two apartments. Well, her apartment and Rose Gorman's house. "This probably isn't the best time for me to be waltzing off and leaving you by your lonesome. How about I call...," Nikki pulled a much-folded piece of note paper from her back pocket and attempted to shake it open one-handed as she lit a cigarette with the other. She fumbled with the lighter and a footlong flame shot out almost singing an eyebrow along with a wayward lock of curly, ginger hair falling over her forehead. "Holy shit!" she muttered around the cigarette while quickly spinning the small wheel on the lighter with her thumb, reducing the flame.

"What's the matter, Nikki?" Mrs. G's voice carried from her living room where she lay propped up on the couch.

"Ah, nothing Mrs. G, give me a sec here." She tossed the lighter on her cluttered kitchen table and, using both hands, unfolded the notepaper. It was covered at different angles with her barely legible scrawl, as well as doodles and a drawing of what was supposed to be the smiling face of an adorable puppy she'd copied off an ad, but which looked more like, well, a pretty shitty drawing of a puppy. "More like the creature from the black lagoon," she muttered, leaving the mess of her small apartment, and entering the pristine of Mrs. G's.

"What's that, dear?"

"Nothing." Nikki crossed to the large floor-unit television and lowered the volume with a twist of a nob. A song proclaiming the wonders of having borax in a certain laundry detergent went from an irritating jingle to a barely audible mumble.

"Thank you, dear. I was about to turn it off but didn't want to get up. I think I'll read for a while." She held up a dog-eared paperback.

Most definitely *not* the Micky Spillane she'd seen two weeks ago.

"So, no General Hospital today? Don't you wonder what that dishy Doctor Hardy is up to?"

The older woman looked at her balefully.

"Okay." Nikki snapped off the set. The various shades of grays and off-whites quickly faded into a single point in the center of the screen before finally vanishing. She sat on the edge of the couch and reached for the older woman's hand.

"What I was saying was I—" She looked around for an ashtray; an ash was about to drop. "Hang on." She crossed quickly back to her apartment, a hand cupped under the cigarette. She pinched off the end and set it in an overflowing ashtray on the counter. "Okay, what I was saying," she said, brushing her hands together, "was it's probably not the best time for me to take off and leave you. It's *my* turn to be the responsible one now."

About two months ago, after Nikki herself had been released from the hospital following her near-death encounter, Mrs. Gorman set about trying to instill some stability into her young tenant's life. A life that had devolved into one of alcoholism and promiscuity. This stability primarily took the form of visits to church, avoidance of waterholes and those who frequented them, a job, and attendance at Alcoholics Anonymous meetings. None of these tasks were easy for Nikki to embrace, but surprisingly, she was finding the frequent visits to St. Margaret's Church bearable. At the very least they offered moments of calm in an existence that was in dire need of it. The maelstrom that had been her life seemed to slow when she entered the stone walls of the church. And it was certainly in need of slowing.

Two years ago, Nikki lost...what? Her boyfriend? Fiancé? Almost fiancé? Recent ex-almost fiancé? Whatever Donald had been to her, he died. Died in a horrible car crash at college. Nikki blamed herself for the rift that occurred during the final days of his life, and while having nothing to do with the accident, the blame for the demise of the relationship fell squarely on her shoulders. Nikki then proceeded on a path of self-destruction.

She was a fixture in the local bars and anyone willing to support her habit could have her. Many did. The behavior continued until Mrs. Gorman finally broke through her mantle of self-hate and rescued Nikki from herself. However, in a small town a young woman, both alcoholic and promiscuous, quickly becomes infamous. And Nikki certainly was. This notoriety almost cost her her life when a lunatic attempted to exterminate yet another piece of filth threatening the God-fearing families of Pendale. Nikki would have been victim number three if not for sheer luck and the timely arrival on the scene of Captain Clarke.

However, that event could not erase almost two years of wildly indiscreet behavior on her part. To say that she was not popular among the women of Pendale would be a colossal understatement. They believed, often accurately, that she may have had sex with many of their men. How many men, who knew? Nikki certainly didn't. She became a pariah. Without the intervention of Mrs. G, Nikki knew she would not have survived the past several months. This intervention began with a trip to St. Margaret's on the day of a killer hangover. That terrible visit aside, Nikki was beginning to accept, if not welcome, the visits to the old church. There certainly had been enough of them. While Mrs. G wasn't a daily churchgoer, she was damn close, and Nikki was expected to join her on these visits. And it wasn't so bad. Nikki wouldn't say she was becoming pious or anything. Hell no. But the muted light through the stained-glass windows, the coolness of the air inside the old structure, the feel of the pew beneath her, it was calming, and Nikki found, if just for the duration of her visit there, she could momentarily put aside the near-constant burdens of self-recrimination she felt for the death of Donald, the demise of their relationship, and her more recent abhorrent behavior.

As far as employment, Nikki had not worked in God knows how long. Showing up at work reeking of alcohol and vomit quickly put an end to that. No more paycheck. No paycheck, no money. No money..., well there was always a way for a girl to drink if she was willing. And she drank. Often and a lot. If it hadn't been for the kindness of Mrs. Gorman, whom she had begun renting from back when she and Donald were still a couple, Nikki would have been on the streets. Despite Nikki's self-destructive behavior and her sordid reputation, Mrs. Gorman had somehow worked magic. Recently, she had persuaded a couple women in town to hire her as a house cleaner. At first Nikki was skeptical. Who in the world would want someone with a rep like hers poking around their house? Then when she heard what she would be paid, it became clear.

"Are you fu—are you frigging kidding me, Mrs. G? I made more an hour babysitting when I was twelve! Are you turning me out in some sort of white-slavery deal?"

"No, Nikki, I am not. And thank you for your attempt at civil language. This is simply a way for you to earn a few dollars—"

"You got the 'few' part right."

"A way to earn a few dollars for items like cigarettes, sweets, things like that."

Sweets? Good God. "Well, it's a good thing smokes are only thirty cents a pack. As it is, I may have to ration them."

"Oh, please, you'll be fine. Not that it wouldn't be a good thing. You know how I feel about them."

"I know." Mrs. G's husband, Carl, had died of lung cancer just weeks after Donald's passing. Nikki thought again of how they were two women, alone, without their men.

"Payment aside, how did you convince anybody to let me into their home? I mean, aren't they afraid I'll raid the liquor cabinet or seduce their teenage sons?"

"I can't speak for the liquor cabinet, but the women I talked to are all older. Even older than yours truly," she said with a smile. "So, there are no teenaged children in the house, no children at all. They're all grown up and living with children of their own."

"Still, I'm surprised. I know you have magical powers of persuasion, but...."

"You underestimate yourself."

"I do?"

"Yes. That night in the garage, that awful night, you showed such courage. There are people who respect you for that."

"No shit? Really?"

"Nikki."

"What?"

"Language."

"Huh? Oh, sh—ah, I mean damn—no, heck! No heck?" She hesitated. "No heck sounds stupid, Mrs. G. It just doesn't work."

"Why not just say, 'really?'"

She thought. "Yup. That one works. So, really?"

The older woman nodded, smiling.

"I don't think there was much in the way of courage that night," Nikki said. "Stupidity, yes, there sure was that. I mean, I knew that nutcase was pretty far out there, and I was definitely a target of some serious hatred. Why I went there on my own is a mystery."

But it wasn't, she knew. Nikki went to confront the person who had said Donald was better off being dead than having to share his life with her. There were probably many in Pendale who would agree with that, Donald having been born and raised there, a "good boy," while Nikki had arrived on the scene just before the two began dating. And one thing the good natives of Pendale did not tolerate was an outsider. But having something like that said to her face? Nikki had withstood a lot, but she couldn't allow such audacity to pass without a response.

"Whatever you believe, dear, there are those who admire your courage," Rose Gorman continued.

"Wow."

Nikki felt tears in her eyes. Dammit! What is it with these crazy emotions she'd been dealing with since, well, since around that night? One minute she's mad as hell and ready to kick the grocer in the nuts for being such a rude prick, next she's bawling over a cute baby smiling at her in the checkout line. For a moment she felt a shred of pride, then she remembered what was being offered as payment, and the feeling quickly dissipated.

"Okay, so what exactly am I going to be doing? Vacuuming? Some light dusting? Remember, I don't do windows. Ha, ha."

"You will be doing whatever you are instructed to do. Colleen, Mrs. Kowalczyk, told me she has any supplies you might need. She did ask if you had any physical limits as to what you were capable of, and I told her you were healthy as a horse and just as strong."

"Oh, boy. I hope she doesn't want me to move a piano or anything."

"I wouldn't think so. I've been to her house; there is no piano. Although from what I recall, the place certainly could use a good bit of cleaning. This will keep you off the streets for a while."

"So, this is no quick job, huh?"

"Probably not. In fact, I hope these few jobs I've been able to line up will turn into many more and keep you busy. It's important you fill your time and don't have to deal with too many idle hours. Work can set one free, they say."

Nikki thought she remembered that line from somewhere, though used in a less-than-positive context.

"When Carl stopped drinking," Mrs. G began, "I remember he struggled in that regard. The drink had taken over so much of his life he was at odds as to what to do with himself. Your apartment," she nodded toward the door to Nikki's kitchen, "was one of the projects he took on in order to keep busy." Mrs. Gorman smiled, "For a man who really had no aptitude for handiwork, I'd have to say it turned out rather well."

"My place was part of his early sobriety?" A word, she thought, until recently, she may have used maybe twice before in her life.

"That's right."

"It sort of makes me feel there's a connection between him and me. I mean concerning his struggles and mine, you know? He was able to overcome them; maybe with you, along with his ghost, his spirit on my side, maybe I can, too."

"I have no doubt."

"Are you sure you'll be okay on your own? I can call...," Nikki peered at the name on the many-creased paper from her pocket, "Mrs. Kowalska and postpone the cleaning. I'm sure she'd be alright with—"

"Kowalczyk, Collen Kowalczyk."

"Yeah?" Nikki looked doubtfully at the paper. "Kowalsick," she said. "Kowalsick."

"Not Kowal*sick*, Kowal*czyk*. Kowal C-Z-Y-K."

Nikki squinted at her scrawl. "Okay, I'll call Mrs. K. I'm sure I can put her off. She's got to know you've been in the hospital, right? Everybody knows everything about everyone in this town. I mean, jeez, you have gas and minutes later someone four blocks over knows it."

"Nikki, really...."

"Okay, sorry. I'll call her. But you look tired, you shouldn't be on your own yet. Let me just give her a ring." She rose to cross to the phone on the kitchen wall.

"Stop," Mrs. G commanded. "Sit and listen." She nodded to the spot Nikki had just vacated.

Nikki sat, hands folded, in her lap.

"I look tired because I recently had a heart attack. I will probably continue to look tired for a while. But I'm home because the hospital believes it is safe for me to recuperate here, right?"

Nikki nodded.

"I was also told I need to work at getting some strength back, right?"

"Yeah, but—"

"Yes, the doctor said to gradually work at getting it back, I know." She took one of Nikki's folded hands in her own. "My walking to the kitchen or bathroom is not going to do me in. I will be fine. You have an appointment, keep it. It's a job, a paying job. Make some money. Maybe one day I'll actually receive rent again." She smiled. "And then I won't have to kick you out into the street."

Nikki grunted. "I'm going to need a hell of a reduction in rent with the pittance Mrs. Kowalski is paying me."

"Kowalczyk."

"Yeah. Hey, what kind of name is Colleen Kowalczyk? It's like the most Irish first name with a *real* Polish last name. What gives?"

"How long have you lived in town? Two years, three? You know it's been Irish/Polish here for generations."

"Yeah. With almost no tolerance for anything else," Nikki said, thinking about Rosaria Donez and the horrible manner the young Puerto Rican girl had been murdered just two months ago.

"Unfortunately, that's very much true."

The two sat in silence for a moment.

"I guess I should be thankful Dad's last name was Greene and not Lopez or something, huh?"

Rose Gorman nodded quietly.

"Really though, it's not a problem staying with you. I know you're not rich, but you don't seem to be hurting for the rent money. And let's face it, I can't even remember the last time I paid it. Truth is, there's a lot I don't remember." Nikki smiled ruefully. "But way too much I *do* remember." She looked down at her hands. "And a lot I wish I could forget." Nikki ran her index finger over the back of Helen Gorman's hand. After a pause she said, "One thing I'll never forget though," she raised her head, tears in her eyes, "is that you saved me, Mrs. G. From everything, from those guys, and from myself." Thank you, she mouthed silently.

"We saved each other, Nikki. Without you to take care of after my Carl's death, I would have died, as well. You gave me a reason to get up and struggle through each day. This is very much a two-way street."

They nodded to each other. "Okay, I'm off to Mrs. Kowawhatever's now." Nikki stood. "Can I pick up anything from Foodtown or Baranowski's on my way back?"

"Maybe some ham from Baranowski's."

"You got it. Should I grab some cash from the cookie jar, or just rely on the old money-maker?" She slapped her rump as she made for the kitchen.

"Nikki, I know you're joking, but I beg you, don't attempt to make light of what you put yourself through. You hide behind your humor. We both know that. But there is nothing funny about that part of your life. It nearly killed you. Don't joke about it. Please?"

A lump in her throat, Nikki nodded. Cookie jar cash it is, she thought.

Nikki waved through the window to Mrs. Gorman as she crossed in front of the house on her way down the street to Mrs. Kowa...ah hell's house. She glanced at the notepaper for the address, Stevens Avenue. Two blocks over and two down toward Broadway. The direction of her old watering holes, the ones that haunted her nights. She felt her face getting warm at the very thought of them.

"Get a grip, Nik," she muttered. "Serenity, serenity...God, grant me some fucking serenity."

SEVEN

"Kevin, Sully, get in here, please," Clarke called from his small office. It was going to be another scorcher today. He swore, this summer had been like a preview of what Hell might be like. Not that he ever expected to experience the real thing. He hoped. The fan above his door offered a bit of respite, but not much.

Sully lumbered through the office entrance. Must be the only time in his life he's been first for anything, Clarke thought. Then he noticed the powdered sugar on the man's lips and the front of his shirt. He'd been downing donuts in the coffee room. No wonder he'd been so prompt.

"Hi, Captain," Sully said, wiping his mouth with the back of his hand. Clarke waited for what he knew was coming next. "Hot enough for you?" He had to say this for Officer Sullivan, he was consistent.

"Yes, Sully, it certainly is. Hey, move away from the fan, would you?"

Well over both six feet and two hundred pounds, Sully tended to take up a lot of space. And space was in very short supply in Clarke's office. The hell with this, Clarke thought. "Let's move this to the coffee room, it's crowded in here already and we're still missing Kevin."

Sully perked up immediately. The coffee room meant Starlite Donuts, his absolute favorite. "Great idea, Captain, meet you there."

"How about grabbing Kevin from the squad room first?" MacDougall had made it a lifetime practice to be punctual. The fact he was making them wait just added to Clarke's concern for him. "The donuts will still be there, I promise."

Sully grinned. "I'm on it."

Clarke headed to the coffee room and eyed the open box of donuts; he saw two of his favorites, crème-filled crullers. He stopped in mid-reach, thinking of his pinched midsection pushing against his uniform belt. Damn. Instead, he reached for a mug and poured his first coffee of the day. He sipped and grimaced, as he heard his two junior officers enter the room. He heard them bantering back and forth, which Clarke took to be a positive sign given Kevin's recent issues. As they entered the room Clarke saw he'd been too optimistic.

Kevin's face was drawn and pale. It did not appear he'd slept much the previous night. His pallor accentuated the almost violet acne on his face. As Sully crossed to the box of donuts MacDougall sat at the old table and ran a finger over several of the many scars carved into it.

Clarke held up his mug. "Kevin?"

"No, thanks, Captain."

"Going to make a grab for the donuts then? Better hurry, Sully's ready to empty the box."

He shook his head. "Not today. But thanks."

Despite his weighing in at less than a hundred and fifty pounds, Clarke knew the young officer could put away nearly as much food as Sully. His refusal was yet another reason to worry.

"Okay." He pulled out a chair for himself. "Sully, grab your donut and park yourself. I need to speak to both of you."

Once everyone was settled and he'd had another sip, he said, "A couple things. Doc Eichen's death. I need both of you to get out to

Catherine Street and the surrounding blocks. Canvass the area and check if anyone has seen anything out of the ordinary." He heard a groan from Sully.

"You take issue with this, Officer?"

Sully's face quickly turned scarlet. "No, Captain. I'm sorry. It's just, you know, usually a waste of time. No one ever knows anything, and if they do, they don't want to tell us. It's almost like we're the bad guys."

"I'm aware it's very time consuming, but sometimes it yields results. It's just something...Wait! Wasn't it you who interviewed that old neighbor after Nora Wilson's death? The guy who named his cat, his *female* cat, after General Patton?"

Sully grinned. "Yeah! That's right! But it was Westmoreland, not Patton. He called her Westy."

"If I remember correctly, his information was very helpful. You did well, drawing it out of him."

"Thanks, Captain. But he was an old, retired guy wanting someone to talk to."

"At any rate, he was helpful. Maybe we'll get lucky again this time. Don't just go through the motions with this, got it?" Sully nodded.

Clarke opened a file and glanced down. "I received word from the medical staff, the ice pick entering his brain was what killed the doc. Surprise, surprise. Apparently, if you penetrate the brain deeply enough and wiggle around the weapon, it's very effective." He shook his head, and the room was silent for a moment except for Sully's chewing.

Kevin said, "Why an ice pick? Who would choose such a weird weapon? And why kill the doc?"

"Good questions, Kevin. Questions we'd better find answers to quick." Clarke looked at both the young men in front of him, and then deliberately closed the file. "Along those lines, there's something else I need to make you aware of."

After a pause, he said, "You know how I've been hounding the higher-ups for another officer in the department. Even prior to the Donez case, I've felt we were understaffed. Well, the publicity garnered from the case and our successful conclusion of it has finally gotten them off their collective butts. We'll soon be seeing a new face around here."

Sully shrugged and took another bite of donut. Kevin looked wary. "Do you really think we need the extra manpower? It's not because we haven't found the doc's killer yet, is it? It's only been, what, a day? I mean, we just solved probably the biggest case this town has ever seen. Everybody seemed really pleased."

"They were, and no, it has nothing to do with this case. However, I do believe we need the extra help. Policing is changing and there is just too much for us to keep up with. You may not feel stretched thin now, but I assure you, in the coming months and years, you will. This way, we're being proactive, so we'll be ahead of the curve. And you know, or should know, I am very proud of this department and how it handled those recent difficult events. But it took a toll on us." He glanced at Kevin who was frowning, still running his finger over the table surface. "So, we're getting some assistance.

"I have asked for and received permission to transfer in an officer from Newark." Sully paused in mid-chew. Kevin looked up. "Newark?" he asked. "Why are we going to the big city for extra help? There are plenty of departments a lot nearer. In Sayreville alone—"

"I realize there are other departments with officers we could draw from, some just a town or two away. However, this department has always been manned by those who were natives to Pendale, or at the very least, are from the region. "Sully, you've been here over twenty years, since grade school, right?" Sully nodded, once again chewing. "Kevin, you were born and raised here. While I realize that it's often a positive, knowing the townsfolk, how they think and act, it also comes with drawbacks. "How long until you outgrow being little Kevvy MacDougall, the boy from school or the kid on the playground?" Sully grinned. MacDougall didn't.

"Was it a problem during that last case?"

"No, it wasn't. What I am trying to say, not too well, I gather, is that while it is an asset having those who are familiar with the town on the force, it will also be beneficial to have someone on the force with no preconceived notions. As I said, I am proud of you. Period. This addition will simply make us even better. That's all."

Kevin slumped a bit. "Okay, Captain. Remember though, this town doesn't do change very well. Anyone with an unfamiliar face is going to draw a lot of distrust."

Don't I know it, thought Clarke. He'd been there almost two decades himself, and he was still the new guy replacing old Captain Delaney.

"There are folks who feel the town is under attack from, ah, outsiders. So much changing in the world: marches, demonstrations, riots, all the war stuff...they're real wary."

"I am aware of that, Kevin, and yes, the world is changing," though not necessarily for the better, he thought, "and Pendale, like everywhere else, is going to have to accept it and change with it."

"We're with you, Captain," Sully said with enthusiasm. "Maybe the new guy can help us out on the PBA ball team. Do you know, can he pitch?"

"Why don't we wait and see, officer." He took another sip and made another face. "That's about all I have, gentlemen. Questions?" Sully shook his head, MacDougall stared again at the tabletop. "Okay, we'll meet back here at four o'clock. Remember, be thorough! Off you go. Kevin, do me favor and check with me at the end of the day before leaving, okay?" Not waiting for a response, Clarke rose, dumped the remaining dregs of his coffee into the sink, and left the room.

EIGHT

Nikki stood in the grease-scented kitchen of the very matronly Colleen Kowalczyk. After one quick look, Nikki knew God was out to get her. The kitchen looked a lot like her own during the worse throes of her drinking. The cabinet doors were smudged with what looked like years of fingerprints, the floor was sticky, and in the corners, Nikki could see a buildup of dirt, grime, and dust balls like tumbleweeds. The sink was stained with who knows what, and while the stovetop was sure to be found somewhere under the layer of grease, exactly where she wasn't certain.

"You can start in here," Mrs. Kow-whatever told Nikki. She waved her arm across the room. "I've let it go a bit. My back, you know," she reached behind and placed a hand just above her ample butt. "There are rubber gloves and cleaning things in the closet, a mop, too, I think. If you want me, I'll be in the living room. Really, the only way to avoid this constant pain is to be horizontal." She grabbed a bag of potato chips from a cabinet and lumbered off. "Try not to bother me. I'll be watching my stories."

Alone, Nikki slowly turned in a circle, taking in the job in its entirety. Holy shit. If I didn't owe Mrs. G my life, I swear I'd kill her for this.

Where to even begin? She tried to remember something she'd heard about where to start when cleaning a room. Work from the floor up? No, work from the top down. Wait, was that for when you were cleaning or painting? Dammit. She looked up. How the hell does someone get grease on the ceiling? Not just over the stove, but the entire fucking ceiling? She opened the closet door where Mrs. K had indicated there might be cleaning supplies. There certainly were a bunch of them. Mostly unopened. She sighed and dragged out a small stepladder, bucket, detergent, and rubber gloves. Nikki shook her head and went to work.

After an hour and a half of craning her neck upward and back to scrub the ceiling, Nikki felt she deserved a break. She stepped outside for a quick cigarette. She could hear Mrs. K's television blaring through the open window. It sounded like a lot of people being very terse with each other punctuated by crashing chords on an organ, followed by commercials for household products.

She rubbed the back of her neck and, eyes closed, slowly rolled her head from side to side, and round and round. This is going to take more than just the remainder of the afternoon, she thought. That Mrs. G was tricky. Keep me occupied and wear me out so all I'll want to do is crash in bed at the end of the day. She took a deep drag and opened her eyes. Across the street and one house down a guy was washing his car. He was looking at Nikki and flashing a knowing smile. Shit.

One of her past benefactors, she guessed. Some guy willing to buy the drinks she swilled in exchange for an hour, hell, usually a lot less than that, with Miss Congeniality. That was the problem trying to get sober in a small town. There were so many people who knew of her drinking, they couldn't be avoided. She didn't even recognize this guy, just one in a long parade, but he sure as shit knew her. Great. Now he was waving her over. Nikki ignored him the best she could, finished her cigarette, and crushed it out. She looked up to see the guy making a drinking motion to her and inclining his head toward downtown. She gave him the finger, turned, and went back to the kitchen.

Two hours later, with the ceiling, cabinet doors, and counters clean, she was ready to call it a day. "Mrs. Kowal...shit. Mrs. K," she called toward the living room. When she received no response, she stuck her head in and saw the woman sound asleep on the sofa, empty bag of chips on the floor next to her. The woman snorted as she exhaled and reached toward the bag in her sleep. "Mrs. K?" Nikki said softly. "Mrs. K?" A bit louder.

Her eyes fluttered open and after a moment focused on Nikki. "Oh, you're finished?"

"Um, no. If you like, I can come back tomorrow morning." There wasn't a prayer in hell she could finish it then.

"Really?" she said struggling to sit up on the sofa. "I would have thought you'd be done in an hour or so. Don't even think about trying to stretch out the job for more pay. I wasn't born yesterday, you know."

Nikki clenched her jaw. "I would never do that, ma'am. If you would rather I didn't come back, that's fine. It *is* quite a big job."

"Oh?" she mumbled and lumbered to the kitchen with Nikki. She looked around. "You haven't done anything! The floor is still dirty. It looks exactly the same!" Nikki pointed upward. "Oh, the ceiling. You cleaned it? Why would you clean a ceiling? Nobody ever looks at a ceiling, they look at what's around them. I haven't given the ceiling a thought in years."

No shit, thought Nikki.

"When professionally cleaning a room, you start from the top and then work your way down. The floor is always the final item taken care of. It's common practice in cleaning circles."

"Really?" Mrs. Kowalczyk asked. "I'd never heard of that. I just assumed you sort of cleaned what was in front of you. I didn't know there was procedure."

"Absolutely, ma'am. The ceiling sometimes takes the longest due to its proximity and ah, the dimensionality of the room. Also, it was really greasy."

"How about that. You know, I barely ever look up."

Nikki held her tongue and just nodded.

"Well, yes, I suppose it would be best for you to finish tomorrow. Just let me get my purse to pay—" She stopped. "Now why don't we wait until the whole job is done and then I'll pay you for both days. I think that would be smarter, don't you?"

Again, Nikki kept her mouth closed and nodded.

As she exited through the kitchen door Nikki saw the jerk across the street was gone. Lighting another cigarette as she walked home, she thought of men in town, and even the surrounding towns, she may have had sex with to support her habit. It's not like she could simply choose to avoid these people; she'd do it in a heartbeat. The problem was she truly could not remember who most of them were. They had been just a means to an end for her. How do you avoid what you can't even recognize?

She tried to recall any men in Pendale, other than Donald, who had treated her with some level of kindness or respect. Her old employer at the drugstore had been nice to her, but she'd always had the feeling the old guy was sizing her up to make a pass at her. Once or twice, she'd turn around and catch him ogling her ass. Horny old goat. No, there really weren't many. Nikki could come up with just two.

Jonesy, the bartender at The Bottle Cap, one of her old haunts. There was never a shortage of eager customers willing to help a girl get drunk there. She recalled Jonesy stepping in on occasion trying to get her to leave before a transaction was paid in full. On her last binge, Mrs. G had come to the bar in search of her. Nikki had been about to pay off some fat, sweaty construction worker for having bought God knows how many shots for her when Jonesy came to the rescue and threatened the guy with a baseball bat. Nikki blushed just thinking about it. She didn't remember much more about that afternoon. It was as though it took place in a mist. Just the fat guy, Mrs. G, Jonesy, and his bat. Later that evening however, trapped in a sweltering garage and being attacked by a homicidal maniac, well, every detail of *that* stuck with her. The heat, the shovel swung at her head, and the breasts. The breasts of those poor girls, sliced away to be used as some crazy fertilizer or something.

And she remembered the policeman, Captain Clarke. The guy who had rescued her on that awful night. She smiled. While she still felt some embarrassment over it, it really was kind of funny. He had initially thought she was a young boy. She'd been covered in dirt, sweat, blood, and at barely five feet tall and not even a hundred pounds, you could forgive the man. That and the fact she was shirtless and wearing only a pair of torn cutoffs probably added to his confusion. She could not remember the last time a man had held her for any other reason than to use her sexually. But he was attempting to give comfort, nothing more. His visit at the hospital the following day, while she knew it fell under the category of "police business," also felt comforting. Her smile widened at the memory.

Mrs. G sat silently in the corner. Her eyes were closed, and her lips were moving as her fingers worked their way around her Rosary. Captain Clarke hesitantly stuck his head into the room and spoke quietly.

"Mrs. Gorman? Rose Gorman?" Mrs. G opened her eyes and nodded to him.

"Could I ask you to step into the hall for a few minutes?"

The older woman hesitated, "I'd rather not leave Nikki. Could we speak later perhaps?"

"Actually ma'am, it's not you I need to speak with, it's the young lady. The nurse's station said she could only have one visitor at a time. It's very important I speak with her while the details of last night are fresh in her mind. I promise not to monopolize her time. The minute I'm through, you can come back in."

"It's okay, Mrs. G, this is the nice man who rescued me." When the woman still hesitated, she said, "Go. He's the police. He'll slap you in a cell for obstruction of justice or something and I'll have to use the cookie jar money to bail you out." She gave a tired smile. "I'll be fine."

"Oh, Nikki." Mrs. Gorman kissed her forehead and before leaving whispered to Clarke, "Please don't tire her; she needs to recuperate. I can't imagine what she went through last night."

"No, ma'am, I won't."

She left and Clarke's eyes scanned the room. The girl was the only occupant. The bed was very narrow, but still provided plenty of room for her tiny body. She barely created a rise under the sheet. He remembered how light she'd felt last night as he held her after he had cuffed and subdued that maniac. He'd thought she was a child, a boy, because of her slight build. The figure in the bed was obviously female. She had been cleaned and was no longer caked in blood and filth. There was a bandage around her head. He could not see her hair, but he thought it was some shade of red. In the madness of last night, the only light in the murky garage was thrown by the squad car's flashing lights and a dim bulb that careened madly off the walls; he really couldn't be sure of the color. The red he remembered could have been blood, there certainly had been enough of it. He wondered just how weak the girl might be today.

Her face was very pale, as were her arms that rested on top of the bedcovers. They were bruised and there was a deep cut on one that had been stitched closed. An IV bottle ran to a needle in the crook of her left elbow. Her nails were chewed to the quick. There was a large bruise on her right cheek and her lips looked chapped and raw. Her eyes though, were very distinct. Above the spray of freckles across her nose and cheeks, their green color was almost startling.

Clarke must have been looking at her for several seconds because she said, "Yeah, I look like Frankenstein's monster, don't I? When I used the bathroom earlier, I caught a glimpse in the mirror and almost fainted. I've looked rough on occasion, but nothing like this."

"Not at all, Miss Greene, just a bit banged up, that's all." The truth was, with her injuries and near-emaciated body, she looked as though she'd spent time in a prison camp.

She gave a tired-looking smile. "I'd like to believe you, Captain, but my guess is you don't usually lie. You're not very good at it. And please, call me Nikki."

"Alright, Nikki. First, is there any family we should contact for—"

"No. Just Mrs. G."

"Got it. Mind if I sit?"

She shook her head a winced. "Ah, hell. No more of that, Nik," she murmured.

Clarke reached into his breast pocket and withdrew a small pad and pencil. Nikki noticed the shirt looked freshly laundered and starched. She thought of the previous night and remembered how tightly she had clung to this man, her near-naked body pressed against him; his clothes had been covered in dirt as well as her sweat, and certainly her blood. His wife must have made sure he looked presentable today. For the first time, Nikki took a close look at the man's face.

He looked exhausted. There were bags under the red-rimmed eyes. She wondered if he had slept at all after the events of last night. Probably not. Even with the drugs the hospital had given her, she'd struggled to sleep herself. Nikki wasn't great at guessing ages, but he appeared older than most of the men she'd recently had in her life by a good decade or so. Maybe forty? Fifty? Sixty? No, not sixty. There was some gray in his almost military-style haircut, but the dark brown there was not being overwhelmed. He had what her aunt would have referred to as "a spare tire" around his middle. He exuded an air of calm. Maybe it was exhaustion, or maybe he had taken some great drugs to deal with the craziness of last night.

"Can you tell me why you were present in the garage?"

"Boy, you sure didn't start with an easy one, did you?" He smiled.

"Okay, why was I there?" She paused. "I guess I was there because I'd been insulted, and I wanted an apology."

Clarke scribbled in the pad. "In the middle of the night?" he asked, not looking up.

"There were a lot of people there earlier. This was a personal thing, and I didn't want anyone else around."

"I don't mean to invade your privacy, but any details you can provide would be greatly appreciated."

"Okay." Nikki sighed. "My boyfriend, Donald Thompson, died about two years ago. If you've lived in this town a while you may have known him or his family. The day of his funeral I caused a scene. It was totally my fault. I let something someone said about me get under my skin." She stopped and smiled ruefully. "I guess I'm just the kind of person who invites rude comments. Anyway, all hell broke loose, and it seems the whole town was there to witness it. Earlier yesterday that...maniac told me Donald was better off being dead than having to spend his life with me."

Clarke's pencil stopped. "That's awful." He looked up. "What would move a person to say such a thing?" Of course, as soon as he'd spoken, he recalled they were talking about a lunatic here.

"I have a sort of reputation in town." Clarke looked at her expecting more. "Wow, it looks like you might not be entirely aware of it. You'll have to unearth the details on your own, Captain. I don't have too many blushes left, but maybe just a couple, and I'm not ready to go there with you right now. Mrs. G could probably help you. Because of this reputation, I'm not too highly thought of in some circles. Hence the remark about Donald being better off dead." Nikki felt tears coming on. She tried to force them down. "So, I went there to demand an apology. It would have been earlier in the evening, but there was a crowd of people around and it looked like the whole yard was being excavated."

"Yes, it was. That was my doing. I believed, uh, evidence relating to the deaths of two young women was hidden there. Unfortunately, we found nothing. It wasn't until later that we put two and two together. I'm so sorry it wasn't sooner. It could have saved you a lot of pain."

Nikki shrugged.

"How did you know where the severed breasts had been hidden?"

"I didn't. I had gone there for an apology and was promised one if I showed *my* breasts, such as they are. I think that demand was intended to humiliate me, to make me feel small, degraded, worthless." Nikki gave a rueful laugh. "As though I needed any assistance in that. So, like an idiot, I went along with it. That's when the...the breasts were revealed to me. That's when I was told mine would join...ah hell." Nikki stopped and tried, unsuccessfully this time, to will back the tears, "I was told mine would be joining them. They'd be used to help make the world a more beautiful place." She forced a weak smile. "Though, in the eyes of that psycho, just killing me would have accomplished that."

My God, thought Clarke, what an ordeal to have lived through. And this young woman seemed relatively calm and matter of fact. This was one tough girl.

"Um, that's why I was half-naked when you showed up. Sorry about that, I hope I didn't embarrass you."

Embarrass *me*? "No, I'm sorry it took me so long to realize...ah ..."

"To realize I was female?" she said with a small smile. "Yeah, well, I do kind of have the killer physique of a sixth-grade boy. But like I said, I don't embarrass so easily these days."

They lapsed into silence.

"I think I'll let you get back to resting. Besides, unless I'm mistaken, your friend Rose Gorman is probably pacing impatiently just outside the door. She seems to care for you very much."

"Yes. She's my best and only friend. I couldn't be luckier."

"I would have to agree. I may want to speak to you again, miss, but that's it for now. Please rest up and get healthy."

"I will, and it's Nikki."

He nodded. "Nikki."

He left the door ajar and Nikki saw him speaking with Mrs. G. She did not know how long they spoke; she'd closed her eyes and allowed herself to drift off.

As she neared home, Nikki found herself in front of the Wilson house. Vacant since that fateful day. Nora Wilson killed and mutilated, and her brother shipped off to the psych ward at some VA hospital. The peeling paint might once have been some shade of blue, but now looked dull gray. A dilapidated aluminum yard chair sat on the porch that itself seemed to be sloping to the left. The front screen door lay on its side near the entrance as it had since that day. That damn day when everybody's life in this screwy town got turned upside down. They had made statewide news, maybe even national news. They'd bumped Vietnam down the front page of the papers. For a day, anyway.

Were things any different now? For her, absolutely. For one, she was sober and was not trolling for a drinking buddy at the Bottle

Cap. And *she* was looking after Mrs. G instead of the other way around. But everyone else in town? Anyone else? Nikki doubted it.

Two women were brutally murdered. One was from a family most of the citizenry wished did not exist. The other, Rosaria Donez, well, the fact that she was Puerto Rican and not Caucasian was reason enough for them not to get too worked up about her demise. If anything, there were those who believed one less of "them" in town was a positive thing, the fact she was murdered and butchered notwithstanding.

Nikki thought she saw a flash of movement from within the house. A shadow passing behind a grimy curtain. She shivered in the summer heat. Like a damn haunted house, she thought, and hurried home to Mrs. G.

NINE

"Come in and sit, Kevin." Clarke rubbed the bridge of his nose where his reading glasses had perched. He'd been getting nowhere trying to draw connections between Doc Eichen and anyone angry enough to kill him. The man seemed to live in a bubble. He went to his practice, then he went home. Period. No social life at all. Until recently there had been a wife in a nearby facility. Apparently, she'd had a stroke and constant care had been necessary. She passed away two months ago.

Clarke thought about the photograph of the attractive young woman he'd seen in the house during his first visit after the murder. A beautiful woman, what a shame. Upon contacting the facility, Clarke learned the doctor had not visited her in years. That hardly sounded like the actions of a loving husband, but the doc certainly did not seem to be shaping up to being one. Rolf though, had been a frequent visitor. On average he visited several times a month, sometimes weekly. Not that the woman had been aware of it. Or, for that matter, aware that her husband had not been there. She was essentially a vegetable.

Clarke leaned back in his chair, continued rubbing his nose, and sighed. "Remember how with the Donez case we felt overrun with suspects? A boyfriend, husband, priest, hairdresser, veteran? We were chasing our tails everywhere?"

"Oh, yeah, I remember."

"Well, we've got next to nothing here. We have a dead doctor and that's it. No coworkers, friends, enemies, the only family is a son and a wife. And the wife was an invalid in a home up in Flemington until she died. Even alive she certainly was never in any shape to kill the guy. So, for the moment, all we've got is the son."

"He's the one who called it in, right?" Kevin asked. Clarke nodded. "Hmm. By calling us in you think he's maybe trying to deflect suspicion away from himself?" Clarke shrugged.

"Maybe our new recruit will jumpstart our brains," Clarke said. Kevin grunted.

"That's what I want to talk to you about. I need you to take this new officer under your wing. It's not easy being the new person in an organization. Everybody is familiar with everyone else—except you. And if you're new to the geographical area as well, it makes it just that much harder. I want you to do this. Do you understand?"

"Yes, Captain. I think the town has been through enough upheaval this summer and the last thing it needs is an unfamiliar face in uniform, but I'll do my best."

"Good."

"I don't know any of the Newark cops; has the new guy worked anywhere else? Is he looking to get away from the big city and embrace small-town life? I'm not sure how many of the small-town residents here will be ready to embrace *him,* but I guess we'll see."

"We certainly will."

"Sorry if I've been kind of whiny about this. I've let stuff get to me maybe more than I should." Clarke sat silently. "I've been thinking a lot about my stepfather and his death lately. I finally started digging into his belongings and it's bringing back memories."

"Bad ones?"

"No, not necessarily. But I have questions I'll probably never get answers to. I think it's been weighing me down. Sorry."

"There's nothing to be sorry about. I have all the faith in the world in you, that's why I want you to mentor our new officer. My only concern is maybe I could have prepped you better for this." He glanced at the wall clock.

"What prep do I need? I'll show him the ropes, just be my normal pleasant self."

"Mmm. I guess that's all I can ask." The rear door to the station, down the short hall from Clarke's office, closed with a thud. "This is probably our new addition now. Sit tight," he said as MacDougall started to rise. "Be right back."

Kevin ran a quick hand over his cowlick and stood anyway. He would be friendly, yet firm, he thought. Show the new recruit the ropes, let him know what the captain expected, what he disliked, try to put the guy at ease, maybe invite him out for a beer later. Yeah. Be a benevolent big brother figure.

He heard the captain's voice down the hall. A quieter one responded to him. The footsteps of the two grew closer.

Clarke rounded the corner into the office. "Officer MacDougall, I'd like you to meet the new addition to our department. This is Officer Reyes, Valeria Reyes."

From behind Clarke stepped a young woman. She was tall, about the same height as Kevin's five foot nine. She was in uniform, and it was obvious she was very strong. Her shoulders were broad, and her belt and holster rested above narrow hips. She stepped forward and held out her hand. "Officer," she said. "It's a pleasure to meet you." She firmly shook the hand that slowly rose to hers and looked him in the eye. Her face showed no expression.

For a moment Kevin was speechless. A girl, a very attractive girl. The captain was bringing in a girl. And she was...oh man. Her skin was dark, a shade or two darker than copper. The hair pinned up under her cap was black, as was the color of her eyes. Not just a girl, he thought, a Puerto Rican girl. Oh, Jesus, he thought. That's all this town needs, a female cop. A female, PR cop. Was the Captain trying to blow the town up? A PR, a *girl* PR, with a badge and a gun. Whoa, boy.

"Uh, hi. Welcome to Pendale PD," he said.

"I asked Valeria to briefly stop in today. She's just getting settled in town and will be starting full time tomorrow." He turned to her, "Kevin is a local, I'm sure he'll be useful with any questions you may have concerning the ins and outs of Pendale. We're not as bustling a place as Newark, but I'm sure you may have questions."

"It seems charming, sir."

Charming? A word Kevin would never have thought to describe Pendale.

"Um, yeah, I can show you around. Do you know the town at all? Friends? Family?" There must be someone here she knows. Why else would she come here?

"Family," she answered.

Kevin nodded. Of course, they all had big families.

"Why don't you give her a tour of the station, Kevin? I have to run. We're glad to have you here, Officer Reyes," Clarke said to her. "Captain Clements at Newark is an old friend of mine, and he was very complimentary of you. He said we would be gaining a fine officer."

"That's good of him to say, sir."

"We're pretty informal here. It'll be Kevin, Valeria," and he pointed a thumb at himself, "Captain."

Valeria smiled. "Yes, Captain."

"I'll see you both tomorrow morning."

He left and the two young officers stood in silence. "Right," Kevin finally said. "Let me show you the squad room and, I guess, what'll be your desk." Later, he could remember little of the tour. He knew he showed her to a desk, the coffee/interview room, the one bathroom, and the shower in the basement.

"There's uh, no ladies facilities. Just the one bathroom and shower. Sorry."

"It'll be fine."

Okay, what else? "Hey, I just thought of something. Maybe you can be in charge of making the coffee."

"Oh?"

"The captain likes his coffee and none of us is any good at making it. Are you?"

After a pause, "I'm a tea drinker."

"Really? I thought coffee was big in Puerto Rico. I assumed everyone drank it."

"I've never been to Puerto Rico. I was born in New Jersey. Like you, I bet."

"I just thought the culture...I mean...they grow coffee, don't they...never mind."

He quickly finished with her and said he would see her tomorrow. "Do you need directions or anything?" he asked, edging toward the station door.

"No thanks, I'm good."

"Are you living over on the west side?"

"Yes, how did you know?"

He shrugged. "Lucky guess. Bye."

Kevin ran out. Valeria stood alone in the empty squad room. She slid a well-doodled-on blotter off the surface of what would be her desk and laid it against the wall. The rest of the desktop was dusty and covered with coffee rings. She pulled open a drawer. It contained assorted pens and pencils, a large pink erasure, and a very dry-looking pizza crust.

Yuck.

Valeria walked to the sole bathroom and ran a fistful of paper towels under the faucet. Looking at her reflection in the mirror above the sink she wondered if moving down the turnpike a few exits had been the right move. Wringing out the paper towels she thought, really, there weren't any choices; it was her only move. It was this or...nothing. She wiped down her desk before using the towels to pick up and discard the pizza crust. The typewriter on the table beside her desk appeared as though it hadn't been used in a while. She pressed one of the keys and the hammer stuck, the "j" pressed to the roller, immobile. Great.

She pulled the battered swivel chair out and sat as she tried to free the frozen "j." She leaned forward and the chair's swivel dropped to the floor with a jolt.

"Damn!" Using the chair's arms, she gingerly pushed herself up, then stood, rubbing the small of her back. Looking at the chair's seat she saw a coating of dust surrounding the surface where she'd sat.

Valeria looked back over her shoulder and examined her backside as best she could. Lovely. She began brushing off the seat of her uniform pants. The motes of dust flew, and she sneezed three times. After blowing her nose on another paper towel, she laughed.

Charming Pendale. Right.

TEN

Valeria eyed the dead geraniums in the two clay pots, one on either side of the front door. She gently poked at one with her toe. It felt almost weightless, dry as powder. She gave the door a short rap with her knuckles and waited. The mailbox attached to the porch rail was overflowing. Valeria tried to pull out a handful of mail, but it was packed solid. Sliding out several envelopes and flyers from the middle of the mass, she was then able to get a grip on the rest. A quick glance told her the mail was from across the spectrum: flyers, bills, some of which looked to be second or third notices, a couple letters, and quite a few cards.

A shriek reached her from down the street. On the corner playground she saw two young girls playing on the sliding board. After reaching the top of the ladder one girl with a mop of curly blonde hair plopped herself on the slide, pushed off, and screaming in joy, flew down where first her feet, then her butt landed in a well-worn trough of dirt. An almost identical girl, wearing a faded pink smock quickly followed her and did the same. Valeria smiled. She thought of herself and her cousin, Isabella.

The two of them had been inseparable. They loved making believe they were members of the Wild Dogs, the gang that ruled their section of Newark. As little girls they pretended to stalk the streets, scaring the hell out of everyone. In the stairwell of their tenement they inked the twisted W and D of the Wild Dogs onto their prepubescent skin, posing and flexing until they dissolved in laughter. The infatuation continued through the rest of childhood and into high school. Valeria's mother was not happy about it.

"You don't need them," Mama had said, "You have a family, a good one. You don't need any gang's support or protection. I'm here, and so are your brothers. You have a true family." Yeah, but Valeria knew her three younger brothers wanted to be part of the Dogs, as well. In fact, Eduardo, who was now sixteen, ten months younger than her, was ready to go soon. Mama didn't know, but it really shouldn't have come as a surprise. Valeria's father had been a member. He was gone now, a victim of the violence associated with that life. When Mama had found out she was pregnant with Valeria, her father's gang status hadn't stopped her from marrying him and then quickly popping out three baby boys. Gangs were a part of life. You didn't think about it, it just was.

One night Eduardo had returned home bloody, beaten, but proud. He'd been jumped into the gang. He ran a gauntlet through two columns of gang members and had withstood their assault like a man. When he staggered through the kitchen door before collapsing in a bloody mess Mama hadn't said a word. She administered iodine, bandages, stitched a cut above an eye, and set a splint for his broken wrist, all without saying a word. In the following days he proudly spouted to Valeria and his younger brothers that now he was part of a second family. Valeria took in his injuries and nodded. Later, he displayed the tattoo he'd received a few days after the initiation, a WD, gripped by thorny branches that dripped blood, right over his heart. He was a Wild Dog.

A few months later she approached Eduardo about joining the gang herself. At first, he said nothing, it was obvious he was torn. "The gang is important, real important. I wouldn't be the same person without it," he said. "But it's not easy getting in, and if you're a girl...." He trailed off shaking his head.

Valeria knew about the initiations. Cousin Isabella was two years older than Valeria and had joined a little over a year ago: she explained it to Valeria. The first way was to get jumped in, just like Eduardo had been. The jumping takes place in a narrow alleyway. Nowhere for the candidate to go, just forward or back, that's it. The gang members form two lines, their backs to the buildings on either side of the alley. It left about three or four feet between the two lines. The candidate had to make it through the gauntlet and come out on the other end still standing. Don't even think about turning back or running away. You'd get labelled as weak or a coward and that would kill any chance to join. It would be a stigma that followed you forever. So, if you chose to be jumped in, you'd better be certain about it. Damn certain.

"What if you get hit in the head and fall or pass out or something?" Valeria had asked. She recalled his head injury when he'd staggered home on initiation night.

"They're not supposed to do that," he said. "Heads are off limits."

Valeria gave him a look.

"Well, a couple of the guys can be jerks," Eduardo said, rubbing the stiches above one eye. "They do what they want, but mostly the guys follow the rules, no heads."

"Were you scared about getting beaten or that you'd fail the test and not be allowed in?"

Eduardo thought for a second. "I wasn't too scared about the beating. I knew it would hurt, but I would eventually heal up. I was way more scared about falling or maybe not making it to the end of the gauntlet. I'd be labeled a weakling, and never be allowed in. Word would get around to other gangs, too. Not that I'd want to be anything except a Dog," he added quickly. Yeah, Valeria knew about getting jumped in the gang.

She also knew of the other avenue: getting sexed in. It was simple. The gang leader orders the female candidate to have sex with the gang members. You can refuse of course, but then no gang membership for you. Isabella had taken that route, but she had never been the strongest person in the world. There was no way she'd make it through a gauntlet. And sexed in, well, Valeria knew her cousin wouldn't have been too put off by it.

Valeria vowed there was no way in hell she was going to be ordered to have sex with anyone, potential fellow gang members or not. But she was curious. "What was it like?" she asked Isabella. "Was it all at once? Was it spread over a few days? A week? What?"

"It wasn't anything I'd like to do again," Isabella said, "but it was okay. I mean, it didn't kill me." They sat on the back steps of Isabella's first floor apartment in the Brick Block projects. "Wait a sec." She ran into the kitchen, the empty screen door slamming behind her. A siren wailed several blocks away, gradually growing softer as the vehicle sped uptown. In a moment Bella returned with a cigar box and began rolling a joint from its contents. She was quiet until she'd licked it closed, lit, and inhaled. She closed her eyes until finally allowing the smoke to escape her lips. "No, I'm good with what happened. No real complaints."

Valeria noted her cousin was rarely without some kind of drug these days. Growing up Bella hadn't ever used any substances. She rarely even drank a beer.

"Honest, prima? It's okay?"

"Yeah. For a while it hurt, but that passed." Valeria raised her eyebrows. Isabella sighed. "Some of the guys wanted things I really wasn't ready for."

"Díos, mia! Didn't the whole thing make you feel...cheap, dirty?"

"For a while." She shrugged. "But that passed, too. And some of them are real good-looking, you know? And I get to do them."

"Wait," Valeria interrupted. You *get* to do them? You mean you're still having sex with them *now*? It's been what, three, four months since you joined?"

"You don't get it. They appreciate me. When they feel the urge, they call me and maybe one or two other girls. Not those skags that have been around forever. I have a... a purpose. Yeah, they need me."

But how long before you're one of those skags, Valeria thought. "What if you get pregnant? It sounds like you're doing it an awful lot."

"Yeah, pretty much," Bella said, and took a final deep pull on the joint before rubbing the tip of the paper between her fingers and dropping it to the ground. "But don't worry. The Dogs got someone who can take care of it. We supply him and he's on call for us."

Great, Valeria thought. A druggie abortionist.

Isabella had never been beautiful, but she had never wanted for male company either. She had the face of a very young girl and Valeria knew a lot of men were turned on by that. And her figure had always been full and curvy; men certainly liked *that*, too. But she'd never been the smartest person. Sometimes she got manipulated into unpleasant situations and then tried to kid herself everything was just fine. It sure sounded like that now.

Valeria looked at her cousin critically. She looked tired, even haggard. There were dark pouches beneath her eyes. Her face was rounder and it appeared she was developing a double chin. A slight roll of fat spilled over the top of her tight jeans. No, it wouldn't be long before she too was one of the skags the gang members no longer had a use for.

"Bella," Valeria began, searching for the right words, "don't you feel, well, like you're being used? Sort of, you know, taken advantage of?"

"You don't get it. I have a role, a job. I'm there for my new brothers."

Valeria needed to ask her cousin a question but wasn't sure how or even if she wanted to hear the answer. "Um, Eduardo, he wasn't part of the...initiation, was he? Being family and all?"

"Yeah, he was, but he was nice. He didn't hurt me or say anything nasty. Real gentle. And don't worry, we haven't done it since."

Jesus. "You guys are *cousins!* Family! How could that happen? How could you allow yourself to be—"

"Allow? How could *I* allow myself? Prima, I had to get in the gang! Don't you understand? This is how it is. You do what they tell you or you're out. There's no choice. One guy, ten guys, or a hundred, it doesn't matter. This is how we get in. Simple as that. If it was such a terrible thing to do Eduardo could have said no. I mean, he's already in the gang, right? He had a choice, I didn't. So don't give me this *allow* shit!"

"Yeah, okay, okay. I'm sorry." Eduardo...jeez. They were cousins. The three of them had played together as babies, known each other forever. Damn.

Valeria touched her cousin's shoulder but was shrugged away. She sighed. "Okay, prima. Sorry, again. I'll see you, huh?"

Isabella just nodded and began rolling another joint, her lips pressed together tightly, concentrating on her task.

Later that evening Valeria pulled Eduardo outside to the stoop and they both sat. "I need to talk with you."

"Okay, shoot. It's got to be quick, though. I have a meeting with the boys tonight."

"Yeah, the boys. It's sort of about them, and you, and Bella."

Eduardo looked up the street and said nothing.

"What did you do, brother?"

"What did I do?" He turned to her. "I did what had to be done, *sister*. You know the rules. They probably haven't changed since Dad's day. You choose to get sexed in and whatever the head guy says, goes. Marco said she does the guys, so that's what happened. She's not the first girl got done like that. You know, a gang thing."

"No, but she's the first girl who's your cousin that you 'done like that' because of a 'gang thing.'"

"You don't get it, it's something you just got to do, that's all."

"You couldn't say no? That you won't do it because she's family? It wouldn't be right. You couldn't do that?"

He looked away again. "No, I didn't feel I could say that."

"But maybe you could have? You didn't even try?"

"You don't get it," he repeated.

"No. I don't. What if it had been me? What if I want in? Would you—"

"What?" Eduardo sprang up. "No! No close family! And before you say something, cousins are different. There's...separation."

"Separation."

"Yeah."

Valeria looked up the street, gathering her thoughts. "Why's it have to be that way? It's not right. A bunch of guys doing Bella, turning her into a hood rat."

"Now that she's in and part of it, nobody's doing any forcing. And believe me, she's real willing."

"Yeah. Because now she's high most of the time, not caring about anything, how she looks, how others look at her, how she feels, what she thinks. You know she's never been real smart. Want to know what she told me today? She said she's 'appreciated and wanted.' She feels she has a real purpose. Oh, Duardo, you and the others have turned her into whore."

"No one made her do anything against her will."

"Yeah," Valeria said, rising from the stoop. "Tell me hermanito, is our cousin a good lay?"

"Fuck you, Val!" Eduardo turned and strode away into the dimness.

Valeria watched her brother's straight back until it disappeared around the corner. What she'd heard from Isabella sickened her. And the fact her cousin seemed oblivious, just made her sadder still.

Yet she knew the importance of acceptance into the Wild Dogs held for Isabella. She felt it too. Their whole lives yearning to become a part of this almost mythical group. Both of their fathers had been gang members. So had Bella's mother. For a brief second Valeria wondered if Aunt Camila had been sexed in like her daughter, but then pushed the thought from her mind. No way could she envision her rotund aunt as a young woman or teenager being passed from member to member.

No way that was going to happen to her. Yes, the gang was still a dream she'd pursue. It could still provide some sort of validation Valeria felt she needed. But she would not be sexed in. Unlike her cousin, Valeria was physically and mentally strong and she wasn't afraid of some pain. No, she vowed, like Eduardo, she would be jumped in.

Another scream from the little girls on the playground brought Valeria back to the present. Playing on a sliding board vs inking gang tattoos on each other's skin: two completely different universes. Neither of these two little girls would ever find themselves in the position of choosing to be jumped or sexed into a gang. Newark and Pendale. Yeah. Two different universes, alright.

After a moment's wait Valeria knocked again and then tried the knob. Unlocked. She opened the door about halfway and stuck in her head. "Hello? Anybody here?" she called in Spanish. There was no response, but she thought she heard a sound from further in the house. "Tía Anita? Alfonso?" Stepping in she closed the door behind her and put the mail on a small entry table. A stack of mail already there cascaded over the top, spilling, creating a pile on the floor next to an already existing one. Valeria stooped and added her handful to the rest. She did what she could to arrange them into small stacks against the wall. Most of it consisted of sympathy cards, she knew. She saw one with her own return address from Newark, sent almost two months ago. Another from her mother, others from various friends and family members whose names she recognized. All unopened.

Standing, she took in the living room. It looked clean enough, just unused, lifeless. She hated the thought of that word, but it summed up the impression perfectly. Valeria walked into the small dining room. The table was set as though for a family meal. Beneath the plates and silverware lay a white lace tablecloth. Valeria's mother had a similar one. It was used for family gatherings and holidays. There was a noise from the kitchen. A pot or something being set on the stove or counter.

"Hola, Tía Anita?" Entering the kitchen, she saw the back of a woman working at the counter. She appeared to be chopping meat with a large knife. A white T-shirt and jeans hung off the woman's body. Unkempt hair, shot with gray, reached down her back. It did not appear to have been washed in some time. The woman's feet were bare.

"Aunt Anita?" she called louder. "Hello!" louder still. The chopping stopped and the knife dropped to the cutting board. After a second's hesitation the woman turned, a look of almost painful hope on her face. Upon seeing Valeria, the face slowly sagged, losing all expression.

"Valeria, I thought for a second...." The words seemed to wear her out and she breathed heavily, sounding almost out of breath. "I thought you were someone else," she finished in a whisper. Anita Donez turned back to the counter, picked up the knife, and continued chopping. "Please sit and stay for dinner. We have pasteles. Lots of pasteles. I make them every day. That old crook of a butcher, Baranowski, is mad at me for buying up all his pork. He says there is none for his other customers." She shook her head. "Rosaria loved my pasteles. Every Christmas she asked, 'Mama, where does it say we can only eat pasteles at Christmastime? Why can't we eat them all year? They're so good!' I told her like I always did, not to be a silly girl and to be thankful we had them at all. Don't be so greedy." She stopped chopping and wiped away some hair from her brow with the back of her wrist. "I was always doing that, scolding her. I look back and see I was such an evil witch to her."

"You were nev—"

"Now to atone, I make pasteles every day. For Rosaria. My poor, lost Rosaria. I make her pasteles, and some days, if I'm lucky, I think for a few minutes that she is still alive and will be eating them with us. Rosaria, me, and little Alfonso." She turned again and faced her niece, "But I'm usually not so lucky." There was a tired, incredibly sad smile on her face. "So, I have a freezer full of pasteles. Alfonso won't touch them, he's so sick of eating pasteles. The neighbors won't take any more. The fridge is loaded with them, too. They'll be going bad soon. When you leave, you need to take some."

"Of course. Let's go in the living room and talk, huh?" She took Anita's hand to lead her away from the counter, then stopped. "Um, Aunt Anita?"

"Yes?"

Valeria disengaged her hand from her aunt's and held it up. It was shiny and smeared with fat from the raw meat. "How about we wash up first?" They smiled and almost laughed.

"How is Alfonso? I know how close they were. It must be difficult for him." The women sat on the sofa, turned toward each other. The aunt Valeria had always thought of as looking so glamorous, like a movie star, was almost unrecognizable. She appeared decades older than the mid-thirties she was. Until recently her hair had been a glossy jet-black, and her figure was the envy of every woman who knew her. It certainly was the envy of Valeria's mother, Anita's sister. She was rounder and shorter than her attractive younger sister and while they shared similar facial features, that was about as far as it went. Valeria resembled her aunt more than her mother.

"For weeks he would not leave my side. I tried to shield him from the details, but this town, it's so small and petty. When he learned what was done to her, he began to close up. Now, days go by when I don't see or speak to him." She saw the question in Valeria's eyes. "No, he still lives here, but he comes and goes at all hours. I am getting concerned about the company he may be keeping."

Valeria felt her stomach tighten and she unconsciously rubbed the left side of her chest through her blouse. She thought Alfonso may have been at least part of the reason her aunt had initially reached out to her.

"I was afraid he would run to that man Rosaria had been seeing, Marcus. They were close, the three of them. But now," she looked disgusted, "if half of what I hear is true, I don't want my Alfonso anywhere near him." Valeria was about to speak, but Anita waved her off, "No. We're not talking about him now, okay?" The younger woman nodded.

"I'm glad you came to a decision about what I suggested. I know it couldn't have been easy. Uprooting and coming to this...place. God, I hate this town so much. It's small and so are the people. They fear or hate anything different. And that's you and me. And Alfonso, and," her voice caught, "Rosaria." She quietly cried. After a moment she said, "That captain though, I didn't see it right away, but he did what was right. I know most would not have cared about what happened to one of us, but he did."

Valeria nodded, thinking of their brief meeting earlier at the station.

"Tía Anita, I know the last thing most of this town wants to see is another Puerto Rican, but to hell with them. We have as much right to be here as they do."She moved closer and put a hand on her aunt's knee. I know this place is far from perfect, but I want to be here. It's an escape from...you know, my past. It's a present, maybe even a future." Again, she unthinkingly rubbed her chest. "I wish I could have gotten Mama to come with me, but she wants to be near her boys. I couldn't stay, though. It was going to mean death for my career, and maybe death for me. So, your call was like a life preserver thrown to me."

"Don't thank me yet, it may be an anchor instead."

Valeria smiled. "Maybe. But it's a clean slate and whatever the future holds, it happens because I'm *here*. It's not based on anything else."

Anita ran a hand over Valeria's hair. "I know, I know. How are *you* doing with what—"

"It's done. I'm fine."

"I know. You're a strong one. But I know the trouble...it came back at you recently."

"Yeah, it did. But that's why I'm here. I'll make it work. Just watch me." Valeria tried to sound more confident than she felt.

"Hmm, I hope so. I don't want to be responsible for ruining your life."

"No matter what happens, you'll not be responsible for anything. I chose to come here. I know almost everyone here is a stranger and I'll have to prove myself, but that's exactly why I had to move. I was labelled in Newark. Too many people knew me, knew what I was, what I had been. I needed another chance." Realizing her hand was still at her chest, she quickly dropped it to her lap.

"Are you...alright?" Anita nodded to the spot she rubbed.

"Yes. For a while it was...it's fine." Valeria felt her face getting hot and tried to will away her embarrassment. "I barely ever think about it."

Valeria steered the conversation away from the topic. "Would you like me to speak with Alfonso? Maybe get some idea what he's thinking and who he's spending time with?"

Anita nodded. "Sí. I don't think I could live if I lost another baby." She stared at the coffee table, tears rolling down her expressionless face.

Valeria nodded toward the pile of mail on the floor and said, "Let me help you get all those cards in some sort of order. Put the pasteles on hold for now, okay?"

Anita nodded. "Really, if I see any more chopped pork my head will explode."

Valeria smiled at her aunt's attempt at humor, scooped up a large handful of cards from the floor and the two women began the task sifting through the sympathetic wishes from loved ones.

ELEVEN

"Have a seat folks. Let's review what we have."

Sully was just entering the coffee room as everyone grabbed a chair. His customary smile froze on his face when he saw Valeria. He quickly glanced at Kevin, then the captain, then back to Valeria. Clarke tried, unsuccessfully, to hide a smile.

"Officer Sullivan, this is our new transfer, Officer Valeria Reyes." Sully remained immobile. "I'm sure she won't bite."

Valeria took the initiative and held out her hand. "Officer,"

He hesitated, wiped his hand on his pants, then shook. "Um, Sully."

"Pardon?"

"Sully. I'm Sully. You're the new guy from Newark?"

"I guess I am."

Clarke said, "I'll be bringing Valeria up to speed today on station procedure and what precious little we have on the Eichen murder. She should be joining you in the field tomorrow."

Sully pulled out a chair for himself, eyes still on Valeria. "Um, do you pitch?"

She raised her brows.

"Pitch. Baseball. Do you pitch?"

"Oh. Not really. Maybe a little when I was a girl."

"Okay." He looked disappointed. He turned and looked at the counter by the coffeemaker. No donuts. His look of disappointment deepened.

Once everyone was settled, Clarke began. "Okay, Kevin, our local oracle, what can you tell us about the doctor? Any details you can add from your childhood? I'll take anything you've got: facts, rumors, speculation, hell, even fiction of it's based in some sort of vague truth."

Kevin's face reddened and he quickly glanced toward Valeria. He then pulled out his notepad and cleared his throat.

"I wish I could help more, sir, but there's not much. He was never my doctor, so I have no firsthand knowledge of anything. From what I recall, it was mostly the old-timers that saw him."

"Old-timer" probably meant anyone over thirty-five, Clarke thought.

"My stepfather saw him a couple times before he passed away. I don't think he was particularly crazy about the guy. I assumed it was because they both came from Poland that Paval, my stepdad, went to him. I don't recall him ever going to another doctor. He was real healthy. Until the very end, anyway," he finished glumly.

Clarke tapped his pen against a yellow legal pad. Valeria too had produced a small notebook. Sully reached to his breast pocket, found it empty and was about to open his mouth, then stopped. Valeria quietly tore off a page from her notebook and slid it to him. He smiled thanks and reached to his other breast pocket for a pencil. Nothing. Valeria gently shook her head and lifted her lone pen an inch or so.

"Anything you might remember from friends or neighbors that stuck with you about him?"

"Not really, other than he was thought of as being a grumpy old cuss, but one who seemed to know his stuff. I remember Mrs. Johnson, a neighbor, telling my mom that her husband was a patient of the doc's and once the doc blew his top with the guy. The doc had been telling him for years he had to lose weight, exercise, you know, get in shape. But Mr. Johnson didn't—lazy, I guess. Then on one visit the doc exploded. He called Mr. Johnson an idiot and told him never to come back to his office. He said he didn't want people knowing he was the doctor of such a physical wreck. He didn't want any connection to him.

"Whoa, man! I see the grumpy side, but what about the 'knowing his stuff' part?" asked Sully.

"Whelp," Kevin grinned, his discomfort forgotten for the moment, "he scared Mr. Johnson so much, he finally started doing all those things the doc had been telling him to do and he lost a ton of weight. Mrs. Johnson told Mom it was as though he was a completely different guy. I remember the two of them giggling about that. Six months after the blowup he went back to the doc to show off his new look, expecting the doc to be impressed and take him back. The old guy refused. Told him to come back in another six months when he'd lost more weight and gotten even healthier.

"Mr. Johnson was shocked, and really, really, mad, I guess. But he kept up his new regimen. He told his wife when the doc saw how great he looked and wanted him back as a patient, he was going to tell the guy to go to hell. But from what Mrs. Johnson said, the doc just told her husband, 'If I hadn't yelled at you and humiliated you, would you have gotten healthy?' Mr. Johnson realized he probably wouldn't have and was grateful as all get out."

"Wow," Sully said. "That really does show the doc's smarts. So, he took him back and they lived happily ever after?"

Kevin's smile widened. "Ah, nope. The doc refused. Mr. Johnson asked again and again, but the doc still said no. The guy kept pushing, asking, 'Why, why? I did what you told me to do. Look at me, I'm a new man!' Mr. Johnson practically begged him to take him back, until the doc exploded again and said all those years of Mr. Johnson ignoring his advice had been an insult to him. He said he was glad Mr. Johnson was healthy so whenever he finally did die the undertaker wouldn't be as disgusted as he would have been."

Clarke and Sully nodded. Kevin added, "Then he called Mr. Johnson a dope and kicked him out again. This time for good."

Clarke mused, "I'm not sure what to think about him."

Valeria was puzzled, as well. Were childhood stories part of everyday policework here?

"I know Captain, I mean, he got the guy to do what he needed to do to get healthy, right? But then boots him to the street and calls him names."

Sully said, "At least Mr. Johnson got healthy. Probably lived longer, too."

Kevin shook his head. "Hit by a bus."

The four sat in silence, Kevin glancing at his notes, Clarke jotting on his pad, Valeria second-guessing the transfer, and Sully alternating between looking at the blank page in front of him and craning his neck toward the similarly empty counter.

"We need to canvass the doc's neighbors, both around the home again and those around his office. Sully, you take the office, Kevin, the neighbors." Sully grinned. It would put him in the proximity of Starlight Bakery.

"But—"

"Yes, Kevin, I know you already did that, but did you speak with everyone? I've never been able to catch one hundred percent of the neighbors home on my first pass through, do you have some powers I don't? Maybe we missed something. Who knows, we might get lucky, and a neighbor will have seen somebody leaving the place with blood on his hands." The others looked at him doubtfully. Clarke smiled. "I can dream, can't I?"

He pushed out his chair. "Valeria, you're with me. I'll try not to bore you too much with paperwork; you guys, let's meet back here at four o'clock."

MacDougall stepped out of the patrol car and looked up and down the street. The captain had them running in circles. They had been through the neighborhood once already and now it seemed they were trying to conjure up something from nothing. Jeez. And how the heck a Puerto Rican girl was supposed to be successful working as a cop in Pendale was beyond him. Had the captain completely lost it? The guy got so caught up in his "teaching moments" and wanting to change with the times. Jesus, did they really need to change? It's not like *everything* was bad. Right?

He rang the bell at 212 Catherine Street, stepped back, quickly lifted his cap, and smoothed down his cowlick. The door swung open and a grinning man, barely up to MacDougall's shoulder, enthusiastically invited him into the living room. The walls were covered with framed photos of dogs. Of one dog, MacDougall realized as he looked closer. A long-haired black and brown terrier sporting a pink bow on its head in many of the pictures. The dog at the beach, on the sofa, sitting in an arranged setting that must have been a photographer's studio. Man, he thought, that's a lot of dog-love.

"Wow, Mr. uh," he looked at his notes, "Walsh? Your dog?" He looked around for the animal.

"Bernadette," Walsh said, his grin wide as ever. "She passed on ten years ago."

"You must, ah, really miss her."

"I truly do." He nodded vigorously. "But she's still with me. When I walk down the street, go to the park, sit in the yard, her spirit's always there."

"Is there a Mrs. Walsh?"

"Died last year." The man nodded to a small, simply framed photo on the mantle, dwarfed by the ornately framed ones of Bernadette. "Can I get you something to drink, Officer? Tea? Coffee? I could perk some right up!"

"Thank you, Mr. Walsh, but no. I tend to drink too much of it on this job."

"I bet you do," Walsh said, nodding, "I bet you do. Can't let yourself get jittery, no sir!" He mimed shaky hands and laughed, then gestured to a chair. He sat on the sofa himself, leaning toward MacDougall. The grin never leaving his face.

"As you know, Dr. Eichen was killed next door. I'm here to ask if there is anything out of the ordinary you can remember about the last few days or even further back. Have you seen any strangers around?" Walsh shook his head, still grinning. Did you hear any arguments from next door, anything like that?" Head shake, grin.

"Okay. Well, as the doctor's neighbor, what can you tell me about him?"

Walsh leaned forward further and, if possible, the grin spread wider. "Nuthin'."

Before MacDougall could open his mouth, Walsh continued. "Nuthin'. I probably haven't laid eyes on the man for more than five seconds at a time in twenty years. Twenty years!" He shook his head, grin remaining in place. It looked as though he marveled at the fact. "The man leaves from the back door, pulls his car out of the garage, drives to work, comes home and vanishes back in the house." He sprang up and walked to a side window. "Come here." He waved to MacDougall to follow. "Look at this hedge."

Outside was a hedge, thick and leafy. "What do you see there, Officer?"

"Ah, nothing."

"Right!" Grin. "What about behind the hedge, on the other side?"

"I can't see through."

"Right again!" Walsh turned, shaking his head. "And he's got another hedge on the other side of the house, and a wall in the back yard. And you know what else?" The grin didn't move. "Even if I wanted to get nosey and be a real peeper, he's got those awnings hanging over every window in the place! A guy would almost have to duck his head under them and press his nose against the glass to see in." The grin left his face. "Not that I'd ever do that, though!" he assured MacDougall. The grin returned. "The guy just doesn't like people. Keeps completely to himself—kept, I guess I should say, him dead and all."

MacDougall made a note or two. "Is there anything at all you can tell me about the man? Anything?"

The grinning man thought for a second. Slowly, the grin dissolved, and he looked almost morose. "His wife was beautiful. Probably the most beautiful woman I ever saw."

He nodded toward the plain photo of his still-unnamed wife on the mantle, "Even the wife thought she was beautiful. Then one day she vanished. An ambulance showed up and took her away. Some kind of heart attack or something." He shook his head. "So damn beautiful."

"Yes. She was institutionalized and died about six months ago."

"A true shame."

"Anything else you can tell me? What about the boy, Rolf?"

"He was terrified of his own shadow. Not that I'm surprised with the father he had. He was a funny-looking kid. Built like a cinder block. Looking like he did probably didn't help him any." Walsh shook his head. "Never saw him play in the yard, never heard him with friends, never saw him and the doc playing catch or anything. Sad." The man now looked positively mournful. MacDougall felt guilty about ruining his sunny outlook.

He rose. "Thank you, Mr. Walsh. I appreciate your time."

"Certainly, certainly. You have a good afternoon, young man."

Kevin descended the porch steps and heard the man call, "And don't you go drinking too much coffee, you hear?"

As he turned to acknowledge him with a quick wave, Kevin saw the grin had returned to Walsh's face.

It made him feel better.

TWELVE

Valeria squinted as she stepped through the doorway and out into the late-afternoon sun. Her soaked T-shirt stuck to her body beneath the extra-large gray sweatshirt she wore. The mid-eighty-degree August temperature added to her discomfort, although the air outside felt about ten degrees cooler than that in the gym.

Diego's Gym was one of the first establishments Valeria visited when she'd moved to Pendale. She'd taken up boxing at the police academy and it had become a passion at which she was pleasantly surprised she excelled. She'd heard about Diego's through the grapevine and wanted to be certain there would be no issues about joining due to her gender. Diego, a grossly overweight middle-aged guy, seemed surprised at her request, but when Valeria offered to pay the first three month's fees up front in cash, he just shrugged, took her money, and gave her a quick tour of the place. It wasn't much. A large room with weights, barbells, benches in the back, a couple speedbags on the far wall to her left, and a heavy bag. Most of the space was taken up by a boxing ring. Off the rear was a locker room with a shower and off that a bathroom. Singular. Both. Valeria got the impression she might have been the gym's first and only female member. She'd dress and shower at home. And relieve herself there, too. Today she'd put in most of her time on the heavy bag, trying to release some of the tension that seemed to permanently reside in her shoulders and neck. Beating the hell out of something usually helped. Today, it didn't. All she did was aggravate an old hand injury.

She walked down the block watching the heat waves rise from the sidewalk. She yanked out the rubber band that held her hair back while she was working out and roughly shook her head. She stopped at her car and fumbled with her keys while trying to unlock it. Valeria shook her left hand in frustration. She'd pushed it too hard on the heavy bag. A couple fingers had been splinted years ago and never healed up right. She slid behind the wheel of the '60 Rambler, bought used just last year. She held her breath and turned the key. After a moment's hesitation it started, and Valeria eased into the street. Most of the businesses she saw were Puerto Rican owned, the pedestrians all seemed to be Puerto Rican, as well. She'd heard the neighborhood, on the west end of Pendale, was referred to as Browntown by many of the town's Caucasian residents. Stopping at a light she looked left and right down the cross street. Nope, not a single white face. Ah, she thought, no wonder that pasty MacDougall knew the part of town she lived in. Can't have us spilling over into nicer neighborhoods. Her apartment was a quick five-minute drive. Once she knew the lay of the land better, she'd probably just jog to the gym.

Valeria clomped up three floors worth of stairs to her apartment. It was above a market in what was once part of the building's attic. It was stifling. The air in the dim hall was hot and close. It smelled like cat urine. Using her sense of touch more than sight, she slid two keys into wobbly locks attached with mismatched screws to her apartment door. There was an empty light socket on the wall across the hall. Got to pick up a bulb, she thought, though she didn't hold out much hope there was power connected there. Wiggling the keys in the locks to get them to catch, she figured she'd better get a deadbolt, as well. Valeria pushed the door open and stepped directly into the living room of the tiny apartment. She dropped her gym bag on the sagging sofa and swung the door shut, not bothering to lock it. What's the use? she thought. A kitten could push through the current locks.

She pulled off the bulky sweatshirt and pants. Standing in front of the small fan on her coffee table she closed her eyes and sighed as the breeze hit her soaked T-shirt and shorts. After a moment, Valeria crossed to the galley kitchen and with little hope, pulled open the rust-speckled refrigerator door. She yanked hard to free the tiny freezer compartment door and peered in. She was pleasantly surprised to see the ice cube tray she'd filled this morning almost completely frozen. Freeing the cubes from the aluminum tray with one hand was a chore, but at last, she dumped them in a bowl and shoved in her hand. She carried the bowl with her and dropped on the sofa allowing her head to fall back, trying to enjoy the fan's slight breeze. She pushed her hand further into the ice and felt another stab of pain. The broken finger had never healed right. Damn it, she thought. A consequence of yet another poor decision from her past.

Less than a year after Eduardo's jumping in, Valeria was ready. It was a long walk to the Central Ward where the headquarters was located. It wasn't an area she'd ever hung around much. Guess that's going to change soon, she thought. She followed Eduardo as he pushed though the dented and graffitied steel door. It was dark, many windows were partially boarded up allowing in only shafts of light. She sensed the presence of others. Almost immediately she felt the eyes of the members crawling over her. Murmurs of cocha, culito, reached her ears. Several of them stood and moved closer. She had to brush against them as she made her way through the room. Eduardo had warned her of what to expect. He assured her nothing would come of the comments, but it hadn't made it any easier. A tall gang member with a scar running from his forehead over his left eye and down his cheek stepped forward.

"Te quiero follar," he said as he reached for her.

Eduardo batted his hand away. The two men were instantly almost chest to chest.

"Seb! Duardo!"

A burly, well-tattooed man of about Valeria's height stood in the doorway. He nodded to Eduardo, stared off the scarred man, then turned to Valeria. His eyes locked on hers. "I'm Marco, top Dog. You want to be a Wild Dog, eh?"

"Yes." Valeria was relieved her voice sounded clear.

"Eduardo's sister?" She nodded. "He's a good man. Strong, brave, trustworthy. He says you are the same." She nodded again. "You know what is necessary to become a Wild Dog. You need to have a member vouch for you." Eduardo nodded at this. "And you must go through the initiation. What do you choose? Jumped in or—"

"Jumped," she said loudly.

Marco gave a slight nod and a small smile. "I thought so."

Grumbling was heard from several members of the gang. The tall scarred one rubbed his crotch and slowly shook his head.

"Bring her tonight, Eduardo. Tell her what to expect." He turned, "Seb, with me. We have details to nail down for this weekend." The tall, scarred man nodded and followed Marco from the room.

Valeria remembered nothing after hearing Marco say the word, "tonight." Eduardo took her arm and steered her from the room, through the murmurs of the members, and into the near-blinding sun on the street.

"Are you okay, Val? Valeria? Hey!"

Valeria suddenly realized they had walked half a block down Market Street and Eduardo was talking to her. "Huh? Si, good, yeah, I'm good."

He shook her arm. "Come on! You got to listen to me! Are you ready for this tonight? Will you be okay? It'll look bad if you don't show up. Are you sure you want to go through with this.?"

She nodded, thinking of the gang's leader, Marco. Oh yeah, she'd be there.

"I got to tell you, I'm glad as hell to be a Dog, and I'd do anything to stay one, but the initiation is rough. You saw me afterward. I was trying to be tough in from of Mama and you all, but I was hurting like a bitch. It's going to be hard. Do you want this bad enough?"

"Duardo, I've wanted to be a Dog since before you knew what one was. Do you really doubt I want this?"

"No, I remember you and Bella drawing the Dog tattoo on each other. I know you've wanted it since then. But manita, it hurts." He hesitated before saying, "You know there's the other way."

Valeria abruptly walked away. Tires squealed as she crossed the busy street. Horns blared along with angry shouts.

"Hey! Hey, Valeria!" Eduardo called over the sounds of the street. After a moment's indecision he ran after her, dodging cars and grabbed her arm again.

She spun on him. "How can you even suggest that? Would you rather I do that? Screw all the Dogs? Are you saying to me, your sister, you would rather I did that? What do you think I am, Duardo, some hoodrat? I'm not Bella!"

"Okay, okay, I'm sorry. I shouldn't have suggested it, I was wrong. I just don't want to see you get hurt. That's all. Come on." He nodded ahead and they began walking again. Valeria kicked an empty soda can and sent it clanging against a spraypainted brick wall depicting a pair of gigantic breasts. One of a series of seemingly endless brick walls on countless brick buildings. Brick City is right, she thought. The city sure lived up to its nickname.

"What can I expect tonight?"

"I wish I could tell you exactly, but my mind was real blank when I did it. I just sort of reacted."

"Have there been any initiations since then? You know, that you've been a part of?"

"There was one about three weeks ago. I was out of town though, on business."

Valeria almost smiled at her brother's use of the term. "What business?"

"Can't say. Dog stuff. Remember when I was away for a few days?"

She did. Mama hadn't been pleased and it was tense at home. Plus, Valeria had to spend a lot of time with Bella. Her cousin had been drunk or high and had decided to put a brick through a Broad Street store window downtown. Valeria shuttled her from one relative to another trying to avoid the cops. That stupid girl had thought it was funny.

"From what I heard though, it was bad," said Eduardo.

"What do you mean?"

"This is why I...this is why I suggested what I did about the other way to join."

"Was it a girl?"

"No, it was a guy, but he went chicken. They told me he got a couple steps into the line, getting hit on both sides, got scared, turned, and tried to run. Man, I'm glad I wasn't there. They beat the hell out of him. There's nothing worse than a coward. No gang wants one. I guess it was good for the Dogs this happened. Who'd want this guy in their gang? He was just a pussy thinking he could be a Dog. They were pissed, though. From what I heard the guy would have been a lot better off moving forward than with what happened."

They walked in silence.

Finally, Valeria said, "What? You can't leave it off there. What happened?"

"I heard they hurt him so bad he ended up in the hospital. Two broken arms, his insides busted up, and head injuries. Once he tried to run for it his head wasn't off limits anymore."

"How long was he in the hospital?"

"Ah, geez, manita." They barely slowed at an intersection before crossing through the traffic, earning more beeping horns and middle fingers. Any other time Eduardo would have given it right back to the drivers, but Valeria saw he was too distracted.

"Is he still in the hospital? Was it that bad?"

"No. He's not still there." Eduardo studied the ground. "He's dead. He died two days after he got there. There was something about it in the news, I think. Cops chalked it up to another disagreement in Crazyville. The jumping was near there."

Valeria thought she remembered hearing about it. But another person in Newark attacked and dying? No big deal. Add to the equation it was near Crazyville? It seemed a rare night when someone *wasn't* getting killed over there. But the Dogs killed him just because the guy turned tail to run? Hell.

"You see? This is serious-ass business. I don't think they'd beat a girl that bad, but I just don't know. I don't want you hurt. I couldn't live with that."

But you could live with the idea of near-strangers screwing me right in front of you? Valeria thought. "I'm not going to run. When have I ever run from anything?"

"Okay. Be ready for me to come by at ten tonight. Don't tell Mama what's up."

She gave him a "no shit" look and said she'd be ready. "Where'll you be till then?"

He shook his head. "Not for you to know, not yet anyway. We're making plans. There's a bad storm brewing. We got to be ready."

She looked at him questioningly, but he just shook his head.

"Okay, see you later, manito. Thanks for the concern, but it's not necessary."

Eduardo turned and ran down the sidewalk until he reached a broken chain-link fence. He slid through and vanished from sight.

That evening Valeria sat on her bed looking into the mirror hanging above her dresser. She had always been told by Mama and pretty much everyone else what a beautiful face she had. Dark, almost black eyes, wide cheekbones, rich coppery skin, a wide mouth which she usually kept closed. After a chubby childhood, she had grown tall and athletic. She was lean, yet not lacking in curves. Since about age thirteen she'd been on the radar of many of the boys in school and the neighborhood. She'd ignored most of them, but not all. At fifteen she'd given herself to a classmate, Alejandro. Bella had pushed her, telling her she was taking too long and getting a stuck-up reputation. Bella was twelve when she did her first guy.

Alejandro was in a couple classes with her at school. He was quiet and didn't really fit the neighborhood. He was one of the few kids in class with both parents still in the picture and he had no aspirations of being a Dog or anything else.

There was something about him though, maybe his quiet, that appealed to Valeria. One afternoon with Mama at the market and her siblings out of the house, she had succumbed. Or rather, he had. She was the one who had initiated the encounter. It hadn't been great, nor had it been awful. It was just something that needed to be done and was taken care of. They continued together for a while, each time better than the last, but Valeria ended the relationship after a couple months. Soon afterward, Alejandro and his family left the neighborhood and that was that. No longing, remorse, guilt, nothing. Since then, there had been no urge to repeat the performance. Not until she'd seen Marco. Valeria felt, well, she felt something she hadn't ever felt with Alejandro. She looked in the mirror and saw an almost guilty smile on her face. She grunted. Enough.

She pulled a couple handfuls of clothes from her drawers and threw them on the bed. What does a girl wear when she's about to get jumped into a gang? Geez, just grab some clothes, eat something light, and visit St. Lucy's for a quick prayer.

Church had always been a grounding for her, a true calming influence and this time was no exception. The gray stone building always seemed to cast a sense of peace over her. Maybe it was the change in temperature, it always felt cooler there. Maybe it was the light streaming through the stained-glass windows. Maybe it was the presence of God. Who knows? She knelt and prayed for strength to get through what was to come. She prayed she would make Eduardo proud and, as she did every night, she prayed for the health and safety of Mama and all her family. An hour later she crossed herself, walked home, and waited for Eduardo.

He arrived and nodded to her to come. It was a long walk to the chosen alleyway, and for the first time Valeria wondered how she would get home afterward. Would she be in any condition to make the journey? Let's just get through it first, she thought.

"What you got to do," Eduardo said as they turned a corner beneath a broken streetlight, "is run through the lines as fast as you can. Don't look back. You look back and you might trip and fall. Then they'll be on you, and you might never get up." She nodded. "Pick something at the far end of the line to focus on. There's an old dumpster I aimed for. You should do that, too. If you somehow get turned around, try to find the dumpster." She nodded again.

Before she knew it, they had reached the alley, not far from Crazytown. She saw each side was lined with about ten or fifteen members, most of them brandished clubs or some similar type of weapon. Only Marco stood unarmed near the head of the narrow lane. He stepped toward her and told Eduardo to join the ranks. Her brother hesitated, then obeyed. He walked to the end of the line, near a large, dented, green dumpster.

"Valeria Reyes, step forward," Marco said loudly. "Tonight you wish to join the ranks of the Wild Dogs." She stared straight ahead, nodding slightly. "Having chosen to be jumped in, you must run the gauntlet. Are you prepared to do this?" She nodded again.

He turned to the two rows of gang members. "Dogs, ready?" There were shouts of assent and the sounds of clubs and bats being banged against the ground and hitting garbage cans. There were several female members in the lines. All looked ferocious and ready to inflict damage, Bella among them. The only other member she could identify was Seb. He was about halfway down on the left. Marco stepped away then faced Valeria. "Begin."

Ayúdame, Jesus, she thought, and dashed forward.

Immediately she was struck across her middle with a club. She almost doubled over, the air driven from her lungs. She was stunned, and thought, how can I do this if I can't breathe? In almost the next instant she felt a sharp pain in her right shoulder. Her upper arms, back, and thighs received a rain of blows, but gasping, Valeria pushed forward. She felt a hand grab her left breast and twist hard. She almost screamed at this intrusion and instinctively knocked the hand away. She rushed onward raising an arm to shield her face and was immediately met with a painful popping sound as two of the fingers on her left hand snapped back. She saw Eduardo in the near distance and lunged toward him, pushing past the final members, and throwing herself against the rusted side of the dumpster. She clung to it, gasping, finally able to suck in a chest full of air. She gripped the top rim of the dumpster with both hands, willing herself to remain upright. She refused to fall.

Still grasping the dumpster, Valeria turned and faced the gang. She squinted as blood ran into her right eye, her chest rapidly rising and falling. Apparently, rules or no rules, she had been hit in the head by someone. Eduardo looked at her with a combination of pride and concern. Marco slowly walked the path she had just taken. When he reached her, he nodded. "Welcome to the Wild Dogs. You have shown you have guts. Eduardo!" he called. "Take her home and care for her." To Valeria he smiled and said, "We'll see you soon."

Blinking through a sheen of blood, her chest still heaving, she nodded.

The journey home was a blur to her; she remembered leaning on Eduardo to the extent that he was nearly carrying her. She hurt everywhere, but especially her left hand and her breast where she was grabbed. She must have been reaching for it because Eduardo growled, "That damn, Seb."

"Who?"

"Seb. He's got his sights on you. I saw him grab your tit. He's next in line for leader after Marco and he thinks he can do whatever the hell he wants. I'll talk with him tomorrow."

Valeria shook her head. "It's not worth it. I'm good."

Once home she fell into bed and when she awoke, she saw her fingers had been splinted and felt a bandage above her eye. She saw Mama standing in the doorway of her room. Valeria smiled weakly. "I'm a Wild Dog, now."

Mama just nodded grimly and turned away.

Pushing her hand deeper into the ice, Valeria wondered why teenagers always seemed to believe everything their parents had to say was complete nonsense. Why the hell hadn't Valeria listened to Mama? It didn't matter now. She had to live with the consequences.

"I'm a Wild Dog," she whispered to no one, the words snatched away in the fan's air currents. "Once a Dog, a Dog forever."

She crossed to the crooked aluminum TV stand and turned on the small portable black and white she'd bought at a pawn shop prior to moving. Using her good hand, she moved the aerial right to left, then backward and forward, searching for decent reception.

"Should have picked up some tin foil for the antenna," she mumbled, then stepped back to get a clearer view of the screen. Pretty bad. Walter Cronkite seemed to be addressing the camera through a snowstorm. The audio was clear though. Cleanup after the race riots in Miami and Chicago. The Russians had just conducted a nuclear test with the promise of more to follow. The Democratic Convention was due to kick off in Chicago soon, the city's mayor giving assurances all would run smoothly, despite the recent riots.

Lots of luck with that, she thought.

Valeria clicked off the set; the snowy image imploding to a single point in the screen's center. She crossed to the miniscule aluminum shower stall and pushed the stained plastic curtain aside. Reaching in she turned on the water, knowing she'd have to contend with near-nonexistent pressure and the water's light brown tinge from rusted pipes. Valeria peeled off her remaining clothes and, averting her eyes from the bathroom mirror, stepped under the shower's trickle.

THIRTEEN

Nikki leaned her butt against the iron handrail bordering the porch steps of 214 Catherine Street. She lit a cigarette and glanced up and down the block. The houses were all large, significantly larger than Mrs. Gorman's and most others in town. About half of them had some version of porch running along the front or, as in the case of this house, one that wrapped around the front to one of the sides. And a porch swing! Awnings, too. Yeah, this was way more upscale than she was used to.

"Nikki! Would you come in, please?"

She'd been dozing on her sofa, not entirely restfully. She was dogged by bad dreams almost nightly. They just didn't want to let go. Behind her eyelids resided a parade of leering, sweaty-faced men eager for what she'd always been willing to offer. She shot up and almost bolted off the sofa. "Here I come, Mrs. G! Is everything okay?" She was at her landlady's side in seconds.

"I'm sorry, I didn't mean to frighten you. I'm fine, in fact I feel like making us some dinner today."

"Uh, I don't know, let me get my bearings a second. Why don't I just put togeth—"

"Nikki. Stop. Look at me." Nikki looked. "Don't I appear better than I have in days?" Nikki had to admit she did. "I am capable of putting together a dinner salad for the two of us."

"Sure, you look great, Mrs. G, never better, you belong on one of those singles beaches where—"

"Nikki."

"Okay, yes, you look fine, but why rush this thing? I can whip up a pot of spaghetti in no time. And I bought a jar of sauce yesterday, so we're fine there."

"No more spaghetti! We have had spaghetti three times this week. I appreciate your efforts, dear, but enough is enough. I'm handling dinner tonight."

"So, you don't like my spaghetti. Why didn't you just say so? I could have made some burgers or boiled up some hotdogs. I can be versatile, you know."

"Of course, you can, but not tonight."

"Is that why you called me in? You wanted to tell me you hated my cooking?"

Mrs. G looked flustered.

Nikki couldn't keep her smile concealed. "Damn, I had you going, huh? I'm awful sick of my cooking, too, so I won't argue. But please, go slow, okay?"

"Okay. But I did want to speak with you about something. Word of your cleaning expertise is getting around. Earlier, I received a call from Rolf Eichen."

"Ralph I can?"

"You really should get your hearing checked, you seem to have difficulty grasping names."

"Believe me, Mrs. G, getting my hearing checked is so far down my to-do list it's practically underground."

"It's Rolf, not Ralph, and Eichen, like, well, Eichen. Not 'I can.'"

The name sounded familiar to Nikki, but she couldn't place it. She chalked it up to the number of brain cells she'd slaughtered. She shook her head. "Not ringing a bell."

Thinking about the letch washing his car, Nikki hoped he wasn't one of her old patrons. She lived in fear one of the sleazes she used to transact with would schedule a house cleaning in hopes of revisiting the past.

"He is the son of the man killed on Catherine Street."

"Oh, yeah. What in the world would he want with me?"

"He wants you to clean his father's house. Apparently, the doctor had been living there alone for many years, and while it hasn't fallen into a pigsty—"

"Like Mrs. Kowchick's."

"Like Mrs. Kowalczyk's, the house does need a thorough cleaning. He said he hasn't spent much time there in recent years so he's not exactly sure what needs to be done, but he said you could name your price and it should be fine."

"Whoa, name my price? That's music to these ears! When does he need me?"

"He said whenever works for you, but the sooner the better. Really, he seems very accommodating."

"He sure does, and you said the word is out about my skills with a scrub brush? That's why he called?"

"How else would he know? Give yourself some credit, my dear. People appreciate you for the work you do."

"I guess." She rather doubted it, more likely it was Mrs. G somehow pulling some strings, but either way, naming her price, yeah, baby! She called and scheduled to meet Eichen at the house the next day.

Nikki considered heading over to the porch swing and parking herself there while she waited but thought seeming too casual as she met her new employer might not look good. Instead, she leaned back and soaked up some of the sun peeking through the leaves of the huge chestnut tree anchored between the sidewalk and the curb. There was a light breeze and Nikki felt a certain peace, something she was not at all accustomed to. Jeez, she thought, could this be that elusive "serenity" she'd heard so much about?

She'd just flicked away her cigarette butt and was digging in her hip pocket for the old, scratched Timex Mrs. G had lent her when a car pulled to the curb. Nikki straightened up, gave her hair a quick brush with her fingers, and conjured up what she hoped was an earnest-looking, hard-working smile. A short man, wearing a light jacket, exited the car and though he really was not noticeably heavy, he seemed to waddle up the curb and sidewalk toward her.

"Hello." His voice was rather quiet. In fact, a car passed as he spoke, and Nikki wasn't at all certain he'd actually said anything. Maybe he'd just moved his lips. He stopped in front of her and just stood. Nikki figured she should make a move.

"Um, Mr. Eichen?"

He nodded.

"Hi." She stuck out her hand and after a second of indecision, he shook it. "I'm Nikki Greene. Rose Gorman told me that you're looking for someone to clean your father's house. By the way, I'm sorry about his passing." She nodded at the house. "It's really lovely. The porch, that swing, what a great house to grow up in, I bet."

"Yes. It's a nice house." His square head nodded barely perceptibly on an almost non-existent neck. "It will need some...well, why don't you follow me?" He passed her and patted his pockets searching for keys. He pulled out a large keyring and after trying a couple keys, opened the front door into a kind of vestibule. There were hooks for coats and built-in benches on each side.

"Wow. These benches are beautiful. Like the pews in church only more ornate, and smaller, of course." Nikki said. "A little room just to put on your coat or sit and pull your boots off. Neat."

"Mmm."

Eichen opened the frosted glass inner door, and they were in the living room. Nikki doubted it had changed much since the forties or fifties. The wallpaper was boldly patterned and looked to be very thick. The ornate wooden legs of the sofa and chairs were all very dark and looked like a ball-in-claw type of design. Must have been the in-thing way back when, she thought.

Yeah, it was like walking into the past. What she perceived the past would look like, anyway. The place didn't appear too dirty, though. It certainly needed dusting, airing out, and maybe the wallpaper could use some scrubbing, but beyond that, not bad. Wow, she thought, look at me, thinking like a true domestic.

"Overall, I don't think there is much you need to do on the first floor. The kitchen, of course, is a mess. The police turned the room upside down. That's where the Doctor's body was found."

What an odd way to phrase it. 'Where the Doctor's body was found'. Not Dad, Pop, or even Father. And didn't *he* find the body? It didn't sound like a real lovey-dovey family.

They proceeded through the first floor: living room, den, dining room, and kitchen. Yikes. That room certainly was a disaster. Drawers were pulled open, and it looked like utensils were just dumped either on the counters or the floor. The contents of each cabinet had been removed and left, as well. The refrigerator door gaped open. The interior light glowed, and the motor still ran, vainly, trying to cool its contents. Whatever was in there had long since spoiled. A stench hung in the air.

"As you can probably see, I have not been back since that day." He closed the refrigerator door.

As Nikki inspected the room closer, she saw powder everywhere, the tabletop, counters, the stove, even clinging to vertical surfaces like the refrigerator door. She was puzzled until Eichen mentioned fingerprints. The police had been searching for ones that did not belong to either the deceased or a family member. "Unfortunately, they found nothing," he said.

They then descended a set of stairs into the basement and were immediately consumed by a warren of trunks, boxes, crowded free-standing shelving, rolled carpets, and God knows what else. Nikki saw an old-fashioned washing machine with wooden rollers to wring out water from clothes. Across the beams overhead ran four or five lengths of clothesline for hanging things dry. How state-of-the-art, she thought. If the guy wanted this place cleaned out would take about a year and a half. I hope he's not expecting me to shlep all this crap out she thought. She immediately received her answer.

After a deep sigh, Eichen said, "I wouldn't worry much about all this. Just leave it for now." She wanted to kiss him. "I've gone through the trunks and many of the boxes. I have already taken anything of value to me. Sometime this week I'll hire some men to haul all it all to the dump."

"Really? There may be some childhood items—"

"There's nothing I want. Let's go upstairs; this mess depresses me."

Well, okay, she thought. Let's.

In the kitchen he reached into a pocket and dug out several bills. "Here is some money to buy whatever you feel you need to do the job." He pressed them into Nikki's hand. "If you need more, call me. I think your friend, Mrs. Gorman, has my number."

Looking at the wad in her hand, Nikki said, "I'm pretty sure there's more than enough. I'll get receipts and any leftover cash back to you."

"Don't worry about receipts. And just apply any of the change toward what I need to pay you." He had been carrying the crowded keyring while they toured the first floor and basement. As they passed the kitchen table, he dropped it amid the fingerprint powder and stacks of crockery from the cabinets. "I can't stay longer, I'm afraid. Keep the keys. They're for the front, back, and side doors. The garage door keys are there, too, as well as the outside basement doors. And I'm guessing there are a bunch of extras opening God knows what. He cleared his throat and continued, "Whatever you can't open, don't worry about it, just let me know." Eichen hesitated and said, "There is an office upstairs; it may be locked, too. If none of these keys open it, just ignore it, and move on. There are three bedrooms, the one being used as the office, a second, the master bedroom, and a bathroom. It's all rather dated, I imagine. I have no idea if they've ever been renovated."

"It's been a while since you've been upstairs?"

"Yes. I haven't been in this house more than a handful of times the past ten years."

Nikki didn't know how to respond.

"When do you think you can begin the work?"

"First thing tomorrow morning if that works for you." He nodded. "Given the size of the house, I'm not sure how long it will take me. To be honest, I've never had a job this big. I mean the size of the house, number of rooms, that sort of thing."

"That's fine. Whenever you finish, call and I'll see about having the real estate people in to price it and put it up for sale."

Nikki was surprised. "You're selling? Not planning on moving back in yourself?" He shook his head. "Well, it's a beautiful house. I'm sure you'll do well. I promise I'll be super careful cleaning. I won't scratch anything and when I want to take a smoke break, I'll go outside." She picked up the bundle of keys and tried to look like the competent house cleaner she doubted she was.

They walked back through the first floor to the vestibule and out the front door. Nikki was surprised at the weight of the keyring in her hand. Who knew a place could have so many locked doors?

"If you don't mind, would you lock up, miss? I'm sorry the keys aren't labeled. You'll probably have to go through quite a lot of trial and error. I'm sure the Doctor knew to what door each key belonged, but I don't." He descended the porch stairs while Nikki fiddled until she found the right key to lock up.

"Gotta organize these things, first off," she muttered.

"Oh, miss!" Eichen called from the sidewalk. "You mentioned about stepping outside for cigarette breaks. You don't need to concern yourself with that. Feel free to smoke in the house."

"Was your fath—ah, was the Doctor a cigarette smoker, too?"

"No. He hated the smell." For the first time, Rolf Eichen smiled. "Smoke to your heart's content."

At a loss, Nikki just said, "Okay. Thanks. I will."

He got in his car and carefully nosed out into the street. Nikki couldn't help but notice he was still smiling.

FOURTEEN

That evening Kevin sat on the sofa, staring at the trunk in front of him. It had served as a coffee table since the death of his stepfather. On it was one of those doily things that seemed to be everywhere when he was growing up: on the arms of chairs, on headrests, on tables beneath centerpieces. The trunk had been calling him for the almost two years since Paval's death. He'd hesitated to answer that call. He wasn't sure why.

He rubbed his tired eyes and thought again about the new addition at the station. Valerie, or whatever her name was, it was going to be a disaster. It was just...too much, too quick. A girl cop. Jeez, the cops in nearby Perth Amboy and Sayreville must be laughing their asses off. No way a traditional, conservative town like Pendale was going to be able to handle such a change. Plus, she was like a robot or something. In the four-thirty meeting she barely talked, answering questions with just one or two words, no facial expression. Was she trying to act superior or something? Because she was from the big city, and they were just a bunch of hicks? And lastly, oh my God, a Puerto Rican? Had the captain lost his damn mind? They had barely been able to keep the town from exploding during the Rosaria Donez killing. Why risk all that crap again?

He sighed and tried to take his mind off this impending disaster, again looking at the trunk that held Paval's, what, his legacy?

When his own biological father passed, Kevin did not remember feeling anything at all like grief. When his mother died it had certainly been difficult, but not as difficult as it could have been, because Kevin still had Paval. The man had become a best friend to his stepson. Paval seemed to have felt the loss more strongly than Kevin and younger man did all he could to help him through his grief, growing even closer to the person who had become the center of his life.

And when he died, it was just Kevin. Sure, he had support from aunts, other family, and friends, but his center was gone. To avoid dealing with his feelings he quickly put the family house up for sale. Furniture, belongings, everything he could not justify saving were either sold or carted to the Pendale dump. Except for the piano and the trunk.

Paval had been an avid reader and writer. Reading English was difficult; anything he read in his new language was at a crawl: newspapers, magazines, whatever. Books often took months to get through. However, Paval was an enthusiastic journal writer. He had several old leather-bound volumes from his days in Poland in which his miniscule scrawl covered each page in entirety. No margins, breaks, or extra spacing. Each page a solid block of words. Polish words. In addition to the many leather-bound journals from Poland, there were newer lined marble-style covered notebooks, the kind Kevin remembered from school, that served as journals in his new country. But he never became comfortable writing in his adopted language. Despite the familiar covers, these too, were gibberish to Kevin. All he could decipher were the dates at the beginning of each entry and those on the cover of every journal.

Kevin looked at the notebooks' covers and smiled. He remembered once asking Paval why he wrote the dates backwards. Or partially backwards, anyway. Kevin had been in grade school where each day was a lesson in survival dealing with those bigger kids who seemed to thrive on intimidating kids like himself. These moments with Paval were a life raft to him.

"Look," Kevin had once said, pointing, "today is June 17th, 1955. Instead of 6/17/55 you wrote 17/6/55. Even if you weren't sure of the date, there are only twelve months, not seventeen. That's weird."

"Oh, is it Kevin? I say weird is the way *you* write it, the way Americans write it."

"What do you mean? Doesn't everybody write it the right way?"

"Not Americans."

"Huh? But we do write it right."

Paval had smiled and run his hand over Kevin's head, smoothing his hair. "What makes something right and something wrong?"

Kevin thought for a minute. "It's right if it's...right. It's the way everybody should do things."

"Oh? Such as?"

"Well...like Sunday being a holy day, a day you have to go to church."

"What about the Greenbaums up the street?"

Rosie Greenbaum was in his class at school and Kevin thought she was the most beautiful girl in the whole world. He felt his face flush. "What about them?"

"Is not Saturday their holy day? They go to the synagogue on that day, no?"

He hadn't thought of that. Some people *did* do things differently. He remembered Rosie talking about Hannukah during show and tell. What a rip-off only getting one gift for each of the days of the holiday. Poor girl. "But if *most* of the people do something one way, then that's the right way. Religion excepted," he added quickly.

"Ah, I see. So, if all the boys and girls in your class do something one way and only one person does it another way, that person is wrong."

Kevin thought about it. "Yeah. They're wrong."

"What if almost every country in the whole world did something the same and one country did it another way. They are wrong?"

"Well," Kevin hesitated, "yeah."

"Okay. I give you an assignment, like homework, but really, more like schoolwork. You go to your librarian, Miss Monroe, a smart lady." Kevin nodded. "Ask her how different countries in the world write the date. I am now to tell you what you will find in your schoolwork. The United States is the only country that writes the month before the day. Everybody else, *everybody*, writes the day first." Paval leaned down to Kevin's height. "You say if everybody does one thing and one person does another, then that person is wrong, eh? So, is America wrong?"

Kevin hadn't known what to say. America couldn't be doing something wrong because, well, just because. But he did not want to tell his stepfather he must have his facts confused. That might be rude. Kevin shrugged and said he would check with Miss Monroe. He did. The next day he quietly approached Paval after dinner.

"Paval," he said in a near whisper.

"Yes, Kevin, sit up here with me." Kevin jumped up on the sofa next to him. "I noticed you were very quiet at dinner. You are not often so quiet a boy. Is something bothering you?" Kevin nodded. "Is it to do with the assignment I give yesterday to you?" He nodded again. "What did you learn in your school library?"

He could barely articulate the words. "We're wrong."

"What? How can this be? The United Sates, wrong? No!"

"Everybody else writes the date with the day first, we're the only ones doing it with the month first." Kevin was silent, then, "How did we get it wrong?"

"You did not get it wrong."

Kevin looked at his stepfather doubtfully.

"Really," the older man said gently. "This country, *your* country and now my new country, it is not wrong in this. It is only different. America chooses to write it different, that's all."

Kevin was quiet for a moment. "So, maybe we do it different to try and make it *better*?"

Paval laughed. "Perhaps. But is it not enough to just think it is different? No one is better than another, no one is right or wrong. Only different, okay?"

Kevin nodded. "Okay!"

After Paval's death, Kevin had promised himself he would get a hold of one of the town's recent immigrants from Poland and have them translate for him. He had gone as far as scheduling a meeting with the butcher's cousin who had just arrived from Europe about six months after Paval's passing, but Kevin then canceled. While he was curious as ever about the thoughts and observations of his stepfather, he felt the words were too personal to share with another. He wanted Paval's words to be between just the two of them, no third party invited. So, he was caught in a purgatory of possessing these words that were so important but having no knowledge of their meaning. It was time though, to take some action. Earlier, he'd called the local college and been put onto a guy who could do the translations.

Kevin was especially excited about reading of pre-war life in Poland. But there was more than just the older stuff. Paval had wanted to talk to him about something before he died. And they'd never gotten around to it. Probably, it was nothing, but maybe there was some mention in the last journal. Maybe it would give him some idea what had been on the man's mind at the very end of his life.

119

Kevin reached into the trunk and began withdrawing the many notebooks, setting them on the carpet next to the sofa. He then arranged them in order, by the backward dates Paval had written on each cover. He made five stacks, four stacks of ten journals and one of eight. He gently pushed each stack against the wall and sat cross-legged on the floor gazing at them, at the memories of the man he had loved more than anyone else in the world.

FIFTEEN

V aleria leaned back, bracing herself for pain. This was the moment she'd dreamt of since childhood. She was about to be tatted with the Dogs' colors. It had been a week since her jumping in and she was healing up. Her fingers were still splinted, but the bandage above her eye had been removed and the bruises on her breast where Seb grabbed her had faded. She was in a back room of the building that served as Dog headquarters.

The tattoo guy had spent time in prison and learned his craft there. Most of the current members, including Eduardo, had been inked by him. Valeria heard him shuffling across the dirty floor. His thin, gray hair hung almost to his shoulders. He rubbed the back of his neck compulsively; he'd rub, pull his hand away and inspect his fingers, then rub some more. Valeria laid back in the ratty old reclining chair he'd steered her toward. The guy, whose real name Valeria never learned, mumbled to her to get comfortable, have a smoke or drink, it was going to take a while. She shook her head. He shrugged and told her to either remove or unbutton her shirt. She had worn a loose flannel shirt and low-cut bra beneath it. She fumbled with the buttons, her splinted fingers clumsy, and opened the shirt to expose the upper part of her left breast. The guy looked at the bra and made a face, then turned and dragged over a floor lamp, and in the glare of the bare bulb, leaned over her for a close look. He sat on a bar stool, its seat heavily taped, the legs on rollers.

He pushed her shirt open further and pulled the bra down an inch or so more. He leaned closer till she felt his breath on her breast, then ran his fingers over the exposed area. Valeria breathed deeply and immediately regretted it. Between his breath and body odor, Valeria didn't know if she'd make it through the session. She turned her head and looked to the corner of the room, searching for something to focus on. The corner where the stained ceiling met the crumbling wall. She stared, trying to think of nothing. Focus on nothing, Be nothing.

"Got nice skin," he mumbled.

"Um, thanks."

"Better than most."

"Okay."

He straightened up. "Be right back."

Valeria exhaled and closed her eyes as she heard him shuffle off. She knew this wasn't apt to be a pleasurable experience, but she hadn't expected the slovenliness.

"He's right. Your skin's great."

She opened her eyes, startled. She hadn't heard Seb enter the room. She reflexively pulled her shirt closed.

"Ha! Don't be so shy. Doc will be back and he'll just pull it open again. He ducked out for a quick hit. Says it keeps his hands steady." Seb sauntered over to her and looked down. "Sometimes he needs a little something to get him through the job. Not the strongest of Dogs, our Doc. Let's help the poor guy out a bit." He quickly reached down and pulled the shirt completely open. Valeria grabbed his wrists before he could do the same with her bra.

"No." She spoke through clenched teeth.

Seb laughed. "Yeah, you're a toughie, alright. Saw that at the jumping in. Shame you didn't go the other route. I got to tell you, there are a lot of guys here real disappointed in your choice." He bent closer, "Yeah, nice looking tit. It sure felt nice, too."

"Seb!" Marco stood in the doorway. "Let Doc work."

"Adios, baby," Seb said straightening. "We'll be seeing more of each other." He gazed down at her body, "a lot more." Then he strolled out, grinning at Marco.

"You ready?" the gang leader asked Valeria.

"Yeah, and—"

"And what?"

"And Seb's an asshole."

Marco laughed. "Yeah, you sure got that right. He's also the best warrior we got in this gang. If I tell him to do something, anything, I never have to worry it won't get done. He don't think, he just does it."

Doesn't think, great. Valeria just nodded.

"Later, when you're done, come show me your tat. It's always nice inspecting the Doc's work." Valeria liked the idea, but wondered how many other girls' tattoos he had inspected.

Doc then shuffled by him holding a metal tray with rags, a series of different sized needles, and several bottles of ink. Valeria's stomach flipped. She was glad she hadn't eaten earlier.

Marco laughed. "Oh, your face right now. If you could see it. Like a ghost." He left.

Doc set the tray on a small table nearby. Valeria saw the tray advertised Shaeffer Beer. Apparently, it was "the one beer to have when you're having more than one." He rolled his stool nearer, pulled the lamp close, and leaned again to about an inch or two from her breast. She held her breath.

"Ready?" he grunted.

Valeria exhaled. "Mm-hmm."

She looked down at her chest as Doc began to trace on her. Oh, shit, she thought, as she felt her stomach roll. She focused again on the space where the wall and ceiling met.

Two hours later Doc grunted; grunts were prominent in his vocabulary. He straightened up and tossed a needle on the beer tray. Valeria pulled her eyes away from their target on the wall and looked at him expectantly.

"Done," he muttered. "You can check it out in the bathroom mirror."

She pulled herself up from her position and, gingerly holding her shirt closed without it touching the tattoo, walked stiffly to the bathroom. A large guy brushed past her as she reached the door. The stench almost knocked her over. She stepped back, gulped some air, and entered.

The bare bulb affixed to the wall over the mirror cast a harsh glare. She kicked the door shut and slowly opened her shirt. The dark green and black of the twisted W and D, weeping drops of red blood, adorned the left side of her chest, over her heart. Valeria stared for several minutes before closing her shirt. This is what she'd wanted most of her life. It was now official. She looked into the reflection of her own eyes. She was a true Wild Dog.

After covering the inked area, Doc gave her aftercare instructions and told Valeria he'd be checking it throughout the week. He then stumbled out again for a hit of something or other. Valeria stood alone in the back room; a feeling of anti-climax enveloped her. She wanted to share her big moment with someone close to her, but Eduardo was out on some mission concerned with whatever trouble was on the horizon. Mama would certainly not appreciate the gravity of the moment. Bella, well, Bella had been drifting away. After Valeria had been jumped in the gang rather taking the route she'd chosen, Bella seemed to want little to do with her younger cousin. There was no one. No one except Marco.

She found him sitting alone in a room that seemed to be his office. A battered door laid across two stacks of cinderblocks served as a desk. Marco sat behind it, a sheaf of papers in one hand, immersed in thought. Valeria watched him for a moment, a frown on his face.

He looked up, saw her, and smiled. "Who would think running a gang would entail so much grunt work? Sometimes I feel like a suit behind a desk, living the life of a damn clerk."

Valeria just smiled.

"You're here to show me what our newest member looks like wearing our colors," he said. Without waiting for an answer, he quietly added, "Close the door."

With no hesitation, she obeyed and listened for the snick of the latch. Turning back to him, she saw Marco now stood on the near side of the desk, leaning against it, arms crossed over his chest. His leather vest over a bare torso showing his powerful arms, shoulders, and chest, adorned with his own Wild Dogs tat.

"Show me," he said.

"Doc covered it to keep it—"

"I know. Show me."

Valeria looked Marco in the eye and slowly unbuttoned her shirt keeping it pulled away from the inkwork. He stepped forward and gently slid the shirt off her shoulders and dropped it to the floor. He reached behind her, unclasped her bra, and it joined the shirt. He looked at her chest and then into her eyes, directly across from his own. He kissed her, massaging her un-inked breast, rolling the nipple between his fingers and thumb. Valeria's felt her eyes flutter.

He pulled away from her, held up one finger, then dragged a chair from the corner of the room, jamming it under the doorknob. He took her arm, led her toward the desktop, then swung his arm and swept it clean; papers, pens, an empty beer bottle, all fell to the floor. Marco lifted Valeria by her hips, laid her back across the desk and deftly began unbuttoning her jeans. For a second Valeria was stunned. Then, she lifted her hips, and using her unsplinted hand, helped push her jeans down before wildly kicking them to the cluttered floor.

She met each of Marco's thrusts with her own. Between his fingers and mouth plying her un-inked breast, the savage union at their hips, and the very intensity of her desire, Valeria climaxed quickly. Thankfully, Marcos did not. But when that moment occurred, Valeria came again as well, her legs wrapped tightly around Marco's hips and her arms clamped around his neck. Valeria felt him twitch inside her. She gasped and half-screamed over his shoulder. They laid chest to chest for several minutes, unmoving except for their labored breathing.

So, this is gang life, she thought, and burst out laughing.

Marco looked down at her with a puzzled smile.

Valeria shook her head, still trying to catch her breath. When she could finally speak, she whispered, "Do you think, um, is there any way...,"

Marco laughed and nodded. And it was even better than the first.

It didn't last. A month later, Marco was dead. Marco and two other Dogs were killed in an altercation with a rival gang. Many were injured, including Eduardo. Valeria had not been present. She and another representative of the gang had been sent to New Brunswick on a mission aimed at convening a summit between as many of the Jersey gangs as possible in an effort to avoid exactly what happened to claim Marco's life. In the aftermath of the incident, Valeria wondered if Marco had ordered her away to ensure her safety. She never knew. The Dogs were left with a vacancy in the gang hierarchy.

It did not stay vacant long. Seb seized the role and immediately began planning a counterattack against those who had killed their leader. Marco's efforts at convening a peaceful meeting with reps from other gangs were tossed aside. In his new role as head Dog,

Seb also tried to lay claim to Valeria. In the days following Marco's death he gave her no peace, her refusals were immaterial. She spent as much time as she could away from him and at the hospital where Eduardo lay recuperating from his injuries.

Valeria sat next to her brother's hospital bed, watching his chest rise and fall as he slept. It had been four days since Eduardo's attack and Marco's death. Inhaling the stale, sterile air of the hospital room she thought of the countless hours as a little girl dreaming of gang life. It was all she'd ever aspired to. In school other little girls, usually the few white girls in class, or maybe the non-gang family Spanish girls, had other dreams. Ballerinas, nurses, teachers. Hell, one girl even wanted to be a doctor. All Valeria had ever wanted was to be a Dog.

In seventh grade Mrs. Diaz, her math teacher, pulled her aside after class one day. She was Valeria's favorite teacher. The woman was strict and took no shit from anyone. Rumor had it she had a husband in prison somewhere and a kid that had been killed in a drive-by. But no one really knew, none of the students, anyway. Her demeanor gave away nothing. She always held herself erect, whether walking down the crowded halls or, like now, seated at her desk, hands folded in front of her.

"Valeria."

"Yes, ma'am?" She stood before the woman's desk.

"I wanted to congratulate you on achieving the highest average in class last quarter. Again." She showed a hint of a smile at the last word. "You and Leigh battled it out to the end, but you did it." Leigh was the hopeful future doctor.

'Thank you, ma'am." She smiled and nodded.

Mrs. Diaz took a deep breath and, if possible, pulled herself even more erect behind the desk. "I'm curious. What are your plans when you get out of school?"

"Well, I've got to babysit my two youngest brothers until my mother gets home from work. Then—"

"I'm sorry. I wasn't clear. I meant what are your plans after you graduate from high school?" Valeria looked confused. "I know it's a long way off, but is there anything you wish to pursue?"

Wish to pursue? The end of high school was a million miles away. The truth was she had given it zero thought. Probably find a guy and maybe have kids. All she knew for sure was that whatever came her away, she would greet it as a member of the Wild Dogs.

Mrs. Diaz continued. "Have you given any thought to going to college? There are young women who attend college, you know."

Not a single friend or family member of Valeria's had ever gone to college. "Yeah, I know, but—"

"No buts. Look at me, Valeria." Her gaze bore into Valeria's eyes. She spoke softly. "You are the most gifted student I have ever taught. Your other teachers feel very much the same way. You have the opportunity to do great things with your life. If you are concerned about the cost, there are grants available, student loans, part time jobs; money should not be an impediment."

"I never...I mean nobody I know goes to college. It's just not something I ever thought about."

"I understand. But you should think about it. You have the capabilities, don't waste them. Should you choose to go that route I promise you I will do everything in my power to help it come to fruition." She hesitated. "I know how difficult it can be resisting what your environment forces upon you. However, there are other options. But you need to search for them. You may know I lost a daughter to violence. She was ten years old. My husband is a victim, too, though in a different way. His life is finished. He's...I will never see him outside of prison again." She pursed her lips and looked down at the immaculate desk. She quietly cleared her throat. "There are other avenues in life than the one you appear to be headed for. Please think about them. You have time, but I promise, the time will go by before you can blink."

"Okay," she nodded, "I'll think about it."

Mrs. Diaz nodded. "Fine. Shall I write you a pass to your next class? It is English, am I right?"

"Yeah, I'll need one. Mr. Mulcahy is a pain about being late."

The woman handed her a pass. "Thank you, Valeria. Please don't forget this discussion."

But she did. Or rather, she actively ignored it. And as Mrs. Diaz had promised, graduation rehearsal was upon her in a flash. She had no speech to make; she was not valedictorian or salutatorian, not even close. Throughout high school, as interests changed and gang life drew nearer, Valeria's grades slid. She kicked ass in gym. And for whatever reason, excelled her foreign language elective, but really, what did grades matter? No one in the Dogs was going to care about her GPA.

She'd been goofing off with a couple classmates in the auditorium, playing with their gowns and mortarboards when she heard a voice behind her.

"Valeria."

She turned. Mrs. Diaz held out her hand. "I wanted to say goodbye and to wish you well."

"Uh, thanks." She took her old teacher's hand, startled. At that moment, their talk of five years ago came back to her. She felt her face getting hot. She nodded. "Thanks," she said again. As the woman turned away, her posture erect as ever, Valeria saw the look of disappointment on her face.

Sitting by her brother's bed she wondered, given a similar opportunity, would Eduardo have seized it? Probably not.

Sometimes you're destined to be what you'll be. But man, at such a cost. She thought of Marco. He'd been a true leader, with the ability to inspire, to motivate...God, what a loss! In another context, his options would be limitless, head of a company, military officer, anything. Valeria felt tears in her eyes.

She heard the door open and quickly wiped her eyes. She was shocked to see Seb and two other Dogs enter.

She whispered, "I don't think he can have so many visitors at a single—" Seb waved away her objection.

"Hey, man," he said loudly to Eduardo. Eduardo, didn't wake. Seb walked to the bed and shook his arm. "Duardo!" Eduardo winced.

"Hey!" Valeria whispered. "Leave him be, Seb."

"Shut it. Remember who you're talking to." He shook Eduardo's arm again.

Eduardo's eyes fluttered open. "Wh, what?" he whispered, his voice filled with pain..

Seb leaned over the bed, "Hey man, how you doing? The nurses treating you right?"

"What?" Eduardo didn't seem to understand him. "Yeah, yeah, good," his breathing labored.

"I saw some of them babes on the way in. Enjoy those sponge baths, my man."

Valeria quickly left the room. She stood outside the door, back against the wall, arms folded across her chest, teeth clenched.

Several minutes later, the Dogs came out.

"Seb, what the fuck are you doing?"

He stopped and stared at her, dead-eyed.

"He's really hurt. He got fucking stabbed. Jesus, give him time to heal up. You want him to start bleeding again? He lost enough blood already. Any idiot knows not to grab and shake him."

He continued staring, then in an instant his hand was around her throat, lifting and pinning her to the wall. He brought his face to hers and whispered.

"Shut your fucking mouth, bitch. Don't you ever talk to me like that again. Never forget who's top Dog now. Marco ain't around to watch over that pretty ass of yours. You will never, I mean never, disrespect me again, especially in front of my Dogs. And know this," he leaned his face to within an inch of hers and whispered, "something's coming your way that's going rock the hell out of you. Better get ready." He squeezed harder for a second before releasing her and turning away.

Valeria's knees buckled, but she stayed upright, the wall supporting her. She gasped, trying to get her breath back.

"Let's go, Dogs." Seb walked away, followed by the other two Dogs.

Valeria fought to breathe as they rounded the corner without a glance back.

It didn't take long for Seb to make good on his threat. Several days after Eduardo was released from the hospital, Seb called a meeting of the Wild Dogs. It was very quiet. Many members, knowing what was coming, waited in anticipation. Eduardo, still very pale, sat with Valeria standing over his shoulder.

After hitting on several topics, Seb announced a new edict. He stood before them, arms crossed over his chest. Maybe trying to emulate Marco, but failing badly.

"There's going to be changes. New leadership, new rules. First change: the Dogs have been allowing some members to choose the way they can join up. It's bullshit. Almost none of the other gangs do that. All males are jumped in, like always, but from here on out, all females joining up are sexed in. Period. They got a problem with that, they'll never be Dogs."

Valeria looked at Seb, her grip tightening on Eduardo's shoulder.

"And any current female members not sexed in, you got to be. You're a Dog, you got to do it. Marco was a pussy giving out choices. No more."

There was a murmur throughout the room.

"The list of those not sexed in is short." He now looked directly at Valeria. "We got one."

Eduardo struggled to stand. "Seb, this is shit, she's a Dog already, no way to make her—"

"Yeah, there's a way. There's a way because I say there's a way." He continued looking at Valeria. "You're a Dog. You're inked as a Dog, you wear the colors, marked forever. Female Dogs got to be sexed. Period. By end of day tomorrow."

Seb gave Valeria a tight smile and strode out. As he passed her, he said, "I'm looking forward to it. Lots of us are looking forward to it." The remaining Dogs trickled out, talking quietly and glancing Valeria's way. She heard one say, "Man, I'm gonna dream good tonight!"

Eduardo was breathing heavily, looking even paler than earlier. "No. I won't let him do this, 'mana. No fucking way. This is wrong, Marco would never allow this."

"No," said Valeria quietly, "but Marco is dead."

They walked home in silence. Clouds raced by the moon, briefly obscuring the weak shadows it threw. As they reached home, Valeria sat on the stoop, gently pulling her brother beside her. She looked up, over the top of the brick buildings before her. The moon had completely disappeared behind a mass of clouds. A darkness fell on them. She asked, "Once you're initiated in the gang, is there any way to leave?"

Eduardo gripped the handrail as he sat. They were close enough to touch. "It's not the initiation. That's real important, sure, that gets you in, but it's the colors. Once you're marked with the colors, you're a Dog. Always, until you die. There's no way out. No way they'll let you walk. You can't just keep the tat covered up. Oh, hell, 'mana," he dropped his head to his chest, "you're trapped." He began to cry. "I'm so, so sorry."

Valeria gently ran her hand over his head and spoke quietly. "There's a way...there's got to be a way."

There was. And she found it. But no one believed she would go actually through with it.

SIXTEEN

N ikki unlocked the trunk of Mrs. G's old Buick and began unloading cleaning supplies: floor cleaner, furniture polish, dish detergent, cleanser for the sinks and tubs, oven cleaner. She didn't remember seeing mops or buckets on her quick tour with Rolf Eichen, so she took it upon herself to buy them, as well. The trunk smelled like the cleaning aisle at Foodtown, lemony and nauseating. It took two trips to lug all the stuff from the sidewalk to the front door of 214 Catherine Street. Nikki paused for breath.

Look at this, not twenty-one yet and gasping, she thought. She walked to the porch swing, sat, and lit a cigarette. What the hell, might as well take my first break. She sat musing as a light breeze gently pushed her in motion. The tips of her sandaled toes hung above the porch surface. Nikki dropped her head back and closed her eyes. Her forehead tickled as the wind gently blew a lock of hair. What was this feeling she had? Could it be contentment? At last?

It had been a hell of a summer. Beginning for her in the same manner she'd spent the last two years: either drunk, trying to get drunk, or screwing some stranger for the price of her next drink. Even sitting there alone, she felt her face blush. My God, Nik, how the hell could you have allowed it to go that far? The answer wasn't hard. Guilt. Guilt and cowardice. Guilt at having caused the end of her relationship with Donald, and the cowardice of running from the consequences of his death shortly thereafter. She hadn't known where to run or who to turn to, so instead, she turned herself out, for the price of whatever she felt she needed.

Thank God for Mrs. Gorman. Without her Nikki knew she'd be dead. Or worse than dead, living as she had been, drink to drink, guy to guy. Mrs. G had once again intervened, dragging Nikki from her downward spiral, and for whatever reason, this time it stuck. So far anyway. Maybe that murderous lunatic was part of the reason, trying to kill her but failing. And somehow, Nikki had emerged stronger for it. Yeah, but was it strong enough? She was having doubts.

Last night had been rough. Ingrained behavior is hard to change. When you've become accustomed to passing out each night, simply drifting off to sleep doesn't come easy. Your mind wanders, hell, it races, focusing on everything you absolutely do not want it to. The feeling of relief when that first drink quells the fierce longing, even though that longing never seems to completely depart. The bars themselves. Their shadowy dimness, lit by random neon advertisements reflecting backward off a shadowed window. The gloom barely brightened by the gray flicker of a small TV perched somewhere above. And the smells: the sharp, almost medicinal scent of the liquor, the mustiness of the rooms, the reek of the sweat and breath of the patrons. It was the smell of what was forbidden, of what she knew would cause her pain, but she longed for it anyway. That smell...it was almost sexy.

Leaving the stark intensity of the outside world where life was all too distinct, passing through the door into the shadows, it was almost as though she felt herself being enveloped by danger, by menace and risk, and she embraced it wholeheartedly. She wrapped it around herself while breathing it in until it both filled and swallowed her. She was one with it.

And the men. Men who thought nothing of using her in any manner they chose and then discarding her immediately thereafter.

Trash to be disposed of when they were through with her. Like something insignificant, of no worth. This was validation. The humiliation, shame, and physical pain she experienced was exactly what she deserved. This was who she was. What she was. It was truth. Why would she question it? Even if she wanted to fight it, it was useless. It was a crazed rollercoaster throwing her blindly this way and that. There was no escape until the ride ended. And it never ended.

The men were all very large. Nikki hadn't really thought about that until now. They were heavy, even obese, and very physical. For whatever reason these were the men she attracted, those with the need to impose their will on her. These men who were two or even three times her weight. She knew she would be physically incapable of extricating herself from their grasp even if she wanted to. And there was a perverse comfort in that. It was easier to accept the futility of attempting to end the degradation, so why bother trying? Simply ride the rollercoaster and try to convince yourself it was what you wanted. You were not the only one being used. You were using them as a means to attain what you yearned for more each day. It was a simple business transaction. Both sides benefitting.

Yeah. That's what she tried to tell herself as she stumbled against a dirty wall in an alley behind some random bar, trying to vomit the taste from her mouth. Alone, as the most recent guy had just zipped up and ambled back inside for a quick one before driving home to dinner with the wife and kids. After a few minutes, she'd clean up the best she could, brush off her jeans, suck on a Lifesaver, run her fingers through her hair, and head back in. Never acknowledging what had just occurred, what was obvious to all. And after a trip to the ladies' room, she could almost fool herself that a quick reset had been hit and when she emerged it was brand-new day. Just a girl out on the town, nothing untoward about it. Park herself at a table in the shadows and before long there's another drink in front of her and another big, grinning guy leering down at her, calculating how many more he'd have to pour into her before leading her out. Maybe, if she was lucky, he'd have a bottle of something at home and Nikki could be comforted in the knowledge that her need, her hunger, would be satiated until morning.

She almost shivered as a gentle breeze nudged the porch swing.

What was hardest to admit to herself even now was that despite the degradation, the acts of humiliation, and the self-loathing it brought, Nikki yearned for it. And now that it was gone, it left a void. One that was barren and endless. Nothing could possibly fill that vast emptiness and satisfy that overwhelming hunger. The only constant in her life now was guilt. It felt like it had been her companion forever. Guilt over wrecking the relationship with Donald, guilt over her actions at his funeral, guilt over whoring herself, guilt over what she'd put Mrs. G through, guilt over the life she was wasting. And sometimes, like now, guilt that she longed for it so much.

She'd barely slept the previous night. Nikki had kept the door between the two living spaces open and every couple hours tiptoed into Mrs. G's to check that the woman was alright. Nikki'd been awake anyway. The cravings. She wondered how long her body would still be screaming for the booze. At her meetings she'd heard it all. Some recovering drunks said it'd be a week, a month, ninety days. One older woman who claimed to have been sober for seven years said she still feels the urge whenever she's overly tired or stressed. Well shit, thought Nikki, I'm overly tired because I can't sleep because I'm stressed because I can't drink. So where does it end? No one could tell her. All they said was don't drink, go to meetings. Terrific.

And the craving for the other? For the men and what they did to her? How can you both hate and long for something at the same time? Knowing at any given minute the longing might outweigh the hatred. One moment of weakness and....

Jesus, she thought, you are one messed up bitch, Nikki. She flicked her cigarette over the porch rail and walked toward the front door and her pile of cleaning supplies. Let's get this party rolling before I start feeling guilty about wasting valuable cleaning time.

After dumping all her equipment in the kitchen, Nikki took a slow tour of the house. It looked in serious need of a woman's touch. Not that she knew exactly what that meant, her own apartment being just this side of a disaster itself. It just *felt* like a man's domain. Aside from the kitchen, which was a wreck because of the police, the remaining downstairs wasn't too bad. She moved from room to room, jotting notes in a small notebook. Very much, she thought, like the one she saw Captain Clarke use when he'd visited her at the hospital. Maybe we both shop the back-to-school sales, she mused.

Most of the furniture looked heavy and solid. The floral designs on the sofa and chairs were garish, though faded through the years. Legs and arms of the pieces were both ornate and dark. She pulled up a corner of carpeting and saw the floor beneath was darker, the sun having discolored the exposed wood. There was a large, two-door cabinet in the living room, its dark wood ornately crafted. She opened one door and saw a rack of records standing in their sleeves. Behind the other door was an old turntable. She looked below and saw speakers. Whoa. Let's see what tunes the old doc was into.

Unfortunately, each of the record sleeves was in a foreign language. Polish probably, she wasn't sure. The covers themselves depicted marching bands, images of parks, a dark castle perched on a mountaintop against a brilliant blue sky. She pulled the record from that one. It was heavy and thicker than any records she had ever played. On the label near the center hole, it read 78 rpm. Whoa! So, this is a 78, Nikki thought. Cool. After a quick search she found the power switch. She dropped the disk on the turntable and gently placed the needle.

Instantly, the room was filled with sonorous brass and Nikki immediately turned the volume down. Don't want the neighbors to get ticked off. Although, if the doc listened at that volume, they were probably used to it. It sounded familiar, but she had no idea of what exactly she was listening to. Examining the record sleeve Nikki read "Der Ring des Nibelungen" it was by some guy named Wagner. The only Wagner she knew was that cute guy on TV who played a thief working for the government. Looking at the picture of the composer on the album sleeve she didn't see much in the way of resemblance to the actor. She listened for a few more seconds before lifting the needle and turning off the turntable. Pretty cool, but no Sergeant Pepper. Kind of scary, really. She shut the cabinet doors and crossed to the den. Looking about she noticed a painting that seemed to dominate the room. It hung directly opposite a comfortable-looking easy chair and above a buffet-style piece of furniture.

The painted scene looked very heavy and forbidding. Beneath a gray sky was a strange collection of buildings, in varying styles of architecture. In the rear were castle or church spires, in the foreground were much lower, simpler buildings, a stone bridge ran between the structures. All these buildings bordered a frozen body of water where a couple horses and sleighs crossed. Finally, there were several people bundled up against the cold. Nikki squinted at a small plaque on the bottom of the frame. She assumed it to be the painting's title. It, too, was not in English. All she could make out was the word Danzig. Hmph. Someplace in the doc's old country? Maybe a little slice of home, she thought. She peered closer. Kind of depressing, though.

Beneath the painting, on the surface of the buffet, were several doily-thingies, on top of which were old photos. One was of a very beautiful, yet sad-looking girl, another was a very dated picture of a severe-looking old woman. A real sourpuss. The doc's wife and mother, maybe? She then bent and opened the cabinet doors of the buffet and gasped.

Jesus.

Bottles of about every kind of alcohol she could imagine. The smell rolled out through the open doors, almost physically assaulting her. It crept down her throat and into her lungs. She could almost feel it settling on her skin and hair.

She slammed the doors shut. But not before a wave of giddiness washed over her. All that booze!

Nikki quickly stepped back. Outside of a bar or liquor store she'd never seen so much alcohol in one place. She hesitated, unsure of what to do. She sat on the edge of the easy chair, her back straight, hands between her knees. Dammit. The split second before she'd closed the cabinet doors her reaction to the sight had been one of almost joy. Her mouth actually watered.

She stared up at the scary painting. Could she handle this? Could she trust herself alone in this house, with all that alcohol? Should she get Eichen's number from Mrs. G and call him saying she wouldn't be able to follow through with the job? Tell him something had come up, she'd forgotten about a previous promised job, something? Crap. She'd already spent some of his money on the cleaning supplies. What if he was ticked off and demanded the money back? He didn't seem the type, but still.... What would Mrs. G say? There was no way she would want Nikki to do anything that might lead her to relapse, that's for sure. So maybe this was the route to go, just back out of the job. But she'd been so pleased, almost proud when she spoke of Eichen contacting her about wanting Nikki's services. And Nikki wanted so badly to please her.

She had no idea how long she sat, trying to decide. Why the hell can't someone just appear from a puff of smoke and tell me what to do? Like that hot-looking blonde genie on TV. Damn. She immediately thought back to her little haram dance in the car with Donald. Oh, Donald, I miss you so much. Nikki knew a few quick belts from one of the bottles wasn't going to make the longing go away, but it might dull the ache. A clock somewhere in the house ticked loudly. Each second seemed a battle between Nikki and the drink.

"Fuck this," she said. "I'll work on the kitchen." She quickly rose and almost sprinted out of the room.

SEVENTEEN

The overwhelming mess of the kitchen was almost a relief. Nikki scanned the ceiling and saw, thankfully, there would be no need for her to scrub away years' worth of grease. She filled the sink with hot soapy water and tossed in as many utensils that had been littering the countertops as it would hold. She would let them soak, hopefully washing away the fingerprint dust, while she cleaned the insides of the cabinets.

After about an hour of work and what seemed like miniscule progress, with her brain returning again and again to the buffet in the den, Nikki thought the job might go quicker with some music to scrub to. She saw a countertop radio next to the toaster and, after rinsing her hands clean, she flicked it on. After a second of so of static a voice in a foreign language intoned something or other. Again, Polish? German? It struck her as what she'd always believed German would sound like. Jeez, the German language always sounds like the speaker is mad at the world. "Mellow out there, Adolf," she said to the broadcaster. Nikki spun the knob. Oooh! Here we go! "Born to be Wild!" That's me, baby!

Standing on a step stool, she shook her hips to the music as she sprayed cleaner into a cabinet and began wiping as she desperately tried to forget what was in the next room. Yeah, got my motor running, alright. She hummed along, making up most of the words as she scrubbed, trying to keep her senses diverted. After about thirty minutes Nikki decided she'd tackle washing the soaking utensils. Her mind kept slipping back to the den. So many bottles. Mr. Eichen said he barely ever came to the house, no way he'd miss one or two.

"No!" she shouted above the music. "No, no, no!" She reached and turned the volume up.

"People everywhere just got to be free!" She shouted along to the music, again moving her hips, trying to lose herself. The minutes dragged. She scrubbed hard, feeling the ache in her shoulders, concentrating on that and the music rather than the pull from the other room. The music segued into something quieter, the sound of waves on the beach reaching her ears.

"Oooh, whoever this sexy-sounding guy is, I'd sit on any dock of any bay with him."

When she'd emptied the sink of utensils, Nikki leaned against the counter. She glanced at the doorway to the dining room and den. She felt an agitation growing and despite what Rolf Eichen had said about smoking indoors, she figured it was time to head out for a smoke break. She shook water from her hands and dried them on her shirt before stepping into the bright backyard. Strands of music carried through the screened door as she lifted her face to the sun. "This Guy's in Love with You." Fat fucking chance, she thought. Nikki lit up and wandered into the yard.

It was small, but nice, well-kept. She tried to focus on the landscape. Privacy hedges along both sides of the property, a detached two-car garage at the end of the driveway. Some fruit trees lining a rear stone wall, pears hanging heavily off the thin, twisted branches. There was also a grape arbor with a short folding table and Adirondack chair beneath the arch. Nice, Nikki thought, looking around. A great place to kick back and get lost in your thoughts. She shook her head, that's the place she wanted to get lost.

Nikki eyed the fruit trees. She remembered Mrs. G mentioning a lot of immigrants planted fruit trees to make homemade wine, sort of a reminder of the old country or something. Did the old doc follow suit? With the trees, the arbor, the stone wall, and privacy it offered, the yard was a little oasis. You could hardly hear traffic from the street. It looked kind of like some sort of beer garden. One of those outdoor places where folks would hang out and quaff a few in the open air. She remembered seeing pictures of them, she couldn't remember where exactly. Probably the only reason the memory registered, Nikki thought, was because it was alcohol-related. Jesus, what a messed-up head.

A gentle breeze blew, and a bank of clouds momentarily blocked the sun creating a cool, fresh respite from the heat. Instead of heading back into the kitchen, Nikki decided to take advantage of the moment and stroll around the property. The lot the house sat on wasn't huge, none of the lots in Pendale were, but this one was larger than most. Forest-green awnings hung over virtually every window. There was even a tiny one over the small first floor bathroom.

Nikki thought again about how charming it all appeared. Charming and private. The old doc probably could have done some nude sunbathing in the yard and nobody would be the wiser. Hmm. She glanced around. Ah, screw it. She had a job to do, and it wasn't flashing her pasty body at the squirrels.

Her eyes needed a second or two to adjust when she stepped back into the kitchen. After a moment she surveyed the room. The cabinets looked good, but about two thirds of the counters and all the drawers still needed her attention. Crap. Jesus, Nik, what have you gotten yourself into? Yeah, she thought, the "name your price" part of the job was appealing as hell, but...maybe it would be best to take a break from the kitchen. She eyed the door to the dining room. Maybe move to another room and start fresh. She could always zip back in here, after a bit of work elsewhere. That'd work.

She grabbed a dry mop and spray cleaner from her pile of supplies. Get rid of all those nasty spiderwebs and dust bunnies along the borders between the ceiling and walls. Yeah. She'd start back in the living room. She glanced at the liquor cabinet as she walked through the den. She sprayed the mop with cleaner. Maybe some tunes would help matters. She thought of the radio in the kitchen but didn't feel she was up to facing that mess. Nikki leafed through the record collection again, looking for anything that didn't seem a hundred years old. Nothing. What she wouldn't do for a Rolling Stones or Cream album.

Ah, well...let's give Wagner another whirl. She dropped the needle to the record and turned up the volume. Might as well go big, she thought.

The cleaning was harder than she'd thought it would be. The constant reaching upward and craning her neck back was taking a toll. Jeez, already huffing and puffing. A sad state of affairs. She was about to take another quick break when the music shifted to another movement. Whoa! A refrain of heavy brass roared through the speakers. It almost seemed to lift her off the ground and it was energizing as hell. All of a sudden she felt ready to tackle the whole house with energy to spare.

But the piece ended way too quickly. Nikki dropped her mop and scanned the record sleeve. Just what the hell *was* that? Running her finger down the list of what she thought to be the titles of the songs, or pieces or movements or whatever, she found what she believed to be the one. Ritt der Walkuren. Well, shit, wasn't that informative?

The music had moved on and instead of being motivating, it had become an annoyance. Nothing sounded as good as the part she'd heard earlier. After a while, she'd had enough. Time for another record. Nikki peeked at the buffet while crossing to the stereo. Leafing through the records again, she couldn't decide which one to go with. The hell with this. She shoved them back, crossed through the den, past the buffet, into the dining room and then the kitchen. She unplugged the countertop radio and tried to ignore the mess.

She returned to the den and looked for somewhere to plug it in. The only free electrical outlet she saw was near the back of the buffet. Nikki put the radio next to the picture of the old lady and dropped to her knees, pulling the cord toward the outlet. Her face now so close to the cabinet she could smell its contents. She felt dizzy. The plug finally slid into the outlet and Nikki sat back on the carpet, almost panting. She studied the closed doors, catching her breath.

The chiming of a clock woke her from her reverie. *Jesus. How long was I zoned out?*

The still, stale air in the house seemed to weigh in her lungs. *God, it was stuffy. I'd kill for a cold beer.* The thought was in her head almost before it even registered. *Shit. And here I am about two feet away from what amounted to a drunk's Aladdin's cave. I know if I open those doors again I might...yeah, but a beer, a cold beer, it's hardly the same thing.* She tried to remember if she'd seen any in the fridge.

She moved to get up and head to the kitchen. "Whoa! What the fuck! Nikki, stop!" she yelled out loud. She almost ran to the stairway, needing to distance herself from that damn cabinet and whatever might be in the fridge.

Let's get the lay of the land up here, she thought. *It's got to be safer.* She dug the small spiral pad from her back pocket, along with a stub of pencil. Pushing the buffet and its contents out of her mind as best she could, she moved from room to room. The bathroom in the front of the house didn't look bad at all. In fact, it didn't even look as though it had been used recently. She made a note to remember to bring up some tub and tile cleaner anyway. Next was a small bedroom. Probably a child's room or a guest bedroom. It too looked as though it hadn't been used in years. She scanned the walls and ceilings. Cobwebs. Dust on all the wood surfaces, the dresser, nightstand. The linen probably needed to be laundered, too.

She left the room and looked up. There was a trap door in the center of the hall ceiling. A piece of rope hung down about a foot, attached to it was a small wooden handle. Most people could have reached up and taken hold of the handle. It took Nikki half a dozen jumps to snag it. She held on tight and as her feet hit the ground the door pulled partially open. She worked to catch her breath. Fucking cigarettes, she thought. She pulled down and wooden stairs folded out until they rested on the hall floor. She gingerly climbed until her head poked above the square trap door opening. She looked around. Sunlight streamed through windows in the attic's front and side walls. Nothing. Not a single thing. Just dust motes floating in the sun. This has got to be the cleanest damn attic on the planet, she thought. She climbed back down and after jumping off the final step she folded up the ladder and let the trap door spring closed. The wooden handle on the end of the rope swung madly.

Next was what she assumed to be the master bedroom. It was very spacious, with windows looking down over the driveway and one set of privacy hedges. The king-sized bed's spread was pulled up haphazardly.

Nikki tried to remember if she and Donald had ever made love in a bed anywhere near the size of this one. She doubted it. There was the smallish double bed in her apartment, and the single in his dorm at school. Occasionally they'd used his old bedroom at his parents' house when they were out. And sometimes too when they weren't. Their first time doing it there Nikki remembered thinking it was almost as though she was violating a child, as they went at it under sports posters tacked to the wall, plastic models of monsters in a low bookcase, and a small cowboy hat hanging on a bedpost. And God only knows how many dead-end roads, turnabouts in the woods, and dark stretches of beach they'd graced. She smiled. Yeah, they had certainly embraced the great outdoors together. She felt herself becoming aroused. Oh, Nik. Just stop it.

The past was such an insidious thing, she thought. You're basking in happy memories, feeling the warm fuzzies one second, becoming horny the next, and then getting clobbered with shame, which was what she felt now.

She shook her head hard. Stop it! Fuck you, past! Back to work.

Okay, wash the bedsheets in here, too. Maybe the spread if it was washable, if not, get it dry cleaned. And, of course, dust everything. Leaving the room, she moved down the hall to the final door situated near the top of the rear stairs leading down to the kitchen. She tried turning the knob. Locked. There was no key sticking out of the keyhole. She ran her fingers over the molding around the sides of the door. Nothing. She returned to the bathroom and grabbed a short stepstool she'd seen under the sink and felt along the section of molding above the door. Nope. It was probably on the keyring Rolf had given her.

Nikki went downstairs, through the living room and den, glancing sideways at the buffet, to the dining room where she remembered having dropped the keys on the table. Moving from key to key she slowly made her way back into the den. She stopped near the easy chair. This one maybe? No, looks like to a padlock, not an interior door. She looked at the Danzig painting, then to the buffet below it. Guess I'll just have to try them all. She moved on and climbed the stairs again, feeling as though she was climbing a mountain. Gotta cut down on the smokes.

After going through all but the final two keys, Nikki finally hit the lucky one. Swinging open the door she wasn't sure what she was expecting, but nothing this boring. The room appeared to be used as an office. There was a desk with an immaculate blotter on top, on a table at its side sat a typewriter, and a file cabinet stood in the corner. Nikki discovered the drawers were locked, but she figured the small key on the ring might open them. She tried it, yup. But she wasn't up to checking it out right now. Finally, there was an easy chair and a floor lamp next to it. It looked comfy. God, she was tired. Time to call it a day. She stepped out, closed the door, thought about locking it back up, but thought the hell with it. She'd just lock up the exterior doors tight.

She slowly clomped down the rear stairs and found herself back in the mess that was the kitchen. She was exhausted. The lack of sleep was really catching up to her. She glanced at the wall clock. Jeez, she'd been there for over six hours. It seemed impossible. She wondered how much time she'd spent, staring at that buffet.

Nikki locked up the back door, left the kitchen, walked through the dining room, and stopped in the den. The painting, the one of Danzig, drew her. She felt she could stare at it for hours. Nikki inhaled deeply and thought she could smell the alcohol, sharp and fresh. The painting my ass, she thought, it's what the painting was hanging above that drew her. She quickly crossed into the living room, through the vestibule, and out the door. She locked up, shook the knob, and almost ran to her car.

EIGHTEEN

C olors. It was all about the colors.

You can't have them bestowed on you, then toss them aside. No. When you're inked, you're inked for life. The tatting was permanent. But Valeria had been right. There was a way.

She recalled one of her uncles, also a Dog, talking to another member over beers in the kitchen. It had been about ten, twelve years ago. They'd had quite a few and their voices were loud.

"Shit," her uncle had said, "it'd take balls the size of melons to do it."

"I heard about a guy over in Asbury Park—"

"Pussies! Those Asbury Park guys are pussies. Don't got the balls of a schoolgirl."

"Fucking right. But I heard about this guy, I don't know why, but he wanted out—"

"Because they're pussies! I told you!"

"Yeah, Jesus, shut the fuck up for a minute, okay? They're pussies, I'm with you. But this guy, he wanted out. So, he took that route. And I heard he had a heart attack or stroke or something, right in the middle of it. They had to throw him on the garbage barge to be dumped in the bay."

"You know why he kicked off, right?" Valeria's uncle asked before belching.

"Yeah, I know. He was—"

"A pussy!" Her uncle yelled, laughing.

During the conversation, they had divulged the process by which one could free themselves from a gang...and the colors. But could she go through with it? Was it worth the cost? Would she even survive it?

Getting sexed in, all she had to do was ride it out. A night, maybe a couple days, not with guys she'd choose to have, but hell, it's not like they'd be complete strangers. They'd be familiar faces, comrades. It wouldn't be rape; she'd be consenting. What was the saying? Just lay back and try to enjoy it. There wouldn't be any enjoyment she knew, but when it was over, it was over. Done. Nothing more to think about. Go on like it never happened.

But Valeria knew she could not live like it never happened. It would always be in her head, refusing to be pushed aside. She would be seeing these guys almost every day for the rest of her life. She wasn't Bella, she couldn't convince herself that it was for the good of the cause, something important and necessary for the gang's well-being. No, there weren't enough substances in the world that could make her ever feel that.

Valeria stood in front of her bedroom mirror. She slowly unbuttoned her shirt and slid it off her shoulders. She unclasped her bra and shrugged it off. She gazed at her tattoo. The twisted vines through the letters, the drops of blood. This had meant everything to her for so long. Being a Wild Dog. She was breathing heavily, her chest almost heaving. She closed her eyes and forced herself under control. She opened her eyes and studied her body in the glass. Her coppery skin, long, muscular neck, wide shoulders, full breasts. She stared for a long while. Could she do this and was it really worth it? She made up her mind.

"You choose this over the other, being sexed in?"

Valeria nodded.

At first no one had believed her, except Mama. Eduardo burst into tears when she told him her decision. "Val, I am so, so sorry," he gasped. "Are you sure? Really sure because...." He couldn't finish.

"It'll be fine, manito," she whispered, pulling him into her arms and stroking his head. "You know I'm strong. It will be fine," she repeated, looking over Eduardo's shoulder at Mama. She had not cried, but the look of pain on her face was immense.

After she led the despairing Eduardo to his room and laid him down, Mama returned to her only daughter. She looked up into Valeria's eyes. So beautiful, so smart. How could this be happening? She hugged her, her head barely reaching Valeria's shoulder. "Mi niña hermosa," Mama whispered, as the two women embraced. Before they drew apart Mama said firmly, "You *are* strong. Don't doubt it for even one second."

The temperature in the old garage was sweltering. The smell of years of spilt oil absorbed into the dirt floor was overpowering. Outdated tools hung off rusted nails hammered into the walls and shimmered in the haze. The old metal can had once held engine lubricant. It was jammed onto the end of a fireplace poker. The white-blue flame of a blowtorch, clamped in a vice at the end of a

153

workbench, completely engulfed the can. A Dog held the poker to the flame like a kid holding a marshmallow at the end of a stick. The metal can and end of the poker itself were slowly beginning to glow, from black to dull orange.

Valeria stood between two large Dogs. Though about ten feet away, she could feel the heat of the flame. She could not pull her eyes from it. She didn't want to watch this, the flame, the glowing, but Seb ordered she be there. She'd made a choice, she lived with the consequences. From start to finish.

Until the last minute, Eduardo argued, then pleaded with Seb to call it off, just let her go. She'd leave the town, the state, anything. No one ever needed to know she was a Dog. Just please, stop this. Seb had him dragged away.

It turned out Doc was the guy who would perform this operation, too. He looked at Valeria and then the poker. "Be right back." He scuttled away for a hit of whatever he needed to get through the procedure.

Valeria was pale and shaking. She prayed as she had never prayed before for strength and courage. Sweat rolled down her face. She felt the heat enter every pore. She tried to avert her eyes from the glowing poker but couldn't. Her entire body shook.

Seb nodded and the two burly Dogs each grabbed Valeria by the upper arm and pushed her toward the flame. They held her, waiting for directions. Seb stepped up, grabbed her by the hair, and backhanded her across the face. He yanked open her shirt and tore off her bra, throwing them both to the floor. He stepped away, allowing all the Dogs to feast their eyes.

Blood flowed from Valeria's nose and over her lips. She dragged her eyes from the poker to Seb. Her mouth was dry, and she fought to keep the tremor from her voice. She spoke loud enough for the entire room to hear. "You're not a tenth the man Marco was."

Seb exhaled loudly. "Where the fuck is Doc?" he yelled, just as the man stumbled through the door.

The two Dogs tightened their grip on Valeria's slick arms, holding her upright as her knees buckled. She felt sweat roll down her back and sides, almost tickling her. Doc hesitantly moved to the glowing poker. He looked imploringly at Seb who just stared back. He grasped the poker's handle and shuffled toward Valeria. He gazed at his inkwork over her bare left breast and mumbled sadly, "Such nice skin."

Valeria's eyes followed the glowing end of the poker and can as it moved from the flame to within inches of her. Sweat flowed into her eyes, blinding her, but not before she saw the poker move forward and connect.

NINETEEN

The pain was like nothing she could have ever imagined. Before she passed out, she hazily recalled the sound of screaming, the smell of burning meat, and then wails of agony. Were they her screams, her wails? Probably, but the smell, there was no question about that. She blearily remembered Seb approaching her, again yanking her by the hair and leaning to her ear. The last words she heard before he dropped her head back to her chest were, "I can still take you anytime I want. And I will, we all will. You did this for nothing you stupid, stupid bitch."

It took months to recuperate; she was barely able to move, much less leave the house. Mama was her near-constant companion. She sat with her only daughter as she endured weeks of agony, then intense pain, then, finally, a discomfort she believed she just might be able to live with. Mama changed her dressings, checked for infection, administered painkillers. They spoke for hours every day, trying to keep Valeria's mind from the pain. They became closer than ever.

Mama whispered, "We must figure out what to do, hija." She sat bedside, holding Valeria's hand, looking into her pained eyes. "When you are better, they will come for you. And this," she looked to the bandages on Valeria's chest, "will have been for nothing. We must think." She wiped beads of sweat from her daughter's forehead with a cool cloth. "You are strong. You can survive almost anything from them, but you cannot survive if they choose to kill you."

Valeria nodded. "I know." She squeezed her mother's hand. "I need protection and strength, some power over them. I have an idea. Let me think about it."

Then late one cold and rainy autumn night, there was a knock at the door. It was Isabella. Valeria was shocked to see her. Since the night of Valeria's burning, Bella had avoided her, wanting to distance herself even more from her traitorous cousin. She stood outside; the rain ran down her face, but it was also evident she was crying.

"Eduardo is dead."

Mama gasped. Despite the pain, Valeria wrapped an arm around her mother. She looked over Mama's head at Bella, waiting.

"It was in Trenton. Him and two other Dogs, Lucas and Mateo, went on gang business. Lucas was killed, too. Mateo made it back. Somehow."

"What happened?" Valeria asked quietly. "Why the hell were they in Trenton?"

Still standing in the rain just outside the doorway, as though she didn't want to contaminate herself by entering, Bella said, "Gang stuff, that's all I know. Mateo said almost the second they stepped into Central West, they got jumped. They turned a corner and a bunch were there, waiting."

"But why were they there?" Valeria repeated. "The Dogs have nothing to do with Trenton."

"I don't know," Bella said. "Gang stuff," she repeated.

"So, Seb knew about it?"

"Yeah, I guess. I don't know."

If it was gang related, Valeria thought, then Seb must have sent them. If Seb sent them, he must have had a reason. And it looked like they were ambushed?

The three women stood unmoving, Valeria holding Mama who cried into her shoulder, and Bella in the rain. "I'm so sorry," she said. "He was a loyal gang member."

Valeria glared at her.

Bella looked down. "And he was a good cousin," she murmured." She turned and trudged away in the rain.

"Again, it happened again, hija. Your father, now our Eduardo." Mama cried on Valeria's shoulder. Valeria did her best to comfort her, but the physical contact, hugging, was excruciating.

In addition to her grief, Valeria had a fear. One she almost couldn't bear to contemplate. She knew Eduardo's pleas to Seb that Valeria be spared, had put her brother in a very bad light with the new leader. Had Seb intentionally put her brother in harm's way? Trenton! Why in the world would he send anyone to Trenton? It was almost begging for trouble, putting Dogs on another gang's turf. And the fact it seemed like they had been expected? Dear God, no. Had Seb set up Eduardo because of what transpired around Valeria's burning? Please don't make me responsible for the death of my brother, she silently pleaded.

At the funeral, Seb approached the family. He smiled at Valeria's younger brothers and spoke a few words to them. The two women stood expressionless as he neared them. It was another cold and blustery day. The wind whipped away the priest's words almost as they left his lips. The low, gray clouds seemed to weigh on those in attendance, lending a feeling of being boxed in, trapped.

"Señora Reyes," Seb said, avoiding even looking at Valeria. He and several other Wild Dogs attended, dressed in gang colors. "Eduardo was a good man, a strong warrior. His death will not be in vain. Even if it takes a war, it will be avenged." He hugged Mama, her body stiff. Valeria stared down unmoving. Seb did not touch her, instead he leaned forward and whispered in her ear, "We'll be seeing you, Val. We all will."

That night they sat at the kitchen table, still dressed from the funeral, Mama looking like an old woman. The coffee Valeria had poured for them, growing cold.

"Hija, you must go. I can't bear to lose you, too. Eduardo...," she sighed. "From the day he joined that gang, it was a matter of time. I know you think his death might be connected to your," she nodded toward Valeria's bandaged wound, hidden beneath funeral black, "to what happened to you. Maybe it was." Valeria felt tears spill from her eyes. "It doesn't matter, it would have happened eventually. Your father, his brothers, Eduardo, and I fear for your other brothers, the little ones." She smiled bitterly. "Not so little. You watched them this afternoon?"

Valeria nodded. At the funeral, Christian and Angel looked enthralled at seeing the gang members up close. The hero worship as Seb spoke to them was almost palpable.

"It is a matter of time, that's all. They will soon join that group. I believe this, and I believe they may eventually die because of it. God forgive me, for thinking this, but I feel this will happen. I accept it." Mama reached for her coffee cup, then withdrew her hand.

"A mother should not have favorites among her children. But hija, if your connection to this gang somehow meant your death, I don't think I could continue living. You are the best of us all. Your father, me, your brothers. If surviving means you must leave, you must. There is nothing for you here. You see that. You must escape what awaits you. If not death, then...something you should never have to endure."

The silence hung between them. Finally, Valeria said, "I have an idea. I don't know if it will protect me, but...if it works, it will give me power over them."

Initially, Mama had been disbelieving.

"A police officer?"

"Sí, Mama."

The police were rarely viewed as anything other than adversaries to most of the Puerto Rican community.

"Why?"

"Can't you guess?"

"Ah, a gun. You carry a gun."

"Yes, but more important, I'll have the power of the law working with me, not against me."

Mama nodded. "But will you be accepted there?"

"Let's see if these new laws are for real. If they are, I think I have a chance to get in. Whether I'm actually accepted once I'm there is another story. The thing is Mama, no one can know what I'm doing. Not Christian, Angel, nobody. If I get in, I can't risk word getting to the Dogs and them somehow wrecking my chances before I even begin."

Just under a year later Valeria graduated from the New Jersey Police Academy in Marlton. Many of her fellow graduates felt she had only been accepted into the institution because of her gender and her ethnicity. They made their feelings clear to Valeria. She didn't care. She worked her ass off, excelled in the field training, and graduated in the top ten percent of the class.

Clasping her diploma, Valeria walked off the stage and made eye contact with Mama in the audience. She was the only family member present.

There had been a single moment Valeria feared might derail her plans before they even began. Her scar. She knew it had to be kept secret. If seen, questions would arise, and the truth might emerge.

There was an initial physical exam prior to acceptance in the academy. She sat on the table in the exam room in a sleeveless T-shirt and briefs. A nurse stood in the corner and middle-aged black doctor, with a completely bald head exhibiting several scars, began examining her. He moved from eyes, ears, and mouth before gently tapping her back while moving his stethoscope across her chest. As he slid it over the T-shirt covering her scar tissue he hesitated and looked into Valeria's eyes for the first time since the physical began. He called quietly over his shoulder to the nurse. "This scope is giving me problems, would you get me another from down the hall, please?"

"Yes, doctor."

When the door closed, he slowly rolled up her T-shirt and examined the hard, shriveled mass of purple and red tissue. He pursed his lips, then rolled the shirt back down. He pointed to his own chest and quietly said, "Black Spades."

Valeria had heard of the notorious black gang. "Wild Dogs," she responded. "Am I out? Does this disqualify me?"

"I've never known a woman to do that." He nodded toward her scar.

"Am I out?" she repeated.

He picked up a clipboard and began making notes.

It's over, Valeria thought. What do I do now?

The door opened and the nurse handed the doctor a stethoscope. "Thank you, nurse." He listened to Valeria's heart through her T-shirt and made more notes.

Talking as if to himself, he said, "Heartrate good, 58 beats per minute. Slight scar on left of chest, nothing to worry about...." He mumbled on. At the conclusion of the examination he said, "Looks good, very healthy, no concerns." He handed the nurse his clipboard, nodded to Valeria, and left the room. Valeria never saw the man again. She would have liked to thank him, buy him a drink, something.

Even after clearing this hurdle, it hadn't been easy making it through the academy. There were very few women in her class. Just two others, both white. They palled around with each other and went out of their way to ignore Valeria. She was fine with that. She didn't want anyone to get too close. And she knew there probably wasn't a recruit in her class that didn't believe the only reason she was there was because of affirmative action. Again, she didn't care. Her race was for once some help to her rather than a hinderance. She immersed herself in studies and physically working out. Any off hours were spent in the gym. She was surprised to find she had a knack in the boxing ring. She was obviously a novice lacking technique, she but had great speed and balance. And for her weight, she was strong as hell. Often being the sole female present, she was usually significantly outweighed by her male opponent. But she could put up a good fight, and sometimes get the best of them. She needed to be strong. She refused to submit to the fear that one day she could be jumped by a gang of Dogs. If it ever happened, she would make sure they would regret it afterwards.

After graduating, despite requesting a posting in another part of the state, she was eventually assigned to Newark. Hell. Probably matching a brown face to a primarily brown populace, she thought. She kept her head down, made no waves, did her job. Valeria prayed she could remain anonymous and somehow evade her past. But it was impossible. Newark was a large city, but not that large. It happened just after her first-year anniversary of joining the Newark P.D.

She'd been partnered with a veteran officer who had been on the force for about ten years. Anders Gustafsson had been barely cordial when they first partnered up. Valeria had been assigned to him after six months of less-than-exciting administrative duty. He was outspoken in his views, especially those concerning the "vermin" found in gangs. Valeria kept her mouth shut. Despite his strong opinions, she had to admit he was a good cop. She was learning from a pro, she could see that. After a month or two they had even developed a rapport: Valeria kept her opinions to herself and Gustafsson spouted his. They worked well together.

They were patrolling the city's Central Ward when they received a call to answer a disturbance at Scudder Homes. Possibly gang-related. "Fucking great. Crazytown," said Gustafsson, hitting the lights and siren.

"A 'disturbance'. Wonderful. That could be anything from two old hags fighting over the last loaf of bread in the bodega to mass homicide," Gustafsson went on. "I swear, I don't know why the hell we don't put a giant fence around the whole ward and just let them kill themselves off." Valeria acknowledged the call and felt her stomach tighten.

This would be the first time she had been back in that neighborhood since the night of her burning. Thus far luck had been on her side. Now she was about to be dropped into the chaos she had once aspired to be a part of.

"Hey, maybe you'll see some relatives, Reyes."

Valeria glared at him.

"Just a joke. Jesus, on top of everything else you people have no sense of humor?"

They skidded to a stop in front of a burnt-out bodega just in time to see a big guy sink a blade into the stomach of a much smaller man. When he saw the car, he turned and ran. The surroundings were deserted. Between the guy with the knife and the police siren, the locals had headed for cover.

"I got him," Valeria cried as she sprang from the car. She heard Gustafsson's first few words as he radioed for an ambulance, but then it was just the sound of her feet hitting the pavement and the measured exhalations of her lungs. She saw the suspect round a corner and almost fall as his foot slid on a flattened beer can. She turned the corner just in time to see him leap up a rusty chain link fence and after a second of scrabbling, pull himself over. Valeria followed suit and made it over the top in about half the time he did. She was now near enough to hear his ragged gasps. He looked over his shoulder, stumbled, and she was on him. She forced him face down and dug her knee into his back as she cuffed his hands behind him. She stood, stepped away and took a moment to get her wind back. The suspect lay on the pavement, his head turned away, wheezing. Looking around at the abandoned brick buildings, boarded up windows, and litter-strewn lots, she wondered how the hell she ever could have desired a life here. Unconsciously, she rubbed her scar through her uniform.

"Up," she said, grabbing the assailant by a cuffed arm and pulling him to his feet. She pushed him along in front of her as she herded him toward the car. He shuffled along, head down, still fighting for breath. Reaching the cruiser, she pushed his head down and shoved his bloated body into the backseat.

Gustafsson was crouched by the victim. In the distance a siren wailed, getting louder by the second. Gustafsson slowly stood, hands pushing off his knees.

"They might as well turn the siren off. No hurry now." He walked to the car and rapped hard on a back window. "Hey, Ratshit, congratulations, you're a murderer," he called through the glass. "You hit the big time. An all-expense paid lifetime stay in one of many institutions constructed for human garbage like you."

The guy spat against the glass.

"You okay, Reyes?" She nodded. "You Miranda him yet?" She shook her head. "Mind if I have the pleasure?"

"He's all yours," she said, and walked toward the body. She heard Gustafsson reading from his Miranda card, while adding a few embellishments.

"You have the right to remain silent, asslicker, and you have the right to an attorney, one who doesn't mind having to deal with no-brain shiteaters like you, you have...." The sirens were upon them now. They switched off in mid-wail, leaving a sudden void, causing all other sounds to seemingly amplify. Gustafsson's voice, her shoe scraping the sidewalk, the ambulance door opening. Listening to her own breathing, Valeria crouched and looked at the victim's face.

"Jesucristo."

It was a boy. He couldn't have been much older than fifteen. And he wouldn't get older, lying curled in a ball on the dirty pavement amid shards of broken glass outside a tenement in Crazytown.

As she approached the car, Gustafsson asked if she was okay. She nodded. "Let's get back to the station and process this guy. Just being near him I want to vomit."

"I hear you. Let me check with the med guys, then we'll roll," he said.

She peered into the back seat. The suspect was slouched as low as the cramped backseat would allow, a smirk on his face.

Gustafsson returned. "Okay." They each got in and began their respective paperwork.

Each officer sat in silence, scribbling their notes.

The raspy voice came from the beat seat. "Hi, Val." She stiffened and slowly turned. "Oh, yeah, I thought so. I wasn't a hundred percent sure, but oh yeah. This is what you been up to, huh? Never woulda believed it."

Valeria looked at him. She recognized something familiar, but...oh no. It had been a while, but beneath a few years of unhealthy living, too many beers, cigarettes, and whatever, was the face of one of the Dogs who had held her upright as Doc pushed the burning poker against her flesh.

"You gotta tell me," he looked to Gustafsson, who was staring at the guy, "she shown you her titties yet? They're yummy. You never saw anything so tasty looking. We sure got a good look at them, right Val? All of us." Gustafsson looked at Valeria. "She didn't show you? Maybe because of her boo-boo. Val got a little boo-boo on one of those pretty titties, don't you, Val?"

Valeria's breathing was measured. She looked at Gustafsson. He stared at her, puzzled but angry. "Shut up asshole!" he yelled over his shoulder, eyes still on Valeria.

"I bet I know why she didn't show you! It's how she got the boo-boo. See, pretty Val, here, didn't want to be a Dog no more. So, she had her tat burned off her little titty. Yeah, that's right, you're riding around town with a ex-Wild Dog. How the hell about that, pig?" He began barking with laughter until being overcome by a coughing fit.

"Gustafsson, let—"

"Shut up, Reyes." His face was hard and much whiter than usual. A muscle in his jaw jumped.

They drove back to the station not speaking, just the sound of wild laughter interspersed with bouts of coughing emanating from the back seat.

It didn't take long for the word to spread. In a day she was receiving sideways glances, by the end of the week she was openly shunned. Then came the day she opened her locker and recoiled, almost retching. Someone had dumped a load of feces inside. It was on her clothes, in her shoes, smeared on every surface.

The other officers around her ignored the spectacle, despite the stench emanating from her locker. They pulled on jackets, tossed belongings into their lockers, told each other to have a good one. She may as well have not been there.

There was no way she could continue to perform her duties as a police officer in Newark. She approached Captain Clements and requested a transfer.

"I'm sorry this has happened, Officer. You should have made me aware of your past affiliations. I'd like to believe nothing would have changed as far as your deployment in the department."

Valeria nodded but believed differently.

"I will have to share the reason behind your transfer from this department with anyone interested in taking you on, you know that." She nodded again. "You have been an exemplary officer. I believe the department will be diminished with your absence."

"Thank you, sir," she said, eyes ahead.

Captain Clements sighed and leaned back in his chair. "And on a personal note, Valeria, you will be missed. I am so, so sorry you have been treated this way. I realize this in no way can compensate for what you've been through, but I know of a department looking for an officer. I have known the captain there for years and can assure you he is a good man. If you like, I'll contact him and make him aware of your situation."

"Thank you, Captain. Yes, sir. That would be fine."

TWENTY

C larke dropped the telephone receiver into its cradle. It felt like he was going nowhere, and he was getting there fast. Doc Eichen seemed to be an enigma. One day in the 40s he showed up in town with his wife and son, shortly thereafter opened up a practice, and that was about all. The man belonged to no organizations that he could find, no clubs, nothing. Clarke had contacted Dr. Silverman, a guy he'd come into contact with during the Donez case, and even he'd been almost no help.

"I'd like to assist you, Captain, but I know very little about the man. Obviously, I know *of* him; this is such a small town, but beyond that...almost nothing. I saw him at one or two gatherings of area doctors in the city, but he never joined any of us for drinks afterwards. We doctors love to chat about the profession and catch up with each other, but he was never a part of that. In fact, I got the impression he rather looked down on us. I chalked it up to cultural differences, his being a relatively recent immigrant, but I don't know. His demeanor...it was like he only tolerated me, all of us really, because he had to. Not because he chose to."

Clarke scribbled notes on his legal pad. "I appreciate your time doctor. Is there anything else you can add that might help us?"

"I don't think so." There was a pause. "I realize this sounds very unprofessional, almost gossipy, but I'll say it. I didn't like him. I can't think of any of my colleagues who did. He was a very condescending man and I know of no one who wanted to be near him. I doubt that's reason enough to want him dead, but there you have it."

"Okay. Thank you doctor. You've been a help."

Silverman laughed. "I doubt it, but condescending bastard or not, I hope you catch his killer."

"Me, too. Thanks again."

Clarke peeled the front of his shirt away from his sweaty body. He thought about what Dr. Silverman had said. No one liked the guy and he seemed to look down on people. No one wanted to be near him. So, who was it that *was* near him? Who was it that caught the brunt of the Doctor's scornful attitude?

He flipped a page and found what he was looking for: Elaine Cook. Someone who'd worked for the guy for years, as a nurse or receptionist or something. That must have been fun, he thought. The woman had been with him for over a decade. That's a lot of time to build up resentment. Enough to kill the guy, though?

What about the son, Rolf? Clarke thought about their meeting on the front porch of 214 Catherine Street. He'd referred to his father, the victim, as "the Doctor." Not much familial affection there. He made a note to check into Rolf's background. His job, friends, how often he saw his father, whatever he could find.

One thing for sure, he thought, looking longingly at the fan above his office door, this had already been a hell of a summer and it didn't seem to be getting any better.

TWENTY-ONE

"Are you feeling alright?"

Nikki sat across from Mrs. G in the older woman's kitchen. Before her was a barely touched plate of Mrs. G's chicken casserole, usually a favorite.

"Just not sleeping, same old, same old." Nikki picked up her fork and ate a morsel.

"I'm so sorry. You also seem very distracted, dear. Have you been working too hard? I know I pushed all this house cleaning on you, now I'm beginning to wonder if it was too much. Every day this week, you're gone after breakfast, not that you eat more than a bit of toast with your coffee, and I don't see you again until dinner, sometimes not till evening. I had no idea the Eichen house needed so much work."

"Don't worry Mrs. G. Yeah, it's a big job, but nothing I can't handle. I mean, the goal is to keep me busy, right?"

"I suppose. I know this sounds selfish, and I feel a bit ashamed saying it after all you've done for me lately, but I miss you, Nikki. I miss talking to you over a leisurely breakfast. I miss you checking to see how I'm feeling throughout the day. I miss talking about my soaps with you." She smiled. "You wouldn't believe what that Nurse Jessie has been up to."

Nikki smiled back. "Aw, shucks, Mrs. G, ya really miss me?"

The older woman nodded.

Nikki felt a lump in her throat. "I'm sorry. I should be done with the doc's place by tomorrow, the day after at the latest. There's more to it than I first thought. Slow going, you know? But have no fear, Ms Clean can handle it." Nikki flashed a small, tired smile. "I just haven't been too hungry lately. I think I may have a bug or something." She nodded toward her plate. "I'm sure it'll pick up. Your cooking is great as ever. Kicks the hell out of my boiled hot dogs."

"That's not a high bar, dear." She smiled. "But I hope you're not allergic to anything in those cleaning materials."

"I'm sure I'm not. You know me, I tend to run hot and cold. I think I'm just in a slump right now. I'll be ready to rock and roll by tomorrow. Just watch."

"Mmm, I hope so. I worry about you, you know."

"Didn't you tell that slob, Mrs. Kowala, that I was strong as a moose, or a bear, or some other forest creature?"

"Yes, and I also told *you* many times, you often try to hide behind humor."

"Thanks, but really, I'm okay. Oh, crap."

"What's the matter?"

"I think I forgot to lock up the Eichen place. I better run over and doublecheck. Maybe I'll do a little scrubbing while I'm there. Gotta rack up those hours, you know. After all, I'm naming my own price. Maybe I'll make enough to book us both on a singles' cruise. A couple hot babes on the high seas? Waddaya say?" She slid away from the table. "Sorry about dinner, I'll heat some up later."

"Don't stay long, alright?"

"Gotcha. Where are the car keys?" Nikki crossed to her apartment.

"Most likely exactly where you left them."

"Well zing! You got me there, Mrs. G." She held up the car keys. "They were on my kitchen counter. You must be psychic. Tell you what, when I get back, we can watch some of the Democratic Convention on TV. That'll put me to sleep if nothing else does."

Mrs. G nodded. "Please try not to be late."

"Yes, Mom."

"Nikki, please promise me to be careful."

Nikki gave her a puzzled look, then quickly crossed and kissed her on the cheek. "I love you," she whispered. She turned and left through her apartment, picking up her shoulder bag on the way out. "Bye!"

Nikki stood on the sidewalk and gazed up at the Eichen house. She slowly climbed the steps, then fiddled to find the correct key, inserting it into the door she knew was locked up tight. She walked through the vestibule and living room without taking notice. In the den she tossed the keys on the buffet, looked at the Danzig painting, and opened the buffet doors wide. Nikki closed her eyes and breathed deeply. Dreamily, she backed to the easy chair and pulled her legs up beneath her. She hugged herself, resting the side of her face against the chair's winged back. As she had been doing for hours a day, she sat and gazed at the lovely bottles, the different shapes, sizes, colors, even textures. And the beautiful liquor, the golds, ambers and tans, caramels, some darker than tea, and others clear as mountain water. Smiling, she inhaled the heady, nearly intoxicating aroma and studied the Danzig painting. Nikki felt as though she was there, gliding across the surface of the ice, lost in the shadows of the spires, virtually lighter than air, completely consumed by the exhilarating fragrance around her.

It brought tears to her eyes.

TWENTY-TWO

Captain Clarke had immediately paired up Kevin and Valeria. The leads to follow were, thus far, limited. Sully was tasked with canvassing the area around the doc's office yet again, hitting on anyone they may have missed in the initial questioning, hoping to dredge up something, anything, they could follow up on. Since this would again put him in the vicinity of the Star Light Bakery, he was more than fine with it. Clarke would plow through paperwork related to the doctor's immigrating to this country. Kevin and Valeria were to interview the former nurse that had served a dual role as nurse/receptionist for the doctor.

Officers MacDougall and Reyes stood before the front door of Mrs. Elaine Cook's house. "If it's not a problem with you I'll take the lead here," he said. "I don't ever remember meeting the woman, but I might be a familiar face, while yours won't. Your face. Or...well, you." His acned face was rapidly on its way to scarlet. Jesus, working with this girl would be murder.

Valeria nodded, expressionless. Does she even have emotions, he wondered.

"Don't be angry or anything, it's just that you're new. Not at being a cop, but here...in Pendale."

She nodded again. "I agree. Seems like a sound strategy."

"Okay, good." The relief on his face was almost scary. He removed his hat and ran a hand over his hair."

Valeria saw he was trying to force down a cowlick with little success.

"Okay," he said, and rapped at the door. "Here we go."

We sure do, she thought.

Standing behind MacDougall's thin frame, Valeria mused this was most definitely *not* like being partnered with Anders Gustafsson. She was uncertain whether that was a good or bad thing.

In a moment they heard very measured steps approaching the door. It was yanked open by a barrel-shaped, white-haired woman leaning on a cane with little extra support legs at its base, glaring up at them.

Kevin opened his mouth to introduce themselves but was cut off.

"You're here because of the Doctor, right?"

"That's right," he began, "I'm Officer MacDougall of the Pendale Police Department, this is—"

"I wondered when you'd get to me."

"Oh, well, good. May we come in and—"

"What's this?" the old woman asked, staring at Valeria.

"I'm Officer Reyes, also Pendale Police."

Mrs. Cook continued to stare. "Hmph. I heard. Didn't believe it though."

"May we come in, Mrs. Cook?" MacDougall asked.

"Yeah, sure." She slowly shuffled back, eyes still on Valeria.

They entered directly into the living room. It was a mass of white wicker, watercolors of the shore, plastic flowers, and crocheted cushions.

"You have a lovely home, Mrs. Cook," Valeria said, her face neutral.

Her eyes had not left Valeria. Almost like she could not believe she had a living, breathing Puerto Rican in her home.

After a minute she said, "Thank you," and waved to the small wicker sofa. "Sit."

Kevin removed his cap, again quickly trying to smooth his cowlick, and sat. Valeria moved toward a chair nearby. The confines of the sofa looking a little too close.

"Where are you going?" Mrs. Cook almost yelled. "There!" She pointed again to the sofa. "I need to be able to see the both of you."

Can't have me sneaking off to grab the family silver, Valeria thought.

Kevin slid as far as he could to his right. Valeria eased herself next to him, aware that their legs, hips, arms, and shoulders pressed against each other. Kevin's face, impossibly, turned a brighter red than before.

The woman sat opposite them, cane set firmly between her knees, hands folded over its handle.

"Thank you, Mrs. Cook. We just have a few questions for you about your time working for Doctor Eichen. He reached to his right breast pocket for his notepad and in doing so his left elbow slid against the side of Valeria's right breast. She heard a sharp intake of air from him.

Quickly dropping his arm, keeping his elbow tight against his own ribs, with eyes averted, he fished awkwardly into the breast pocket with his right hand, finally pulling out his notepad. After a couple tries, he shook it open and eventually found the page he wanted.

"Okay. Okay, um, Mrs. Cook, when did you—"

"Officer, if you want to question me you could at least have the courtesy to get my name right."

"Wait," he said, "you're not Elaine Cook?"

"I am."

He glanced from his notes to the woman, then back again. "But Mrs. Cook, I don't under—"

"It's *Miss* Cook. I never married."

Shocker, thought Valeria.

177

"I apologize, *Miss* Cook. I'll make a note of that." Realizing he would need to use both hands, one to hold the pad, the other to jot down the information, he stopped. "Later."

"I'll make note of it, Officer MacDougall," Valeria said. "And notes of the interview with *Miss* Cook." She deftly pulled a notepad from her shirt pocket.

"Thank you, officer." Relief in his voice.

He began, "How long did you work for Doctor Eichen, Miss Cook?"

"Sixteen years. Nineteen fifty to sixty-six."

"Long time. Can you tell us anything about the doctor that maybe we don't know? Any casual infor—"

"No."

"No?"

"No. I went to the office at 7:30. I worked. I went home at five. On Tuesday and Friday, he worked half-days. I didn't. I worked till five, bookkeeping. Then I went home."

"Okay. In your capacity as nurse/receptionist, did people who were not patients ever stop by? People he may have known from outside the office?"

Miss Cook glared at Kevin. She nodded. They waited.

Jesucristo, thought Valeria.

"Can you tell us who these people were?" he asked.

"No."

"No?"

"No."

Again? thought Valeria.

"Mrs. Cook," he said.

"*Miss*."

"*Miss* Cook, I apologize. Can you tell us anything at all about these people?"

She just stared at him. "Miss Cook?"

"Person. It was one person."

"A man?" She nodded. "Did he come often?"

"No."

"Do you remember how many times he visited?"

"No."

"Please, Miss Cook, try. Estimate."

"Maybe six times, maybe seven."

"So, almost every two years."

"No." This time, Kevin waited. "Maybe up to eight times, but no pattern. Sometimes twice the same year. And I think they met other times, someplace else."

"Oh? Why do you think that ma'am?"

"I heard them talking. It sounded that way. I remember them talking about meeting other people, in the city."

"They spoke freely in front of you?"

"No, but I heard."

"And there was nothing out of the ordinary about these conversations? Nothing to make you believe they wished them to be private?"

"Oh, they wished them private, alright."

The two officers waited.

"Why do you say that Miss Cook?"

She stared again at him and said, "Tell me, young man, sprechen sie Deutsch?"

He sat, confused. "What—"

"Ich spreche Deutsch," Valeria said.

Miss Cook's head snapped to Valeria as fast as her geriatric neck would allow. She opened her mouth to speak, but made no sound. Her knuckles gripping the cane turned white.

Kevin looked at Valeria, confused. "What...." He tailed off.

"Are you saying that the doctor and his visitor spoke in German?" Valeria asked. Her pen poised over her notepad.

Miss Cook nodded, eyes fixed on Valeria.

"And I am led to believe from your question to Officer MacDougall that you speak German, as well?"

Another nod. Valeria made a note.

"But the two men did not know you were conversant in German and spoke to each other freely, unaware that you understood them. Is this correct?"

Another nod, accompanied by an almost whispered, "Yes."

"And the entire time you worked for Dr. Eichen, he was unaware you knew German?"

"Yes."

"Sixteen years." Valeria smiled and said, "My hat's off to you, Miss Cook. Few people could keep something quiet for so long."

Miss Cook's chin rose, and a thin smile touched her lips for a second before she pushed it down. "Knowledge is power."

This time it was Valeria who nodded.

"Okay, Miss Cook," Kevin said, trying to rejoin the conversation. Do you know the name of this man?"

Miss Cook slowly dragged her eyes from Valeria. "Yes."

Not waiting for another pause, he asked, "Will you tell us his name, please?"

"Stephen Smith." Valeria made note. "Now."

She looked up. Kevin said, "Pardon, ma'am? Now? What do you mean?"

"I mean," she emphasized the word, "That's what his name is *now*. Apparently, he had a different one. Stefan Schmidt." She shook her head. "The doctor used to make fun of him for changing his name to a new one that amounted to the same thing."

"I want to be sure I understand here," he said. "Doctor Eichen met a man named Stephen Smith, formerly Stefan Schmidt, and while together they spoke in German?"

Miss Cook nodded.

"Are you sure it wasn't Polish? I mean, the doctor and his family emigrated from Poland.. Maybe the two languages are similar?"

Uh-oh, thought Valeria.

"Are you insinuating I am feeble to the point where I can listen to a conversation between two people speaking in one language, and then, in my dementia, transpose it to a completely different language, one that I don't know? Is that what you believe happened, officer? If so—"

"No, ma'am! Absolutely not! I'm just trying to understand—"

"German. The two spoke German. And if you want my opinion, the two *were* German. Polish, hmph. Anyone who spent any time with the man would know that wasn't the case."

Valeria's pen moved quickly over the page. The three didn't speak for a moment. Finally, Kevin said slowly. "Miss Cook, at any time when Doctor Eichen and Mr. Smith were speaking, and you were listening to their conversations without their knowledge, did you ever hear anything that might lead you to believe someone would want to hurt, want to kill, the doctor?"

"Maybe."

I may strangle this woman, Valeria thought. She said deliberately, "Miss Cook, this is a murder investigation. We need to collect all the pertinent information we can. You must tell us all you know. Please stop being difficult."

The woman looked shocked, then gave her a frosty glare.

Miss Cook angled her body an inch or so away from Valeria and toward MacDougall. "I don't know of anyone specific who wanted to kill him. I *do* know the two of them had enemies. They spoke a lot about them. Said they were dummkopfs. And I'll tell you this, they sure didn't think much of us."

"Of us?"

"Yes, young man, *us*. Americans, our country. The country I'd bet they slunk into for safety. They ridiculed the government and they thought all Americans were fat, lazy, dummkopfs. Idiots."

Valeria said, "People like Officer MacDougall, and you, and me, Miss Cook? Regular Americans? That's terrible."

The woman's expression remained frosty. She did not respond to Valeria.

"Okay," Kevin jumped back in. "Do you know who exactly these enemies might have been?"

She shook her head. Then looked at Valeria and said in a monotone, "No. I do not know who these enemies might have been."

Valeria asked, "Do you have an address or telephone number for Mr. Smith?"

"No, I do not have—"

"When was your last contact with Doctor Eichen?" Valeria asked.

She didn't think the woman was going to answer. Finally, she said, "Almost two years ago. When he fired me after I fell and hurt my back. It limited what I was able to do." She nodded to her cane. "He told me I was now 'useless' and 'could no longer provide a service' so he let me go."

"Did he hire someone else after you left?" Kevin asked.

Miss Cook shook her head. "No. When I left, he was only doing about half the work he did in 1950. I guess he thought he didn't need the help anymore."

The two officers looked at each other and rose. "Thanks for speaking with us, Miss Cook," Kevin said as they walked to the door. Before stepping outside Valeria turned to the older woman and smiled.

"We appreciate the public assisting us in our efforts. Information from any citizen may be important, no matter how insignificant it or they may seem to be." She turned to leave, then stopped, looking around the room. "I love your decorating. You have a flair."

Miss Cook glared, looking confused, until the closing door blocked her from view.

As they walked toward the car Kevin said, "I don't think we made any friends here."

"Probably not."

"It's not in our best interests to annoy the public, you know?" he said. Silence. Jeez, is this what it's always going be like with this girl? Pissing off people until they're even more anti-cop? "I guess we eventually got some decent information from her, though."

"I think we did."

Grudgingly, he said, "You speak German, huh? That's amazing."

"Not really. I needed an elective freshman year. Other than what I said today, about the only thing I can say in German is, "Can I have a beer?""

They got in the car. Kevin sat, looking forward, his hands gripping the wheel. He seemed as though steeling himself for something. His face was getting very red again.

"I..." He cleared his throat and began again, "I'm very sorry."

It took a second for Valeria to realize what this was about. She looked out her window to hide her smile.

"It was inadvertent, I think you know that, though it doesn't excuse it. I want you to know it will never, ever—"

"It's fine," Valeria said, face still averted. "We're good."

Relief flooded his face. "I'm so glad, because I—"

She turned to him. "It's fine. It's done."

He exhaled. "Oh, thank God, I—" He caught himself. "Nope, done. Got it."

Valeria nodded. "Let's head to the station, huh?"

TWENTY-THREE

"Bye," she called into Mrs. G's kitchen. "I promise I'll try to make it back for lunch today." She grabbed the large denim shoulder bag, emblazoned with a rainbow peace sign, and slid it over her shoulder. "I'm taking a couple dollars from the cookie jar to put gas in the car."

"Fine, dear, I'll see you later." She watched Nikki cross from her kitchen to the back door. "Yesterday I noticed you took a shoulder bag, too. I don't think I've seen you with one in, I don't know how long."

"Yeah, pretty cool, huh?" She waved it and flashed two fingers. "Peace, Mrs. G."

"Thank you dear, but why start carrying one now?"

Nikki reached in and pulled out a T-shirt, underwear, and a pair of cut-offs. "After a few hours of scrubbing I'm sweating like a pig. There are a couple fans in the house, but they don't do much; maybe the cleaning frenzy I create is overwhelming them. Anyway, it's no fun spending the rest of the day in stinky, sweaty clothes. So, I go prepared."

"Very smart."

"You bet." She pulled her Mets cap over her curls then pointed to her head. "It's not just for hats, you know?" Mrs. Gorman laughed.

The screen door slammed behind her, then Nikki tossed her bag on the passenger seat and slid in. She leaned her forehead against the wheel and took three, slow, measured breaths. After a moment she looked into the mirror, searching for guidance, advice, anything. Nothing looked back but a pair of frightened green eyes.

An hour after arriving at 214 Catherine Street, cigarette between her lips, Nikki clomped up the back stairs off the kitchen, carrying a dust mop, rags, and furniture polish. Squinting against the cigarette smoke she stumbled and fell forward, landing on her stomach and sliding down about half a dozen steps back to the first-floor landing. The mop and cleaning supplies flew everywhere.

Jesus, what a klutz. I haven't done that since I was about five when it was fun. She stood and rubbed her bruised hip bones. Not much in the way of padding. Lately she'd been eating even less than normal, and the effects were becoming apparent. Looking at her sandals, she saw one of the thongs had ripped out of the sole. Great, just a walking disaster, she thought.

After tossing out the cigarette, she gathered up her supplies and carefully made her way back up the stairs. She stood before the locked office door and examined the clump of keys on the ring she held in her hand and sighed. Still gotta get these organized. Miraculously, on just her second try she found the correct key. Whoa. Things are looking up! She then slid it off the ring and pushed it into her hip pocket. This one and the file cabinet key get put on their own ring she told herself. After opening the door and dumping her cleaning equipment, she tossed the clump of keys on the desk.

She sat in the office chair. Her toes dangling, Nikki pushed against the desk and gently spun.

She didn't know how much longer she could hold out. Every day was getting harder; even Mrs. G was sensing the strain. If she hadn't been spending half the day in front of that damn cabinet, she'd already have the house looking like new. Everything felt so muddled. Nikki rubbed her temples and tried to yawn. Wasn't that supposed to clear your head? Or was it your ears? Whatever. She looked around.

The room looked the same as before. There was not a whole lot to do up here. Maybe the blinds could use some dusting, run a mop over the floor, not much else. She slid open a few desk drawers, mildly curious what a dead doctor might have in his desk. Nothing of much interest it turned out. Other than the desk and the small table next to it, there was just a bookcase that looked full of files, medical journals and stuff like that, a file cabinet, an easy chair, reading lamp, and a door to what was probably the closet.

Nikki crossed to it and grabbed the knob. It would not turn.

"Are you fucking kidding me?" she said. "This is locked, too?"

Has he got a stash of dirty magazines he didn't want anyone seeing? The guy lived alone for God's sake, he could leave his smut out on the dining room table and nobody'd know. Once again, she tried key after key until she found the winner. She swung open the door.

A whole lot of nothing. Just an almost-empty closet. The three interior walls were covered in the same pattern wallpaper as the rest of the room. There were a couple pegs in the back wall to hang clothing off, and that was it. She'd never seen such an empty closet. "Pretty damn anti-climactic, doc," she mumbled, closing the door. She pulled the key from the lock to add it to the two others for labelling, then hesitated.

She thought again, she'd never seen such an empty closet. Ever. She reopened the door and looked. Just pegs, an old jacket and a flannel shirt hung off two of them. The others were empty. So, what's the problem here? After a moment it hit her. Well, duh, Nik, there's no bar running horizontally between the side walls for coat hangers. And no shelf above that non-existent bar, either. Weird, really weird.

Nikki leaned into the closet for a closer look and her torn sandal slid from beneath her. She crashed headlong into the rear wall with a muffled "thunk."

"Fuck!" She sat on the closet floor, rubbing her head. A walking disaster is right, she thought. Everything was so hard! Just getting through a normal day took so much effort. And now, she can't even clean a damn house without turning it into the biggest temptation ever. Hell, why bother fighting it? Just go back downstairs, curl up in the chair, gaze into the liquor cabinet and dream. Nikki began to cry. She pulled her knees up, rested her head against them and sobbed.

"It's too hard! It's too hard! It's too hard!" she screamed, slapping her hands against the floor. "I can't do this!"

She made up her mind. "Fuck it. This isn't worth it. A couple swallows isn't going to kill me. No one will ever know."

She moved to stand and, once again, her sandal slid from under her. This time, she caught herself against one of the closet's side walls before she crashed into it. "And I haven't even had a drink yet," she muttered. Nikki clamored upward, bracing herself against the side and the rear walls.

Wait. Just wait. She placed her palms against the right-side wall and pushed as hard as she could. Nothing, real solid. She did the same with the left wall. Same thing, solid. She then pushed against the back wall. She couldn't be certain, but she swore there was a bit of give there. Nikki rapped against it with her knuckles. 'Thunk, thunk.' She rapped again, harder. 'THUNK, THUNK.' She then rapped hard on the left wall. 'THICK, THICK.'

"Ow!" She brought her knuckle to her mouth. "Shit, that's one solid wall." She tried the right side, knocking softer. 'Thick, thick.'

It was solid, as well. She knocked once again on the back wall. Again, 'thunk, thunk.' It didn't sound solid, at all. In fact, it sounded pretty damn hollow. She pushed against it, hoping one side or the other might swing inward. No dice.

Nikki dragged the floor lamp as close to the closet as the electric cord would allow. She pulled off the shade and clicked it on. In the stark light she ran her eyes over every inch of the wall. Nothing. She knocked again. Yeah, hollow, no doubt. It was a false wall. She saw no knob, no handle, nothing to use to pull, or push, the wall open. Just the pegs running horizontally at about eye level. She was stumped.

Nikki stepped away and pulled the desk chair to the closet. She sat, gently swiveling back and forth. She rubbed the rising lump on her head where it had hit the wall and stared into the now brightly lit closet. Ten minutes later she stood. She went to the peg furthest to the right. A flannel shirt hung there. She pulled it off and wiggled the peg. She tried twisting it right and left. Nothing. She replaced the shirt and moved to her left, from peg to peg. She reached the fourth and final peg. She twisted it and felt it turn upward, revealing a small keyhole beneath it.

"Well," she whispered, "how about that?"

After fumbling yet again with her pile of keys, Nikki found one that fit. As she turned it in the lock, the left side of the rear wall sprang back toward her a couple inches. She slid her fingers into the gap it created, and slowly pulled. The wall swung open like a door and Nikki found herself looking at a set of stairs ascending into darkness. She peered up into the gloom, wondering why the hell a respected, small-town doctor needed a secret room.

About three steps up she saw a light switch on the right. She kicked off her sandals, carefully climbed, and flicked the switch. Above her, a dim light shone. Not enough to see what lay ahead, but enough to manage the remaining stairs safely. Nikki moved a step at a time, her hands held ahead of her, palms out, as though ready to fend off...well...whatever.

Reaching the top step she stopped and squinted, unsure of what she was seeing. Another easy chair? Man, this guy loved his comfy chairs. A lamp stood next to it. There were some bookcases. The walls were just shadows, but there seemed to be a lot of stuff hanging on them. She walked to the closest wall and examined what hung there. What the hell?

"No. Oh, no," she whispered. "I'm not seeing this." She felt her way toward the lamp, clicked it on and immediately a cone of light illuminated the chair, one of the bookcases, and the wall in question. She looked again. "Jesus."

Motes of dust floated before her eyes, moving through the light, then into the murk of the room's shadows. Nikki couldn't believe what she was seeing. She backed away and turned to run down the stairs then froze, transfixed by what she saw displayed above them.

"No, no. Oh, fuck, no."

She gasped and rushed down the stairs as quickly as she could, tripping yet again, and falling on the hard office floor. She jumped up and slammed closed the secret door. She turned the key in the lock, then did the same with the closet and office doors. Clutching her sandals to her chest, Nikki forced herself to carefully descend the back stairs to the kitchen. She felt her breathing beginning to hitch and as she crossed into the den she burst into tears.

Wiping her eyes, she hefted her bag over her shoulder, locked the front door, and gingerly made her way down the porch steps before slowly walking to the car. She placed her bag on the backseat, then sat behind the wheel, wondering what the hell to do about what she'd just seen.

Ten minutes later Nikki crept into her kitchen through the back door. She laid her shoulder bag on her bed and tossed a pillow over it. In the bathroom she splashed cold water onto her face, rubbing it hard. Drying her face she noticed her towel was beginning to smell gross. She looked in the mirror, pasted a smile on her face, then rapped lightly on Mrs. G's door before gently pushing it open.

"Are you decent in there?"

From the bedroom she heard her landlady's voice, "Very funny. I was getting worried. Come in here."

She was propped up in bed, her finger between pages of a paperback, marking her spot. Again, *not* Micky Spillane. Maybe Micky's her guilty pleasure, Nikki thought. Christ, I'd kill for such low-level guilt.

"Hey, Mrs. G."

"Nikki, you look exhausted. Come here."

"Are you going to feel my forehead?"

"I just may. Sit here." She patted the bed and examined Nikki's pale face. "I want you to finish with that house. I was wrong to push you into accepting that job. It's taking a toll on you."

"I'm fine. Like I said before, I'm just in a rut or something. I'll get out of it. And the house is almost finished. I'll be getting rid of the keys soon." As quick as I can, she thought.

"Good." The older woman took Nikki's hand, still scanning her face. Nikki tried to rise, but Mrs. G held on firmly. "You know, I lived with Carl for many years while he was drinking, right?" Nikki nodded. "I know when someone is drinking and trying to act as though they weren't."

"Mrs. G—"

"I don't believe you're drinking. But I am concerned. 'Ruts' always preceded relapses with my Carl. He became distant, preoccupied, very much like you're acting."

"You're such a worrywart, but I'm fine." Nikki rose and disengaged her hand. I need to shower then I'm going right to bed."

Halfway back to her apartment she stopped, walked back and kissed Mrs. G on her head. "Thanks. I love you, too."

Twenty minutes later, wrapped in a towel, with another around her head, she crossed to her bed, lifted the pillow, and gently set her shoulder bag on the floor before her dresser. She quietly slid open the bottom drawer and pushed aside her meager assortment of winter apparel. Kneeling, Nikki reached into her bag, withdrew a T-shirt and tossed it on her bed. She then slid out one of the beautiful bottles she'd first seen in the Doctor's buffet.

She held it up to the fading light streaming in through her window and watched the color reflect off the glass and the liquor inside. She gently placed it in the drawer, nestling it in an old sweater. Nikki pulled a second bottle from her bag, and carefully placed it alongside the first, making certain they would not clink against each other. She then pushed aside more clothing from the drawer and looked at the array of beautiful bottles she'd already hidden there. She sat on the floor, her back against the bed, gazing into the drawer, tears streaming freely down her face.

They were so beautiful.

TWENTY-FOUR

C larke hung up the phone, more than a little puzzled. Why the hell would Nikki Greene want to speak with him? It had been almost two months since their last contact. The circumstances of their initial meeting were unique, to say the least. Him saving her from that lunatic and cradling her, half naked, in his arms before even realizing she was female. He had interviewed her briefly at the hospital the day after that awful night in the garage, and then again, a few days later. He had come away impressed.

After the hospital interview he delved into the police records to learn what he could about her, about the "reputation" she had alluded to. He was shocked by what he found.

Clarke read in disbelief. No, this couldn't be the same person he'd held in his arms just hours ago. A half dozen drunk and disorderlies, a couple disturbing the peace, and what was this Kevin had scribbled in a margin? 'Lewd and lascivious?' Jesus.

"Kevin!" he called through his open door.

When Kevin finally appeared, he looked like he hadn't slept. The dark circles under his eyes and pale pallor accentuated the dark purple acne scars on his cheeks. There was none of his usual buoyant enthusiasm, not that Clarke had expected any. Not after what they both witnessed. He entered the office quietly and sat before the desk. Clarke studied him before speaking.

"Would you like to take the day off, Kevin? Maybe try and get some sleep?"

He just shook his head.

"You sure?"

"Yeah." His voice was hoarse. He cleared his throat. "Yes, Captain. I'm sure. I'd rather be here, working. If I'm home, I'll just be focusing on...you know."

"Okay." Clarke felt the same; the last thing he wanted was to be home alone with nothing other than those damn visions from the night before. "Okay," he repeated and grabbed a legal pad from a drawer then asked briskly, "What can you tell me about the young lady at the garage last night? I understand you've had some contact with her in the past. Disturbing the peace and so on?"

He nodded. "Yeah. She's something else, alright."

"Specifics please."

Kevin straightened in his chair. "Yes, Captain. Over the past year and a half, maybe longer, she's been a fixture at many of the bars downtown. She causes a lot of trouble."

"How so? She's a tiny little thing, how much trouble could she cause?"

"It's not what she does exactly, it's the ah, situations she tends to create. Although she's certainly at the center of it all. Boy, is she ever."

This made no sense to Clarke, but Kevin was beginning to sound a bit like his old self, so he nodded for the officer to continue.

"She gets drunk. A lot. Almost every day."

Thinking of the small woman he'd held the previous night and her pale, almost translucent face today, it was difficult for Clarke to envision, but he nodded again.

"She picks up guys. Or they pick up her." Clarke's eyebrows rose. "She latches onto guys who'll pay for her drinks. From what I understand she doesn't have a job, hasn't had one in a while. And in payment for the drinks, she uh, well, has sex with them."

What an awful existence, Clarke thought.

"Okay, but what how did it come about? She couldn't have been at this long, she's too young."

Kevin sighed. "It's kind of a sad story. Not kind of, it *is* a sad story. This woman, Nicole Greene was engaged, sort of, to a guy I knew, Donald Thompson. He was a good guy, really popular in school, a couple years younger than me. Anyway, he was a decent person. He treated everybody well."

Clarke remembered Kevin telling him what a hell high school had been for him. Anyone, younger or not, who treated him well must have made a huge impression. "Go on."

"Like I said, he was a good guy. A big man on campus if there is such a thing in high school. He always dated the prettiest girls, cheerleaders, prom queens, you know. Well, he met this woman, Miss Greene, and it seems he fell head over heels for her. I was out of high school at that point, but I guess a lot of folks were wondering what the heck he was doing with a scrawny thing like her. I mean, if you could have seen some of the girls he had hanging off him in high school.... God knows what he saw in her."

Clarke nodded. Whatever it was, he had seen it, as well.

"I heard they dated awhile; she moved into an apartment on Augusta Street, at the back of the house that woman, Rose Gorman, owns. I think the two were engaged or engaged to be engaged, when Don went off to college at Lafayette. He died in an awful car accident, and she disintegrated, just turned into a drunk willing to do whatever was necessary for a drink. She's really put a lot of strain on some marriages in town. She'd do whatever with whoever, whether they were married, had kids, it didn't matter. Whoring for a drink." He shook his head. "What some women will do."

"Kevin," Clarke said quietly, "she could not have done what she did without the assistance of others. The men in this equation aren't guilt-free, you know. I hardly believe this tiny girl strong-armed anyone into having sex. There must have been consent, probably rather eager consent."

Kevin shifted in his chair. "Well, sure, but you know, women shouldn't act that way. And when they do, what can you expect the guy to do? It's only natural he follows his instincts."

His instincts. At any other moment Clarke would not have restrained his frustration. But knowing what Kevin had just been through, what *he'd* just been through, he let the moment pass. It would, however, need to be addressed in the very near future.

"What about this 'Lewd and lascivious?'"

"She flashed me. Out on the street." Clarke's eyebrows rose. "I was trying to pull her out of the Bottle Cap one afternoon. They had a new bartender who wasn't familiar with her antics. It was about three-thirty in the afternoon and she could barely walk." He shook his head, disgusted. "She started yelling something or other about police brutality and taking liberties with defenseless females. Anyway, we're on the sidewalk and she pulls up her T-shirt, screaming at me. Saying this was what I was really after. It was bizarre. Believe me, she's got nothing to see. I wouldn't even have noted it except for the fact a woman and little kid were walking by, and the woman started giving me an earful about the police being so lenient with drunks.

"About then, one of the bar patrons came out and said he'd see her home. I was hesitant at first, but by then I just wanted her off my hands. If this guy wanted to come to her rescue, maybe he earned what she usually doled out for the price of a couple drinks. The guy walked her to his pickup, almost had to carry her really, tossed her into the passenger side, then drove off. End of story."

"Except it probably wasn't. What probably happened was a young, inebriated woman, in no condition to say no, was driven off and likely sexually violated."

"Violated! Captain, you're only seeing her as the victim in the garage. Believe me, there's a lot more to her than that. And it's not pretty, at all. You have no idea what she'd do for a drink. Or *who* she'd do."

Clarke sighed. "You're right in one regard, Kevin, I only know her from last night. But no matter who she is, she commands the same level of respect from us as any other citizen. Got it?"

Kevin nodded, picking at a thumbnail.

"I really am concerned about you. I know I didn't have the connections you did with the individuals in this case, but I was part of it. I was there with you. Can I help?"

"You know my stepfather died a while ago, right?" Clarke nodded. "It's been a couple years now and I suppose I haven't really addressed his passing."

"How do you mean?"

"He was more than a stepdad. I mean, that's what he was, but more. He, he was my best friend." His face flushed as he said this. "I have other friends, of course, but he was special."

"I remember you telling me once that he taught you to swear in Polish."

"Yeah, he did. There was something, something toward the end of his life he wanted to talk with me about, but he put it off. I think it may have been connected to the past, maybe Poland. I wish he'd shared.

"Paval first saw Mom at a VFW picnic and almost instantly fell in love with her. I remember him telling me all about it when I was younger. Dad had died in Korea a couple years earlier and I guess Mom was beginning to get on with her life." He grinned. "Enough to go to a VFW picnic and enchant a new immigrant who barely knew English, anyway. I remember him saying he fell in love with her beer-foam mustache."

"He sounds like a very special person."

"Yeah, he was. I wonder what bit of wisdom he could give me during this crappy time.

"I wish I could provide some wisdom in his absence." Clarke hesitated for a second. "Whether it helps or not, thanks for the conversation. It felt a little like it used to."

"Yeah, it did. Thank you. I really mean it, Captain. I think I needed it." He left, grinning.

TWENTY-FIVE

Clarke sat in the diner's booth and glanced at the menu. The plastic was stained in one corner, obscuring the price of the tuna melt he'd briefly thought of ordering. Looking out the window to the side parking lot he watched the heat waves rising from the pavement. Yet another scorcher. Thank God the restaurant had AC. He'd arrived about ten minutes ago, declining anything to eat or drink until his dining companion arrived. He half-listened to the radio emanating from the kitchen as he continued perusing the menu knowing he'd probably just order the usual. He closed the menu and slid it away. What did that song just say? Something about a cake left in the rain? He sighed. He'd never understand this new music. Clarke instead thought about the phone call that had both puzzled and intrigued him.

Nikki had sounded close to frantic, asking if they could meet. He asked if he should stop at her place or would she rather come to the station.

"Not here!" she almost shouted, before regaining control. "Mrs. G is still recuperating. She had a heart attack recently. And at the station, uh Jeez...."

Clarke remembered the older woman watching over Nikki at the hospital. The voice on the phone sounded tense, ready to erupt.

199

"Okay, two things. First, I'm sorry about your friend. I know you love each other very much. I hope she makes a speedy recovery." He could hear a gulp, then a mumbled, barely audible, 'Thanks.' "And it doesn't sound like the station holds any appeal to you. How about a neutral site?" He'd suggested the Peterson Diner and she gratefully accepted.

It wasn't long before a pale, green Buick pulled into the parking lot and slid into the vacant spot next to his police cruiser. Usually people avoided parking directly adjacent to a police car. Clarke wasn't sure why. Maybe afraid of denting the door and getting in trouble. Whatever the reason, he usually had a buffer of a space or two between himself and others.

He watched her slide out from behind the wheel, place a hand on her lower back and stretch upward. Clarke wondered if she had sustained a back injury during her altercation earlier in the summer. She wore sunglasses and a battered Mets cap beneath which spilled several inches of curly, ginger hair. Despite the sunglasses, Clarke could see the tension in her face. She reached into a back pocket of her faded jeans and produced a small metal case. Sucrets, Clarke bet. She popped it open, pulled out a half-smoked cigarette and lit up. Even at this distance Clarke could notice her hands were less than steady. She took a heavy drag and leaned back against the driver's door. She immediately jumped away, rubbing her backside. She squinted at the sun and appeared to mumble something. After several puffs she flicked away the cigarette and from her other back pocket produced half a roll of Lifesavers. She thumbed one into her mouth and hurried up the diner steps.

Clarke was immediately struck by how thin she looked. He remembered the night he first saw her, sans most of her clothing: her prominent ribs and collarbone, jutting pelvic joints, and overall near emaciation. He wished he could believe otherwise, but she did not look any different now. In fact, maybe worse. A faded T-shirt hung from her thin shoulders and showed absolutely no sign of breasts beneath it. She really *did* look like the twelve-year-old boy Clarke believed she was when he first saw her, covered in blood and filth on the dirt floor of a garage.

She entered the diner and peered around the room, searching for Clarke. As she approached, he heard her sandals slapping against her heels. One of them appeared to be mended with masking tape.

"Hi, Captain," she said, a bit of an embarrassed smile on her face. "I'm sorry I kept you waiting. One of my many faults is I'm the least punctual person I know. I needed to take a quick shower before heading out here. Believe me, you would not have wanted to share my company if I hadn't."

She slid the glasses off. It looked like she hadn't slept in a while. Her eyes darted around the room, at him, the table, the diners at the counter. He thought of her quick smoke break outside. Maybe she was trying to calm herself. She sure looked on edge. He smiled. "It's not a problem, I have the opposite issue, I'm forever showing up early for everything."

She shook her head. "I can't fathom that." Seated across from him in the booth she continued looking around. "I've never been here. The Peterson Diner? I don't think I even knew it existed until recently. I've been sort of self-involved for a while." She smiled, but it quickly slipped away.

"I thought it might be more relaxing here. Also, the food is good."

"Okay." She nodded, opening the tri-folding menu and completely vanishing behind it. "I want to thank you for agreeing to meet with me so quickly. I'm sure you're a busy person, being a cop and all...I mean policeman. Being a policeman and all. Sorry about that. I know we only spoke briefly once or twice and that night in the garage, well, we were distracted." Her voice emanated from behind the menu. It was almost as though she was hiding, he thought. "Usually, any contact I have with you guys in blue is because I got into some sort of trouble."

"That certainly isn't the case today, Miss Greene. In fact, I feel like I owe you."

The menu lowered several inches and Clarke found himself looking into the most intense green eyes he'd ever seen. "Really? How so? And it's Nikki."

"Really. I think if I had been able to figure out who had been responsible for the killings a little earlier than I did...well, maybe I could have prevented a lot of pain. Prevented what you went through that night."

Her eyes didn't move. "Wow. A cop, ugh, sorry, a policeman, feeling he owed *me*. I never would have thought. But don't go beating up on yourself. I was there of my own accord. No one's to blame but me."

"There's no reason for *you* to beat up on *yourself* either. And don't worry about the "cop" thing. That's often how we refer to ourselves anyway."

He sensed her relaxing and the menu rose again. "What do you recommend here?"

"I usually order the Reuben."

"What's that?" asked the voice from behind the menu.

He told her.

"Nope. Not a corned beef fan. Are the burgers good?"

"Yes, they are."

She closed the menu and laid it on the table. "We'll go that route, with fries and a Coke."

"And coleslaw?" She made a face. "Okay, no slaw."

The waitress arrived, took their orders, and sidled away. They sat in silence, Nikki looking out the window. She seemed to be trying to make up her mind about something. Clarke cleared his throat and was about to speak when he thought he felt the booth swaying.. He must have reacted to it because it immediately stopped.

"Sorry. That was me. When I'm nervous I swing my feet. I wasn't aware I was doing it."

"You what?" He leaned and looked under the table. The girl's sandals dangled a good six inches above the floor. "Oh, I get it. Your feet don't touch," he said, stating the obvious.

"Nope. And I don't anticipate they ever will. I'll try to keep them still, though."

"I apologize if I make you nervous. If anything, I would wish I could make you feel more comfortable." Did that sound weird?

Nikki arched an eyebrow. "Being asked to lunch by a police captain doesn't fall under the category of everyday occurrences." She smiled at the look on his face and almost laughed. "I'm sorry, Captain, I'm just playing you. But man, if you could see your face! I know I'm the one who initiated this get together. I haven't spent a whole lot of time in the Pendale Police Station, but more than enough. Past experiences, you know. Your suggesting we do this away from the station is very kind.

"You may be giving me more credit than I deserve."

"Maybe, but I doubt it. Thanks for the suggestion of lunch. I could probably use a decent meal. Despite the fact Mrs. G is constantly shoving food at me, lately my appetite has been off." She peered out the window. "A lot's been off, way off." A muscle in her jaw began to twitch.

Clarke felt the booth sway again, despite her intentions. He smiled. "Feel free to smoke if it makes you feel better, it won't bother me." He nudged the tin ashtray away from the napkin dispenser and toward her.

"Thanks," said Nikki, relief in her voice. She reached into her T-shirt's breast pocket for a battered-looking pack of Lucky Strikes. She must have seen a look on Clarke's face. "Yeah, I know, not the typical young lady's brand, but since that night we, uh met, I've kind of thrown caution to the winds and upped the ante on indulging in certain addictions that seem to steady me, another one being sugar. If that waitress doesn't show up soon with my Coke, I'll start chewing the veneer off this table."

Almost in response, the waitress appeared with her soda and two glasses of ice water. Nikki quickly downed about half her drink before the woman had gotten two steps away.

"Miss?" Clarke called her back. "She would like another Coke," he nodded to Nikki, "and this time, less ice please. I'll have some coffee, as well."

"Thanks, Captain. Man, I hate it when they load up a glass with ice and then pour a little trickle of soda over it. What a fu—a damn rip-off. Trying to screw over the customer."

Clarke smiled and nodded.

Nikki peeled the straw from its paper cocoon, jammed it into her glass of Coke-flavored ice cubes, and knowing a second drink was on its way, sucked it dry. She then lit up a Lucky, turned her head, and exhaled out the side of her mouth, away from Clarke. "So...?" she said.

Clarke felt the booth sway. "I suggested the lunch, but you suggested the meeting. So?"

"Yeah, I did." The motion of the swaying seemed to accelerate. Nikki again peered out the window. Her profile was almost lost in a shroud of smoke. "How's the Doctor Eichen murder case going?"

This certainly wasn't what he'd expected. He didn't know what he *had* expected, but not this. "Since you ask, rather slowly. There's not a lot of information available on him. The doctor appears to have been a very private man."

"I bet."

Clarke raised his eyebrows and waited.

Nikki seemed to brace herself and then began speaking. "I have this job cleaning houses." She paused and sucked on the cigarette. "Mrs. G set it up for me. Just some neighbor people who can afford to have someone else clean up after them, not much, believe me." She exhaled a stream of smoke at the window. "It's pretty much scraping off grease, cleaning ovens, and scrubbing toilets. Just the job for these delicate hands." She wiggled her red, chapped fingers with chewed nails. "And this is what they look like with me wearing gloves. Those long rubber ones that go up to your elbow. They say you're supposed to be able pick up a dime while wearing them, because they're so thin, but that's a load of bull. I tried: no dime, quarter, nickel, nothing. When I'm gloved up all loose change in the world is safe. Another example of lying to the customer."

Clarke nodded, waiting her out.

"You wouldn't believe the slobs some people are. They may look neat and clean when you see them face to face but get in their bathrooms, gross." Nikki reached for her cigarettes, realized she already had one going, stopped and began drumming her fingers instead. "There was this one lady's place, grease in places you wouldn't believe."

He nodded again.

The waitress approached with her second Coke and his coffee. "Your meals will be right out," she said.

Nikki tore open her second straw and sucked greedily. "Thank God," he heard her murmur under her breath.

She drained half her glass. "So, yeah, if you want the old Pendale Police Station spruced up, I'm your girl."

Was that what this meeting was about? Looking for a job? "We already have a service the town pays for, thanks, but—"

"Wait. No, Captain. I know it sounded like I was trolling for work. I'm not. Truthfully, I have more than I can handle at the moment. Listening to myself babble I know I'm not making sense. What I'm trying to say is, when I'm in a person's house, I see what most other people, those on the outside, never see."

"I would imagine so. Sort of like peering behind the curtain in the Wizard of Oz and seeing what the wizard's really like."

"Exactly."

Their meals arrived and they prepared to dig in. Nikki pounded the bottom of the ketchup bottle trying to dislodge the remnants and add to a puddle she'd already poured onto her burger. Clark turned, reached back to the vacant booth behind, and grabbed the nearly full bottle from the table. She took it gratefully and proceeded to douse her fries. She then enthusiastically began wolfing down her meal. Clarke had gone with the usual Reuben and coleslaw. He watched her eat, marveling. The food seemed to vanish inside her tiny body. He was not yet halfway through his sandwich as she mopped up the last of her ketchup with her final fry. She leaned back, then noticed Clarke's progress.

"Oh, hell. I really bolted that down, didn't I?"

"There's nothing to worry about. I'm a slow eater. Slow, but very steady, too steady." He patted his stomach. "If you see the waitress cruise by, why don't you order some dessert. The cherry pie is great."

"Cherry pie. Yeah, sounds good." She reached for another cigarette in the interval. "I haven't eaten like that in, well, I can't remember. You sure are great for a girl's appetite."

"Good. You probably needed it then."

"Ha! Yeah, this frame of mine could use some padding."

"So, Nikki," Clarke said, setting down his coffee cup and looking her in the eye, "why did you want to see me?"

"Okay, yeah." She ran a hand through her hair and pursed her lips. "I've gone over this about fifty times in my head, and now I'm stuck. I don't know how to start. I can't just jump into it...it's too damn far out. It's almost unbelievable. But I swear, it's true. You'll see."

"Start small. Try to slowly lead up to it. Before you know it, you'll be there."

"Got it."

The waitress took their plates. Nikki asked for some pie, Clarke, a refill on the coffee. The booth swayed madly.

"Mr. Eichen asked me to clean the house."

"Which Eichen, the doctor before he died, or the son?"

"The son."

"Okay, continue." Clarke reached into his breast pocket and pulled out his notebook and a pen. Nikki watched and hesitated.

"Um, it was a few days after the death, I guess. It was certainly after you guys had been through the house. You sure dusted the hell out of that poor kitchen. Anyway, I'm not sure how, but he, young Eichen, heard about me cleaning houses and called Mrs. G to ask about my services. I'm a girl in demand, you know." She attempted a smile.

"Do you know the exact date?" Clarke's head was down, making notes.

"I think it was the day after you finished with the place. I'm not sure what date that was."

Clarke nodded. He looked up, expectantly.

"Oh, um, he took me on a little tour of the place, basement, first floor, and second floor. Not the attic."

"You won't have much to do there. We looked through the trap door in the hall ceiling, it was completely empty. It seems the doc used the basement for all his storage. I recall it was quite packed."

"Yeah," Nikki reached for another cigarette, her hand trembling a bit. "It was a real rat's nest, all right. The son didn't want me to do any work down there. He said he was just going to have it all brought to the dump."

He nodded. Waiting.

"It's been about a week or so and I've been going over there every day." Clarke saw her jaw twitch again and noticed a tremble in her hand. "It's been slow going. It's a big place, and there are certain distractions." She took a mighty inhale and knocked her ash in the direction of the ashtray. "Sometimes," she again was addressing the window, "sometimes, a couple hours go by, and I don't even realize it. It's scary."

"What is it that distracts you?"

She closed her eyes.

"Well, there are records. These old 78s with the craziest music ever. And a creepy painting of a place called Danzig and some other stuff."

After a moment's silence Clarke said, "I'm guessing there's more you want to tell me?"

"Yeah." She turned to face him, unsure of how to continue.

The waitress saved the day. "Here is your coffee, sir, and some pie for your daughter." She smiled and set both down before them.

"I'm not his daughter."

"Niece?"

Nikki shook her head.

"Ah." The woman turned away.

As she retreated, Nikki burst into giggles.

Clarke stared at the waitress's back as she departed. "Another of life's busybodies."

After a moment Nikki was able to catch her breath. "I'm sorry, Captain, but that was just too good." She picked up her fork and began eating her pie. She nodded her head and after swallowing said, "And you're right about this pie, it's amazing." Looking toward the waitress and then at Clarke, Nikki said, "I'm about to join the ranks of the busybodies."

"Oh?"

"I have some dirt on the doc I don't believe you have." She was about to go on but hesitated. "First though, you have to wait until I finish this pie."

Clarke laughed. "I understand."

Nikki quietly proceeded to clean her plate.

"Okay," Nikki said. She pushed her plate away and looked him directly in the eye.

"Okay?"

"You know how you just told me to sort of creep up on what I have to say? That's not going to work. I could creep for hours and never get to the point. You'll just have to see it for yourself. Follow me over there after lunch."

Clarke looked at his watch. "I'd love to Nikki, but I have a meet—"

"Cancel it. Postpone it. Whatever. You really need to see this right away. I probably should have just asked you to meet me there." She smiled. "But then I wouldn't have tasted this amazing pie."

"It's that important I be there with you?"

Her smile slowly faded as she nodded.

Their waitress was working the register when they approached to pay. As they stood before her, Clarke collecting his change, Nikki couldn't resist sliding her arm through his and looking up at him with adoring eyes.

"Thanks for lunch, babe," she said. They exited under the baleful eye of their waitress.

Nikki held it together for as long as she could, then erupted as the heavy glass diner doors shut behind them. She bent forward, her arms crossed over her stomach, her entire body quaking.

"Oh my God, oh my God, oh my God, I'm going to wet my pants," she laughed. She collapsed against her car then yelped and sprang away. This brought on another round of laughter.

Clarke stood at the cruiser, watching her, bemused.

"I am so sorry, Captain. I know I shouldn't have done that without your knowledge, but..." she gulped a lungful of air, "it was just so damn funny." Another bout of cackling erupted.

Clarke began to laugh.

"The look on her face," Nikki wiped a tear away, "the look on *your* face. Oh, I can't remember the last time I laughed so much." She truly couldn't, one thing for sure, it was certainly before Donald had died. "Oh man, I've got to pull it together here." She slid her sunglasses on in an attempt at regaining composure. Clarke squinted at the sky and reached for his own glasses in his breast pocket.

"So, we're off to the Eichen house?" Nikki nodded at him.

"Want a ride or should we meet there?" Clarke asked.

Nikki eyed the cruiser. "Why don't we just meet up, huh? More convenient for when we're leaving. And, well...your wheels really aren't my style. Plus, I have a feeling you may be wanting to stay there a lot longer than me."

"You really think so?"

She grew serious and peered into the back of her car at her peace shoulder bag nestled on the seat. "I really do."

"Whatever you say. See you there."

She nodded, jumped in her Buick, and, with a squeal of tires, exited the parking lot.

TWENTY-SIX

They entered through the frosted glass doors of the vestibule and Nikki asked Clarke to wait a minute. "I really did almost pee myself at the diner. Let me use the bathroom quick." She ran toward the kitchen.

Clarke walked through the living room and den. His initial reaction of a week ago was confirmed. Pretty outdated, but nice. He stopped and looked at the picture of the young woman again. On the wall above it hung a dark painting. He leaned forward and squinted; he could make out the word "Danzig." This must be the spooky painting Nikki had referred to. He squinted again, it certainly was unique, he thought. As well as damn depressing.

He heard a flush and a moment later Nikki entered from the direction of the kitchen. She grabbed his arm and dragged him away from where he stood in front of the buffet. "You should see what a nice job I did cleaning the kitchen. Your people left it a wreck. Come on."

"Okay, okay," he laughed. The kitchen certainly did look spic and span. He looked around and nodded. "Truly lovely."

She beamed. What was it about this young woman that made Clarke want to make her happy? He knew he was dancing around in a minefield. She was less than half his age, and what he knew of her,

211

they certainly didn't seem to have much in common...other than the fact they both have spent time in a police station.

"There's something you want me to see?"

The smile faltered. She nodded. "Upstairs."

They stopped in front of the first door at the top of the rear stairs. "This was initially locked. The only room that was." She pulled a short piece of pink string from her hip pocket. On it hung four keys. One standard sized door key, one small key that looked like it went with a file cabinet, and two that were sort of between them in size. She slid the standard key in the lock and opened the door. She tentatively stepped into the room, feeling Clarke close behind. She walked to the center and turned.

"An office." She gestured self-consciously with her hands. "The file cabinet is locked, but I have the key for it." She held up the pink string. "I haven't opened it up, but I fitted the key in and sprang the lock. It's the right key alright. I didn't feel up to looking through the files and stuff."

"Didn't want to be nosy?"

"No. After what I found, I didn't want to know what might be in there, what the Doctor felt needed to be locked up."

"Okay." Clarke had no idea what she meant by that. He scanned the room; it looked very much like a typical home office might look. There was a pretty comfortable-looking easy chair with a reading lamp on one wall, its shade removed and sitting on the floor. In addition to the desk and chair was a file cabinet and a side table on which sat a typewriter. Nothing appeared extraordinary. He looked at Nikki expectantly.

"The closet. You'll need these." She handed him the string with the keys. "It's the one I marked with tape."

Clarke slid the medium-sized key with a bit of masking tape on its head into the lock and opened the closet door. It was nothing special, just a couple pieces of clothing hanging off hooks on the back wall. That was it. "A lot neater than any closet in my house," he said.

"What's missing?"

Clarke looked again. "Well, I don't know what he would normally keep in here, so I don't know if—hey! There's no bar to hang hangers on. And no shelf, either." He stepped in and ran his hands over the smooth walls. "What an odd closet. I've never seen one like this."

"Me neither." Nikki approached and stood just behind Clarke in the entrance. "It seemed weird to me, too. I poked around just like you're doing now. I was about to close it up when I slipped and fell into the back wall." He looked at her, surprised. "Yeah, on top of all my other issues, I'm a klutz."

"Ah, are you alright?" Clarke said.

"Just a little bump on the head. You can't even see it under my hair." Silence.

"Good, good." He paused, "I have the feeling there's more to this story, but I'll be damned if I know what."

She sighed. "Knock on the side walls." He did. Now knock on the back wall." It sounded distinctly hollow when compared to the others.

"What the hell," Clarke murmured, running his hands over it.

"I'll save you some time. Turn the clothes hook on the far left." Clarke did and beneath it saw the keyhole. Nikki removed the pink string and keys from the closet door lock and handed them to Clarke. "The last one."

He looked at her, then at the string and keys. He slid the final key into the keyhole on the back wall and turned. There was a click, and the left side of the wall sprang out.

Nikki stepped back to give Clarke more room. He slid his hand into the gap. The back wall swung open with a long, low creaking sound. He pulled it completely open and looked in. A set of worn stairs led up to a dimly lit...what? A part of the attic Clarke had not known existed. Clarke turned and looked at Nikki.

She took a step backward and slowly shook her head. "The light switch is on the right about three steps up. I left it on when...," Nikki said. "I'll wait here."

Nikki quickly crossed to the desk chair and sat, her hands tightly gripping the arm rests.

She heard his steps and the sounds of the stairs creaking. They ceased for a moment and then she heard Clarke's muffled voice.

"Oh, my God."

Nikki sat listening to Clarke's footsteps above. After several minutes she realized she had been gripping the arms of the chair with all her strength. She let go and gently shook her hands, the palms were wet with sweat. Nikki wiped them on her jeans and began chewing her nails. The sounds of Clarke's steps would stop for a moment and Nikki would think she heard him say something, but exactly what, she had no idea. Then the steps would continue. After about twenty minutes she heard Clarke ponderously descending the steps. When he stepped out of the closet and into the office, his face was pale. He wiped the sweat off his face with the shoulder of his shirt.

"How long have you known about this, Nikki?" His voice was quiet, almost ominous.

"Since yesterday. I didn't know what to do at first. I wanted to ask Mrs. G, but I couldn't." She looked at Clarke, tears coming to her eyes. "She just had a heart attack; I didn't want to get her upset. I was afraid this might be too much. I know it's selfish of me, but I love her too much. No, that's not even the truth, I love her, yeah, but I *need* her. See, I don't know if I could stay alive if anything happened to her." She wiped away a tear that had slid down her cheek. "I know you don't get it, but it's the truth. So, I didn't tell her. I laid awake most of last night. I realized you needed to be told about it, so this morning I called. I just thought we'd talk at the station, I'd tell you what's up there, and you'd take over. Really. But you suggested lunch so I could avoid the station. It was so nice of you, and I didn't tell you right away at the diner because I didn't want to think about it because it scares the crap out of me, and then the great cherry pie, and playing that joke on the waitress...." She sniffed, pulled up the bottom of her T-shirt and wiped her nose. "I'm sorry," she said in a small voice. Damn emotions, she thought.

He looked at her in silence, then said, "Don't be. It was just a few hours. It couldn't make any difference. This," he nodded to the stairs, "this isn't going to vanish into thin air because you had a piece of pie. I'm sorry I sounded so grim. It's just so shocking, so—"

"Completely unbelievable."

"Oh, it's believable. Having lived through it once, I can assure you of its believability. But here, in Pendale...." Yet as he spoke the words he realized, of course, why not Pendale? Why the hell not?

"I need to call into the station. It will take a few minutes. Do you want to wait here until I get back?"

"I'd rather not. Can I go downstairs?"

"Of course."

She nodded, walked past him and down the stairs to the kitchen. He did not follow immediately. When he finally joined her, he said, "I wanted to lock up that closet." He held the pink string and keys in his hand. "Are there any other sets of keys to that room or the closet?"

She shook her head. "Not that I know of."

"Okay." Clarke slowly looked around, deep in thought. He then sighed and gave her a small smile. "This kitchen truly does look terrific. You did a great job."

"You really are so damn nice. While you call the station or whoever, I'll wait here in my pristine kitchen like a good little hausfrau."

He turned to head to his car. "Wouldn't it be more comfortable waiting in the other room? I was looking at that painting in there, and it *is* a bit spooky. I can see why it made an impression on you. But that chair looks comfortable."

"Uh, yeah, it is. I sit in there sometimes."

"Be right back."

Clarke headed to the car and Nikki walked to the den and stood before the buffet. With Captain Clarke here she felt better. Safer. Stronger. She bent and slowly opened the cabinet doors. She inhaled the aroma and gazed at the handful of beautiful bottles.

Clarke reentered the house to find Nikki sitting back in the easy chair facing the closed doors of the buffet, her legs crossed at the knee.

She asked, "What's the right phrase for something like this? Setting the wheels in motion?"

"I suppose so. This will make more of a splash than our little department can handle, though. There will be quite a few wheels put in motion."

Nikki sat up straight, looking concerned. "Okay, but this is your case, isn't it? You're the top cop in Pendale, and this is all about a murdered guy in Pendale. So, it's your jurisdiction, right? No other cops are going to swoop in and take over. You'll be the guy in charge?"

Clarke smiled. "It's not about me or the department getting credit for bringing this thing to light, if that's what concerns you. It's a hell of a thing to want credit for." Nikki nodded. "But we'll be in the mix for sure. We'll certainly make headlines, and not just those in the local Pendale Citizen. We'll be national news," he sighed, "again."

Nikki looked at him, almost sympathetically.

"First, we're news because of a crazed killer carving up young women," Clarke said, "now we hit the big time because we have a murdered doctor, a prominent town citizen, who appears to have been a Nazi. And a rather important Nazi, at that."

TWENTY-SEVEN

F rom her chair Nikki watched the parade of police enter and
leave the house. Some local, others, she guessed, from different
jurisdictions and agencies. She saw that skinny one with the bad
complexion, the one she had dealt with on numerous occasions
downtown. He caught sight of her in the easy chair, hesitated, then
proceeded up the front stairs to join the others.

A big, doofy-looking officer showed up a bit later. He looked
familiar, but that's about as far as it went. Even at a distance
Nikki could see powdered sugar on the front of his uniform shirt.
Following him was an officer she was certain she had never seen.
A young woman. She was tall, dark-skinned, with thick black hair
pinned up beneath her cap, really beautiful, Nikki thought. Damn,
if I could have a tenth of what that chick's got going for her, I'd die
a happy woman.

After about an hour, Clarke descended the stairs and told her
there was really no need to stay. "I will be needing to speak with you
more about this, but I know where to find you. You can head home
or to another cleaning job if you want."

"I'm kind of enjoying my afternoon away from work. Is it a
problem if I stay? I promise not to leave this chair unless I have to use
the bathroom or step out for a smoke break." She smiled. "And even

if I want to smoke, I can stay right here. The son, Rolf, said I could smoke to my heart's content in the house. The old doctor wouldn't have liked it, but really, who cares what a fu—uh, damn Nazi likes or doesn't like."

Clarke laughed and said, "Okay, stay. Be warned though, since you're available on the premises, you may get questioned at some point."

Oh boy, Nikki thought, extra face-to-face cop time. "I'll be fine," she said. The truth was this was the first time since she had discovered the contents of the buffet that she felt any measure of control. Knowing she was not alone and not having to fight it one on one, afforded her a feeling of ease. A slight one, anyway.

Clarke turned to leave, then said, "Rolf told you it was okay to smoke in the house, despite the fact the Doctor probably would not have liked it?"

"My impression is there was no "probably" about it. According to his son, the old bastard hated cigarette smoke. Though who knows, Rolf said he hadn't been back here in years; maybe the doc had lightened up a little."

"Hmm. Maybe." He nodded and headed back upstairs.

Nikki fired up, inhaled deeply, and sent a long plume of smoke towards the painting of Danzig. Take that you fucking Nazi.

"We'll need to set up a command center with access to a phone line," Clarke spoke to a counterpart in the State Police, both men peered up the steps in the closet.

MacDougall called from the hallway. "The master bedroom has a phone, Captain. And it looks like a king-sized bed so there will be a lot of surface area to work with."

A king-sized bed? Damn, Clarke thought. That dead Nazi had certainly lived well.

"Sounds good, Officer. Get on the radio and have them send any additional equipment we'll need ASAP, lighting, technicians, whatever." He called up the stairs, into the attic. "How many people have we got up there?"

"Hang on," came a muffled voice. In a moment a heavy tread was heard coming down. Sully, head ducked, stepped into the room. There were sweat stains on his shirt front and under his arms. Clarke had never seen the usually unflappable officer looking so serious.

"Are you alright, Officer?"

"Yes sir." Sully nodded, his face pale. "It's just, you learn about this, you hear about it from relatives and those who served, but this makes it real. Really real." Clarke nodded. Sully hesitated, then continued, "My dad liberated Dauchau. He told us about it, but not details, you know? I don't think he wanted to dwell on them. But this, here in Pendale, a guy, a doctor for God's sake, who's been here for years, decades, living right under our noses." Clarke simply nodded again. "I think I need to go outside for minute, if that's okay, Captain."

"Certainly. I believe Officer Reyes is looking through some of the files that were locked up. She's in another of the bedrooms up here. Find her and send her in. She needs to see this, as well."

"Roger, got it."

"Who else is up there now?" Clarke nodded to the closet.

"Just Pete Page, a photographer from Sayreville P.D. He's taking a bunch of photos. He's really good. Last summer he took some of me and my dog down on the beach. Got a great one of Spewer catching a frisbee in his mouth."

"Spewer?"

"Ugh. Digestive issues. Both ends. It's rough."

"Fine. Get Reyes, please."

Clarke peered up the stairs. There was a bright flash of light, followed in a few seconds by another, then another and another. "Officer Page," he called.

"Yeah?" a voice called down.

Yeah? "It's Captain Clarke."

"Sorry, Captain."

"I'd like to send up another officer to look around. It won't crowd you, will it?"

"Not at all. Even having Sully up here it was fine. There's probably space for three, four people."

Valeria entered the office. "Yes, Captain?"

"I'd like you to go up and take a look, Officer. I'm not expecting any in-depth analysis, but the more sets of eyes, the more we may see."

She nodded, pulled out her notebook and slowly ascended the stairs. Before reaching the top step, Valeria could see two high-intensity portable lights had been set up. Stepping from the dimness of the stairs to the well-lit attic room was like stepping into a bright summer day. She reached the top and stopped.

"Dios, mío."

She stood at the entry of what appeared to be a shrine to the Third Reich. The walls were covered with pictures, many of soldiers. Photos of both large groups and individuals. In some, the subjects looked menacing and severe in their high-necked dress uniforms, in others, they were grinning and seemed to be very much enjoying themselves, almost like boys at play. What looked like dinner plates were also mounted on a wall. One exhibited a raised profile of Hitler, others a swastika, some, an iron eagle. There was a large poster advertising a Pro-American Rally in Madison Square Garden from 1939. It was sponsored by the German American Bund, whatever that was, and some guy named Kuhn was scheduled to speak there. There were swastikas printed in each of the poster's corners.

A Nazi rally? In New York?

Bookshelves lined two of the walls. Valeria approached one and turned her head to the side to read the spines. Karl Marx, Hans Grimm, Agnes Miegel, Gottfried Benn, Valeria had never heard of most of them. There's no way she would have been able to read them anyway; judging by what she saw on the spines, they appeared to be written in German. Hands on her belt, she leaned in for a closer look.

"Hey! No touching!"

She looked over her shoulder.

The guy pulled his face away from his camera and looked at her, scowling. "Hands off! It's a crime scene."

Valeria didn't respond. She peered closer at the photos. There were several of a dark haired, handsome-looking young man. In the photos where he was shown smiling, Valeria noticed a gap between his front teeth. Several depicted this man and another. Some shots were posed, others caught them in action. These appeared to be taken in a hospital, some in what appeared to be a laboratory. The other man looked familiar. He too was young, his hair looked to be light and was combed straight back. He wore wire rimmed glasses. In several photos, he seemed to be looking at the gap-toothed man almost in admiration.

After a moment, it hit her. The young man in the glasses was a young Doctor Eichen. Valeria had seen the morgue shots of his corpse. It had been difficult to pull her eyes away from his damaged eye socket, but she was pretty sure about it. She leaned closer.

"Don't touch! Are you deaf?"

"Do you know who this dark-haired man is? The guy with the gap?" She pointed, finger well above the glass frame.

"Of course, I do." Officer Page returned to snapping photos.

Valeria took a deep breath and exhaled slowly. "Would you please tell me who he is?"

221

"I'm busy."

Valeria stepped in front of his lens. "Who is he, please?"

"Hey, I'm trying to work here!"

She didn't move. "Who is he, please?" she repeated.

"Mengele. Dr. Joseph Mengele. He experimented on prisoners in the camps. After Hitler, probably the most infamous Nazi in the world. Jesus, what do they teach you people in school?"

Another doctor. A famous one.

"Now can I get back to work? Some of us actually have to work at our jobs, you know? They're not just dropped in our laps."

She brushed by him and continued looking. When Valeria turned, she saw, hanging above the stairs and in direct view of the upholstered chair, a large Nazi flag. Deep red, with a black swastika on a white circular plate in the center.

The good doctor's reading room, she thought. Come on up, settle into an easy chair, peruse a little propaganda from the old days amid the photos evoking memories of a long time past, and bask in it all while gazing at the symbol of what would have been the Reich's thousand-year existence. Valeria felt sick to her stomach.

"Thanks for your help," she said to Page and descended the stairs to the office.

"This is tough to take, Captain." She emerged from the closet as Clarke reentered the room.

"It certainly is."

"Who's the officer taking pictures up there?"

"Officer Page from Sayreville. You didn't introduce yourselves?"

"No, but I think we had a unique give and take thing going on."

"Good! I'm glad to hear it. We'll be needing a lot of cross-department cooperation in this case."

Oh, good, she thought. "Is Officer Sullivan alright? He looked upset when he told me you wanted me."

"He has family, his father, who played a significant role in the war. I think this was a bit of a jolt to him. A realization, or at the very least, a reminder of what his father went through."

Valeria nodded. She was hit with a realization herself. That Sully may not just be the clumsy, oaf she'd assumed he was. There was obviously more there than she'd first thought.

"I need to speak to Miss Greene. Please stay here until either Officer MacDougall or I come back."

She nodded. "I think he's just a couple doors down putting together the command center. Who is Miss Greene?"

"You may have seen her when you first arrived. She was sitting downstairs. She first discovered this." He waved a hand at the stairs. "She was hired as a cleaner and stumbled upon it by accident. As you might guess, I'm less than pleased we didn't uncover this when we searched the house initially. But that was before your arrival. There's certainly no blame on you."

"There is absolutely no way I ever would have discovered this, sir. It's just too well-hidden. I hope no blame falls on Officers MacDougall and Sullivan. Or yourself, for that matter." She nodded at the closet door. "It's ingenious."

"Thank you, but ingenious or not, it's our job to find things like this. I'll be downstairs with Miss Greene."

Footsteps were heard coming down from the attic. "Ah, here comes Officer Parks. Maybe the two of you can discuss what you saw up there. A little give and take, right?"

Valeria nodded and smiled.

"Nikki, let's head into your pristine kitchen. I need some details on exactly how you discovered that attic entrance and I'd like to take notes. Sitting at the table will help."

"Mind if I smoke?"

"How could I say no?"

She grinned.

"Is there anything in the refrigerator to drink? I'm dry as a bone," said Clarke.

"You mean like a beer?"

"More like a soda, or maybe lemonade, something along those lines."

She shook her head. "Sorry. I'll get us some water. She ran the faucet, waiting for it to get colder, then reached to the freezer door and pulled it open. "No ice cube trays. I guess we drink it at faucet temperature." She set two glasses on the table.

Hence the need for the icepick, he thought. "That's fine." He reached for his glass and took a long swallow. "Thank you."

Nikki reached into a cabinet for a saucer. She placed it on the table, sat across from him, lit up, and waited.

Clarke organized his thoughts and began. "You discovered the entrance to the room yesterday,"

"Yes. I wanted to clean the office the previous evening, but, uh, ran out of time. So, yesterday afternoon, I finally got to it."

"Sounds like this place has kept you busy. You work evenings, too? Do you ever take a break?"

"Well, I wasn't sure if I'd locked the front door when I left. That's why I came back that evening. And I thought while I was here, I might as well put in more cleaning time."

"Very ambitious of you." Clarke smiled.

She shrugged, knocked an ash onto the saucer, and examined her chewed nails.

"Why were you in the office upstairs? Unless you've already cleaned in there, it looked to be in pretty good shape."

"I was just being nosy, like I said earlier today. That bedroom door, the office door, was the only one in the house that was locked. I was curious why. I went through the bunch of keys Rolf Eichen gave me and finally found the right one. I remember being disappointed when I just saw a regular-looking office, nothing exciting at all." She shook her head. "I sure read *that* wrong, huh?"

Clarke nodded, jotting furiously into his notebook.

"Same thing with the file cabinet. I'd noticed the tiny key on the ring, so I tried it in the lock. It fit. I thought I would look through it later." She paused. "I'm kind of ashamed saying that. I know it's really none of my business, but I've been spending so much time here, it almost seems like I'm part of the house. And the Doctor was dead, so...what harm could it do?"

"And the closet door?" Clarke did not raise his head.

"The same. Another locked door. Another reason to wonder why."

"And the lock on the false door, the same? Tell me about your fall."

"Um, yeah, same with that lock. What fall? What do you mean?"

"You said you stumbled, fell, and hit your head. That's when you realized there was a hidden door."

"Oh, yeah. It's just a bump. Want to feel it?" She leaned forward, pointing to a spot about two inches into the hairline above her right eye.

Clarke did not look up from his writing but smiled. "I'll take your word for it."

Nikki reached for her cigarette and tapped it several times against the saucer.

"This key was on the original keyring, too?"

Nikki nodded.

Clarke, intent on writing, missed it. He looked up. "The same ring?"

She nodded.

"Then you went up?"

"Yeah." She drew on the cigarette and nodded. "It was still afternoon so there was some light coming in from the small window up there. Everything was really dim though, the pictures, stuff hanging off the walls, I saw it all, but I figured it couldn't be what I first thought it was. That would be crazy. It wasn't until I turned on a lamp and saw the big flag that I knew what it was all about." She exhaled shakily while she talked. Her face behind a cloud.

"I figured I had to get the hell out of there. I locked everything up and drove home. I put the four keys on a piece of string instead of leaving them on that crowded keyring where it was murder to find them. It seemed like it took a year, my hands were shaking so much."

"You went right home?"

"Well, I grabbed my bag. It was in the den."

"But then you went right home, you didn't touch anything else? Didn't remove anything from the house? No detours or stops? You didn't share this information with friends?"

There are no friends, she thought. "There was no sharing with anybody until you saw it."

Clarke wrote on for a few seconds, then dropped his pen on the pad. "Okay. That's it for now. You probably ought to head home. It's got to be getting close to dinner time anyway."

She nodded. "I'm sorry I didn't tell you about it the minute I got to the diner. But for a couple minutes, I felt like I had a life again." Clarke looked puzzled.

Nikki blushed, looked down at the saucer and slowly turned it in a clockwise direction. "I got to be in a public place doing a public thing, just like a regular person." She smiled sadly. "You see, after Donald's death, I fell apart. I'm not a shrink, so I don't know exactly why, but it's pretty clear I wanted to hurt myself. Or humiliate myself, whatever. Anyway, my little quest for self-annihilation was very lonely. Oh, I was with people, a lot of them, and all the wrong kind, but I always felt incredibly alone. Now, things are much better and I've got Mrs. G looking out for me. But it's still just me and her. And she's getting over her heart attack, and I'm cleaning houses, so we're not together as much as we used to be. And even back when we were we never went out much. Oh, we'd go to the store, but never to a restaurant or diner like today. Once to a movie, though.

"Hey," she looked up, "did you see that 2001 space movie? Was it as weird as I thought, or was I still drunk?"

Clarke shrugged and shook his head. "I heard about it, but I don't get out much either."

"Mmm, anyway, I think maybe Mrs. G was trying to shield me from people. The people I saw when my life was bad, or people who might be angry at me now for my actions then." She paused, frowned, and reversed direction on the saucer.

"Here I am, rambling to you again. Sorry. You gave me an opportunity to be a person. Someone who goes out to eat, has a conversation with their companion, leaves. I haven't had that in years. It was incredibly special. Being honest, that's why when you suggested we meet away from the station and grab lunch, there's no way I could have said no. I was Nikki again, not some disgusting slu—slob you have to be careful around because you never know what might send her back down the rabbit hole. I don't get many opportunities like that." She then laughed. "Hell, until today, I didn't get *any* opportunities like that." She halted with the saucer, and smiling, looked up to him.

"And that pie!" she rolled her eyes in ecstasy. "I am sorry, though, I should have spoken up about that," she nodded toward the stairs, "sooner."

"It's fine. Like I said earlier, there's no harm done."

They walked through the dining room to the den. "Is this the bag?" Clarke pointed to the large cloth bag with a peace sign and a long shoulder strap. He quickly picked it up and handed it to her. "Heavy. You're not stealing the family silver, are you?"

227

She took the bag from him with both her hands. "Don't I wish. No, Mr. Eichen is paying me enough. I'd never take anything from here."

"Bye, Nikki."

She turned and walked away. When she had reached the small vestibule, Clarke said, "I enjoyed lunch, too." She smiled and waved as she passed through the door.

The smile dropped from Nikki's face as she slowly descended the porch steps, one hand holding the railing, the other tightly clutching her bag to her chest. Why Nik? she asked herself, why did you just lie to Captain Clarke?

TWENTY-EIGHT

"I would like some krupnik please."

Rolf Eichen sat, staring at the scarred table, palms flat against the damaged surface. Clarke had him brought to the station to see what he knew about the Doctor's Nazi past. There was no way the son could be completely in the dark. Let's see what he knows and what he may be hiding.

Kevin looked at Captain Clarke. "Um, coop-what? I'm not sure what you mean."

"Not 'coop,' there is an 'R'. Like chicken coop, but with an R. Krupnik."

From the doorway, Clarke said, "You're going to have to be more specific, Mr. Eichen. We have no idea what you're talking about."

A ghost of a smile formed on the man's lips and was gone almost instantly. "That's right. Such a big part in my family's life for as long as I can remember. It's a drink, a sort of liqueur. It's Polish, made from vodka and honey, I think. The Doctor swilled it like it was water."

"Yeah," Kevin said, a look of realization on his face. Clarke looked at him questioningly. "Not about your father, about mine, my stepfather I mean. I remember him talking about that stuff. Croop-what?"

"Krupnik."

"He said they always drank it around Christmastime back in the old country. I don't ever remember seeing him drinking it more than once or twice. He said it kicked harder than the horses he used to shoe back in Poland."

Eichen nodded. "Yes. It was a staple in the Doctor's diet. He had Szlosek's Liquor Store import it especially for him. I can't count the number of times I was sent down to pick up a bottle for that man." He shook his head. "I swear, he must have paid for Slzosek's boat."

"Mr. Eichen," Kevin said, very business-like, "we are not going to supply you with alcohol in order to obtain your testimony. This is a police station, not a tavern."

Eichen gazed silently at him before saying, "I am ready to be driven home."

"Mr. Eichen," said Clarke. "Am I correct in assuming if we do not give you your drink you will not assist us in answering questions which may lead us to find who murdered your father? However, if we do, you will speak with us?"

"Yes, Captain, that is correct."

"Officer MacDougall, please take some money from petty cash, head over to Szlosek's, and make the purchase."

Kevin gave his captain a 'you gotta be kidding' look and left the room.

"Thank you, Captain. Believe me when I say I am not doing this to be difficult. The krupnik plays...well, Poland plays a very large role in the story. I would be remiss not to include it."

Clarke nodded. "I'll take you at you word, sir." He left and headed to the squad room to join Kevin. He said, "Officer Reyes, would you please remain with Mr. Eichen until we're ready to join him? And then I would like you to be a part of the interview."

Valeria blinked and rose from her desk. "Of course, Captain." Her lips twitched as she left the room.

The look from a moment ago was again on Kevin's face. "You sure about that, Captain?" he asked quietly. "I mean, you know, she's, well she's—"

"New?"

"Um, yeah."

"So were you. So was Sully. You've now worked with Officer Reyes for several days, do you feel she is in any way incapable of her duties?"

"Well, no, but she learned in Newark, a big city. This is Pendale. Wouldn't it be better if...." He withered under Clarke's stare. "Okay, right. Well, what about getting Eichen his croop-stuff? What about that? Where would we be if we bought every suspect the booze of his choice before he spilled his guts in interrogation? Number one, we'd be broke, there's only about ten dollars in the cash box—"

"If it runs more than that I'll reimburse you."

"But on top of that, it's, it's just not professional." Kevin almost italicized the final word with his voice.

"Kevin, sit down for second." Clarke sat at his desk and his chair creaked as he leaned back.

"We have a viable suspect ready for questioning. A very viable suspect I'd say. Our *only* suspect at this time. Would you agree?" The younger man nodded. "We need to elicit information from him, right?" Another nod. "Thus far, his behavior has been impeccable. He agreed to join us, he's quiet, puts up no fuss, and until a moment ago has given us all we've asked for. He has made a request. Yes, it's out of the ordinary, but not completely unheard of. Remember the bucket of chicken we bought last month for Charlie Groski? And all we wanted from him was info as to where he'd parked a stolen car. This is a much bigger deal, right? So, what's the problem?"

Kevin squirmed for a second before finally answering. "It's *alcohol*. If we do this for everyone it's going to be like Friday night at the Bottle Cap around here."

Clarke exhaled audibly. "Kevin, how many suspects are in interrogation?"

"Um, one."

"One. There is no 'everyone' we're going to do this for. This is it, a one off. You'll probably never hear another suspect ask for croop-whatever, again. I know it's a first for me, and I've been around a while. It's a means to an end, Kevin. You know what would be unprofessional? Having this man in interrogation, knowing he is willing to share information with us, and then creating an obstacle in attaining that information. Relax. Go to Szlosek's and buy some of this stuff. Okay?"

Kevin nodded and headed out.

"Smallest bottle they've got!" Clarke shouted at his back.

Rolf Eichen was in interrogation for the simple reason that other than the elderly secretary who used to work for the doctor and the mystery German-speaking Mr. Smith, he was the sole human being, other than a few patients, who had been in contact with the doctor. And it was rather clear there was no love lost between the two men. The son's insistence on referring to the deceased as "the Doctor" was evidence of that. Coupled with Clarke's belief that there was no way in hell the son could not have been aware of the man's Nazi past, there may have been a distinct reason for animosity on his part.

Kevin returned and fifteen minutes later the interrogation, as it was, began. Eichen and Clarke sat opposite each other at the old table. MacDougall stood against a wall, Valeria, in a corner, hands folded in front of her.

"I suppose the reason for my being here is that you now know the Doctor's secret. He is not a Pole who fled the Nazi's during the war. He was one himself. He, my mother, and I fled Danzig, hid in Washington, then eventually settled here in Pendale. Being a German living in hiding was a shame I was forced to live with my entire life. One that, ironically, was a complete falsehood." MacDougall looked puzzled. "I will explain momentarily.

"So, you were aware of the Doctor's past?"

He did not answer directly. "Allow me to tell you a story, a true story." Eichen lifted the bottle of krupnik and smiled weakly at the label. "I suppose it all begins with the Great War. What most in this country refer to as World War I. As you all know, the war did not end well for Germany. It lost quite a bit of territory, some of which became a part of Poland. Oh, Poland had been in existence for hundreds of years, but not until 1918 did it come to be as we now know it. In addition to land, Germany lost many, many men in battle. Almost an entire generation died in the foxholes of Central Europe."

"Mr. Eichen, while this is—" Kevin began, before catching a look from Clarke.

"Please continue, Mr. Eichen," Clarke said.

"Moving ahead to the 1930s when Adolf Hitler began his rise to power, we know one of his goals was obtaining "Lebensraum," living space, for his countrymen. He would need this Lebensraum because he also intended to make up for the loss of the generation that had died." He shook his head and set the bottle on the table. "Tragically, he looked east to Poland for both. Lebensraum translates to living space, there is a similar word which addresses the second problem."

"Lebensborn?" Clarke quietly said.

Rolf looked at Clarke, mildly surprised. With the barest trace of a smile on his lips he said, "Yes, Captain. Lebensborn." He broke the seal on the bottle and poured an inch or so of the krupnik into a glass Clarke had provided. He took a deep swallow and leaned back in his chair, gazing at the amber color of the remaining liquid in the glass. "Where did you learn about this? It is not commonly known."

"After learning of the Doctor's secret, I did a bit of research. Miss Cook at the library was very helpful. I'm not sure what she thought of my search, but the information is there, for all to see; you just have to want to find it."

"That's right. The wanting to find it. There lies the difficulty. How do you find something when you have no knowledge of its existence?"

Clarke wasn't sure if the question was intended for him, or if Eichen was speaking to himself. He chose to answer it.

"I didn't know of it per se, but the first clue that nudged me in its direction was when I was in your living room last week. In the den I saw a photograph of a woman I took to be your mother. It struck me that you bore very little resemblance to her. While you were both fair, that's about as far as the resemblance went. Her hair was curly, yours is straight. She had a rather pointed chin while yours appears more squared off. Also, the shape of your faces, hers was, I guess you would have to call it a very vertical face, where yours—"

"Where mine looks square, like a block. Like my entire head. The Doctor referred to me as a blockhead for as long as I can remember. Just another of his little jibes at me. I really do not remember a time in my life when he did not refer to me in this manner." He took another drink. "But there was a time, a very long time ago, when I was not called this. Such a time *did* exist."

Clarke nodded. Eichen looked at him expectantly. "Please continue, Captain. Surely there is more."

"The fact of you and your mother looking dissimilar means nothing on its own. However, I coupled it with a feeling I had. Nothing tangible, just a gut feeling."

Kevin was familiar with Clarke's gut feelings. These feelings were partially responsible for them apprehending the murderer earlier this summer. On that occasion Clarke had told Kevin not to dismiss those feelings. They were another tool to use in their work.

"Over the years I've seen you and your father around town. Separately. I don't believe I have ever seen you together. In fact, until his death, I didn't know you were related." Eichen looked like he was about to speak but didn't. "I have never seen a father and son more different from each other. He struck me as being very confident in all he did. He was almost aggressive in his daily dealings with people. An arrogance came through. You seemed quite the opposite. While I don't know you well, you strike me as much more...gentle, and excuse me for saying it, timid."

"Yes," the young man said, nodding. "This is true. You are an observant man, Captain Clarke."

"It comes with the job. Say, would you mind if I had a drink of that stuff? It's been a long day."

Valeria and Kevin looked surprised. Rolf nodded. "I would be happy to drink with you."

"Officer Reyes would you please get—no. Officer MacDougall, please get me a clean glass from the washroom. Give it a quick rinse if necessary."

Kevin walked, expressionless, from the room. A trace of a smile appeared Valeria's face.

"But really, there must be more to this gut feeling than you have shared. I don't look like my mother, and I don't act like the man known as my father. Anything else??"

"Well, you really don't look like the Doctor either. But you're right, there's more."

Kevin reentered the room with a clean glass.

"Thank you, Officer." Clarke slid the glass across the scarred table for Eichen to pour him a drink. Clarke then held it up to the light, gave it a tentative sniff, his highbrows rising at the smell, and took a healthy sip.

"Whoa." He blinked several times and nodded his head. "That is *something* alright."

"It certainly is," Rolf agreed, smiling.

235

"Is that honey I taste?" asked Clarke.

"Yes. It gives it its color, as well."

"So, tell me, how or why does krupnik figure into this story?"

"Not the krupnik itself, but the fact that it is a Polish drink. One the Doctor, I am sure to his everlasting disgust, developed a taste for."

"Why might he feel disgust?"

Rolf drank the last of his glass and looked over the rim at Clarke. "I think you know why, Captain."

"Perhaps, but tell us anyway."

"Lebensborn. The 'Fount of Life' is the literal translation. Sounds quaint, doesn't it? Almost Biblical." He took a long breath and slowly let it out. "The first world war decimated the male population of Germany. The birth rate fell over forty percent from just after the war to the early 1930s. As you know, Hitler came to power in 1933. In order to Aryanize Europe, as he planned to do, this genetic shortfall had to be addressed. So, he came up with a plan. We know how Hitler loved his plans, yes?" Rolf poured another glass of krupnik and took a long drink.

"There were actually several parts to Lebensborn. Did you know that, Captain?"

Clarke sipped his own drink. "Tell us about it."

"First things first. What Hitler needed to do right away was make certain existing German pregnancies did not go for naught. He put a stop to any abortions pursued by women who were deemed to possess desired Aryan traits. When a woman became pregnant out of wedlock, because this was normally looked upon as a shameful thing, she might pursue an abortion. But Hitler's friend, Heinrich Himmler, came up with an idea. If the woman believed her child might possibly possess desirable racial traits, she could continue her pregnancy in comfortable, private facilities. Once the child was born, it was then placed in the care of a Nazi couple and raised to be a good German. The biological mother, while carrying the child, was treated like a piece of china. The woman was well-treated, well-fed, given good medical care, all things which would be unavailable to her elsewhere. These places, maternity homes, began popping up in various locations. Desirable Aryan women were producing desirable Aryan babies. A success! These unmarried, pregnant Aryan mothers were corralled, then coddled until they gave birth. But it was not enough. Do you know what those bastards did next? They created a breeding program." He saw the reaction in Valeria's eyes and said, "Yes, Officer. They did.

"They had the Leaders of the League of German Girls recruit young women from that organization to be potential breeding partners for SS officers. Like sifting through this country's Girl Scouts to find the most desirable, and then impregnating them! And would you believe it? This too was a success. These girls were convinced it was an honor to be selected. They were the chosen ones, giving birth to future generations of the Third Reich. Necessary, of course, because the Reich was going to last for a thousand years, correct? These girls would be the matriarchs of a new civilization.

"And these young women who were chosen for their Aryan qualities did not just perform their national duty with a chosen officer once and then retire. No." Rolf drank again and made an effort to collect himself. "No," he repeated. "They became breeding stock. They coupled with multiple officers who were chosen for *their* 'Aryanness.' In reality, I rather think it degenerated into those officers with the most power choosing the most desirable of the females. This was not viewed as the "free love" that is spoken of today. It was viewed as duty! It was a nationalistic breeding program that rewarded all participants involved. The young, impressionable women, barely more than girls, and the powerful, not to mention eager, male participants." He added sourly, "True patriots, all."

He looked from Clarke to Kevin to Valeria. "And unbelievably, it *still* was not enough." He drained the rest of his glass and said, "I need to use the men's room." He rose. "Excuse me, where is...?"

Valeria was first off the mark. "This way, sir." She gestured to the hall. "Down and on your right."

A moment after he left the room Kevin said, "This is crazy. Have you ever heard of this stuff before, Captain?" He looked at Valeria who shook her head. "I know *I* never learned about it. Do you think he's making it up?" Clarke was silent. Exasperated, he pushed on. "Really? Okay. So, is he about to tell us he's a child of one of those chosen girls who had no problem slutting around with Nazis?"

"What about those Nazi officers? Weren't they 'slutting around' too? Valeria said.

"What? I don't know. I mean, they were Nazis, right? Capable of anything?" Kevin said. "Anyway, it's just different with men."

"I'm certain it is," Valeria said.

The sound of a toilet flushing reached them. "Alright, officers, I think we may be getting close to much-needed information. And no, Kevin, I don't believe he was a product of this breeding program."

"Then what—"

Clarke shook his head as Rolf Eichen reentered the room.

He sat again and reached for the krupnik, then hesitated. "Perhaps I should wait. It is indeed a strong drink, am I right, Captain?" He dropped his hand to his lap.

"The breeding part of Lebensborn still wasn't enough, you were saying," Clarke prompted.

"No, it was not. It is here that the Nazis sank to even greater depths. Almost unimaginable depths."

Jesucristo, thought Valeria, what could possibly be worse?

TWENTY-NINE

"What I have told you and what I am about to tell you I learned from the Doctor himself. It was a night of far too much krupnik, and I believe he was feeling melancholic, missing his native land. I too, had done some research, Captain. There are aspects of my life I will go into shortly that led me to do this. I confronted him with this Lebensborn information. I believed he would be shocked I knew. Foolish me, instead he simply laughed and confirmed it. He took pride in the fact that his government, his countrymen, were forward thinking enough to implement just such a program. What will follow is a story as much of myself as it is of the Doctor.

As you know, despite what he wanted people in this country to believe, he was not simply a Pole fleeing his homeland during a time of chaos. He was part of the chaos. He was a Nazi, and a member of the SS, an elite section of the Nazi party, believed to be the chosen among the chosen.

"We lived in what is now known as Gdansk. It is an area that has changed hands over the years. During the war, when the Germans occupied Poland, it was called Danzig. It has long been populated with both Poles and Germans. Its location as a port on the Baltic Sea made it an important city. The Doctor's family had lived there for generations. However, as an officer in the war he was stationed all around Germany. We lived in many cities, and he met many people." Eichen hesitated, then said, "While stationed in Frankfurt he practiced side by side with Joseph Mengele."

Kevin looked puzzled. Valeria said quietly, "A Nazi doctor in the camps. Experimented on many of the prisoners. Very well-known."

He mouthed silently, 'Whoa.'

"Yes. Auschwitz's Dr. Mengele. He had not yet become the infamous Joseph Mengele he is today, but according to the Doctor, his experiments in eugenics were already underway. The Doctor also knew Heinrich Himmler, the brains behind the whole Lebensborn program. The man known as my father was acquainted with some very interesting people."

Rolf seemed to change his mind about the krupnik and poured another. He took a long drink before gently placing the glass on the table. He slowly turned it round and round between his palms.

"He was proud of his relationship with Mengele. Can you imagine? The man who, after Hitler, embodies all the horror the Nazis stood for. He was proud to know him! He once told me Mengele was the most brilliant man he had ever met, and he regretted the fact they did not work together longer. He hoped one day the world's political situation would change, and he could again work with the man and expand on the work Mengele had begun in Auschwitz. If those damn Jew-dogs didn't hunt him down first, he said.

"And I lived most of my childhood under the same roof as this man! Can you imagine existing in the presence of such evil?"

"Most of your childhood?" Kevin asked. "Not all? Were you an adopted child?" He thought of the captain's observations that Rolf looked unlike either of his parents.

"No, Officer. I was certainly *not* adopted," Rolf answered quietly before taking another drink.

Kevin thought the guy better slow down. The level in the bottle was down to almost nothing.

Rolf sat, gazing at the far wall.

After a moment Clarke asked, "Would you like to take a break, Mr. Eichen? Collect your thoughts or maybe take a short walk to clear your head?"

Eichen almost barked out a burst of laughter. "Clear my head? Only in my prayers could I have a clear head. However," he slowly stood, "I would appreciate stepping outside for some air. Do you mind?"

"Of course not. Officer Reyes, would you escort Mr. Eichen outside and keep him company?"

She nodded. "Yes sir. Mr. Eichen, after you, please."

Rolf smiled at the young officer, nodded, and slowly walked out of the room.

Once the door had closed behind the two, Kevin asked, "Do you think she'll be okay with him? Has she ever had to guard anyone before?"

"I have no idea, however I don't believe it will be an issue. And it's not as though she's 'guarding' anyone. Eichen isn't going to make a break for it. And even if he did, do you really doubt Valeria would be able to catch him before he went ten yards?"

"Mmm, probably not."

Kevin lifted the diminished bottle of krupnik, peered at what little was left, and sighed. "He's probably a little tipsy from this stuff, too." He gave the bottle a gentle shake before replacing it.

"I would agree."

The two men sat in silence until Kevin asked, "Eichen just used a word, 'yoojen' something. I didn't want to ask, but what—"

"Eugenics. Selective breeding. Breeding in desirable traits while eliminating those that might be considered undesirable. The young Aryan women and the SS officers. Supposedly a lot of desirable traits in that mix. But the genes found in races of people looked down upon for some reason? Eliminate them."

Kevin thought a moment. "We're talking Nazis so nothing should come as a surprise, but treating humans like they're breeding show dogs, and using their Girl Scouts, too? It's hard to wrap my head around."

"I agree. I had heard bits and pieces about this before, a few years after the war, but it's not until my recent research that I learned the full details of Lebensborn. If I'm not mistaken, we'll be hearing more when he returns, and yes, it's even worse."

"Worse." Kevin thought of Paval and the horrors of the war he felt he needed to hide from his stepson. "Fount of Life," he said bitterly, shaking his head.

After several moments of silence, they heard the outside door thunk shut and the steps of Rolf Eichen and Valeria returning.

"Are you ready to continue, Mr. Eichen?" The man nodded. "Whenever you're ready, sir."

Eichen looked as though the fresh air had revived him. He sat and poured a bit into his glass. Kevin rolled his eyes. "A refill, Captain?"

Clarke shook his head.

Eichen emptied the remains of the bottle into his glass, took a swallow, leaned back, and seemed to settle in. There was a grim smile on his face.

"As the Nazis proceeded to wage war on Europe by invading their neighbors in Poland, do you know what they were shocked to find?" He looked to Clarke, then MacDougall and Valeria. Eichen seemed to be settling into the role of a professor dispensing knowledge to his pupils.

"Aryans. Or, at the very least, people who looked Aryan. But how could this be? The Poles and so many others were deemed to be of inferior races, an insignificant people to be conquered, how could there be so many who resembled what the master race should be? Could it be they were mistaken in their belief there was so wide a gap between themselves and the 'vermin'? Was there really so little difference between them?" He paused, looking at his students.

"Of course not. That would be unthinkable for the Nazis.

"The only explanation acceptable to them was that somehow, over the generations, true Germanic people with their superior traits, had intermingled with the dreaded Poles and the result was a mix of the two. Certainly, there were many who exhibited more Polish features, but there were also a significant number of seeming Aryans, as well. The thought was that while it was unfortunate there was any racial mix, these people who appeared Aryan, with proper education and reprogramming, their true Germanic nature could be enhanced while simultaneously, the undesirable nature is diminished. Or even better, completely wiped out. Make them believe they are, in fact, Germans, have them speaking German, not Polish. Knowing German history and civics, believing the Fuhrer to be a god, living with the knowledge the Reich would last a thousand years. But how to do this? You can't simply drag a man or woman from the street and demand they forget everything they have come to know and believe about themselves. Their name, family, language, past. You cannot erase twenty, thirty, forty years of a person's memories and simply insert new ones. So," he drained his glass in a long swallow and brought it down hard on the table, "how could they make this come to pass?" He looked from officer to officer.

"Children," said Valeria in almost a whisper. "They stole and reprogrammed the children."

THIRTY

"Yes, Officer Reyes, the children."

Valeria appeared startled she had spoken aloud.

"While not exclusive to Poland, much of this heinous practice occurred there. The Nazis seized young children from their homes, from the only environment they had ever known, and proceeded to brainwash them and win over any 'good blood' they might possess. And in this process, of course, obliterate any perceived 'tainted blood.' These children were often taken in full view of their parents. The parents themselves were seized and sent to camps. Either way...the children's lives as they had known them, were over."

Eichen paused and examined the label on the now-empty bottle. "The Doctor loved this drink. I think he felt a certain shame he found this specific Polish drink so much to his liking. He used to say this was the sole thing of any value that came from that vermin-infested country. The absolute only thing."

The alcohol certainly seemed to be having an effect on Eichen, but not to the degree Kevin would have thought. If he had drunk half as much, he'd be either laying under the table or puking in the toilet.

"Since hearing those words from him I have made an effort to embrace all things Polish. Including," he nodded to the empty bottle, "krupnik." He seemed to run out of steam and sat staring, glassy-eyed, at the bottle.

"Kevin," Clarke said quietly, "go back to Szlosek's for another bottle."

"Um, I don't think there's enough in petty cash and I don't have—"

"Here." Clarke dug into his pocket, pulled out a bill, and handed it to him. "Go."

"I think it's about the time he closes up for the day," Kevin said, looking at the wall clock.

"Then you'd better *hurry*, right?"

"Right." He scrambled out of the office.

"Sit tight, Mr. Eichen. Officer Reyes, would you come into my office for a moment?"

They entered the small room and Clarke sat at his desk. The oscillating fan affixed over the door gave some relief. He shut his eyes as a wave of breeze swept over him. "That stuff he's drinking, the uh...,"

"Krupnik."

"Yeah, it's dynamite. I don't know how he's still upright. The little I drank raised my temperature about twenty degrees. Hopefully, it will loosen his tongue a bit more without pushing him to the point of passing out."

"He likely has a tolerance for it, sir."

"You're probably right. It seems to be working, though. If we can keep him upright, we may get something valuable out of this."

"What exactly are we looking for, Captain? Do you think he may have killed the Doctor? Killed him for being a Nazi that's in some way connected to this Lebensborn thing?"

"I don't know. I would say he is certainly justified in hating the Doctor. Enough to kill him?" He shrugged. "What I do know is he is the one viable suspect we have. Let's see what else we can learn. Right now, we're just gathering information about the deceased and his life. We'll see if it has any value later. Do me a favor, peek out and make sure Eichen hasn't taken off on a drunken stroll."

She stuck her head out the door. The man appeared not to have moved since they left him. He was slumped in his chair, gazing at the empty bottle.

"He's fine. I can't imagine living so long with such evil."

"Yes. I used to believe some people treated others so poorly simply because they feared those who seemed to be different. But with each passing year I feel it's not just fear, but active dislike and even hatred. Where it stems from, I have no idea. It gets to the point of dehumanizing those who seem different, not even thinking of them as people, but rather, as things. Like what our friends, the Nazis, did with the Jews in the camps, exterminating vermin rather than committing mass murder." He remembered the town's almost nonchalant reaction when Rosaria Donez was killed earlier this summer. Hell, some residents weren't nonchalant at all, they were almost gleeful. As long as it wasn't a white girl, and it decreased the numbers of *them*, they were more than okay with it.

"I certainly agree about the hatred part. It's hard to miss."

Clarke looked at the young woman standing in front of him, exuding such strength and confidence. Would Rosaria Donez have matured into such a person? There was no way of ever knowing and that was the tragedy of it.

"How are you dealing with life here in Pendale? Are the residents giving you any cause for concern?"

"It's fine, sir, nothing I can't handle." She smiled. "The white residents aren't giving me any problems. They're very wary and are keeping me at arm's length."

"Oh?"

"I think the fact I'm one of *them* and I carry a gun has them a little off-balance. No, they're fine." Her smile then faded.

"However...," said Clarke.

"However, the Puerto Rican community is another matter."

247

"I thought that might be the case."

"Did you? It sounds stupid, I know, but I didn't give it much thought until it started happening. I guess I thought coming to Pendale would be like starting with a clean slate. No one knows me or anything about me, it's a new job, new colleagues, new everything. I thought I could be judged just for what I am and what I do. Let my actions define me."

"That would be ideal, wouldn't it?"

"It sure would, but I was being naive."

"Forgive me for saying so, but I agree."

"To the majority of the town I'm just another brown face intruding into what was once all white. To those like me, I'm some sort of traitor, having crossed to the side of the enemy. At work—" she stopped.

"It's fine, Valeria, please continue. I know what I would like the job to provide for you, for all my officers, but I would also like to know the reality of it."

She hesitated, then continued. "In Newark, before it all hit the fan anyway, I felt like some of the guys on the force thought I might revert to my *true colors* one day and open up on them with my sidearm in retaliation for all the wrongs I perceived they may have done to the Puerto Rican community. Others looked at me like I was trash because of, because of some past choices I made." She hesitated, "I don't know how much you know about that."

"I have your personnel file from Captain Clements in Newark."

"Then you know I once was part of a gang, the Wild Dogs." Her hand went unconsciously to her chest before she caught the motion and angrily pulled it away. "I left the gang, but that didn't matter to some people." She smiled bitterly. "Once a Dog, a Dog for life. That's what they believe. The truth is, I'd heard that my whole life, and it was always said with pride. I never thought how others might view it."

"But you realized it wasn't right for you; you outgrew it."

"That was part of it anyway," Valeria said, thinking about Seb's edict that she would be sexed in if she wanted to remain with them. "And then there were the women."

"They were an issue, too?" Clarke asked, his eyebrows raised.

"Oh, yes. Maybe the biggest of all. There weren't many women on the Newark force, just a couple. But they made it clear I was viewed as nothing more than a threat to whatever relationships they had with their men. One of them was married to an officer on the force, the others were seeing guys in the ranks. It's frowned upon, but it happens. From the moment I showed up I was a potential homewrecker," she said, shaking her head. *As though I would want to have anything to do with those shlubs,* she thought.

"I hadn't thought of that angle," Clarke said.

"Yeah, well, you know what they say about us Puerto Rican girls." Valeria omitted the fact that it was not only the women who seemed to hold this belief, but an uncomfortable number of the males, as well. They made it their mission to test this theory, daily it seemed.

"That was Newark, how about here?"

"I'm happy to say, sir, that I feel fine with you, comfortable and respected."

"I'm happy to hear that, too. And the others?"

"Well, I think Officer MacDougall feels threatened to a degree." She hesitated, trying to formulate the best way to continue. "I think he views me as a threat to his position here. We're close to the same age, and I feel he may think I'll jump past him, get promoted first, something like that. Maybe he's threatened because I'm both a woman and a minority and believes I'll get some kind of break that he, being a white male, wouldn't."

"That's a possibility." Clarke recalled a conversation with his junior officer several months ago when the younger man espoused very similar beliefs.

"Also," Valeria tried to hide her smile, "I don't believe he's had much experience with women. Being around women, I mean. I'm a puzzle for him in that respect, too."

Clarke nodded.

"And last...," Clarke looked expectantly at her, "I think he fears I may somehow take his place in your eyes, sir. Or at the very least, he might have to share that place."

"Hmm, interesting observations to be sure. How about Sully?"

Valeria couldn't help a short burst of laughter. "Oh, Officer Sullivan is fine, sir. Treats me like one of the boys. No problems there." Sully was oblivious to the majority of the intrigue around him.

"Well, I'm glad of that," said Clarke.

"About Kevin, I feel you should be aware of a couple things. First, his stepfather died a little while back. Some time has passed, but I know they were very close. And there's something connected with his death that seems to be distracting him. Also, the murders here earlier this summer, Rosaria Donez and Nora Wilson, not to mention the death of Angela Castille. Working the case was a traumatic experience for us all, but especially for him." Clarke hesitated before continuing. "How well do you know the facts of the case?"

Valeria said, "It was certainly news around the state, probably nationally, too. The killer decided to rid the world of women deemed unworthy to live. They were mutilated as well, their breasts hacked off." She looked to Clarke for affirmation.

"Yes. What you probably don't know is that the killer was someone Kevin has known his entire life. A friend of his family." Valeria's eyes raised, surprised. "It really knocked him off balance. It made him question his beliefs about virtually everything he knew. Which brings me to my final point. He is a product of his environment. He has spent almost his entire life within the confines of this town. His values as well as beliefs have been shaped here. Yet he saw how little the citizenry cared about the death of a minority girl and it troubled him. These were the people he's known forever...so he's struggling with a lot right now."

Valeria nodded. She knew MacDougall was a Pendale native but had not given it more thought. She'd lumped him with those she believed resented her for her ethnicity among other things. Coupled with the fact she believed he'd never seriously engaged with a female in his life, she'd been dismissive of him.

Then a startling realization hit her.

Valeria had grown up with the belief that being in a gang was an important part of a person's development. You weren't considered grown or whole, until you were a part of one. It wasn't until Marco's death and Seb's subsequent actions that she belatedly realized she had been misguided in her beliefs. She had changed, but paid a dear price for it. Maybe Kevin MacDougall had a past that haunted him as much as Valeria's haunted her.

"Would you please check on Mr. Eichen again?" Clarke asked, nodding toward the door.

"Hm? Oh, yes." She looked again. "Same as before. I really find myself feeling for this guy."

"Did he say anything when you escorted him outside?"

"Um, yes," she said, embarrassed. "He said the Nazis would not have found me to be genetically attractive." She did not add he also said it would be a tragedy a lovely young lady such as herself would be deemed unworthy of living.

"The rear door of the station thumped shut. Kevin had returned with the krupnik.

"Old man Szlosek wasn't thrilled to see me again. He was locked up, but I could see him through the glass, cashing out the register. I pounded on the door until he opened up for me. He said he'd thought he'd sold his last bottle of this stuff," he raised the bottle, "when the doc passed away. Now two in one day. He asked if I thought he'd need to order more from his supplier. I told him maybe, Captain Clarke had sampled it and might develop a taste for the stuff." He grinned.

Clarke grunted. "He may want to hold off on that order." He rose from his desk. "Okay, let's get back to it."

Kevin stepped aside so Valeria could exit first. "Thank you, Kevin," she said as she passed.

He blinked, caught off-guard.

THIRTY-ONE

"Are you up to speaking for a little while longer, Mr. Eichen?"

The man looked up, his eyes red, glazed, and tired. "Yes, Captain, I am. This is something I feel I need to share. I have carried this information for many years; it has been very difficult not being able to voice it, to share it."

"Yes, sir. We've got some more krupnik if you'd like." He put it in front of Eichen.

With a tired smile, Eichen said, "Not at the moment, thank you."

The three officers resumed their positions in the small interview room.

"I have always had a very active dream life, especially in childhood. These dreams are all very much alike, not the same dream, but aspects of the dreams are very similar. There is a farm. The farmhouse is white, and a tree grows in the front yard. I don't remember exactly what kind, but it is some type of fruit tree. I remember chickens, and I see myself as a boy, running after them, scattering them, and laughing as I do this. And a cow. An enormous brown cow with a pale white ring around one eye. In my dream her name is Janina. Yes, the cow has a name. Also, I remember the name Karol." He paused, and said again, "Karol."

"And there is a woman. Her hair is black, but with bits of gray. She is large, not tall, but wide. Her face is wide, too. I realize I may be making her sound hideous, but she is anything but that. She is kind; she makes me feel safe and loved. She gathers me to her bosom and hugs me very tight. She laughs as she does this. Pressed against her I can feel the laughter inside her body. And it makes me laugh." He almost whispered, "It is extraordinary."

He reached for the bottle, looking at the label yet taking no notice of it. "I have never felt so safe and secure as I did then." He cleared his throat. "These dreams lasted throughout my childhood, gradually fading in frequency from being almost nightly to several times a month to very rarely. Their effect, however, remains, as you can tell. I told my parents of these dreams, of course. My mother seemed worried by them. She would hold me in her arms, rocking me, telling me to forget them and just know how much she loved me. I remember feeling comforted, but not as secure as I did with the woman in my dream.

The Doctor was dismissive. He told me instead to focus on real childhood memories, our red house in Danzig, the gardens there, my school. I tried to do that, I truly did, however those thoughts always brought distress. I once burst into tears as I thought of the school. I recalled what seemed like countless rows of beds of children. It was a boarding school. And just like me, all the children were frightened and crying. I remember endless days being drilled in history, reading, writing, civics. The days seemed to stretch forever. It was as though the school itself was our home.

"It is so confusing. Everyone wanted to be elsewhere, but where exactly they wished to be...no one really knew. They wanted home, but what was home? We were told that the school was home, but we were also told that soon our parents would arrive and take us back to our true homes. Home to our caring family that loved us and would help us grow to be good Germans worshipping our Führer.

"Sometimes the men and women, couples, came to the school. They looked at us all, pointing at who was best-looking, who looked like children they already had, just...pointing and commenting. Much like one does when they are in a pet store choosing which kitten to bring home. Is it friendly? Does it behave well with other children? Is it housebroken?"

Kevin shook his head.

"Yes, Officer, this is true, it is an actual memory. A very stout SS officer came to the school with his wife, an extremely thin woman with teeth like a horse. She said she needed absolute assurance that no child she took into her house was a bedwetter. She could not abide them." He laughed bitterly. "I haven't thought of that woman in years, decades. In a high-pitched whinnying voice she said, 'I cannot have a child wetting the bed in my house. I simply will not abide it.' Smiling he shook his head and broke the seal on the bottle of krupnik. "I remember that night in the long dormitory room, every few minutes some boy would whinny in the darkness. The call would be taken up by another, and another, until I think each one of us had whinnied at least once." The smile faded. "That may be the single positive memory I have of that place." He slowly poured krupnik into his glass.

"I wasn't shaking my head in doubt, Mr. Eichen," said Kevin, "I was shaking my head because of, well, because of what some people will do to other people."

Valeria looked at him.

"I apologize, Officer. There are elements of these 'dreams' I sometimes find difficult to believe myself. I remember on the night of the whinnying being thankful that couple did not take me home with them. Though I was not a bedwetter," he said with a trace of a smile, "I would have pissed in a hundred beds to avoid those two." He hesitated and looked at Valeria, "I apologize, Officer, for my language. I think perhaps the krupnik...," he said, gesturing to the bottle and glass.

Eichen looked at the glass and seemed surprised it was not empty. He grunted quietly and slowly drank what remained. "Sometimes students, we were called students because this was supposed to be a school after all, would leave with no explanation. No, allow me please to amend that statement. They would not *leave*, they would vanish. One day Piotr would be sitting next to me in class, eating at my table in the dining hall, sleeping in a nearby bed. Suddenly, he was gone. He was not taken by one of the couples who visited the school, certainly not the one with the whinnying woman. Piotr was not an attractive child and there was something wrong with one of his feet. A clubbed foot maybe? I can't remember...there is so much I can't remember! After he was gone, those in charge would not acknowledge Piotr. It was as though he had never existed. No, he was not 'adopted,' instead he simply vanished. Like there had never even been a boy named Piotr.

"When I was in high school, here in lovely Pendale, I remember reading a book about something similar. It was about a world where those in charge decided what the citizenry should believe, whether it be factual or not. They would claim the nation was at war with, let's say, the Blue country, and allied with the Red. But that could not be true because you knew the nation had been at war with Red and allied with Blue. Not true, the government claimed; we have *always* been at war with Blue. Always. But you have your memories, specific memories of the opposite. Yet, those in charge insist, over and over, the country had always been at war with Blue, and Red had always been our ally. And shockingly, people believed this!

"I remember thinking that it was impossible, people are not that foolish. They would remember who they fought against and who was an ally. But no. With enough insistence, enough pressure, enough false proof, people can be swayed to think whatever you want them to think. You thought we were at war with Red? But the newspaper says we are fighting Blue, so your memory must be false. The newspapers and books all reflect we have *always* been at war with Blue. Soon, even in your head, you begin to doubt the past you know to be true. And once this happens, those truths will cease to exist. If they ever did."

"Orwellian."

"Yes, Captain, it is. I found when I read that book, *1984*, it brought back confusing memories of my childhood. Imagine, you are a four or five-year-old child and the adults around you are telling you your loving, German family has dropped you off at school for the term. Eventually, you will be rejoining them in Berlin, Danzig, Bonn, wherever they claim is your home. This is reinforced every day along with the lessons in mathematics, writing, and history. German history, of course. How long until the child believes all they are told?" He sipped again and sighed. "And Piotr? He did not exist. He never did. Those adults in control told us so."

Kevin hesitantly said, "So you're telling us, you are one of those children? A...Lebensborn child?"

Eichen continued as though he had not heard. "The school was located near the town of Kalisz in occupied Poland. One day, it was late, and I remember this couple coming to inspect the children. The man looked very severe and seemed impatient. The woman was pretty and very kind. She crouched and spoke to me, asking my name. I almost said Karol, but I had been told repeatedly that was wrong. My name was Rolf. She spoke very softly, and while I do not remember exactly what she said, I do know she made me feel safe for perhaps the first time since I had been in the school. The next thing I remember is being bundled into a large black car and leaving the school with them. I did not know where I was going but I was happy leaving that dreaded place. I remember crying, not in pain or fear, but in relief. I later learned my new home would be Danzig.

"It was clear her husband, a physician I would soon know as the Doctor, had not wanted me. Oh, he wanted a son, but certainly not one like me. His wife was unable to conceive. That was why they 'adopted' me. I remember for years his railing at her for being 'defective' and not able to produce strong German children. I think he would have left her if she had not been so physically beautiful. If Hitler had had the talent to create a painting of the quintessential German woman, it would look like my mother. He didn't though. He was a lousy painter." Eichen ran a finger over a deep scar in the table's surface. "Her name was Ingrid. She was, indeed, very lovely. And she loved me.

"The children in those Lebensborn schools were divided into three categories, those that were desirable, those acceptable, and those less so. I, apparently, fell into the second category. Piotr, my friend that disappeared, that had never existed, was eventually placed in the last category. While I had some appealing Germanic features, they appeared to have been watered down by generations of Polish blood. As you can see, I am not tall, my head, my whole body, is rather square. It is certainly *not* the prototypical Aryan physique. Yet my mother, Ingrid, wanted me. Perhaps it was a matter of embracing the ugly duckling, who knows? However, I know that I owe her my life. Without her insistence I am certain I would have eventually been shipped to one of the camps, Auschwitz, Treblinka...from what I have learned, that was likely the fate of the woman in my dreams. The large woman who held me to her bosom. The woman who I believe must have been my true mother."

Valeria cleared her throat and asked softly, "Is there any way to check the records to see if that was the case? Maybe she's alive somewhere."

"The Nazi's were, indeed, great record keepers, but only of records they deemed to be of importance. The woman had no name, none that I could remember. She probably became no more than a number, a number tattooed on an arm. A number perhaps copied on a list that was lost or destroyed as the tide of the war turned against the Germans. No," he shook his head, "I have no illusions of ever finding her."

Clarke said, "I'm amazed at the amount of information you have been able to accumulate. Much of what you've told us certainly doesn't fall under the category of common knowledge. How do you know of it?"

"Ah, Captain," Eichen said blearily. "Again, I have Ingrid to thank. Much of what I have shared with you came directly from her. Not only had she probably saved my life, but she also gave me my past."

THIRTY-TWO

"She told you all this? I would think that's a rather daring thing to do. Living incognito in a new country and stating, even to her child, that she is the wife of an SS officer," Clarke said.

"She did not tell me directly, Captain. A moment ago I stated that the Nazis were avid record keepers. Perhaps it would be better phrased if I said record keeping was a very German trait. My mother, Ingrid, was an avid one herself. She was an enthusiastic writer. She kept diaries for as long as I can remember."

Kevin was visibly startled. He asked, "If I remember correctly, your mother passed away about six months ago but had been institutionalized for some time. Did she leave her diaries to you?"

"No. If she had planned to do so and the Doctor had been aware of this, I am certain he would have seized them. And as you said, she had been hospitalized for years. While I was away at college, she suffered a stroke. That is what I was told. It was Christmas break, and I was returning home from my first year away at college, missing home and...well, missing my mother, anyway. I struggled at school. I am not the most social of people and I felt rather ostracized while there. My accent. Though I only lived in Germany very early in my life, sharing a house where both adults spoke in heavy accents, well, it was obvious to all I was an outsider. I certainly did not sound

American. I have felt out of place my entire life. We moved here while the war was still raging. Think about what it would be like for a child to be called a Nazi, Hun, Kraut, whatever. Here I was, unknown to even myself, a Pole brainwashed to be a German, now pretending to be a Pole. I sometimes wonder why I did not kill myself. I certainly contemplated it many times." He smiled blearily. "I know why. Because I am a coward. That is what the Doctor would tell me. I think on this occasion he may have been correct."

Clarke glanced at Valeria, then Kevin. Both were riveted by Eichen's account.

"At Christmas break I arrived in Pendale, and no one met me at the train. I am not sure what I expected, but I had assumed someone would greet me, almost certainly my mother. I lugged my heavy suitcase several blocks and when I arrived home, no one was there either. Just a note from the Doctor, looking as though it had been scrawled hastily, stating he would be home in several hours and not to mess up the house in the interim." He raised his glass to his lips and quietly said, "Such a loving man, no?

"When he arrived I asked where my mother was. He stared at me for several seconds before telling me of her stroke. Of course, I was shocked and wanted to see her immediately, but he said there was no rush, she would not be going anywhere anytime soon and she was very comfortable where she was. It was then I learned the stroke had occurred weeks ago. Imagine it, no one had told me. When I confronted him about it, he was dismissive. 'What good would it have done? Just an interruption to your studies. With your grades that is the very last thing you should want. I did you a favor, but you are too stupid to recognize it.'

"The Doctor had those weeks between my mother's stroke and my return to destroy any of her belongings he chose. I am sure he did destroy many of them, but it is a testament to the scant attention he paid her over the years that he did not realize there was much he missed." Eichen took another short sip. "All through my childhood I remember her writing, writing, writing. She never explicitly told me that what she wrote was a secret and the Doctor could never know, but somehow, I understood. After her stroke, when the Doctor was at his office, I searched for the writings. All those boxes in the basement? She had hidden the diaries among them."

Clarke thought of the packed nearly floor-to-ceiling collection of crates, bags and boxes and wondered how the hell Rolf Eichen could have found anything in that mess. It must have taken him weeks.

"You said she gave you your past. This past, I assume, you learned from her diaries?"

"Yes. I learned of the Doctor being an SS officer. I learned they lived in many places before Danzig, now called Gdansk,. Well, names change, as I am certain the Doctor's did. I learned of Lebensborn, the fact that I had been taken from my real home, brought to Kalisz, and then indoctrinated to believe I was a good German boy." A tear rolled down his cheek. "I cannot stress how important this was to learn. It finally gave some credence to the dreams I had experienced my entire life. I was not crazy or unhealthily imaginative as the Doctor had told me; what I dreamed was real, it had actually happened! The woman, the house, the farm," he smiled and wiped away the tear, "the cow. Until that moment, reading the diaries, I truly did wonder if I was insane."

"I'm so sorry, Mr. Eichen. It must have been an awful shock, returning from college and learning about your mother."

He nodded. "Yes, Captain. I called her mother, but it was then I learned that though she had showered me with love and kindness, she was not, and never had been, my true mother. I call her mother because, well, I suppose because I need some semblance of a family to cling to. She did after all, participate, though in a passive way, with the entire Lebensborn 'adoption.' So, she is not without blame herself."

"She saved your life," said Valeria. "You just told us if she had not selected you, ugly duckling or not, likely you would have ended up in one of the camps. Surely your life, even with having to put up with your fa—the Doctor, surely that life is better than the one awaiting you in Auschwitz or wherever." Valeria's voice was becoming more assertive. "You say she is not without blame, okay, she's not perfect, but from what you just told us, she was your savior. You should pray to God and thank her for what she did for you."

She stopped, surprised at what had come out of her mouth.

"Officer Reyes," Clarke began quietly before he was interrupted by Eichen.

"You are, of course, correct Officer. Here I sit, marinated in krupnik, and place blame on the one person in my life that has shown me love and affection. And yes, she saved me." He pushed away the glass and buried his face in his hands. "My God." He began to sob.

Kevin and Valeria both looked at Clarke with 'What now?' expressions on their faces. Clarke shook his head and mouthed, 'Wait.' He rose stiffly and walked to the bathroom. He filled a relatively clean mug with water and set it in front of Eichen.

"Thank you, Captain," he said, and pulled a handkerchief from his pocket. He wiped his tears, blew his nose, and took a sip of water. He smiled weakly at the mug, "Certainly not krupnik."

"You have been talking for some time, Mr. Eichen, would you like to continue, or should we pick this up tomorrow?"

"I think continuing would be best. I am almost to the end of my tale. It is very difficult, saying all this out loud to virtual strangers...although perhaps the fact you are strangers makes it possible. Yes, let's finish, I would rather not go to bed tonight knowing I will have to return to this tomorrow."

Kevin knew it was likely the man would be returning to repeat his recollections several times before the investigation concluded.

"So, where...ah, yes, the day I returned from college. I demanded he tell me where she was hospitalized. He finally informed me of the institution in Flemington."

Clarke immediately thought of his own father.

"I took the car keys and drove there immediately. After an argument with the nurse, I was eventually allowed to see her. I learned later they had called the Doctor and he had given his reluctant permission.

"I was led to a small ward. It was getting dark outside and with the lights on all I saw in the windows was my own reflection, someone lost, searching. There were six patients in the room. My mind immediately went to that school of my childhood and the dormitory room there. I looked from patient to patient and was about to tell the nurse she had brought me to the wrong room.

"Then I recognized her. Her bed was furthest from the window, near a door to what I assumed was the bathroom. She sat upright, her back against several pillows. There was a bandage around her head and a gauze patch covered one eye. The wisps of hair protruding from below the bandage were gray. She had begun to gray when I left for school, but it looked now that she might be completely gray. The bedsheet and blanket were folded back, and her hands rested there. Her wrists and palms faced upward, almost as though she was waiting for something to be dropped in them. Her face was...completely vacant." Eichen looked at Clarke, then quickly to Kevin and Valeria. "There was nothing there. No expression, no recognition of me, nothing. It was as though whatever made her who she was had been poured out. The body before me was completely empty.

"I don't know how long I stood there, staring at her. I felt a hand pull gently on my sleeve. "Sir?" It sounded as though the voice may have repeated itself several times before I was aware. A nurse led me away from my mother's body, out of the room, and toward the nurse's station.

"Your mother suffered a severe stroke, sir. I am very, very sorry. Despite the fact your father is a doctor and did all he could...even being her physician, knowing her medical history, there was no hope.

"No, that's wrong," I said. The nurse smiled patiently. "I mean, he is not her doctor. I can't remember her doctor's name, but it's someone in Perth Amboy. She would never allow the Doctor to be her primary physician."

The nurse looked confused. "She would not allow a doctor to be her doctor? I'm sorry, Mr. Eichen, I know this is upsetting—"

"No. What I mean is *the Doctor*, Dr. Eichen, is not her doctor, she wouldn't have it."

The nurse pulled a chart from a rack of others and examined the top page. "It states here he is her doctor. It's not common for a spouse to be one's primary doctor, but it's not unheard of. Perhaps she tired of the other doctor. Maybe it was simply easier having you father in that role."

I shook my head. "Can you tell me, was there any warning? Of the stroke? Was it sudden?"

"I was on duty when your mother was admitted. Your father was inconsolable. He said that recently she had gotten clumsy, tripping over things, and would have to repeat words because she spoke unclearly. These are tell-tale signs of a stroke. Frankly, I'm surprised your father missed them." She glanced at the chart again, "But really, given her relatively young age, it's possible he just didn't put it together."

"Why is her eye bandaged?"

"She fell." The nurse glanced at the chart again. "Yes, it seems she fell and hit her face on the corner of a countertop." I must have looked confused. "Oh, this was at home, when she had the stroke.

The eye was badly damaged. Your father found her when he returned from work and saw what must have happened."

"Will the eye get better, or will she need the patch forever?" Why this concerned me I had no idea. "And is this how she'll be for the rest of her life? Just vacant?"

"To answer your second question first, yes, this is the condition she will remain in for the rest of her life. The eye should heal. Your father has been diligent in examining it every few days. What a devoted man. He must feel awful about what happened."

"*He's* examining her? Aren't there other doctors here?"

"Well, yes. It is rather unorthodox, but your father has requested he be able to look in on her. I understand he and our chief physician, Dr. Shultz, are friends. Or at the very least, they know of each other. Dr. Shultz gave his permission and informed the staff to assist your father in any way we can."

Eichen sighed and looked at Valeria. "I visited her each day for about a month. I took a semester off from school, very much against the Doctor's wishes. The woman who had saved me, nurtured me, and loved me, was gone and an empty shell remained. It was soul-crushing. My visits became less frequent, I returned to college and eventually graduated, barely. My life, such as it is, went on. On my last visit she appeared completely unchanged. Other than the gray hair, it seemed as though she was not aging, simply remaining frozen in time." He slowly pushed back his chair and delicately stood up. "Seeing her reminded me again, as if I needed reminding, of how much I hated the Doctor." He turned, needing to grip the chair for balance. "I am finished talking. Whoever killed him, I would like to shake their hand. He deserved it. Now, would it be possible for the charming Officer Reyes to drive me home? I am tired, and I think, rather drunk."

Clarke nodded to her. "This way, Mr. Eichen." Valeria ushered him out of the room. They were silent until they heard the back door of the station close.

"Wow."

"I would have to agree, Kevin."

"The doc is a Nazi and part of this Fount of Life thing."

"Lebensborn, yes."

"He never wanted Rolf as a son to begin with. And the woman who pretty much raised him as a son his whole life ended up a vegetable, then died."

"Yes."

"With the Nazi thing and the Lebens-thing, you'd have to say the son had a pretty decent motive for killing the guy."

"I would agree, but if everyone who had a problem with a parent killed them, we'd—"

"Oh, come on, Captain! A Nazi! One who sort of indirectly stole his original family. Isn't that pretty strong motive?"

"Yes, but we need more, you know that. Something to tie him directly to the murder weapon. A witness, stronger motive, something."

"Yeah." He sat glumly, thumbing graffiti carved into the tabletop. "You think Val's going to be alright with him? I mean, it's not just a couple steps out on the sidewalk. It's transporting our only suspect. Alone. She might not be up to it."

Clarke slowly stood and straightened his back. He could feel his vertebrae crackling. Jesus, this aging stuff is for the birds. It was only about nine-thirty, but he felt he'd been at it all night. He pulled his sweaty shirt from the small of his back. Ah well, he thought, it's all about pacing yourself. He might not have youth on his side anymore, but hopefully he had wisdom. Time to impart some. "Let's go back to my office, Kevin. The fan's there."

"Mind if I grab a soda first?"

"Go for it. If there's anything in the fridge other than that stuff you drink, grab one for me. Got to get the taste of that krupnik out of my mouth." He lumbered to his office and sat in the much more comfortable desk chair. The oscillating fan was heaven. He pondered the best way to approach the upcoming conversation with Kevin.

"Okay," Kevin said, as he entered the room. "Got a ginger ale for you." Clarke was pleasantly surprised; he hadn't expected much of anything. "And a Dew for me."

Yea, Gods, Clarke thought, how the hell this kid's insides aren't rotted out is a mystery. He took a gulp of the ginger ale, belched, and leaned back in his chair.

"We need to talk, Kevin. We need to talk about your problem with Valeria."

"There's no problem, Captain. I just worry about her competency, that's all."

"Her competency."

"Yeah." He took a guarded sip of soda.

"And you've seen what exactly to merit your concern about her competency?"

"Well, nothing...yet."

"Yet. Tell me, what are you expecting to see?"

"Come on, Captain, you know what I'm talking about here. Why are you making me say it?"

"Because I want to hear it. Let's go, officer, I'm losing patience."

Kevin squirmed in his chair. He hesitated, then sighed. "Okay. She's a girl. She's got no place here. This can be a dangerous job. I mean, look at earlier this summer. People can get hurt or killed. She might not be up to keeping the peace and protecting the public. Not only that, but being female, she might get hurt herself. It's just not right. That's how I feel." He gulped some soda, placed the can on Clarke's desk, and waited for a response.

"So, you're saying she might not be able to protect the public."

Kevin nodded. Clarke pulled a manilla folder from a desk drawer. "This is Officer Reyes' personnel file. It was sent to me from Newark when I was searching for a new officer. I will share one or two bits of information with you, none of which I believe to be personal. I want you to get a more rounded view of her than you seem to be capable of."

"I've got nothing against Val. I'm sure she—"

"Stop. Her name is Valeria. Unless I missed something, I don't recall her okaying a nickname."

"It's hardly a nick—"

"Did she say to you, 'You can call me Val?'"

"Well, no."

"Kevin, have enough respect for her to at least address her by her proper name. It's not up to you to decide what to call her. Alright?"

He sighed. "Okay, Captain."

"You're concerned about her not being able to take care of herself. And that's because of her gender, right?"

"Right. They don't have the upper body strength that men do. They could get hurt, or be disarmed, who knows what. Girls don't—"

"Women."

"What?"

"You were about to say girls can't do something simply because of what they are. But we are not discussing girls, we're discussing women. A woman is an adult, a girl is a child. Officer Reyes is an adult; therefore, she is a woman, *not* a girl."

"Okay," Kevin muttered.

"You may think I'm being picky, Kevin, but if you can't even properly address the topic of the conversation, we're not going to get anywhere. Valeria Reyes is her name, not Val. She is a woman, not a girl. Okay?"

"Okay."

"Now, you're worried about her physically being able to handle the job."

"Right. Yes." Kevin said. Relieved it seemed they were moving on from terminology.

Clarke opened the folder and glanced at a page. "It may surprise you to know that Valeria is a boxer."

"What! A girl boxer? No way."

Give me patience, Lord. "No, Kevin. A woman boxer, one who seems to be pretty darn good at it, too. Captain Clements from Newark filled me in. They have a good-sized gym at the department and there's a boxing ring. Apparently, Officer Reyes has yet to lose an exhibition."

"She boxes? Wow. But did she just fight other gir—ah, women? Or did she fight real fighters?"

"I'm sure whoever she fought was 'real' and not a fabrication, but that has little to do with it. The file states several of the male fighters on Newark's force were very impressed with her skills. She often trained with them."

"I bet the guys' wives or girlfriends loved that."

Clarke sighed. True. Nothing new is ever easy, he thought. "The point is, she can take care of herself. Very well."

Kevin took a thoughtful swig from his soda before placing the empty can on the desk. "Okay. But will others respect her? That's a big question."

"Yes, it is. I'm sure there will be people in Pendale who will not. But I have no reason to believe she will not hold herself to a high standard. Probably higher than you or me, because she knows to be respected, she must be just as good, if not better, than her male peers."

"I hear what you're saying, Captain, she's got to be really good for people to accept her because they're already expecting her to fail. Got that. But there are reasons for these expectations. Women just don't work in jobs like ours, they aren't made for it."

"Some people will believe that, but *you* don't have to be one of those people, Kevin. That's what this conversation is about. I want you to judge her on her merits, what you actually see in front of you, not your preconceived beliefs."

"Okay. I promise I'll try, Captain."

"That's all I can ask."

"But then there's...you know."

Here we go, Clarke thought. The heart of the matter. He waited.

"Come on, you know." Silence.

"I suppose you better enlighten me, Kevin."

After another moment he said, almost whispering, "She's not white. She's a PR."

"That's right, Kevin, she is. And you're Polish, Irish, and probably at least some Scottish with that last name of yours. I'm Irish, as is Sully. Mrs. Barton on the switchboard is Hungarian, I think she told me once. What's the point?"

"The point is a lot of people think way too many Puerto Ricans have moved into town. They feel they're taking over. And now there's one on the force. Folks already think we're cutting them too much slack, giving them breaks they don't deserve. And now, well...."

"Well?"

"Putting them in control. Giving them power. A gun."

"Do you believe that's the case? Have you seen Officer Reyes acting in a way she shouldn't?"

"Well, no, but I'm not with her all the time. Who knows what she might be up to when she's out on her own."

"Kevin, this has got to stop," Clarke said quietly. "You are a better man than this. I know. I've seen it. I realize you're going through a rough patch, but it's no reason to revert to those prejudices you've grown up with. You're just parroting racist nonsense you've probably heard most of your life. The truth is you have seen nothing, *nothing* to lead you to believe Officer Reyes is incapable of doing a stellar job. Nothing related to gender, or race. Am I right?"

Kevin squirmed a bit before answering, "Well, yeah."

"I hadn't planned to share this with anyone, but Rosaria Donez was a cousin of Valeria's. They were relatively close. Part of the reason she wanted to join this force is because she was impressed with how we handled that investigation. And you were a very large part of that. She felt we treated the case like any other and it did not matter that the victim was Puerto Rican, or the killer was white. We saw beyond that and did the job right. You did, Kevin. Please don't go backsliding on me here. This force needs you to be the best you can be. I need that, too."

Kevin exhaled and ran his finger through a scar on the table in front of him. After a moment he looked up at Clarke. "I promise I'll try, Captain. I can't do more than that. Can I?"

"No, you can't." Clarke had absolutely no idea if anything he'd said had made an impression. "Okay. It's late. Why don't you head home? I'll wait for Valeria. We'll meet tomorrow first thing and discuss what we learned from Eichen tonight."

Kevin headed toward the door. "Got it. See you later, Captain."

THIRTY-THREE

At eight o'clock the next morning, Captain Clarke and Officers MacDougall, Sullivan, and Reyes were back in the interrogation room. Clarke had picked up a box of Starlite Bakery donuts and Sully was reaching for his second. Clarke dragged the box a few inches closer to himself.

"Anybody want some coffee? I made it first thing this morning," Kevin said.

"I'll take a cup," Clarke said. "Sully?"

The big man shook his head and said through a mouthful of donut, "Nope. I'm good."

"I'll get it," Valeria said, rising. She poured and placed the mugs for Clarke and MacDougall in front of them and then poured one for herself.

Kevin said, "I thought you drank tea."

She shrugged, "Expanding my horizons."

Kevin reached for the sugar and powdered creamer that must have been hiding behind the donut box. She watched him dump enough of each into the mug until the level of the coffee had risen to the brim. He pushed the sugar toward her. Valeria shook her head. "Creamer?" Another shake. "Wow. You take yours like the captain. I've got a wicked sweet tooth."

"Your tastes may change, Valeria, once you drink some," Clarke said.

"Thanks a lot, Captain," said Kevin. "But yeah, I guess it can be strong. Or weak. I don't know, I never seem to be able to nail it." He nodded to Valeria. "Maybe you can make it better." He hesitated, then rushed on, "I mean because I'm so bad at it, not because you should be doing stuff in the kitchen because you're, you know, a girl. Woman! A woman." His face began to color. "And it's not really even a kitchen. It's got a fridge, that's it. And a couple counters and cabinets. And a coffeemaker, of course. I mean that's what we're talking about, you making coffee." His face was getting redder as he struggled. "Or *not* making it. That's good, too. Whatever you want. We're not expecting you to do it, but you can. If you want."

"Okay, Kevin." Valeria smiled and took a sip before gently setting her mug down. "I'll give it a try tomorrow. Definitely."

He nodded, looking from her to Clarke and back again.

"Okay," said Clarke. "Let's review. And I have some new information to share. Sully, listen up and take notes seeing as how you were absent last night."

Sully nodded and reached to his breast pocket. His face froze as he pulled out a nub of pencil, but no pad. Valeria tore off a couple pages from hers and quietly slid them across the table. He mouthed, 'thanks'.

"It seems the Doctor was not Polish, as I believe everybody here was led to believe," Clarke began. "From what I understand, it was assumed, and I'm sure reiterated by the Doctor, that he was a Polish refugee fleeing from the Nazis. I don't believe he ever claimed to be Jewish, but I think most of the local citizenry assumed he was being targeted for his ethnicity or religion back in Europe."

Clarke reached for his coffee, changed his mind, and continued. "He arrives in Pendale. Why here? Who knows. He is embraced and welcomed. He has a beautiful young wife, a small boy, and quickly becomes an important, if not exactly loved, member of the community."

"How'd he get away with it?" asked Sully, wiping his mouth with his hand. "He's German, not Polish. Didn't he sound German when he talked? Thinking about it now, I know he sounded German to me. Why didn't I notice it? Why didn't anyone pick up on it?"

"He claimed to be from what is now Gdansk and what used to be called, when the Germans controlled the territory, Danzig. That region has been a German/Polish mix for years, centuries maybe. I'm sure a resident there would speak a dialect that sounded like a mix of the two languages."

"Captain," asked Valeria, "why didn't anyone question his background when he first arrived? Surely there were protocols regarding immigrants."

"It was well before my time here, but I have a theory."

"Shoot, Captain," said Kevin.

"My guess would be he had assistance from people here that were sympathetic to his cause."

"Wait, you mean there were townspeople who knew what he really was and snuck him into the country anyway? Are you saying these townspeople were German, too?"

"There *are* Germans in Pendale. Not many, but some. Just because they have German ancestry doesn't mean they are supportive of the Nazis. But I'm not referring to them."

All three of the young officers looked perplexed.

Sully asked, "What else could it be? It's not like regular Americans were going to sneak in a Nazi undercover."

"Does the date February 20th 1939 resonate with any of you? You don't remember it from history class at Pendale High, Kevin?" Silence. "I know none of you had been born yet, but does it ring any bells at all? No? Well, don't feel bad. Most people wouldn't recognize it. The war was going on in Europe. Here in the States we knew it was not looking good for the Allies, but we had yet to join. Not until—"

"Pearl Harbor, 1941," Kevin piped up.

"That's right. The Germans hadn't invaded Poland yet, that was coming later in the year. We knew what was happening in Europe, but since it had no direct impact on us…, well, out of sight, out of mind." Clarke paused. Ah, the dramatic effect.

"February 20th 1939 was the night of the Pro-American Rally at Madison Square Garden."

That poster, Valeria thought. In the attic.

"Well, okay," Kevin began, "what's the big—"

"Except it wasn't."

"Wasn't what, Captain?" said Valeria.

"It wasn't actually a pro-American rally. It was called that by those who sponsored it, but it wasn't that at all. It was a celebration of the rise of Naziism in Europe." Silence. "Yes. Those in attendance, primarily Americans, were there to celebrate what Hitler was doing in Europe."

Kevin looked disbelieving, Valeria, pensive, Sully stopped chewing for a moment.

"No way, Captain, uh-uh, I don't believe it. No way Americans would celebrate what the Germans were doing," he said.

"Well, the entire story hadn't yet unfolded in Europe, but it was pretty obvious Hitler's intention was to grab all he could, using whatever means necessary."

"Yeah! It was obvious. So how can you expect us to believe that Americans would…condone or celebrate all this master race stuff?" Kevin said.

It was silent for a few seconds. Valeria opened her mouth, then hesitated. Clarke spoke quietly. "Kevin. Remember two months ago. The first murder, Rosaria Donez. How did the citizens of Pendale react to this terrible crime? Patriotic Americans, each and every one. Remember? No outrage, no fury, not in the white population, anyway. Her tragic death was just...accepted. And in some circles, I imagine, quietly celebrated. All because she was different from most of the population, thus making her death less worthy of the fury or outrage that would have been felt if she was white. So, is it really that great a leap for people to accept, and perhaps celebrate, those who believe one race is superior to another? I can think of one or two locals who might fit the bill. What about it? Sully? Kevin?"

Sully shook his head. Kevin sat staring at the scarred tabletop, his face and neck becoming redder and redder. "Yeah," he mumbled. "Excuse me a minute." He stumbled out of the room. Valeria looked after him, concerned.

Hell, thought Clarke. This lesson most definitely was *not* supposed to go like that. So much for a big teaching moment. "Let's take ten, folks. Get some air, have a drink, definitely *not* this coffee, maybe something to eat. That is if Sully leaves us anything." He forced a smile at the two remaining young officers. Sully leaned forward and peered into the box. "There are a couple left. I don't like the cream-filled."

Clarke laughed. "Thank God for that!"

Valeria made a quick reach for one of the remaining donuts. "I love the cream-filled," she said to Sully before she left, munching.

Valeria chewed as she headed toward the squad room. I'm going to have to be careful working in this place, she thought. Donuts, krupnik, who knows what else these guys may be ingesting. Gotta put in extra ab work at the gym.

She looked around, the room was empty. Through the window she saw Kevin standing out on the sidewalk, hands in his pockets, eyes closed, his head tipped back as if to soak up the sun. That boy better watch it with that skin of his, he'll be looking like a radish in no time. She watched him for a minute, trying to decide exactly what to do. She jammed the last piece of donut in her mouth, brushed her hands on her pants, and pushed open the front door.

When the door thumped close behind her, Kevin did not move. Still chewing, she sidled up next to him, looked upward and closed her eyes as well. After a moment she said, "You guys usually eat and drink so well here?"

"What?" He sounded surprised and looked at her. "Oh, no, not usually. Well, we *do* have donuts a lot. Sully could live on them and even though the captain complains about how much Sully seems focused on them, he likes them, too." Kevin smiled. "He's always moaning about his waistline, but he's usually the one buying them."

"And krupnik during interrogations?"

"*That* was definitely a first."

"I figured."

There was a moment of silence before Kevin spoke. "Hey...Valeria, I need to say something." She nodded. "First, I'm sorry if I sounded like a dope with that coffee thing. Here's the one hundred percent truth. Yeah, I figured you might make the coffee. Yeah, it's because you're a gir—, because you're a woman. It was wrong of me; my mind just went there. I suppose I was raised where that's how things go. Woman in the kitchen, you know. I'll really try not to be that way."

Valeria nodded. "Okay, thanks Kev—"

He rushed on, "But I know I'll probably still mess it up. The captain is constantly hounding me to think before I talk. You know, think how people might feel. I'm trying, but it's a slow go."

"Thank you, I appreciate you telling me this." After a pause she added, "I know that how we were raised, what we were led to believe when we were young, really follows us into adulthood. For better or worse." She reached toward her chest, then dropped her hand. "So, Captain Clarke serves as a mentor as well as being a superior officer?"

"Oh, yeah. When I heard the door close just now, I thought it was him. I thought I was going to get another one of his teaching moments. I'm glad it wasn't him. I'm glad I got to apologize to you about the coffee thing."

"I owe you an apology, too. I hate tea. I just said I drank it because I was aggravated about the coffee expectations." She smiled. "I really, really hate tea."

"Ha! Me, too. But my coffee is pretty bad, there's no getting around it."

"We are in complete agreement on that, Officer MacDougall."

"Val—hey, do you prefer Valeria, or Val?"

"The only people who call me Val are family members and people I hope to never see again. So, it's Valeria."

"Okay, got it. Um, if you stay here in Pendale, and there's no reason to think you couldn't, unless you decided not to, of course. I mean, you'll do what you choose, just like anyone else. It's your right." Kevin's face started to redden. "Some people might give you a hard time, the woman thing, being a P..., being um, a minority in a mainly white town. But you seem tough enough, I mean strong enough, no girl wants to be called tough. Do they? Woman! No woman does...unless they want to! Because they, you, anyone, should be able to want and be and do whatever they choose, tough, not tough, whatever." MacDougall exhaled. "This is what I mean about not getting it right. Not at first anyway. Sorry."

"It's fine. It looked like you came out here to do some deep thinking. Anything I can help with?"

"Huh? Oh. Yeah. The big case we dealt with a couple months ago, when Rosaria Donez was killed. Oh, I know she was a cousin of yours, I'm sorry for your loss. The killer was a friend of my family. Someone I've known my whole life. I'm having trouble with that.

It makes me wonder just what kind of environment I grew up in. What does it make me? Why do I think like I do? Is there a whole other way of thinking I have no idea about?"

"I'm not sure what to say."

"You don't have to say anything but know when I say something or act in a certain way, I'm trying to get it right. I really am. It's just the past really doesn't want to let go."

"Oh, boy. That's the truest thing I've heard you say." Valeria paused once more. "Okay, here we go." Kevin looked at her expectantly. "If I stay in Pendale, you and I will learn about each other. You'll probably hear why I left Newark and transferred here. You're right about the past. It hangs on like a lion. I'm trying to escape my lion, but it's powerful, real powerful. I hope you'll give me the benefit of the doubt when some facts come to light. Because I think I may want to stay here. I didn't think that a couple days ago, but I do now. I have family here. I have distance from my past—to a degree. I have a job with coworkers I think I can learn to trust, and hopefully like." She looked up and down Broadway. "It's not heaven, but it might just end up being home."

"Well, I hope you stay. It's definitely strange having you here, but we could use a girl like you on the force. Ugh! Woman! We could use a woman! Jeez!"

"You just keep trying, *boy*. Come on, let's go in before Sully and the Captain empty that donut box."

They were too late. The box was jammed in the trash can. Sully was chewing while trying to brush away the powdered sugar from his shirt. There was a plain cake-style donut on a napkin in front of Clarke. He must have hidden it away. Despite his words earlier, it looked like he'd poured another mug of coffee and was readying to dunk his donut.

Kevin and Valeria shot each other a look and smiled.

"What's up guys?" Sully asked. "You both look guilty as hell about something."

Kevin grinned. "Mind your own business."

"You missed a spot." She pointed to his shirt.

"Oh, thanks," Sully said. His previous remark forgotten.

"Okay, lady and gentlemen, let's pool our resources and see what magic we can create," Clarke said. "By the way, early this morning I was in touch with colleagues in the New York Office. It seems that Steven Smith, previously, Stephan Schmidt, died two years ago. So, one individual we know was in contact with the Doctor is off the table. Incidentally, the reason we know about him is because he was part of the German American Bundt and one of the organizers of the Pro-American rally in '39. That's why he was on the radar of the city cops. Who knows, he may have given the doc that poster in his attic as a gift. That leaves us with exactly one suspect, Rolf Eichen, son of the deceased."

"But not his biological son. His son by adoption," Sully said.

"His son by theft," Kevin muttered.

"True, but as far as the law in this country is concerned, Rolf is legally, if not biologically, the son of Jan and Ingrid Eichen."

"I feel terrible for him. Abused his whole life by the man supposed to be his father, dreaming of a previous life, and thinking he's crazy for doing so. The poor, poor man," Valeria said.

"I agree, but did those circumstances lead him to murder? That's what we need to focus on, not how bad his life has been, but whether he killed because of it."

Kevin said, "Yeah, but Captain, where will we get the proof we need? All we've got is what he told us. Do you really think he's going to put his own head in a noose? We can get him drunk on croop...."

"Krupnik."

"Thanks, Valeria. Krupnik. But then, is anything we get from him admissible? I know last night you seemed to have had a pretty good idea of what he was saying, or even about to say, you know, about the leeb, leeb," Kevin sighed and looked to Valeria.

"Lebensraum and Lebensborn."

"Yeah." Kevin finished.

"That's about it as far as my Nazi repopulation knowledge goes. So yes, you have a valid point, where else can we look for more information? We can get a German translator to pour over the information from the file cabinet in the bedroom office. We already have the names of some members of the Bundt," he referred to the pad in front of him, "our friends who sponsored that rally in Madison Square Garden and who may have also assisted him in entering the country, but there's nothing at all that points to why he received an ice pick in the eye."

"It's such a specific manner to kill someone," Valeria mused. "Why not just whack him on the head?"

"Or shoot him," added Kevin.

"Or cut the bastard's throat." They all stopped and looked at Sully, the generally gentle giant.

"That's how I feel. He deserved the worst he could get. The icepick was too merciful. That's my opinion anyway."

"Let's reel it back in folks. I agree, the Doctor was a terrible human being, but we still need to find who killed him. There is, after all, a murderer presently on the loose."

"I'd like to buy him a beer," Sully mumbled.

Clarke ignored him. "Where else can we look? Our trouble is the time element. His days as a Nazi officer were over a quarter century ago. Did someone know about them and just waited before dealing out retribution?"

"Revenge is a dish best served cold," Valeria said.

"Whoa," Sully said under his breath. "That's deep."

Valeria blushed.

"I see your point, officer, but twenty-five years is a long time. My feeling is it's got to be something more current. Maybe connected to his Nazi days, but more up to date."

The three sat thinking. Clarke sipped his coffee and grimaced.

"Captain," Valeria said slowly. "We're focusing on the son, Rolf, because he's really all we have, right?" Clarke nodded. "But Rolf was living in the dark, regarding his past anyway, until he learned about it after his mother's stroke." Kevin and Sully nodded. "And he obtained that information where?"

"His mom's diaries!" Kevin said. "Why didn't I think of that?" he asked Clarke.

Clarke said, "Let's get a warrant to seize those diaries. I'd say we have grounds for suspicion. Judge Farrell is usually amenable. I'll reach out to him. There seems to be a lot of hate built up in the younger Eichen. Pray he hasn't destroyed them."

"No way, Captain," Valeria said. "They're all he has left of the only person in his life that showed him love."

"Let's hope you're right. We'll break for an hour. I should have an answer from Farrell by then."

THIRTY-FOUR

Two hours later, they had the diaries in their possession.

Eichen was furious. "These are all I have of my mother! How dare you do this!"

Kevin and Valeria had executed the warrant. "We will not do anything to desecrate the memory of your mother," Valeria said. "These will be examined and if found to be inconsequential to the case, returned." She stood in the living room of the modest home while MacDougall carried in an armload of diaries from another room.

Eichen looked at her in disbelief. It was a look she had received before, from both whites and Puerto Ricans. Near-astonishment she could be capable of such actions. Whites not believing she should be trusted enough to be a cop, her own people believing she was betraying them by becoming one. And now, Eichen's disbelief that she was carrying through with these thuggish actions despite being an oppressed member of society.

"Ah, you!" He waved her away. "I believed you were better!" He watched MacDougall place the diaries in a cardboard box whose side advertised fresh-picked strawberries. "Don't you damage those!"

"No, sir," said Kevin. He scrawled a quick receipt for the diaries and carried the box out while Valeria stood near Eichen, her eyes forward.

"Get out, Officer Reyes!" Eichen shouted in her face. "You're as bad as them. No! You're worse. Because you should know better."

"I'm sorry, sir."

"You're much, much worse!"

She slid into the passenger's seat, removed her cap, and wiped the sweat from her forehead. "Let's roll."

"You okay?"

Looking straight ahead she nodded. "Yup."

They had procured the services of an adjunct professor at Middlesex College to translate the diaries from German. She was just arriving as they entered the station with the box. A petite strawberry blonde woman stood inside the front door, holding a small case and looking excitedly around the squad room.

"Professor Pinkton?" Clarke crossed to her.

"Yes. Please, call me Alice." She held out her hand. "I understand you have some work for me." She wore an eager-to-please smile.

"We do." He shook her hand. "Please sit down for a moment." He gestured to an empty desk in. "We'd like for you to translate personal journals, some diaries. We have no idea what information you may find, however we may have to use some of it in a criminal investigation. So, whatever's there is strictly confidential. We will ask you to sign a document stating your understanding of this and that you'll be breaking a law if you disclose any of what you find."

"I understand, Captain."

Clarke smiled. "I apologize if I am being redundant. You've done similar work before?"

"No. This is my first time translating for the police. It's rather exciting." She smiled eagerly and looked around the squad room. "Wow. This is sort of the nerve center, huh? Will I be working out here?" She glanced around, soaking up the details.

"Um, no. We'd like to give you a bit more privacy. This way, please." He showed her to the coffee room. "It's not much, but it's marginally more private than the squad room."

"My." She took in the small room. "Yes, it's private." She looked at a spill of powdered creamer on the table from earlier in the day.

Clarke leaned forward and blew the powder away, then gestured for her to sit. "Do you need a pad or writing utensil?" She shook her head and nodded to her bag. "Maybe something to drink?"

"No, Captain," she answered, still scanning the room. "I think I'll be fine."

"Good. I'll get that non-disclosure form. The diaries have arrived. I'll have them brought into you."

He waved in Kevin. "Officer MacDougall will get them for you. We have no idea how or even if they are organized. Any assistance in that area would be appreciated, as well." She nodded. "I'll leave you to it." She smiled and again, nodded.

"How did it go?" Clarke asked Kevin when he entered the office.

"About as well as can be expected, I guess. He didn't want to part with his mom's belongings, and he let us know it. I collected the diaries and carried them out, Valeria dealt with him. She caught most of the blowback."

Clarke nodded. "Where is she?"

"She wanted to splash some water on her face. She'll be right out." Kevin hesitated, "It was a tough situation, but she was real professional, and understanding, as well. She showed, um—"

"Empathy."

"That's it! I always get it mixed up with sympathy. Anyway, she showed it. I'm starting to think having her on the force is a good idea. Sort of a woman's touch, you know? Good in situations like this one."

"Maybe, but you'll be dealing with your share of similar moments. Valeria's not here to carry that burden."

"No, I get it. I just wanted to say she was good."

"Thanks, Kevin. I'm glad to hear it. I'll speak with you after our translator makes some headway."

"Got it. Later, Captain." The bathroom door thudded.

"Officer Reyes, may I speak with you? My office, please."

Valeria peeked in at the translator as she passed the room. She entered Clarke's office. "Yes, sir?"

He gestured her to a chair. "Are you alright? Kevin mentioned that Eichen targeted most of his wrath at you."

"I guess you could say that. He was upset. I think it's a natural reaction, I'd be the same way."

"Kevin also said you were very empathetic."

"He said that?"

"Maybe not word for word."

She laughed. "Well, it was still nice of him."

"Kevin aside, it's no fun being on the receiving end of someone's anger. If you feel the need to speak about it, I hope you won't hesitate to do so."

"I understand, thanks. I lost a brother a few years ago and I think if I was asked to part with any of the few tangible items of his I have, I'd come out fighting, too."

"Yes. I know that must have been a very traumatic time for you and your family. I'm very sorry." She looked at him, surprised. "Personnel file," he said. She nodded.

"I think Officer MacDougall is close to being in your corner, if he's not already there."

"Yes sir, we had a discussion earlier and reached an understanding. I think we'll be fine. I hope so, anyway." She never would have believed she might have anything in common with the guy.

"Okay. That's it for the moment. Keep your fingers crossed we find something of value in those diaries."

Several hours later, Professor Pinkton entered the squad room. "Hello? Hello?"

Valeria was at her desk trying to unstick her typewriter keys, her hands gripping the roller.

"Yes? May I help you, Professor...?"

"Pinkton." She crossed to Valeria and stuck out her hand. "But please, it's Alice."

"Yes?" Valeria nodded to her inked hands on the typewriter.

"Oh. Um, I have a question or two." She glanced around the room, licked her lips, and leaned forward. "These diaries are connected to that murder, aren't they? The doctor?" Valeria was silent. "I thought he was Polish, not German. That's what the papers said, Polish. But it looks like they got it wrong, like they always do. And not just German, but a 'Nazi,'" she stage-whispered the word, her eyes gleaming. She looked around the vacant squad room, then dragged a chair over and sat, poised, hands clasped in her lap, leaning slightly forward, ready to dish. "I'm only into diary number three, but I can barely pull myself away. Oh, what an awful man! It almost makes me glad he was killed. The papers didn't say exactly what happened...." She waited, got nothing, then gushed on. "Was it violent? Of course it was! It was murder! Duh! Silly Alice! Was he shot? Oh, just listen to me go on, I'm just a Curious George, I guess."

"One moment, Professor."

"Oh, Alice. Please."

Valeria left the squad room and stuck her head in Clarke's office. "Captain, do we have a signed non-disclosure form from our translator?"

"Right here." He grabbed a paper off the top of a stack and waved it. "Why?"

"No reason. Thank you."

"Professor, let's go back to the coffee room." Valeria led the way. Once the translator entered Valeria gestured to a chair and pushed closed the door behind them with her foot.

The woman sat. "Professor—"

"Really, I prefer Alice."

"Professor." Valeria stood gazing down at the woman. Valeria was expressionless, her voice was matter of fact. "Prior to beginning this translation, you were asked to sign a non-disclosure agreement, correct?"

"Oh, sure, I told your captain—"

"I won't insult you by asking if you understood the agreement, you're a college professor after all. Of course, you understood." The professor nodded. "You realize that any information you come across may be used in a police investigation and it is imperative that this information remains confidential. Which brings me to this question, Professor—"

"Al—"

"Professor. Why are you trying to—"

There was a knock on the door.

"Occupied!" Valeria yelled over her shoulder.

From the other side of the door came a hesitant, "Occupied? What?" She heard MacDougall and Sully speaking quietly to each other. One whispered, "The kitchen's never been occupied." The other whispered back, "Maybe you should try again." But the conversation died away.

Valeria placed both fists on the table and leaned over the woman. "Why are you trying to elicit information pertaining to this investigation?"

"What? Oh, no, I'm really just—"

"What you need to do, Professor, is—"

"I prefer—"

Valeria held up an inked finger to silence her. The woman gulped.

"What you need to do *Professor*, is translate to the very best of your professional abilities, remember what you signed, and never, ever tell anyone what you read in those diaries. It doesn't matter that you're a Curious George. George's monkey ass can get slammed in a cell just easily as anyone else's."

Pinkton stammered, "Why don't I just leave? I think maybe—"

"Stay still," Valeria commanded. "I'll tell you why you won't leave. Because that will lead us to ask ourselves the reason for your departure. Why wouldn't she continue assisting us? Is the reason in any way connected to the diaries? Whatever could it be she saw there? It would certainly look suspicious to us."

Alice's eyes widened. "No! You can't, I mean, that's—"

"I think the best way to handle this is for you to deliver an accurate and cohesive translation, with you adhering to the rules of the document you signed. It'll be a win-win. You get paid, we get information that may help us, and nobody outside of our little circle ever learns of the diaries' contents. Sound good, Professor?"

"Alice," she said sadly, in almost a whisper.

Valeria smiled for the first time since entering the room. "Fine, Alice. Can I get you anything? A Coke, a bite to eat, anything?"

"No, I think I'd better get back to work."

Valeria nodded. "Sounds good to me."

Valeria left the door open as she headed back to the squad room, leaving two inky smudges on the table in front of Alice where her fists had been.

Sully watched as she sat at her desk. He seemed to be trying to make up his mind. "Is everything okay?"

Valeria returned to trying to free her typewriter hammers. "Absolutely. Why do you ask?"

"The kitchen has never been, uh, occupied before. And you sounded sort of upset."

She looked up from the typewriter and smiled. "Not at all. Just chit chat, me and Alice. Girl talk. We love our privacy, you know."

"Oh, yeah, I get it." He wrestled with whether to ask more. "You sure sounded mad."

"Nah. Hormones. You'll get used to it."

Sully shut up.

Late the next day, Professor Alice Pinkton finished translating the last of the diaries. She presented the final tally of her hours and scurried out of the building, never to be seen again.

"Nice lady," Clarke said after she left. He looked at the stack of diaries. "Hard worker."

"Absolutely," said Valeria.

As she had completed each diary entry, Alice produced the word for word translation, written in impeccable cursive on yellow legal pads. And at the conclusion of each, she had written a concise synopsis.

After about an hour's reading, Clarke tossed the pad aside. He slid his reading glasses off and rubbed the bridge of his nose. He stared down at the translation on his desk and sighed. He now had sufficient grounds to arrest Rolf Eichen on the suspicion of murdering his father.

THIRTY-FIVE

C larke looked at the synopsis of the first of Ingrid's diaries. It began in 1940, shortly after the two were married and her husband had become a member of the SS. The newly-wed wife was in awe of this handsome doctor who seemed to travel in such lofty circles. Once, while accompanying the Doctor to a social gathering, she had even met Heinrich Himmler! Later when she expressed her astonishment at this, her husband was dismissive. A stupid chicken farmer, he'd said. The man did, however, have the ear of the Führer, so it was wise to humor him.

Sticking with the synopses, Clarke read on.

After seemingly endless postings about Germany, they'd finally settled in Danzig. It was a far cry from Berlin, where she was born, but it was certainly better than some postings. Ingrid had especially disliked Frankfurt. Not the city itself, but her husband's constant regaling of his colleagues: one in particular. The most gifted man he'd ever met, he had said. He will revolutionize the medical field.

At yet another social gathering, Ingrid met this young doctor. He certainly was handsome and perhaps even as intelligent as she'd been led to believe. But Dr. Joseph Mengele had radiated condescension and scorn. His arrogance was off-putting. He had grandly taken Ingrid's hand, raised it and then circled her, gazing at her as though inspecting a prize heifer. "Yes," he'd said. "The quintessential German beauty." He lowered her hand, kissed it, and continued to gently massage the back of it with his thumb. "Johann, you are indeed a lucky man," he had said to her husband, "to plant the seed of the Reich's perpetuation in such a perfect Aryan specimen."

At last, he released her. Ingrid, mortified, remained smiling as long as she could before retreating to the ladies' room. She could not remember ever experiencing such humiliation. Part of this humiliation was based on the fact that try as they might, they had been unable to conceive a child. Rather, as her husband pointed out repeatedly, *she* had been unable to conceive one. The night of Mengele's pronouncement, Johann had gotten very drunk. Despite her repeated requests to leave, he refused. He wanted to show off the beautiful wife he possessed. Had not Mengele declared her magnificence to all present?

Clarke pushed aside the synopsis and rubbed the back of his neck. He was disgusted as well as intrigued at what he read. It was like a behind-the-scenes peek at one of the most evil chapters in history. He lumbered to the bathroom and splashed water on his face. He grabbed a handful of paper towels and rubbed it dry. He stared at his reflection in the mirror. That war had been a long time ago, but he recalled the daily reminders of the evil loose in the world and that freedom always came at a cost. Jesus, that was almost twenty-five years ago! Just who was this exhausted old guy looking back at him from the mirror? Damn! Jowls! I'm turning into Richard Nixon, he thought. God help me.

"Old man," he whispered at the mirror.

He returned to his desk, picked up another pad and read from the verbatim translation this time.

Jan dragged me out of the ladies room by the arm. He was drunk and I felt embarrassed for both of us. He led me to a group of young women. All attractive, one very much pregnant. He said her name was Lea and she worked for him at the hospital. He said theirs was a very special working relationship. I knew what he was implying. I did not think it possible, but I felt even more humiliated. He said she, not I, was the true quintessential Aryan woman, successfully performing her role in perpetuating the Reich.

I fled again to the ladies room, staying there until he barged in and dragged me to the car. We did not speak during the drive, not wanting the driver to overhear. I don't know what I would have said anyway. I was getting angrier with each passing mile.

Once home he continued to drink. He had not yet said a word. I knew he was angry, as well. I had seen it before. The drink, the silence. I knew how this would finish. My inability to conceive a child would be of no importance. He would take what he wanted, with or without my consent. I only hoped he would drink himself into uselessness.

Then I said it. I don't know why. I knew there would be consequences, but I could not help myself. I told him he looked so proud to have impregnated that bitch, but could he ever be sure the child was his? She obviously was not very discriminating when it came to choosing partners. A mistress to one could be a mistress to many.

He slowly walked to me and gently caressed my my cheek. That caress frightened me more than anything I had ever felt before. He kissed me and then punched me hard in the stomach. I fell to the carpet, unable to breathe. I thought I would die. I could get no air! I don't know how long I lay there, curled in a ball, gasping for breath. I remember him stepping over me to get another drink. He said if I ever spoke to him like that again he would carve up my body until even I would be unable to recognize it. As long as he left my face alone no one would ever be the wiser. And If anyone did see my body, certainly no one would believe a word from a self-mutilating woman, demented by her inability to bear children.

Laying there with my cheek on the hearth rug, I realized what he said was true. I was trapped.

Jesus, Clarke thought as he read. We lived with this guy in our midst for over two decades! The journals continued, into the early 40s, chronicling Rolf's "adoption" pretty much as he had described it to them. When it became apparent Germany was not going to win the war, Eichen contacted individuals already living in America and arranged an exit plan. The Bund temporarily placed him in the Washington, D.C. area. He worked in hospitals there for several years alongside doctors who would later dramatically influence his life. One doctor in particular. One on the cutting edge of new procedures in psychosurgery.

Clarke read on. Oh, my God, he thought. Oh, my God.

He dropped the translation to his desk and sat, stunned. He did not know how long he sat. He was completely blank. Finally, he felt he could read on. It was a fight to keep the tears from flowing.

Eventually, the family settled in Pendale under the guise of being a Polish family fleeing Nazi oppression. Having lived in Danzig, so close to Poland, they were familiar with the language and local dialect. It was deemed he and Ingrid spoke well enough to risk being dropped into an area with a Polish population. If there were questions about their accents, they were simply to tell the truth. They had lived in what was now Gdansk and the dialects from both sides of the border were present in their speech. And the ruse worked.

An hour later Clarke entered the squad room. Sully was on the phone; he held a takeout menu in his hand and it sounded like he was ordering a dinner to be picked up on the way home. "You might want to put a hold on that, Sully." The big man mumbled into the phone, and looking dejected, hung up. Valeria had her hands wrapped around the roller of her typewriter, looking as though she was strangling it, ink up to her wrists. "Valeria, I'll order you a new typewriter tomorrow. Maybe not brand new, but certainly better than that disaster."

"Thanks, but no, sir." A string of Spanish profanity escaped her as her hand slipped and she scraped her knuckles. "Nope, it's personal now." She gritted her teeth and nodded at the machine. "One of us is going down and I'll be damned if it's me."

He sighed and shook his head. "Where's Kevin?"

"He said he had some literature he needed to pick up," Valeria said, wiping her hands on a wad of paper towels on her desk. "I didn't know he was a big reader."

Sully said, "He likes old detective stories. You know, the guy in the trench coat, smoking a cigarette, fedora pulled low."

"Really? How about that, our own Sam Spade."

"Valeria, call Kevin—never mind, your hands are a mess. Sully, get him on the radio. Have Mrs. Barton do it if necessary. We need to talk about Mrs. Eichen's diaries. All of us."

They sat around the old table in the coffee room. Valeria was the last to arrive, coming from the bathroom after trying, unsuccessfully, to clean up. Sully looked at Valeria's blue palms and the matching patches of ink on the backs of her hands. "You're almost tattooed."

She examined her hands. "Mmm. I suppose so."

"Looks like you might be stuck with it forever," he said, grinning.

She slowly nodded. "Maybe. Hopefully not."

Kevin sat quietly, seemingly oblivious to the surroundings.

"Okay, people. I've read the translations of Mrs. Eichen's diaries. We believe we have enough to arrest Rolf Eichen on suspicion of murder." Instantly, he had a captive audience. "Not one hundred percent proof, but enough to move forward."

"What did they say, Captain?" Kevin leaned forward, now paying attention.

Clarke was gratified to see the old, eager Kevin.

"Let me start near the beginning and move chronologically.

"They begin around 1940. Johann Fiedler and Ingrid Graf are married." The three younger officers looked puzzled. "These were the real names of the Doctor and his wife. Ingrid's family lived in Berlin. They had once been wealthy, but the First World War wiped them out. To Ingrid's near-destitute family, Fiedler was considered quite a catch. Handsome, brilliant, and a rising star in the medical field. The marriage, however, could charitably be described as loveless. I'll let you read the translations in your own time. Without going into detail, I lay most of the blame at the feet of the Doctor."

"Surprise," said Valeria, under her breath.

"As he rose through the medical ranks, Fiedler and the family lived in various German cities before finally settling in Danzig. In his travels, it seems our good doctor did some work with Josef Mengele. He had not yet become the infamous character we now know." Clarke added dryly, "The Doctor and Mengele got along well."

Sully looked puzzled. Kevin whispered, "Famous doctor at the camps. Really evil." He looked at Valeria with small smile and shrugged.

"Fiedler was a member of the Nazi party and then the SS. They adopted a son through the Lebensborn program. It was very much as Rolf described it. Incidentally, at the time of the adoption, Ingrid learned the boy's original name had been Karol." There was silence for a moment.

"Not only does the poor kid lose his family, his home, the life he knew, he also loses his name. Jeez, that almost upsets me more than anything else." Sully shook his head.

"A name reflects an identity," Valeria said. "They stole that, too. They were trying to wipe the slate clean, to do with it what they chose. And except for his dreams, they were successful."

"When it looked like the Germans would lose the war, Fiedler, like many others of the master race, fled with their tails between their legs. He had contacts in this country, most notably in the German American Bund. They assisted him and his family. They were originally placed in Washington, D.C. where he became Jan Eichen and encountered another infamous figure, Dr. William Colson. In the mid-forties this man became known for his work in neurosurgery. Apparently, our Dr. Eichen was an enthusiastic follower. This is important.

"In 1948 the family moved to Pendale. Why here and why then isn't mentioned. Perhaps the proximity to New York and other contacts there, I don't know. He opened a practice, and the Doctor, wife, and son became a part of the fabric of Pendale under the guise of a Polish family fleeing Nazi oppression.

"As I said, it wasn't a loving marriage. The Doctor was both verbally and physically abusive to his wife and son. Ingrid and Rolf were extremely close. I believe they had to be, simply to survive. When Rolf left for college, Ingrid may have had some type of breakdown, I'm not sure. Her writing becomes very erratic, large blocks of pages don't make sense. It's very difficult reading and very tragic." He paused and looked at his officers. "However, what becomes obvious in the text of the diary is that Ingrid came to a decision. She was going to expose the Doctor."

"Whoa," Kevin said, "but wouldn't that be putting herself at risk, too? I mean legally?"

"More importantly, wouldn't that be putting herself at physical risk with the Doctor? You just said he was abusive; might this push him to the point of homicide?" Valeria asked. "He's a Nazi. Part of the SS. A buddy of Mengele. Please tell me she didn't inform the Doctor of her plans."

"Unfortunately, it seems she did. I can only guess that with her son away at school and having to live alone with that man, she wasn't in the best state of mind to make informed decisions. Her final entries mention her desire to reveal his identity and how she would confront him about it."

"What came next?"

"There was no next."

The three officers sat staring at each other. "But wait!" Kevin said. "She had a stroke. It wasn't fatal. She lived for years more. What did he do? You can't give someone a stroke, can you? I mean, intentionally? I don't get it."

Clarke said quietly, "The Doctor needed her silence; he could not have her speaking to anyone, correct?" They nodded. "He didn't necessarily need her dead, he needed her incommunicado. A moment ago, I said that Eichen's connection with Dr. Colson in D.C. was important." They nodded again. "Dr. William Colson is very well-known in medical circles. He's known for one procedure in particular, in the area of transorbital surgery."

The three officers looked puzzled, then Valeria's mouth dropped open. "Dios mío," she whispered. They all looked to her. "Lobotomies. Through the eye. Icepick lobotomies."

"You mean he...," Kevin could not finish. "But how?"

"Apparently, it's a simple procedure. Colson used to perform them in his office. My guess would be the Doctor caught her unaware, and with one quick thrust.... We'll never know for sure. He could then have inflicted more damage to the eye after the fact. Done something that would mirror what could have happened to her in a fall. He waits an hour, maybe two, calls for an ambulance, and by then it's over. Ingrid, for all intents and purposes, is gone. Just a shell remains. After learning of her intent to expose him, perhaps he pulled whatever strings necessary to reflect that he was Ingrid's primary doctor, thus ensuring access and control over her medical case. Maybe someone in authority at the facility where she was placed was sympathetic to the Doctor's unique world view. Again, we'll probably never know. All we know for certain is Ingrid Eichen lived for many years without ever saying a single word to anyone. As long as she remained mute and her diaries never came to light, Eichen would be safe. And he was. For a while.

"But unfortunately for the Doctor, Ingrid finally died. Rolf, after avoiding his father for years, returns to slowly sift through the many boxes, trunks, and cases that might contain memories of his mother. At some point he must have discovered her diaries and taken them. I very much doubt the Doctor knew of their existence. It had been over a decade since Ingrid had been institutionalized. The Doctor probably felt very secure.

"So, Rolf removes them, takes them home and begins the painstaking process of discovering the truth. The truth about his family, about himself, and I believe, about his mother's death. He surely had not read much German since arriving in the States twenty-some years ago. It must have been slow going for him, deciphering exactly what his beloved mother had written." Clarke looked at Kevin. "We hold very dear the words of those we love.

"What we have in Ingrid's own words, are specific reasons why Rolf might want to kill the Doctor. The lobotomy is speculation, but I don't think it's too far a leap. It's such a specific manner to kill." The four sat in silence before Clarke said, "I wonder if he was shocked by what he saw."

"I would say not, Captain." Valeria continued, "He knew the players. He had lived it all. His entire life. That horrific adoption. The 'school' where he was housed with all those other poor children. His dreams of a real mother, a real home, even a cow for goodness sake! The abuse he suffered his entire life at the hands of that man. He may not always have known about the Nazi past then, but he knew what a terrible man his adoptive father was."

"I think," Kevin slowly began, "that maybe he didn't realize it earlier because it was just too monstrous to believe. His mother, Ingrid, is pretty much dead. This one person who loved him, supported him, gone. What's left is just someone that looks like her. Can he move from the unbelievable grief he's feeling to the awful realization that his other parent is responsible? I don't know, I think it would be hard. It's too...monstrous."

"I may agree with you," Clarke said. "During the war in Germany, Jews were being rounded up and shipped away. The 'regular' German citizens were told they were being moved for safety's sake. Property was confiscated, homes were seized, but supposedly it was nothing other than simple relocation. This was believed. These citizens saw the Jews being beaten, jailed, treated like they were less-than-human, but moving from that reality to another where they are being mass-slaughtered was too far to journey. It could be explained away. Relocation. Even the stench from the camps could be explained away. Many thought, 'Of course, this awful thing you're contemplating can't be true, it simply can't. It's beyond comprehension.' Well, maybe this was beyond Rolf's comprehension. It was just too far a leap." Clarke looked again at the yellow legal pad before him.

Sully said, "So, what we're thinking here is Rolf read in his mom's diary that the doc once worked with an icepick lobotomy guy, and that his mother had been about to spill the beans about the doc's Nazi past. Rolf makes the leap, finally, that his father attacked and, what, lobotomized, his mother to silence her. Then he decides he'll kill his father the same way. Am I right? Did I miss anything?"

"No. I think you summed it up well. I don't know if there is any way to prove beyond a reasonable doubt that Rolf did this, but the manner in which the Doctor was killed, it's hard to think otherwise," Clarke answered.

"Do we go pick him up?" Valeria asked.

"No, let's wait a bit. While I would be fine with arresting and charging him, I doubt we have enough evidence to hold him for any length of time. We'll keep him under surveillance to make sure he doesn't go anywhere. And we'll get moving on the paperwork in that file cabinet. I doubt it will shed any light on Rolf and his actions, but I would love to unearth a name or two of someone who may have assisted him in relocating here."

Clarke stood, the meeting now over, "It's slow going through all those files, especially since so much of it is in German. I called Professor Pinkton and asked if we could pay for a few more hours of her services, but she declined. She said she was swamped with work. I even offered time and a half. She worked so diligently on the diaries. I sure wish the Professor was available now. It's a shame."

"Yes," said Valeria, also rising, "She was very enthusiastic." She paused then added, "Though she preferred Alice."

Clarke nodded. "True."

THIRTY-SIX

C larke pulled the squad car to the curb at 642 Feltus Street. He then killed the siren, leaving on the flashing lights. He nodded to Valeria and they exited the car, hands on their firearms. They each circled a side of the house and met in the rear. Nothing.

A neighbor alerted the station that a gunshot sounded as though it had come from the residence of Rolf Eichen. Clarke and Valeria had not spoken a word during the drive to the house. Normally Clarke would have used the occasion to quietly utter several words of procedure to any young officer who was accompanying him. He did not feel that necessity with Officer Reyes. Nor was he up for any conversation.

They slowly climbed the steps to the back porch, firearms at the ready, prepared for any danger they both knew was not present. Reaching the back door, Clarke called into the house identifying themselves. After a moment's silence he nodded to Valeria and pushed open the door to the kitchen. Neither officer doubted what had occurred, and if they did, the doubt was immediately dispelled.

Seated at the kitchen table was the body of Rolf Eichen, slumped back in his chair. On the wall behind him, above a portable dishwasher, was a dark red splatter. Valeria crouched, looked under the table, then nodded. "To his right, under the other chair."

Clarke bent and saw the small handgun. Straightening, he said, "We need to search the premises." Valeria nodded and they searched basement to attic. There was no one else in the house. Before returning to the kitchen, they walked to the car and Clarke called to request the crime scene unit and an ambulance. "No siren necessary, Mrs. Barton. Over."

"Oh, dear, that's a pity."

Clarke sighed.

"Over," she added.

Valeria stood several feet away, looking up the street, her back to him. When she turned Clarke saw her lips moving. "Did you say something, Officer?"

"No, Captain."

"Oh, I thought I saw—"

"A prayer. Spanish thing."

"I didn't know you were particularly religious."

"I'm not. It's just, this whole case, this mess, makes me so very sad. I'll take any assistance from above I can."

"Sounds like a good idea."

"I know he was a murderer," she nodded toward the house, "but my God, I can't say I wouldn't have done something similar. He killed a monster. Speaking as a human being and not a cop, I think he made the world a better place when he killed that man. And I'm so very sad he felt he had to end his own life."

"Speaking as your superior officer, I don't want to hear such an observation." Valeria looked him evenly in the eye. "But speaking as a fellow human being, I would agree with everything you said. Just please don't broadcast it." She nodded.

"Let's go examine the crime scene."

They entered at the front door and walked through the first floor to the kitchen. A closer look at the wall behind Eichen revealed bits of brain mixed with the spattered blood. On the table before him were several pieces of paper covered with different styles of handwriting. There was also a sealed envelope. On it was scrawled 'Captain Clarke.' The two officers looked at each other.

"We leave it until the crime scene people are through," Clarke said.

One of the other pieces of paper appeared to be a receipt for the diaries they had removed from the house several days earlier. Clarke recognized Kevin's's barely legible scribbles. There were other papers covered in a very feminine-looking script. Some in English, some in what they perceived to be German.

"His mother's?" Valeria asked. Clarke shrugged, but nodded.

They each circled a side of the table, and, touching nothing, took in all they could. Valeria let out a small moan. Clarke looked up quickly.

"I'm okay. It's just...look." She pointed at the floor beneath the dangling left arm of the corpse. The fingers hung a foot or so above the tile. Beneath them lay a scarf. It looked delicate, almost shear with a very subtle design.

"His mother's," Valeria said. "He must have been holding it. He wanted to have something of hers with him when he...." She shook her head, eyes tearing. "He didn't have her diaries anymore. We took them. Everything was taken from him. His real family, his childhood, his country, the woman who raised him as a son, and what he had to remember her by—the diaries. We took the final vestiges of anything positive he held from his past. We were just the last to take from him." She felt a catch in her throat she angrily tried to quell, but it became worse.

"Excuse me, Captain." Valeria turned and walked stiffly out the back door into the yard.

Clarke stared at the scarf puddled beneath Eichen's fingers. Ah, Christ, he thought. They had followed procedure and in doing so had aided in destroying an individual who had already experienced more hurt and loss than anyone could imagine.

They were supposed to do what was right. They were supposed to be the good guys. To protect and support those who needed that protection and support. But even when attempting to do this, they sometimes got it so wrong. Was Valeria right? Were they just last in the line of monsters to destroy this man's life?

He thought of the debacle at the convention in Chicago. The cops purportedly keeping the peace. He wasn't on the scene, but he sure as hell knew what he saw on TV. An army of well-armed, well-organized thugs, dressed in blue, advancing on and attacking a bunch of virtually unarmed protestors. Sure, a motley-looking group of protestors, but they didn't deserve what they appeared to get. And they were Americans, after all. They were doing what Americans had been doing since before 1776. Protesting.

If the news footage had been grainier, he swore he could have been looking at Berlin thirty years ago. When did it become acceptable to attack the weak under the guise of keeping the peace? Clarke couldn't believe it of himself, but he wondered if those war protestors and race rioters might actually have a point. Maybe the powers that be were too satiated with their power and too eager to exercise it. Simply doing so 'because they could' was a poor reason, but one that seemed to become more prevalent every day. God, he could use a drink. Even that croop-whatever stuff.

Valeria was standing in the rear of the yard, her head inclined upward, appearing to look at the branches of a small pear tree. Her back was to Clarke and he wondered if she was even aware of what she was seeing. "Officer?"

She turned. "Yes, sir. I apologize for my reaction in the kitchen. I let my emotions cloud the fact that the victim was a murderer himself. It wasn't professional and it won't happen again."

Clarke wearily shook his head. "Officer...Valeria, please don't. You're a person first, and a police officer next. Don't ever completely shut out your personal beliefs and emotions. It's sometimes necessary to temporarily shove them aside, but never lose them. They're part of what makes you who you are." He sighed and gazed into the branches Valeria had been staring at. "The truth is, we do what we believe to be best. Sometimes it works the way it should, other times, it doesn't. I've just been thinking about what we could have done differently. Truthfully though, I would have done everything the same. We needed those diaries for translation, just as we needed to have the contents of the file cabinet translated. And there was no reason yet to arrest Mr. Eichen. If we had, he probably would have been back home in twenty-four hours anyway. We needed to gather more evidence. I believe, I want to believe, even if those diaries had remained in his possession, he still would have done what he did." He turned to her. "I have to believe that."

"I believe it, too. Standing here I came to that realization. I believe he would have sat there surrounded by all those diaries, clutching that scarf, and still shot himself. He was at the end of his journey. It began in Poland, and through no fault of his own, ended here in Pendale. Most of his life had been stolen from him, but he was still capable of making choices. He chose to punish the man who had tormented him, the man who destroyed the only woman he knew truly loved him. Once that was done, it was over. Sitting in the station, telling his story, drinking all that krupnik, he struck me as someone who was tired of life. What did he have left? Really, Captain," she continued, "his life was over."

"Thank you for saying that. I'd like to believe it."

"Believe it." Valeria smiled at Clarke.

"He didn't have your strength."

Valeria's smiled slipped a bit.

"That's the difference. Rolf Eichen allowed his hellish past to dictate his present life. He *had* no present life, so he chose to end it. But you made a different choice; you chose to move onward. I won't pretend to know what you went through when you were younger, or to understand the choices you made, but you took control of your future. You used your intelligence and strength to, hopefully, make a better life both for yourself and those around you. We're fortunate to have you here."

They stood silently, both now gazing up through the branches and at the pristine blue sky. They heard a vehicle pull up in front of the house, then several car doors slamming. "Sounds like the crime scene people are here, sir."

"Yes." They walked toward the driveway together. Clarke said, a bit apologetically, "I have the tendency to be a bit pedantic. I'm afraid I sometimes sound like a boring old teacher. Kevin has probably warned you."

She shook her head. "Not a bit, sir."

That evening Clarke sat at his kitchen table. The back door and windows were open, giving a hint of cooling breeze. He'd grabbed a beer from the fridge and it sat on the table in front of him. Next to the bottle was the envelope Rolf Eichen had left for him. It had been dusted and examined and the crime scene people had turned it over to him. How long he sat he didn't know. He barely registered the soft breeze and sounds of insects bumping against his back porch light. He eventually noticed the ring of condensation around the bottom of the beer bottle had spread and was now in danger of dampening a corner of the envelope.

Better get moving or it'll be warm, he thought, and took a long swallow from the wet bottle. Not warm yet, but not exactly cold either. He wiped his wet fingers on his shirt, opened the envelope, and unfolded the note.

Captain Clarke,

I trust by now you know the facts behind the death of the Doctor. Perhaps you do not yet have enough proof to come for me but I believe eventually you will. You strike me as a very intelligent man. At some point you will find what you need, and then you will come. I will not wait for this.

I wish to thank you. For years I have wanted to tell the story of my childhood...my life. I was not searching for pity, or even understanding, I simply wished to share. I needed someone to hear, just to be aware of what happened. In the sharing came the final realization that they were not dreams, it all had indeed happened. I no longer doubt these memories, and the sharing of them and seeing your reactions leant them even more weight, more substance.

I rid the world of a monster. He killed the only person I can truly remember who had any love for me. Yes, she lived on, but she, the woman who loved and raised me, was dead. I look back on my life and see it is barren. My few actual memories are lost in a haze of fear and hate. I have taken just a single action in my life that I can honestly say had a positive impact on the world. Now it is done, there is nothing left for me.

I will soon be with my loving, Ingrid. We will walk the path beneath the fruit tree to the white farmhouse of my dreams. We will gently scratch between Janina's eyes, and we will both be embraced by the woman I know to be my mother. This is my dream.

And last. Please apologize for me to Officer Reyes. I realize in coming for Ingrid's diaries she was simply doing what she believed was necessary. In killing the monster, did I not do the same?

Speaking to you was a rare pleasure for me, Captain. I wish you a long life, full of joy.

Karol

"Ah, jeez."

Clarke slowly stood, lumbered to the back door, and stared into the night.

THIRTY-SEVEN

K evin sat cross-legged on his living room floor. The moment had finally arrived. It had cost him what he thought was a small fortune, but all of Paval's journals had been translated and he'd even sprung to have them printed and bound between some impressive-looking covers. He had before him a small stack of about ten yearbook-sized volumes. Each contained somewhere between two and three of Paval's journals.

The translator told him he had tried to be concise in the translation. If Paval had repeated himself, if there were grammatical errors, he translated them exactly as written. These were Paval's exact words.

Kevin opened the first volume and saw it titled: 17/11/34. He smiled and perused the first several pages, delving into life of 1930's Poland. It appeared the young Paval had been quite a ladies' man. And while he was never overly graphic in descriptions of his liaisons, there were enough details to make Kevin uncomfortable. He knew Paval must have had a romantic life prior to meeting his mother, but he'd never given it much thought. Now, seeing it in black and white was a bit disconcerting. He seemed especially obsessed with a girl named Ilka.

317

Kevin closed the volume and sighed. Maybe snooping into Paval's distant past wasn't the greatest idea. Not now anyway. He had enough problems dealing with his own and didn't feel his current state of mind could handle much more craziness. He reached instead for the last volume. Maybe he'd get some insight into what had been bothering his stepfather toward the end of his life. What was the problem from the past he'd mentioned, but not had the opportunity to share?

He looked toward the back of the volume, flipping pages until he found what he was looking for.

19/1/66 Have been feeling poorly. Earl in maintenance says I should see a doctor. Hate them. Ever since that drunk doctor cut off my toe in Poland. Whoa! Kevin had no idea Paval had been missing a toe. *Called doctor's office today. Will see the old Pole. Will be first time meeting him. Maybe we will have much to talk about! Getting older is tiring, but if Clara could be with me, it would be a joy.*

Damn, Kevin thought. Yeah, that would have been a joy for all of us.

21/1/66 No. I must be wrong. This can't be. This cannot be the man I think he is. He is much older, yes, but the voice. It is the same man! He is no Pole. He is a monster! I must be certain. Next week I will know. I won't let him treat me. I don't trust him. Should not have allowed the injection today he said would loosen my chest. But I wasn't sure yet. I am now.

Jesus. Did Paval recognize the doc for what he really was? After so many years? Had they known each other in Poland? Is it possible? Why not? They had both lived in Gdansk or Danzig or whatever it was called at the time. What injection?

26/1/66 It is him. The monster in the black car. The one being driven like a lord to and from the hospital. The man who killed my brother. Filip rushed to the hospital. Doctor treated him like an experiment. What did the nurse whisper? She said he waited to see how long one could live with a burst appendix before it was fatal. My poor little Filip. Why is this man here? How is this possible? Why does no one see him for what he is? How did I not see him? Do we unknowingly shield our eyes from what we wish not to see? Is it possible to be so obvious that one is invisible? The evil has followed me across the ocean! I must be careful. He cannot know. I will investigate him. Soon I will confront him. This damn illness! My chest feels in a vice. I will see him again on Monday.

Another tie to Eichen, Poland, Gdansk. The past won't let go. God, no, Paval. Please be careful.

31/1/66 There can be no doubt. No one else sees what I see. But no one else is from Gdansk. I tried to speak about the old country with him today. He said very little, there is no mistaking that voice, though. I don't believe he suspected me, but I must be careful. I wish my chest would improve. I must talk to Kevin about my suspicions. Maybe someone at the police school will know what to do. But not yet. I don't want to frighten him. He is such a good boy. Ha! Young man! When he comes to dinner this week we will talk.

Could this be what you wanted to speak to me about, Paval? You recognized a monster from the past? Please God, please, please, this can't be why he died. Please.

4/2/66 Chest is worse. Took day off from work. First time. I will nap before dinner with Kevin.

8/2/66 Did he know? I thought I hid my feelings well. Maybe no. The way he looks at me today. He studies me. Like I am an experiment. A lab rat. Like Filip. What was in that needle? Should have talked to Kevin. I am so tired. Tomorrow.

There were no more entries.

Kevin sat immobile. Could it be true? It couldn't, right? Twenty-five years, on the other side of the world, how could the Doctor remember Paval? No, it was impossible. When Paval was brought to the hospital it must have been apparent something had been done to him. Didn't the other doctors see this? They must have known something was wrong. They must have.

But they hadn't with Ingrid. They believed everything Doc Eichen told them about her accident. Why would this be any different? If he, as primary doctor, signs off on Paval's death, would anyone question it? Would anyone investigate what was in that injection he'd given Paval? Why on earth would they? It was just another cancer-related fatality of a Breyerton Refinery worker.

Rolf Eichen, and Lebensraum and Lebensborn, and Joseph Mengele, and that lobotomy doctor in Washington. And Ingrid Eichen, frozen in time until death mercifully took her. Kevin wished he'd never heard of any of them. Paval dying was difficult enough. This, this was unbearable. He could barely put the thought to words. Doc Eichen murdered Paval. There was no question in his mind. He killed the person Kevin had loved more than anyone. Just as he had done when he'd killed Ingrid, Rolf's only love.

Kevin walked through the kitchen and only then took notice of the radio he'd turned on shortly after he got home. The hourly news report told of the aftermath of the bloody convention in Chicago. Will it ever end, he wondered?

He thought of the dead: Rosaria Donez, Nora Wilson, Angela Castille, Ingrid Eichen and the doc. And Martin Luther King, Bobby Kennedy, and God knows how many thousands in this damn war. What the hell was happening? How can such chaos exist?

The screen door slammed behind him as Kevin stepped out into the late August evening. The heat was still present, but there was just a scent of water in the air. Maybe some much-needed rain was on the way. He sat in a lawn chair and worked his bare toes into the grass, something he'd done since childhood that always made him feel good. Far above was the vapor trail of a plane on its way to somewhere much more important than Pendale. Kevin wondered where.

Pendale was his universe: birth, childhood, school, job, and probably death. Maybe, if he was lucky, marriage and kids somewhere in there. This town dictated who and what he was. For better or worse. Would he ever be able to overcome the thoughts and beliefs that until recently he hadn't even known existed? Those which bound him to the past?

Paval had tried to overcome his past as well. Leaving his family and beloved Poland to come to this New Country. He had been lucky. He found Clara, his angel with the beer foam moustache. And they lived happily. Not happily ever after, but for a while though. Then the past caught up to Paval. The evil he thought he could escape from and leave on the other side of an ocean reared its head and killed him.

Does it ever let go? Can you ever escape?

Kevin continued to watch the plane, his head tipped back, tears running from the corners of his eyes.

THIRTY-EIGHT

"Mrs. G?"

Nikki stood in the doorway between their two apartments. She nervously twisted the bottom of the T-shirt that hung loosely off her.

"Mmm? Yes, Nikki?" The woman sat on the sofa, book in hand. She looked up and was shocked. Framed in the doorway, Nikki stood, shoulders slumped, looking so fragile. Mrs. G hesitated to say anything more. Nikki looked like a frightened animal, seeking comfort, but ready to bolt at any moment.

"I feel bad asking this. Especially so soon after your heart attack. And God knows you've done so much for me already, but I...I need your help." She avoided looking directly at Mrs. G.

"You know about the attic at the Eichen house and what's up there?" Mrs. G nodded. "I guess everybody knows now. There's more, though. And it's bad." Her voice quavered on the last word.

"Dear God, worse than the fact we've been living with a Nazi in our midst?"

"Yeah. It's not Nazi-bad, but for us, well, for me, it's bad."

Mrs. G waited.

"I tried so hard," Nikki said, barely audibly. "I really, really did. It's just, it's too much." Tears began sliding down her face. "I know I'm weak, but I thought I could do this. It's been two months, right? I was doing it, but it's harder than I thought. Way harder."

"You said you *were* doing it?" Nikki nodded miserably. "You mean you've been drinking? At the Eichen house?"

"No! Not yet, but...oh, God."

"Tell me, Nikki. What's going on?"

Nikki tried to catch her breath, close to sobbing. "I'm...I'm...."

"Dear God, oh, Nikki, come here." She held her arms open. "I am so sorry I didn't see this. I pushed you too hard. I failed you."

"No!" The word sounded like a gasp. "No! It's me failing. You did so much. You kept me alive when I would have rather been dead. I failed, not you. Oh, God, I'm so worthless! I can't hug you now."

Mrs. G looked bewildered.

"Because...."

"Because why?"

Nikki looked at her, helpless.

"Oh, Nikki, you need to be hugged more than ever. And I need it. Please, for me, come here."

Nikki ran to her and collapsed into her arms, her body nearly spasming with sobs. They remained this way, Nikki curled tightly against her landlady, almost wailing in pain, until Mrs. G asked, "What can I do? What can I do to help you?"

Nikki pulled away, stood, and held out her hand. Mrs. G rose and Nikki led her through the kitchen, to her own apartment's bedroom. It was there Mrs. G thought she could just barely discern an odor of alcohol. Nikki dropped to her knees, moving like an old woman herself, and slowly slid open her bottom dresser drawer.

Mrs. Gorman saw several sweaters she vaguely remembered seeing Nikki wear at some point. Nikki lifted them away and, nestled on other clothes, lay almost a dozen bottles of various types of alcohol.

"Please, Mrs. G, please help me get rid of these. I can't do it. I've been trying, I really have, but I can't do it."

"Leave, Nikki."

Nikki looked startled. "L-leave?"

"Don't be afraid. I'm not kicking you out. Just go outside. Sit in the car while I take care of this. I'll get rid of them. You won't have to. Just sit and wait for me." Nikki nodded and laboriously rose from her knees; she slowly trudged out of the room.

Rose Gorman gazed at the bottles before bursting into tears herself. How God? How did you allow me to be blind to this? She wiped her eyes and got to work.

Nikki sat in the passenger seat, her eyes closed, hands folded on her lap. She felt almost lifeless. There was no longer the borderline panic she'd been living with for the past week. She had confessed the worst so the fear of being discovered was eliminated. That burden was off her. She had put it on Mrs. G. Nikki felt some guilt about that, but really, more than anything, she felt...nothing. She was a bare landscape. Gray and deserted. She pulled the nothingness around herself and hid there.

Later, she didn't know how long, there was a quiet knocking on the car window. Mrs. G opened the door, took her hand, and led her back into the house. Nikki smelled a sharp odor of pine cleaner. They sat on Mrs. G's sofa. "It's all gone. I poured it down the drain, rinsed out the bottles, and they're in the trash. You have to tell me what happened. Please, Nikki?"

Nikki sat quietly for several seconds. "I'm not really sure. I saw them when I was cleaning. For a couple days I just sat and looked at them."

"Looked? What do you mean?"

Nikki slowly shook her head. "Just that. I sat in a big comfy chair and looked at them in their cabinet. They were so, so pretty," she almost whispered. Mrs. G looked alarmed but remained silent. "It was like that for a couple of days. I'd do some cleaning, then I'd sit and look at them, then I'd clean some more, and then more looking." She smiled weakly, "Man, if I had spent every second over there cleaning the whole place would be glowing bright."

Mrs. G waited.

"A couple days ago I figured since I was strong enough to just sit and look at the bottles at the house, why couldn't I do the same here? It's not like I was drinking, right?" She sighed. "So I smuggled a few bottles each day in my shoulder bag. I put extra clothes around them so they wouldn't make noise."

"Oh."

"I'm sorry I lied to you about the bag." She wiped her nose with the back of her hand. "I don't like lying to you," Nikki whimpered.

Mrs. G gently nodded.

"It's so...so, what's that word?" Mrs. G waited. "Insidious. Yeah, insidious. It just creeps closer and closer until...." She gently shook her head. "I thought because I was just looking, it was okay. But I wasn't just looking. I was spending hours and hours curled up in that chair in front of the cabinet. I was bathing in the smell. All those bottles, their fragrance filled that cabinet, and when I opened the doors wide it rolled out and wrapped me up. It was so comforting," she finished quietly.

"I wanted that comfort here, too. So, I brought them home with me. I would open my dresser drawer and sit and gaze at them half the night."

Nikki's nose looked red. She took a deep breath and said, "I started unscrewing the tops on some of the bottles. I'd inhale and it was like a sharp knife clearing everything else out of my brain. For just a second, I had no worries, no fears, no shame. It was just me and, well, the booze. It felt so private and so...beautiful." She attempted a small smile and failed. "Pretty pathetic, huh?

"Finally, even I could see it was just a matter of time before I was at it again." She shook her head. "It's so damn sneaky. It feels so comforting and then...I think in another day, maybe two, I wouldn't care anymore. I'd just say, fuck it and head back downtown to the bars." She wiped her nose with her shirt bottom. "I'm sorry about my language. It slipped out."

Mrs. G patted her knee.

After a moment's silence, Nikki said, almost whispering, "There's more, though. My life before, when I was drinking, yeah, the booze was a big part, the biggest, maybe. But it wasn't everything." More tears slid down her cheeks. "Jeez, this crying is crazy. I feel like a fountain or something." She again wiped her nose. "Yeah, there was more. Oh God, I'm so ashamed of this." She choked back a sob. "The men," she said, almost dragging it from her throat. "They're a part, too. Oh, I feel like such a piece of garbage, but I...I miss it."

"What do you mean?" Mrs. G asked, whispering as well.

"What they did," she whimpered. "What I did to pay for the drinks. It was, it was sort of like a dance. One part flowed into the other. They bought the drinks, I drank them, then we left and went...oh, hell, it doesn't matter where we went, but I did what they wanted me to do." Nikki rubbed her forehead with the heel of her hand. "It was terrible. And a lot of times, most of the time, all the time, degrading, but because it was part of the dance, I did it. Now it's gone and I miss it. And I think I feel I deserved it. The pain, the humiliation, all of it."

"Oh, Nikki." Mrs. G hugged her.

"Jesus, I crave being treated like shit by those men. I'm exactly what those neighbor women say I am. I was starting to think maybe I wasn't, but I am. Them calling me a cheap slut is right on target. Hell, maybe that's going easy on me."

"No," Mrs. G said, adamant. "You are not some, some fallen woman."

Nikki almost smiled. "If I'm not, then I can't imagine who is."

"All right. You've fallen, but you pulled yourself up again. That's what's most important."

"You're my biggest and only fan."

"Nonsense. Many respect you and admire you for what you're doing to help yourself."

Doubtful, Nikki thought. Only Mrs.G and maybe Captain Clarke, but who else?

Mrs. G disengaged from their hug and looked Nikki in the eye. "Maybe, maybe there is more than just alcohol you need to deal with. You may need to ask for help in other areas."

"Oh, God, Mrs. G. So now instead of just going to meetings where I have to say, 'My name is Nikki and I'm an alcoholic' I'll have to say, 'I'm Nikki and I'm a mangy whore?' I don't think I could handle that, truth or not."

"No, I'm not saying that. But you certainly seem to have issues with self-worth. Perhaps there's someone you can talk to about that."

"Yeah." She sighed. "I'm tired of feeling broken. I just want to be fixed. It doesn't have to be perfect, just back into some semblance of working order."

"You will be, I promise."

"Promise?"

"Nikki," Mrs. G laid both hands on one of hers, "I give you my solemn word."

Nikki burst into new tears and clung desperately to her best friend.

THIRTY-NINE

Valeria climbed the sweltering hall stairs. She felt out of breath, totally wrung out. She struggled out of her sweaty uniform, turned on the fan and stood, completely limp, feeling the breeze on her moist skin. From the window came the murmur of Spanish voices, shouts of good-bye, punctuated by muffled slams and banging noises. The market below was closing for the day.

She could not stop thinking about the case. After a quarter century of hiding, Doctor Eichen was finally dead. Brutally murdered, but still better than he deserved. The hell he had spread during that time…the hell he created for Ingrid and Rolf, had finally caught up with him. His destruction of Ingrid's life and the theft of Rolf's, including his home, his family, his childhood, his country, his name. And hadn't that theft of a past, proven to be more than Rolf could bear? Dios mío. Could we ever be free?

She slowly walked to the shower, reached through the curtain, and turned on the water. Standing under the cool trickle she willed herself to think of nothing. Like when she had focused on the corner of the wall while being inked. Just turn off. Think of nothing, feel nothing, be nothing.

Eventually, she became aware of the phone ringing. How long it had been doing so, she had no idea.

Valeria stepped out of the shower, quickly wrapped a towel around herself, and crossed the living room to pick up the receiver. It was Mama. Bella had just left. Seb was dead. His body had been found in a dumpster near Crazytown. No one knew who was responsible, a rival gang or maybe even someone within the Wild Dogs. Either way, the Dogs were turning on themselves; Bella feared the gang might destroy itself.

After hanging up, Valeria wondered, Is it over? Had she eluded her past long enough to finally feel safe? She honestly had no idea.

Valeria had made choices, and for the rest of her life would be faced with the consequences of those choices. It was a steep price. Very steep. All that was left was to try and live her life on her own terms. She hoped this was possible. Hope, and prayer, were all she had.

She said a silent prayer then walked to the bathroom and stood before the mirror. She opened the towel and let it drop to the floor. Staring into the mirror she poured a palmful of lotion into her hand, brought it to her chest, and rubbed.

Acknowledgements

The author would like to thank Renée Bondy and Tanya Healy for their time and constructive input. And of course, I wish to thank Manon for the countless hours she worked editing and formatting all my work. This bus would have never left the station without her gentle prodding and support. And also, thanks to Pablo, for helping to get me home from Coral Springs.

Leave a Review for Break with the Past

Thank you for reading *Break with the Past*. If you would, please write a few lines of review. These reviews are one of the best ways for authors and their works to receive exposure. Below are links to *Break with the Past* at Amazon and Goodreads. Your review is greatly appreciated.

Leave an Amazon Review:

Leave a Goodreads Review:

Where to Find the Author

Website: www.jemullane.com

Mailing List: www.jemullane.com/contact/

Blog: www.jemullane.com/blog/

Facebook page: www.facebook.com/JEMullane/

Instagram: @jemullane

About The Author

The author is a former schoolteacher who lives with his wife and action-challenged cat in New York State's Adirondack Mountain Park. In a previous millennium, he received his English degree from St. Bonaventure University and his graduate degree in education from the State University of New York at Oswego. In addition to *Break with the Past,* he is also the author of *Beneath the Surface* and *Disturbing the Dead*.

A lover of noir, both on-screen and on the page, he is also a fan of smart-ass dialogue with a strong dose of dark humor. Who says despicable characters can't show their funny sides?

When not camped in front of a laptop, he enjoys the activities his unique home region has to offer. In the colder months he enjoys snowshoeing and hunkering down by the fire. In the brief window of warmer weather, he can be found among his beehives, harvesting honey and beeswax, splitting the hives, and producing queens. Whenever possible, he'll be hiking or kayaking.